Praise for the Novels of

HEIDI JON SCHMIDT

The House on Oyster Creek
. . .

"This novel shimmers with the light of a summer day in New England. Schmidt expertly explores the complexities of domestic life and the tug of forbidden love, and plays them out against the subtly drawn accuracies and realities of class in a small Cape Cod town."

—Elizabeth Strout, *New York Times* bestselling author of *Olive Kitteridge*

The Bride of Catastrophe
. . .

"Comically beautiful. In polished, nearly Austenian prose, Schmidt blurs the line between inanity and tragedy." —*Village Voice*

"There is line after line of hilarious and desperate truth here—what a joy to read." —Elizabeth Strout

"Energetic, garrulous, and funny, with characteristic affectionate yet biting wit. Our heroine may be a long way from mastering her life, but she has an enviable command of the book of love." —*The Washington Post*

"Will comfortably share the shelf with works such as John Irving's *The Hotel New Hampshire* and Paul Theroux's *Mosquito Coast*." —*Library Journal*

continued...

"Schmidt has a keen eye for detail and a sharp sense of humor."

—*Publishers Weekly*

"Offers a number of pleasures, including . . . the exuberant attitude toward experimentation that was the hallmark of the 1970s."

—*Booklist*

Darling?
. . .

"Brilliant, very, very funny. . . . It is impossible to disentangle the comic from the tragic in Schmidt's writing. . . . [She] is incapable of cliché." —*The Washington Post*

"Generous, poignant, an unsparing eye and a keen wit: Alice Munro throwing her arm around the shoulder of J. D. Salinger. One doesn't often raise the banners that say profound and enormous fun over the same book, but here we can and do." —Elinor Lipman

"Sharp, yet lusciously written . . . full of shocks, beautiful images, and new ways of seeing things." —*The Guardian/Observer* (London)

"Here is that rare and welcome book about love that's less concerned with how we find love than what we do with it, a book that deals not in moments of passion, but in moments of grace, a book about the frustrating, hilarious, embarrassing, transcendental business of living with love. Heidi Jon Schmidt's stories are filled with delightful wit, spellbinding feeling, and an emotional intelligence that rises to the level of essential wisdom." —Peter Ho Davies

"This collection has so many shining moments of humor, of heart-break, of grace that readers might find themselves asking: Why aren't more stories this good?" —*Publishers Weekly*

"Schmidt creates a mood not unlike the tenor of modern life, lurching from giddy enthusiasm to embarrassment to frustration. Schmidt's take on contemporary phenomena is bracing." *Booklist*

"[Schmidt's] precise and elegant prose is smart and artful, indeed."
—*The New York Times*

The Rose Thieves
. . .

"A graceful journey into the individual life of a young woman and the collective life of a family—and a fine debut."
—*The New York Times*

"Laugh-out-loud comic and really tragic at the same time. Beautifully, evocatively written " *The Boston Globe*

"The stories are standouts." —*Chicago Tribune*

"Captures the rueful humor in family ambiguities."
—*Publishers Weekly*

"Delightful . . . precise and elegant." —*Library Journal*

OTHER NOVELS BY HEIDI JON SCHMIDT

The Rose Thieves

Darling?

The Bride of Catastophe

The House
on Oyster Creek

HEIDI JON SCHMIDT

NAL
ACCENT

NAL ACCENT
Published by New American Library,
a division of Penguin Group (USA) Inc.,
375 Hudson Street, New York, New York 10014, USA
Penguin Group (Canada), 90 Eglinton Avenue East, Suite 700, Toronto,
Ontario M4P 2Y3, Canada (a division of Pearson Penguin Canada Inc.)
Penguin Books Ltd., 80 Strand, London WC2R 0RL, England
Penguin Ireland, 25 St. Stephen's Green, Dublin 2,
Ireland (a division of Penguin Books Ltd.)
Penguin Group (Australia), 250 Camberwell Road, Camberwell,
Victoria 3124, Australia (a division of Pearson Australia Group Pty. Ltd.)
Penguin Books India Pvt. Ltd., 11 Community Centre,
Panchsheel Park, New Delhi - 110 017, India
Penguin Group (NZ), 67 Apollo Drive, Rosedale, North Shore 0632,
New Zealand (a division of Pearson New Zealand Ltd.)
Penguin Books (South Africa) (Pty.) Ltd., 24 Sturdee Avenue,
Rosebank, Johannesburg 2196, South Africa

Penguin Books Ltd., Registered Offices:
80 Strand, London WC2R 0RL, England

First published by NAL Accent, an imprint of New American Library,
a division of Penguin Group (USA) Inc.

First Printing, June 2010
1 3 5 7 9 10 8 6 4 2

Copyright © Heidi Jon Schmidt, 2010
Conversation Guide copyright © Penguin Group (USA) Inc., 2010
All rights reserved

The author gratefully acknowledges permission to reprint lyrics from "Waiting on Gramma,"
copyright © Jerry Beckham, 2009.

REGISTERED TRADEMARK—MARCA REGISTRADA

Library of Congress Cataloging-in-Publication Data:

Schmidt, Heidi Jon.
The house on Oyster Creek/Heidi Jon Schmidt.
P. cm.
ISBN 978-0-451-22992-2
1. Self-actualization (Psychology) in women—Fiction. 2. Mothers and daughters—Fiction.
3. Wellfleet (Mass.)—Fiction. I. Title.
PS3569.C51554H68 2010
813'.54—dc22   2010003857

Set in Albertina • Designed by Elke Sigal

Printed in the United States of America

For my sister Laura Ann, whose struggles as a shellfish farmer inspired this book, and whose success as a mother daily inspires me.

And for Marisa, who combs her hair with codfish bones.

1

A LETTER FROM FATE

Charlotte had known when she married Henry that he would inherit Tradescome Point. It helped weave the little veil of romance over him: He was the only child of only children, from a long line of Maine Puritans whose names he knew only from the stones in the family plot. They'd been shipbuilders, ship captains, and his grandfather, having sailed around the tip of Cape Cod to avoid a gale, had found this crooked finger of land in Wellfleet and decided to retire there. Tradescome Point, called Mackerel Point back then, looked south over the serpentine estuary known as Oyster Creek, which opened into Mackerel Bay and then into Cape Cod Bay. The island at the bay's mouth had been named Billingsgate because fish seemed as plentiful there as in Billingsgate Fish Market in London. Lobsters washed up in heaps after a storm, and a man could rake in bushels of scallops at low tide, like leaves. And of course there were the famous oysters, reefs of them in the shallow water, and cod, and mackerel drying in sheaves on every one of the wharves that bristled out all along the shoreline—every fisherman was proud as a king.

By 1902, when Isaiah Tradescome arrived, almost every last

mackerel had been caught. The big wharf at the end of the point had been swept off its pilings in the Portland Gale, and there was no reason to replace it—there were no mackerel left in Mackerel Bay, and the point, accessible only by water or by the narrow cart way alongside the creek, which lay under two feet of water at high tide, was of no use to anyone. Isaiah bought it, all eleven acres, for a hundred and eighty-seven dollars, built his house, and lived there the rest of his days.

Henry spoke of the place slightingly, as the last relic of a tradition he'd managed to escape. He was the last Tradescome except for his father, who lived in a nursing home outside Boston: a staring old man who crimped the edges of his blanket with nervous fingers all day and all night, waiting for death.

"Hold his hand," Charlotte prompted Henry the last time they visited him. It was four hours by train from Grand Central; they'd sit with his father and spend the night in a hotel, reassuring each other about what a good place they'd found, how clean and bright it was, how the nurses seemed genuinely concerned. Charlotte had put up pictures of Henry Senior, looking up from his desk at his insurance office, showing off a wire basket of littlenecks he'd dug out of the tide flats off the point. She wanted everyone to remember that he had once been a whole, living man.

"Or just rest your hand on his head, so he can tell you're here."

"He doesn't know me," Henry said with profound irritation. One of his hands had been weakened by polio years ago; the other was tensed along with his jaw at his wife's notions. She believed in the healing power of a touch, and other banalities.

"He'll feel it; he'll sense something, some deep memory. It'll comfort him even if he doesn't know it's you."

"Conventional wisdom," he said, seething. *Conventional* was his worst insult—he pronounced it with such contempt that Charlotte feared it as she would a red-hot poker. Emaciated, translucent, his father looked up at them with watery, frightened eyes.

"It can't hurt him," Charlotte insisted.

Henry gave in and took the crooked fingers in his. A little frown troubled his father's long, pale face and the old man pulled his hand away. One corner of Henry's mouth turned up—now did she get it? Tradescomes came from cold granite; they did not want comfort against life's blows.

"You're young, that's all," Henry said to Charlotte, with a chuckle. "Your view will darken; give it time."

Before she'd had Fiona, Charlotte had believed this, and most of the rest of what Henry told her. He was twenty years older than she was, an author, a staunch and learned man, and she'd been grateful to have him as a guide. Charlotte was made of empathy; she would accidentally glimpse the hopes and fears of the stranger behind her in a supermarket line. Her heart went out to people and she could never get it back. Henry's heart seemed to have hardened until it cracked; she'd been sure she could restore it, bring it back to life again. It hadn't occurred to her that Henry might not want that.

The phone call woke them all. The light on the Empire State Building was out; it must be after midnight. Charlotte took Fiona up from her crib and settled back in bed to nurse her.

"Thank God," Henry said. "Yes. No, there won't be a service. There's no one left to mourn him." He gave his characteristic bleak laugh and hung up, breathing a long sigh.

She reached her free hand out to him, and he allowed it to sit on his shoulder for a moment before picking it up and returning it to her.

"It's hardly bad news," he said.

"Still it's sad." Fiona was drifting off again and Charlotte's nipple popped comically out of her mouth, though she kept trying to suck, making fish lips in her sleep. To think that Henry's father had been someone's baby; someone had gazed down at his face with this wondering love that amounted nearly to prayer. . . .

"An old, stale sadness," Henry said.

"So, sadness has, like, a shelf life?"

He did smile at that. "No," he said. "Which means it will still be there in the morning, so you might as well get some rest." He got up and went to the bathroom for the hot water bottle, pulling a T-shirt of Charlotte's out of the laundry to wrap it. The warmth and smell would trick Fiona back to sleep in the crib.

"Is this too hot?"

Charlotte pressed her wrist against it. "Just right," she said. Henry was nothing if not helpful. Getting the rice cereal to the perfect consistency, or the water bottle to the exact temperature, these duties he undertook in earnest. And he would hold Fiona whenever Charlotte needed a free hand, though always with a slightly rebellious look, as if just because there was a baby here in the crook of his arm didn't mean he had to feel anything for it. Certainly not.

He leaned down to make up the crib—his naked backside was poignant, two stick legs supporting his thick torso and the head of gray hair he raked with his good hand all day, racking his brain for exact phrases. His back hurt him, the doctor said he needed a new knee, and the bad hand hung strangely as always, an unclenchable fist, proof of the cruelty of life. He settled the water bottle in, smoothed the wrinkles out of the sheet, and Charlotte tiptoed behind him, leaning into the crib, careful to keep the baby tight against her until the last second. Fiona didn't wake up, just snuggled closer to the hot water bottle, and they stood over her, watching her sleep. It felt like they were a real, whole family, the kind where each brings his own spark so there's always a soft light burning, even in the darkest time.

"I'll read awhile," Henry said, going into the living room and turning on his lamp. It had been a bare bulb when Charlotte met him, shining harshly on the jammed bookshelves, the piles of books on the floor beside the armchair, the table where he pushed the books aside to make a bit of room for his dinner plate every night—usually scrambled eggs. He'd read until his eyes felt "like boiled owls," then go down the six flights of stairs and around the corner to McClellan's Tap. "He lives like an Athenian," one of his acolytes at the newspaper had explained. "His life is in the marketplace. Home is just a place to sleep."

Charlotte had been another of those admirers, in awe of his devotion to work and thought, his stark austerity. She'd been so young, embarrassingly young, with no idea what mundane materials lives are made of. Wanting to distinguish herself, do something brave and important, she had gone to work for a pittance at the *East Village Mirror*, which Henry had started printing on a mimeograph when he first saw the danger looming in Vietnam. Now he was the visionary-in-residence, whose purity of journalistic heart made all the rules and tricks Charlotte had learned in grad school seem tainted. The *Mirror*'s tiny circulation did not trouble him—better to address a small group of serious readers than be a cog in some big, shining wheel. Did you see more deeply into the subject? Did you find the details that would etch the story absolutely into the reader's mind? Then you could hold your head high; never mind the byline, the prestige. His chin was always stubbly, his sweaters worn through at the elbows: He didn't waste a thought on such things. The trace of a Maine accent left in his speech added to the sense that he belonged to an earlier and much better time, and his left hand, flaccid at his side, gave a certain glamour, giving the easy explanation for his ferocity, his steely refusal to take part in the ordinary round of life. Everyone was curious—the men drank with him; the women slept with him. They made a myth of him and loved him for it. Only Charlotte, whose brand of hubris was emotional, had tried to get to know him.

And she'd succeeded; she'd made her way into his heart. And been so smug about it too, being favored by the great man. Henry was almost the age her father would be now. Her father had remarried soon after her mother's death (he was one of those men whose wife *was* his soul; he couldn't live long without one), and been absorbed into the new family, leaving Charlotte as a sort of fifth wheel. She'd call him on holidays, and they'd have a bit of conversation, but she wouldn't have thought to confide in him, and when he died one morning as he was setting off on his postal route, she'd felt only a dull, distant grief, an echo of something so old it had become ordinary. By then she had made this strange marriage and didn't know what to do.

She had only herself to blame. She and Henry had taken a trip to France together, in those early years. Provincial creature that she was, she was attracted to everything that glittered: Henry pulled her down alleyways into restaurants that seemed like caves, full of students smoking Gauloises. Paris had been Disneyfied beyond recognition, he said; only the beauty of the women was worthy of note anymore. Away from his desk, he was unmoored; nothing pleased him and he barely spoke, though his face would knot suddenly with fury and he'd address some bitter expostulation to the editor of the *International Herald Tribune*. Holed up in the garret hotel room with him, Charlotte had suffered a loneliness so bleak it seemed almost physical. On the train to Marseilles he went to the men's room and never came back; after an hour she went to look and found him in a differ-ent car, reading a history of the Dreyfus affair and looking fit to kill. She tiptoed back to her own seat, thinking she'd get off at some stop midway and go on alone. Except that Henry, having never owned a credit card, was carrying only a hundred dollars in traveler's checks. She couldn't abandon him, any more than she could have left a child alone. They alighted in Marseilles as married as ever. Charlotte saw a young couple striding past, deep in conversation, and Henry, watch-ing her watch them, said with perfect tenderness: "Poor girl, that's what you ought to have had."

Now, with Fiona safely asleep, he tucked an old wool blanket (his father's) over himself and tried a few pairs of glasses from the side table before he found the right ones. The cat jumped into his lap. Bunbury was the ugliest cat Charlotte had ever seen—a square head, a mean face, and fur stiff as a bottlebrush—but he and Henry had some kind of understanding, and as Henry started to scratch behind the cat's ears, Charlotte saw grief overtake him. His shoulders went rigid, he clenched his fist, that was all. Charlotte tried to sleep—Fiona would need her again in a few hours—but it was impossible. She lay there trying to piece the dead man together, from the bits she knew. The man in those pictures, his linen suit and trim mustache, a certain energy and pride in his face . . . had he gotten some of what he hoped for, before he died? Face to the pillow so Henry couldn't hear, she cried for him. Somebody had to.

He had structured it all so smoothly, before he lost himself to dementia—probate went without a hitch. The nursing home had ab-sorbed most of his savings, and after the taxes there was barely a dol-lar left. But Henry was the only heir, and they received by registered mail the key to a safe-deposit box that contained such jewelry as Charlotte could not have imagined—blue diamond teardrop earrings, a gift to Henry's grandmother on the occasion of his father's birth, and a cameo depicting a barefoot woman on horseback, thrusting a spear into the breast of a lion.

"Ship's captains," Henry said, barely glancing, as Charlotte held the brooch under the light. It was translucent pink, carved from a shell. "They brought things back. . . ."

They were shut up in the anteroom off the safe-deposit vault. It was paneled in gleaming mahogany, and about the size of an elevator. "Dross . . ." Henry said under his breath, pushing aside a packet of old letters. Underneath, there was a set of brass knuckles, well used.

"Mutineers," he said with a gleam, trying them on his good hand. "You had to be ready for them. You have to be hard as a ball bearing, Grandfather used to say." He made a quick, tight jab in the air, with real hatred on his face, as if his enemy were right in front of him.

"Is this the deed?" Charlotte asked, to turn the subject. Clearly it was—a fold of thick, brittle paper, covered in tendriled script, tied with a stained satin ribbon. It looked like a letter from fate.

"'Know all men by these presents . . .'" she read out. "'In consideration of one hundred and eighty-seven dollars, I, Luther Travis, do hereby grant unto the said Isaiah Tradescome, his heirs and assigns forever, a parcel of upland and meadow in South Wellfleet, being about ten and three-quarter acres more or less, bounded northerly by the Oyster Creek cartway, seventy-three lengths of fence as the fence now stands, and southerly by the waters of Mackerel Bay, extending eastward to the bridge beside the boat meadow, and westward to Sedgewick's Gutter. . . .'"

"Point Road was still the cartway when my grandfather bought the place," Henry said, rigid in the shoulders. "The road came later, after the automobile." He was the only person Charlotte had ever heard speak the word *automobile*, and he said it with some suspicion, as if it was still a newfangled idea as far as he was concerned. "Sedgewick's Gutter, I don't know."

"The Boat Meadow?"

"Oyster Creek is only full at high tide. It runs through the marshland—you can take a canoe through the channels but there's high grass on all sides, so it's as if you're paddling through a wheat field. I used to spend whole days in there. In some places the cordgrass is ten feet high. It's mysterious; you don't know what's around the next bend."

His voice was soft and distant, and he slid the brass knuckles off and took the deed out of her hand as if he might see himself there, a boy kneeling at the edge of the marsh, keeping still enough that the life of the place would continue, the hognose snake slithering off the bank and across the water, the fiddler crabs popping out of their holes.

"So, you do remember something from before you were twelve," Charlotte said. He'd always insisted that his first memories were the things he could see in the mirror over the iron lung, the year his parents took him out to Wellfleet to try to escape the polio outbreak. Nothing from before that mattered, anyway—it might as well have been someone else's two-handed life.

"I don't," he said, looking up from the deed. "A few flashes maybe—being out in the canoe, or all the women like black statues at my grandfather's funeral."

"And the game," Charlotte prompted. He'd lived for baseball back then, had begged until he was allowed to stay in Boston to pitch the first Little League game of the year. If they'd left when they wanted to, he might not have gotten sick; everything might have been different. "The one that was nearly a no-hitter."

"I do remember the game," he said. "I felt like I could fly."

This was a jeer at the naive boy he'd been. The one who emerged from the iron lung a month later had only scorn for such innocence. He'd kept hearing how lucky he was—how he should be grateful to God for sparing not only his life, but his right arm as well. That the left one hung there helpless was a very small thing when you thought of what might have happened. Of what happened every day. He'd had nothing to do but read while he was in the machine; he'd discovered all kinds of things. Things like Auschwitz

"Lucky to be alive," he said now, treasuring the foolish phrase. "I'd believed in God up till then . . . But there was the minister saying God had been watching over me. He sounded like a salesman. . . . I thought: 'This man must never have seen a newspaper.'"

Charlotte laughed. It was funny how people who had just been kicked in the teeth by life would go on profusely thanking God. It was not funny that Henry had lost hope when he was twelve and never seemed able to catch a glimpse of it again.

"A boat meadow," she said, hoping to change the subject before a rant could get started. "Fiona would love that, floating through a boat meadow."

Henry looked over the top of his glasses, amused. Fiona had just taken her first steps. He had no experience of children, no inkling how fast she would grow.

She went on reading the deed:

"'All of these boundaries, except the waterlines, are determined by the court to be shown on the plan, as listed in the Barnstable County Registry of Deeds, book seven, page two seventeen. . . .' Well, we're landowners."

She spoke with the light drama Henry used to love, fifteen years back when she was the eager girl in the corner of the *Mirror*'s tiny newsroom. She could bring the sparkle and mystery out of things, she'd seemed at first to be the cure for him, but she mostly irritated him now. She had no gravitas; had never fully accepted his authority, though he was vastly more experienced, better read than she was. When he refused to let her write the bigger pieces at the *Mirror* (nothing personal, it was just that she didn't come up to their editorial standards) she had, inconceivably, left the paper altogether to take a job at *Celeb* magazine, a fashion/gossip weekly Henry had never even looked at except once when he was waiting for a root canal.

"Landowners," he echoed, contemptuous, his dark gray eyes darkening further, his mouth pursed. He did not traffic in landownership, but in ideas. Well, she had wanted to please him, had tried for years, but having never been able to measure up, she'd turned it around and learned to enjoy flicking the red flag, watching him charge off in a rage. If you can't join 'em, beat 'em. She'd made real money at *Celeb* while he was holding the fort for serious journalism in his dark little office. She bought an orange patent-leather handbag, red stiletto heels with shark's teeth painted on the side, like hot rods for your feet. All very irritating, but calling him a landowner was the worst thing yet.

"By the waters of Mackerel Bay," she went on. "It's poetry! A 'boat meadow'? The idea of it . . ." Wellfleet was just a word to her, a word from that seminal text, the Oyster Bar menu—Wellfleet, Chincoteague, Blue Point, gusts from the seaside, where the lowing of foghorns, the fresh cold wind off the water, could make loneliness seem like a beautiful thing.

"We're rich! I can't believe it."

She knew this would drive him crazy. His glance was poison and he put a finger to his lips. Was that what she cared about, money? If they had to be rich, she could at least keep from mentioning it, and most certainly from trumpeting it while fanning herself with the deeds to their seaside properties, et cetera.

"It's only the truth, Henry." She laughed. "We . . . well, you . . . have inherited the place. What are you going to do with it?"

He sighed. He'd walked up the endless stairs to his rent-controlled apartment every day for thirty years, from the time he started the *Mirror* through the era of his little renown as a political reporter and critic, to today, when there would occasionally come a volume in the mail, a first edition of his collected essays, discovered at a garage sale, which some supplicant was begging him to autograph so as to fill out his (always *his*) collection of the representative works of the Vietnam era. These little packages made him shudder, reminding him of what he'd meant to become. And the shudder itself infuriated him—his ambitions had not borne out, so what? He could hardly call himself disappointed—he had expected little from life. At the *Mirror* he was the wise man, unfailingly thoughtful, open to all points of view. Charlotte was too young for him, lighthearted, light minded too. He'd had more serious, sophisticated women who would have made much better companions, but some idiot instinct had compelled him in this direction, caught him in this subliterary life. Fiona's crib stood where his desk used to be.

Back in the city, Charlotte looked down over Houston Street, where flocks of black-garbed young people were picking along through the icy puddles. It was the winter of 2003; she still couldn't help stopping at the corner of Sullivan to stare south, toward the empty sky where the Trade Center used to loom. The billboard across the way showed a woman whose stony face made a strange contrast to the breasts welling softly from her lace brassiere. If you bought the brassiere, maybe your face would get that hard and nothing would hurt you;

maybe that was the point. Whatever, Fiona needed a wider view. She was a squiggle in a yellow sleep suit, who must sip up sweetness and strength until she blossomed into the whole, capacious creature Charlotte willed her to become. Yes, willed. Charlotte's own natural disquiet, that sense that any minute she'd put a foot wrong and fall off the edge of the earth, which she had prayed to transcend by becoming an adult, a journalist, a wife, had finally been stilled with her first look at Fiona's face (as she was lifted, bloody, from between Charlotte's thighs by the obstetrician). Of course. You walk toward the light, keeping the little hand tight in your own. That's all.

"So, what are we going to do with it . . . Tradescome Point?" she asked Henry.

"I am not going to *do* anything with it," he said, pressing his temples. "I have work to do. It's been closed up for years, and as long as it doesn't ask anything from me, I'll let it stay that way."

"It's land, Henry; they're not making it anymore. . . ."

"What would we 'do with it'?" he asked, his patience stretched to breaking.

"Float through the boat meadow, on the tide!"

If he'd laughed, or made any response, she'd have gone along. It was one of her gifts, the ability to go along. But instead he shuddered, a little spasm of disgust that touched the sorest spot in their marriage.

"We could live there . . ." she said lightly.

"I live *here*," he said, with icy finality.

Then he gave a small, spectral laugh: "I sounded just like him then—my father."

2

THE BOAT MEADOW

Charlotte had, accidentally, been a good student. She aimed to please, and she would divine her professors' peculiarities, what fascinated them, where they hesitated, and find her own interests flowing naturally in with theirs. Everything she wrote was in some way a personal appeal. She had graduated from journalism school with honors before she realized that newspaper reporters were charged with knocking on strange doors and asking impertinent questions, exposing weaknesses, deflating egos, laying blame, and generally making people miserable. It was too late to change course; her loans were coming due.

Her first assignment at the *Mirror* had been a feature on fall day trips—who could screw that up? But standing in a pick-your-own jack-o'-lantern patch, she had noticed that the pumpkins were already cut and lay evenly spaced alongside vines that looked to have shriveled sometime before.

"You can't really pick them by hand," the proprietor explained. "The vines are too thick." Charlotte had knelt down to see this closer, trying to match a pumpkin to its stem, when the woman cried out suddenly: "It's been a drought year! So we bring a few in from New Jersey, so what? My God, all that's wrong in the world, and you're out here muckraking in a pumpkin patch? . . . Get out; get off my property. . . ."

Charlotte stumbled away, calling back over her shoulder to say she could see the woman was both honest and enterprising, that the vines looked wonderfully strong, that had there been enough rain everything would have been entirely different, and it was extremely thoughtful and generous of her to preserve the joy of the pick-your-own-pumpkin experience by importing out-of-state squash. That was her real gift—guessing what people needed to hear, and saying it. She could darn them up like socks, using a bit of her own wool to strengthen the weak spot.

Journalism did not need her. Henry did. She moved in with him a few months after they met, convinced him to get a telephone, cleaned ten years of dust off his venetian blinds. At first it had all been so sweet—to be with this man who'd been so cloistered among his books he'd missed half of life's substance and could be introduced to things like . . . bread pudding, or an Etch A Sketch . . . by a woman who could have been his daughter. She grew basil in a window box; she knit him a sweater.

"If you'd told me you were going to take two sticks and a ball of wool and make . . . this . . . out of it . . . I wouldn't have believed you," he said.

"That's the thing, Henry!" He was lacking some instinct, some sense as pervasive as taste or smell, and this was just the thing she had to give. And sex, of course—what a cheerful glutton he'd been, as if the secret of happiness were right there in her body. She knew this was the way with men who couldn't speak out their feelings. She was glad of it; it was her best evidence of love.

He gave her the collected Yeats, Stendhal in his preferred translation, and she read and was amazed: He was spreading his world at her feet.

"Just trying to educate you," he corrected her. "To plug up a few of the larger gaps. I barely remember any of it. One gives up fiction after a certain age." She sang while she was cooking or doing the laundry, but it grated on Henry's nerves. "It would be one thing if you had any kind of a voice," he said, "but I'm trying to read." Sometimes he was trying to read her newspaper pieces, and they repulsed him: He'd slash his big fountain pen across a paragraph or a page as if he were bringing down a whip.

And she, agreeable creature, would be stricken to the center of herself with shame at her deficiency. She became quiet, then almost silent, kept her poor attempts at journalism to herself as much as possible.

"You're being brainwashed, idiot," her friend Natalie said. "You're like some kind of supplicant nun. You hang on every word that guy says, even when he's insulting you!"

Natalie had been her roommate the first year of J school, but she'd dropped out midway through. She was a shameless snoop and found work immediately as a police reporter. Charlotte finished her degree, started at the *Mirror*, and found Henry, worrying every minute about whether she was good enough, whether Henry loved her, whether she should stay with him, whether she should stay at the *Mirror*. . . Meanwhile Natalie was scooping everyone in sight. By the time Charlotte screwed up her courage to break up with Henry, Natalie was writing for the *Daily News*, living down near City Hall, where she could keep an eye on the police department. She took Charlotte in, but Henry kept turning up on the doorstep, asking Charlotte for a recipe or whether she still had his *Leaves of Grass*. He was losing weight and his usual intriguing dishevelment had progressed toward actual filth. While Charlotte scribbled down a list of lentil soup ingredients, he did Natalie's dishes and peered into her bookshelves, shaking his head sorrowfully over her reading habits before pocketing the recipe with the penitent gratitude of a man who deserves his exile. It was difficult for Charlotte to stay entirely angry at him, and Natalie, who hated doing dishes, was won over entirely. On Valentine's Day she made a card for Charlotte, with cutout pictures of William F. Buckley, Nick Nolte's mug shot, Dick Cheney, Bin Laden. *Charlotte, don't go back to Henry!* it read. *Be OUR valentine!*

She had put the problem succinctly. Her own boyfriend was a detective whose schedule was the opposite of hers, a perfect situation. If Charlotte could get a little distance from Henry, Natalie was sure things would change. She helped Charlotte apply for the job at *Celeb* ("Is this a cover letter, or an apology for your existence?"she'd had to ask).

Meanwhile Henry himself had an idea—they heard his knock one evening and instead of coming in he asked if Charlotte would come take a walk with him. Halfway down the block he took a pork chop out of his shirt pocket and offered her a bite.

"No, thanks, I ate already. But . . . go ahead."

"I was trying to make dinner, and I realized we ought to get married," he said, gesturing with the chop.

"Why would you want to marry me? You don't like anything about me!"

"I should be shot," he said.

"Nothing so glamorous," she said, so wearily she could have cried for the loss of her old self, the self that had nearly skipped up the eighty stairs to their apartment in the days when she was setting off on a brave new life with the brilliant and eccentric Henry Tradescome.

"The truth is, I can't bear to lose you," he said. He seemed stiff and gray, frozen with grief.

"And we can have a baby?"

"I guess we'll have to," he said, with a sort of giggle, such as a man might make when buckling himself into his space shuttle seat. Then, he—or not he, but some small, feeling being locked up inside the towering critic—whispered: "Please come back. Please."

"I love you, Henry," she admitted. It seemed like her very worst flaw. She held him tight on the street corner, feeling the chop bone press into her chest. No one would ever need her the way Henry did.

And she had loved him so, that miserable October day when they were married at City Hall, he in the usual balding corduroys and his father's suit jacket, which he kept on hand in case of a funeral, she in a white dress that trailed in a mud puddle on the way back to the subway, where people had smiled to see this happy, bedraggled bride. She gave her bouquet to a wide-eyed little girl just before they got off at Prince Street. In the stairwell there, they found a stray cat, yowling, and it followed them home, where Henry opened a can of tuna for it and tucked an old sweater over it as it curled up to sleep in the bottom bookshelf. They were a family; the rain streamed over the window.

His problem resolved, Henry went back to his desk. He was a single-minded, not a wholehearted man. By the time the baby was born, their troubles were part of the habit of married life. Henry's gloom abated during Fiona's infancy, but returned in force as she grew into a creature of wants and needs, running afoul of him at every turn. Why couldn't she sit still in her chair? What was the absurd aversion to peas? There they were just out the door when she was in tears suddenly—because they had left some filthy stuffed animal behind? He clenched his fists—that he, Henry Tradescome, was fumbling through his pockets for the keys to go back into the apartment and retrieve this thing, he who had been called "the incandescent conscience of his generation," before his generation forgot him . . .

He thrust the bear at Fiona, making a furious face that frightened her right back to weeping.

"Now, Henry," Charlotte said, "it's not polite to make faces. Can you use your words?"

He could not, especially not to apologize, and he'd live in a silent fury for hours, only to spend the next day in penitence, undertaking an immense grocery shopping, and cleaning the bathroom tile with a toothbrush.

Living in that apartment with him had begun to feel something like living in his mind, which was like that fabled Venetian cell where the prisoner could neither sit, stand, nor lie. (Henry knew about many such places—he was writing a study of cruelty throughout history: *The Torturer's Horse*. It would justify his long silence, when it appeared.) That morning they'd been making love—or Charlotte tried to see it as making love, not as some sort of exertion Henry performed for his health—and when she had smiled up at him, the gaze she got back wasn't tender or even lascivious—it was more like contempt.

"I think I'll go up to Wellfleet," she said. "Just to get the lay of the land."

They—she and Fiona, asleep in her car seat, one sweaty curl stuck to her forehead—arrived at Tradescome Point in the late afternoon of a golden September day, after driving for what seemed like forever. She had the directions written out—entering Wellfleet you'd see the big screen for the drive-in movie looming, and the next left, across from the SixMart, took you down Point Road. The woods along the highway opened suddenly to show a creek winding through a field of tall grass toward the sea. Oyster Creek—the boat meadow—of course. Waves were breaking way out, and the trees at the edge moved in the wind, but the creek itself was still as a mirror, and so high it spilled into the grasses on either side.

And the light—Charlotte had forgotten how much light the sun could give when you didn't have to wait for it to strike just the right angle between two high buildings. It felt like home, New Hampshire, when the fields were going over to goldenrod and the new school year would begin. School, September, had always held such magical promise for her. She'd felt alone as a tree in the desert, standing at the bus stop on the crest of the hill, the sun yet to rise, the milkweed pods twisted like claws, fluff wafting east on the wind. . . . "The meanest flower that blows," echoes of English class, where hope lived. Her dog had died of ear mites—ear mites!—he had clawed through his skin trying to get at them, while she had stumbled along changing her mother's dressings and trying not to think about . . . anything. She needed to keep going to school. A miracle would come to compensate for all of this, to make it worth something. Maybe a love miracle, or someone who would recognize her true heart, her original vision . . . Poor, idiot creature, she had really expected something like this! But without those dreams she might have lost heart entirely; settled in, keeping house for her father, she'd still be there now. Looking over the salt marsh, the creek winding its strange way through, she felt a breath of that old expectation stir in her forty-two-year-old heart.

Around the next bend was the SixMart, a gas station/convenience store with a lighted sign that read simply, GAS. A man in canvas work pants was filling his pickup truck at the pump.

A hand-lettered sandwich board set out in front added: STRONG COFFEE; COLD BEER; NIGHTCRAWLERS AND SEA WORMS.

Point Road turned left there, between a roadhouse on one side and another low building—a Masonic lodge—on the other. Behind the buildings on both sides was a wretched forest cluttered with fallen trees, then a few small houses, with boat trailers in the driveways, lobster traps in piles, maybe a dog behind a chain-link fence. Henry had talked about the summer people, authors and sculptors and psychiatrists. She had not expected to find hard, New Hampshire–style poverty. The road went over a one-lane bridge, whose sign cautioned drivers it would be underwater at extreme high tide. At the moment the water was just lapping up beneath—driving over, Charlotte could see the wide expanse of the salt marsh again. On the inland side was a colony of little cottages set among scrub oaks and chokecherries. A sign that read, DRIFTWOOD CABINS, HOUSEKEEPING, BY THE WEEK, hung crooked at the entrance, grown over with vines. The cottages looked tired and run-down, with laundry hanging from lines strung between them and plastic toys upended in the yards. Two teenage girls in tight jeans and sweaters were standing there at the roadside, talking, tossing their hair, waiting for someone to drive by and notice them, maybe rescue them.

And then the macadam ended, and seeing the house rear up ahead Charlotte laughed out loud. Of course this was Henry's place, of course! It stood starkly alone on the grassy expanse of the point, a plain, spare building with a high peaked gable and a side porch whose bits of gingerbread trim were sorely in need of paint. The windows were boarded, one of the front steps had rotted through, and the lawn was grown up with clumps of thorny roses. There was an oak tree grown low and wide like an apple at the front, and a thick stand of lilacs to the east, along the oyster shell driveway that ran straight down the beach.

Fiona woke up as the car crunched to a stop on the shells. "Ma . . .

Ma . . ." she fussed, waving her little hands around as if to bat consciousness away. She was a funny-looking child: her little face had Henry's huge nose in the middle, and her hair stuck straight out of her head like a just-hatched chick's. "Mama, what?"

Charlotte lifted her out of the car and settled her on her hip—she was the perfect weight, just the ballast to keep her mother sailing smoothly. As long as Charlotte was holding her, everything seemed right with the world.

"We're here!" Fiona cried, waking up enough to look around. "We got here! What is this place?" She squirmed down and was running toward the beach as fast as her bowed little legs would carry her, and Charlotte just barely managed to catch up with her before she threw herself in.

"Hey, silly, do you want to go swimming?"

"Yes! Yes!"

"Actually, that was a rhetorical question."

But Fiona saw no impediment, and Charlotte held her just long enough to unsnap the corduroy overalls and pull off the sopping diaper. Then she waded in behind, jeans pulled up to the knee.

"It's cold!" they said at once. Charlotte meant they should get out, but Fiona was only announcing a fact. The water was intensely, brilliantly blue and cold, and she jumped and splashed wildly, thrilled by it, though Charlotte's feet were numb.

"Okay, okay, that's enough; we don't want to freeze," she was saying when a truck pulled into the driveway, an old white pickup that had been patched with a blue fender and door.

"Excuse me? Ma'am?" The driver had gotten out and was coming toward them—a burly workman in canvas pants who seemed to think he owned the place.

"Hello?" Charlotte said.

"Um . . . can I help you?" He was standing at the wrack line, so she could see who he was, more or less—a guy like her high school classmates, the ones who'd stayed in New Hampshire as if they were rooted there, who became carpenters or housepainters, while she went off to school. Rough-hewn, strong, with a broad face and a head of unruly hair going gray. A "galoot," Henry would have called him. Fiona, who had picked up Charlotte's discomfort, came up from the water and took her hand.

"Can I help *you*?" Charlotte asked. Neither of them sounded very helpful.

"Ma'am, this is private property. There's a public beach in town, if that's what you're looking for." His eyes were avid: searching, questioning, figuring; the eyes of a predator, or a baby, and he looked her up and down, taking everything in, the rental car, the half-naked child, the blue leather satchel, gift of a *Celeb* advertiser, lolling open so her wallet and her little flowered makeup case, gift of another *Celeb* advertiser, were showing. She saw that once he took these things in, he would despise her.

"No, thank you, I'm not looking for a public beach," she said, prim, offended, because he seemed to see her as the woman she was dressed to resemble. "In fact, this is my place," she said, in a tone appropriate to the woman he had mistaken her for, some Upper East Side type whose face-lift had left her stuck on haughty.

"Henry Tradescome owns this place," he said.

"Yes, and I'm his wife."

He did a real double take, and peered into her face with a frank, unnerving perplexity. "Henry Tradescome is, like, old," he said. "And I don't think he's married."

"Yes, that's a common doubt," she snipped. Henry was a hermit, a sage, a hobo—anything but a husband. If by some chance he did have a wife, she'd be locked in some literary attic, with gray hair down to her waist, bad teeth, wild eyes.

They'd reached an impasse; neither spoke. Both were still bristling, but suspicion was going over toward curiosity.

"I'd think Henry would have mentioned me," he said. "Since I've been taking care of the house all this time."

"Yes, I suppose you would think that. I'm sorry, he hasn't."

"I'm Darryl Stead. I live up the road. My father knew him . . . um. . . . your husband."

"I'm Charlotte . . . Tradescome." She still felt uncomfortable calling herself Tradescome. She was Charlotte Pelletier, the mailman's daughter, the too-intense girl whom no one quite knew what to do with, the one whose mother had died.

Fiona, who had been peeking out from behind Charlotte's leg, emerged, half-naked and entirely wet. Charlotte pulled her up on her hip. "And this is Fiona, my—our—daughter." So there. "In fact, I was just about to go inside," she said. "I've got the key in my purse."

"The doors are boarded over."

She turned back—it was so.

"Well, then, would you kindly . . . unboard them? I'll pay time and a half." This was an insult, revenge on him for calling her ma'am.

"I don't get paid," he said. "I use the driveway to get down to my oyster claim. We all do." He gestured toward the bay like a farmer toward a field, though she could see nothing but water, shaded pale green to deep blue to something darker, almost purple. For all his heft he was still gangly, his arms hanging too long from his shoulders as if heavy work had stretched everything out. "So we watch over the place. And I will take the boards off the door for you."

This he did, moving faster than Charlotte would have thought possible, undoing the screws and pulling down the plywood to set it aside. He took the key out of her hand and worked it into the lock, lifting the door so it would turn. When he pushed the door open, a wave of stale air rushed out at them, smelling of mildew and mouse.

"I've got a flashlight in the truck," he said.

She wanted to refuse it, but the electricity was off, of course, and she couldn't see a thing inside. "Thank you."

"I'll get out of your way," he said, handing it to her. "You can just leave the flashlight on the porch. I'll pick it up at the next low tide."

"People are so damn rude," she said to Fiona as he drove off. At least she'd stood up for herself. But she felt as if she were going to cry. People were so damn rude, the way they saw how she'd grown away from herself, become someone she'd never wanted to be. She leaned in the doorway, trying to collect herself, not to upset Fiona. She had a piece to write when she got back . . . the secret signals women send out with their handbags. She let out a little sob, turning it into a laugh. "Fiona, isn't it pretty here? Wouldn't it be fun to live right beside the water?"

"Dark in there!" Fiona said, cowering.

"Yes, because the windows are covered, see?" Charlotte whispered this, an old maternal trick to make things seem mysterious instead of frightening. "Let's see what it's like inside. Are you ready?"

Fiona's eyes were wide now, and she nodded, clinging tight around her mother's neck. They walked in the path of light from the door, through the kitchen to the parlor beyond. The flashlight beam lit on a corner china cabinet, a sextant beside the mantel, and as Charlotte's eyes adjusted she could begin to make out shapes, a sense of the place. She laughed—of course Henry had lived here. Ahab could have lived here in his few days on land. The horsehair sofa, the big nubbly lamps, the pipe rest beside the chair—she half expected to see Henry's father still sitting there, reading the *Times*'s V-E Day special edition. The kitchen had a real old icebox built into the corner under the staircase, which was steep and narrow and had, instead of a banister, a heavy rope strung along the side. She started up but it was pitch-black, and thick with cobwebs. "Never mind," she said to Fiona, mostly to break the silence. "We'll look upstairs after we move in."

Because that's what they were going to do, she and Fiona anyway. Henry could come if he liked, but he wouldn't want to. At first they'd call it a "long-distance relationship." He'd mean to visit, maybe he would one time, but gradually he'd find he was alone with his work again and be glad.

Back on the porch, they were dazzled by the sun. The delicate fretwork around the roof (some woman's attempt to soften the lines of the place) was all broken, and a corner of the floor had rotted through.

"We've got some work to do here," Charlotte said. It was a beautiful idea, working to make this place solid instead of writing for *Celeb*, coming up with ways to convince women to buy things. If only she had any skill at all . . . She looked down through the hole in the floor and saw something move there—a skunk's tail.

"Okay, so now we will tippy-toe down the steps," she said. Fiona was reaching toward the water with both arms, as if she could swim through the air. Where would Charlotte work; how would she manage it? Well, she would; she'd just have to. A boat was passing the channel marker at the mouth of the bay—a fishing boat, she supposed, with a cloud of gulls hovering. Generations of women had scanned the horizon from this spot, hoping to catch sight of a familiar sail. Charlotte and Fiona were going to join them.

3

CHARLOTTE'S HOUSE

Henry looked at her as if he thought she'd gone mad. Wellfleet? What was she thinking? How would they ever accomplish such a move? Where would the money come from? What would they do there? He couldn't leave the *Mirror*. He'd lived in this apartment for thirty years!

When Charlotte was standing in the front yard at the point, thinking how Fiona would climb up into the oak tree with its thick, low branches, it had all seemed clear, but now, back in the city, she couldn't help agreeing with Henry that it was a foolish, crazy idea. His life, their life, was here. Tomorrow she'd trip uptown in some pair of insane heels, go through the weekend's photos to see which star was carrying which handbag.... She'd have a drink with Natalie after work, the whole city glittering around them as she complained cozily about Henry and got the full and unrepeatable scoop on the police commissioner's love life in return.

"How would we ever get all these books down the stairs?" Henry asked, meaning to seal the question shut. And Charlotte's heart rebelled as if it were throwing off a straitjacket. Were they going to spend their lives in a sixth-floor walk-up because they couldn't figure out how to get some stuff down the stairs? She saw her father walking his postal route, wrapped up in the Red Sox so he wouldn't be menaced by troubles that couldn't be contained in Fenway Park. And her mother, so fragile she'd seemed almost grateful when death rescued her from the difficulty of living. New Hampshire, the stony fields, the fears turned to habits, then beliefs . . . the sense that whatever was beyond the border was unworthy of notice. New York was no less provincial!

"We will throw the books out the window," she said. Fiona, who had been coloring at the dinner table, laughed out loud to hear this, and ran to the window to see how they might fall. "Then we will sell a piece of the land, a building lot, and we can live on that money while we get our footing."

"How on earth would we accomplish that?"

She seemed to feel the ground eroding beneath her, but swallowed and pushed on.

"I don't know, but I can look into it. We could sell the piece to the east, on the other side of the driveway—so we'd still own the point itself. It's a beautiful piece of property; someone would be thrilled to have it."

"Very interesting, if true," he said, lifting his newspaper. "The vote on a bill to combat global warming by raising emissions standards . . . rejected, fifty-five to forty-three. The Republican Congress signs our death warrant, with a flourish."

He spoke with dread and satisfaction both. The news might be awful, but it confirmed his basic sense of things. The planet was getting hotter and hotter, the ice caps were melting, the water was rising, the people in power did nothing to stem the tide. Despicable. Yet somehow it seemed that as the waves closed over the Empire State

Building, Henry would not be grieving, but gloating. It would prove he'd been right all along.

", . . and we'd have that money in the bank," she went on. "We'd fix up the house, insulate it and such . . ."

His eyes came up over the top of the paper, incredulous. Could she really be serious?

"There's a feeling in the air up there . . . a feeling of people making money in real estate," she said. "Really. At the coffee shop, the people in line to buy doughnuts were talking about bidding wars."

His eyes bored into her, the way they did when she wrote something inexpressibly stupid. Who did she think she was, that she'd decided to take up real estate development? What next, brain surgery? She faltered—he was quite likely right. Then she looked around. She'd agreed with him when he thought she wasn't good enough for the *Mirror*; she always agreed with him. She had wanted to agree, to keep safe with him, more than she wanted any job.

"Well, I'll just try it, one step at a time," she said. Her wants had changed. She had to blaze a brave trail for Fiona, even if she was shaking every step of the way.

She'd seen a law office on Main Street, with its name—Nittle, Speck, and Godwin—lettered in a gold arc on the front window. It looked straight out of the fifties, when trustworthiness had been in fashion. Nittle wasn't taking new clients, and Speck had passed away long since, but Skip Godwin, the new partner, would be happy to help her. Yes, the land could be subdivided; in fact, the east side would split off quite simply. "You'll never miss it," Godwin said. There were maps to be drawn, papers to be filed, the zoning board would have to be appeased, a well dug, electricity brought down from the pole. Every time she made a phone call, her heart slammed—she'd be unmasked as an imposter, a child in dress-up clothes—but she inched forward; she had to. It was one of those feats such as happen in wartime, when you, who mostly loved a bubble bath and a silly novel, found you could carry your whole family fifty miles on your back. One day, the job was done. They put the lot on the market, and sold it just about instantly, for a hundred thousand dollars over the asking price. She resigned from her job. She bought a new car: a Volvo station wagon.

She was sitting at the kitchen table filling out the post office forwarding form when she became aware that Henry was standing at a respectful distance, his hands folded, waiting patiently for her attention.

"May I come with you?" he asked.

"May . . . ?" He must be the only man on earth who would politely ask his wife if he might live with her, in the house he'd just inherited. She looked up at him—his ferociousness had melted away; he seemed nearly abject.

"It's your house, remember?"

"Not anymore," he said, an escape artist who's slipped his chains and holds his palms up to show how easy it all was. Charlotte had done the work; thus the house was hers. He was relieved to be rid of it. In fact, the place suddenly became beguiling to him, freed of its WASP taint, the sound of his mother's lockjawed voice, explaining again that Miles Standish's daughter had married John Alden's son, "and that's the trunk of the family tree." Wisps returned to him, like fog off the bay: the view through the beach grass to the water; the eternity of a child's summer morning. He took a year's leave from the *Mirror*—he would still write reviews and the major obituaries, but now he could concentrate on his book. In Wellfleet there was a real office—the same low basement room he'd retreated to during the summer vacations, reading furiously, ignoring the catboat his parents had bought him so he could follow the Tradescome seafaring tradition.

"Of course you can come with us," Charlotte said. Leaning toward her with both hands on the table, his right elbow coming through the hole in his sweater, he looked into her face openly as he hadn't done in years, and she caught a wistful flicker, as if someone were waving to her from an impossible distance away.

They moved in just after Fiona's fourth birthday, a cold April day. Henry was driving, hands clenched tight exactly at ten and two on the wheel. He never saw an automobile without picturing a twisted wreck. Approaching a green light, he would stamp on the brake with the certain knowledge it was about to turn red. On the highway he crept along, swerving occasionally at a premonition of the inevitable catastrophe. It wouldn't do to have Charlotte at the helm in such a dangerous situation. The cherry trees were blooming in the city, the forsythia in New Haven, but past Providence the red-budded branches were the only hint of spring, and when they reached the Cape Cod Canal they saw the Sagamore Bridge arching up into a fog dark as smoke, the cars ahead of them seeming to disappear into oblivion one by one—just past a billboard that read, DESPERATE? in enormous letters, giving a phone number for the desperate to call.

"Flowers!" Fiona cried, reaching her plump little arm toward a bunch of daffodils affixed with pink ribbon to the bridge railing. Someone must have jumped there.

"Aren't they pretty?" Charlotte said, glancing across at Henry.

"'All the instruments agree,'" he said grimly, quoting Auden, a line that finished: "The day of his death was a dark, cold day." Good cheer had not been held in high regard among the Tradescomes; it suggested a superficial turn of mind, which would lead to an unpleasant afterlife. Henry rejected any notion of an afterlife, of course, but gloom was his family tradition.

"I think it's supposed to clear up, late afternoon," Charlotte tried, but he shook his head.

"Weather doesn't improve over the course of a day," he said. "It can cloud over, but you'll almost never see—"

"Henry? Are you serious? You've been looking north over Houston Street way too long."

She laughed; he brooded. "It's like this out here more often than not," he insisted.

"You didn't have to come," Charlotte said. "No one twisted your arm."

"No," he echoed. "No one twisted my arm."

Fiona was telling her bear a little story in the backseat. After Hyannis they were nearly alone on the road, the Volvo excruciatingly shiny compared to the old pickups they passed. Mile after mile, they drove through fog so dense Charlotte lost her bearings and was grateful to see a water tower rear up above them, proof they were still on earth. She could see on the map that their course was a spiral—the cape pushed forty miles into the sea and then began recurving toward the mainland, narrowing all the time. The highway ran down the middle, between two forested banks, no sign of water. Henry looked ashen, muttering between his teeth.

"What?" Charlotte asked, but he shook his head.

"That I spend my life . . . like this . . ."

"Driving with your family to your new home on Cape Cod?" But this was disingenuous—she knew it counted to him as defeat. He'd intended to write twenty books; instead his spirit had flagged after the one. So the newspaper would be his legacy, the record of his uncompromising, eagle-eyed view over the neighborhood, the city, the world. Meanwhile, the neighborhood, the city, and the world had changed in directions he couldn't have dreamed—the last survey had shown that readers of the *East Village Mirror* turned first to the restaurant reviews.

Rounding the rotary in Orleans, they found themselves in a ghost civilization—shuttered clam shacks and cottages, a parking lot full of shrink-wrapped boats, minigolf courses with their mini-windmills forlornly turning. They passed a little church with gothic-shaped boards over its windows and a sign that read, JESUS LOVES YOU. SEE YOU IN MAY. Charlotte had been singing "Old MacDonald" for the better part of an hour, but Fiona was losing interest, and suddenly she undid her car seat safety belt and lunged forward between the seats into her mother's lap.

"No, honey, it's not safe." Charlotte reached back to buckle it again but couldn't manage it at that angle, and Fiona, whose rosy cheeks and soft blond halo could make her look like an angel, showed a devil's determination as she launched herself forward again.

"Stop it!" Henry grabbed her wrist with his left hand, the bad one, gritting his teeth as if he were willing it to be strong enough to hurt her.

"Mama! *Mamaaaa!*"

"Henry, what are you doing?" Charlotte screamed, pulling Fiona by the waist into her lap, and grabbing the steering wheel, because the car had swerved into the other lane.

"She'll kill us all," Henry said, pulling off the road.

"*She'll* kill us? You'll kill us!" Charlotte said. Fiona was shrieking, in fear, and hurt, and outrage. "If there'd been another car? That'd be it; we'd be dead."

But there wasn't, not one. They were all alone out here.

"Daddy didn't mean to hurt you, honey," she said, controlling the damage, holding Fiona tight, rocking her back and forth as she waited for Henry to explain further, that he was afraid for her safety, had lost control of himself. When nothing came, Fiona's little body melted into tears. "Henry, can you tell Fiona you're sorry?"

Fiona gave a ragged sob and looked up timidly at her father.

"I didn't *hurt* her," he said. "She has to learn to stay in that car seat. It wasn't even my good hand."

"The expression on your face was plenty."

"It wouldn't matter what I did; you'd make a federal case out of it."

"If you touch her in anger again . . ."

Henry's face was set. He was furious now; he'd be penitent later. He wasn't going to hurt anyone physically. The damage he might do to his daughter's heart . . . well, Charlotte would have to figure it out, make it okay somehow.

"Here, I'll come sit next to you, how about that?" She went around and got in the backseat beside Fiona, who was puzzling, trying to understand what had happened. Henry turned back onto the road.

"Entering Wellfleet!" Charlotte said, reading the sign out cheerfully, hoping to steer them back into the light. "Look, here we are!" There it was, the boat meadow—scruffy as a lion's coat now, thick in some places and worn nearly bare in others, all shades of dull gold. The channel had cut itself so deeply, all the layers of earth were visible; now there were only a few inches of water trickling out.

"Here's where we turn," she said, seeing the SixMart's lit GAS sign. Then: MERMAID TAVERN, in neon as they turned past the roadhouse down Point Road. "There you are, Henry. It's your dream come true." She couldn't make herself sound warm, but she was managing to sound less angry. Everyone has some grounding force, something that feels right and familiar. For Henry it was gloom. For Charlotte it was forgiveness. When she forgave she felt she was doing right, and this steadied and calmed her.

"Finally," Henry said, taking the chance to cover the breach. "Somebody did the obvious thing. 'Souls of poets dead and gone / What Elysium have ye known / Happy field or mossy cavern / Choicer than the Mermaid Tavern?'"

Keats, not that Charlotte would have known this if it weren't for Henry. His dream of elbowing in between Shakespeare and John Donne in some eternal tavern—if she could have gotten it for him she would, the same as she'd find a way for Fiona to live in her storybooks.

"See," she said. "A good omen."

"Omens," he said, shaking his head. Evil portents counted as realities, good ones as superstitions.

Two mud-splattered trucks passed them on the road, and as they came over the little bridge they saw more trucks parked on the mudflats, men in waders pulling heavy rakes through the sand, the tide streaming out in silver rivulets around them.

"Raking clams," Henry said. "The tide goes out half a mile at the new moon."

Charlotte had seen what she'd thought was low tide the day she came up for the zoning board meeting. It hadn't looked anything like this—the bay was nearly empty now, exposing a whole landscape of seaweed beds and shoals. The oyster racks were lined up in squares of nine or twelve, like rusty bed frames in a dormitory. Each square was someone's farm and the trucks were parked between them.

"Look!" Charlotte said. A heron took flight with three huge flaps, its prehistoric silhouette rising over the marsh and the men. Hope rose with it. Things could change; this place could change them.

· · ·

The shutters were off the house, and this, along with the few daffodils blooming by the side door, softened the look of the place so it seemed welcoming in its own grim way. Wind as much as water had made this landscape: The tall grass was brushed neatly west to east, and the oak tree had grown so slowly against the wind that it split into branches only a few feet from the ground.

Henry got out of the car and stretched, pulling one knee and then the other up to his chest like a flamingo. "It's nice here," he said, seeming surprised.

"I told you it would be," she said, lifting Fiona out of the car seat, settling her on her hip. Fiona could hardly bring herself to look up for fear of coming face-to-face with her father. He went over and picked one of the daffodils.

"This is for you," he said, offering the olive branch, but there was no warmth in his voice, and Fiona shook her head against Charlotte's shoulder.

"Look me in the eye, please," he said—commanded. Even he looked disappointed to have lost the thread of the apology.

"Fiona, I think Daddy's saying he's sorry he hurt you before. Can you say thank-you?"

"No! No!" Fiona kicked both feet, wild with fury. She tore the head off the flower and threw it, and Henry shot Charlotte a victorious glance—did she see what a monster she was raising?

"Fiona! Calm down! What's wrong?"

"Can't take that flower," she said. "He'll know I love him!"

And what could anyone say to that? Anyway, now they had something beautiful to look at during their wretched silences. From here they saw the bay from an entirely new angle, the estuary snaking out from the east, opening toward the sea. Some of the trucks they'd seen on the tide flats were right out in front of their house. The men moved quickly—carrying heavy sacks back and forth between racks as the tide licked up around the edges of the shoals.

"This is really our house?" Fiona asked suddenly. She always recovered first. Everything Charlotte and Henry said to each other echoed down through years of efforts and angers and hopes and disappointments. Like a corridor, where one door after another has been slammed shut. "And that's our tree?"

"I planted that tree," Henry said. "My father and I did, when I was about your age. So it must be . . . fifty-eight years old."

That he would admit he had once been Fiona's age—it was a truer peace offering than the daffodil. Charlotte felt Fiona relax, felt her spirit come back, and suddenly she was scrambling down and running at the tree, trying to climb it by throwing her arms around its trunk, as if she expected it to reach down and pick her up.

"That's a good start." Charlotte laughed, running to lift her up onto the branch.

"Look! Look at me! I climbed the tree!" Fiona cried.

Henry darkened. "No . . ." he began, but Charlotte could talk louder than he could.

"You've made a great beginning!" she said. "You'll be climbing it yourself in no time."

"What will become of her if you praise her for no reason?"

Charlotte set Fiona back on the ground. "Run over, honey, and count the daffodils so I know how many there are, okay?" Then, to Henry: "If we're angry and critical, she'll become angry and critical. If we see the best in her, she'll learn to see the best. If we believe she'll succeed, she'll have the strength to try."

The great critic looked startled, as if he had never heard of such a thing, and rubbed his temples, maybe trying to push the idea into his mind.

The sky over the horizon was thick layers of gray, as if torn from blotting paper, and now the sun burst out beneath so that an intense gold light blazed between dark clouds and dark water. Even the oyster farmers stood to see it. Whatever was wrong—and nearly everything seemed wrong—they were here, on their own piece of ground. From this tree Fiona would look out to see the world change day by day, year by year, and no matter how far she traveled, in her dreams she would be walking back down Point Road on a summer evening, toward that place of absolute comfort and absolute mystery: her home.

"Seven! Seven daffodils!" Fiona said, running back to give this news—she'd done her job.

"Good counting! Look how beautiful the sunset is." Charlotte might already have seen half the sunsets she was entitled to—she hated to miss a single one—but for Fiona there were infinite beauties ahead, and she paid no attention. It would be years before the sight of a heron angling up from some marsh would flood her with memories: of her father so alone and upright and unable to yield; of her mother with shoulders squared and hair tangled in the wind, her eyes fixed on the opposite shore.

4

WASHED ASHORE

The key wouldn't turn until she remembered how the caretaker had done it, lifting the door by the knob. They walked into the kitchen—and another century. The evening light streamed in through the wavery old windowpanes, past curtains printed with potted geraniums, over a saltcellar in the shape of a hen on her nest. A spring of grief opened in the back of Charlotte's throat and she pressed her knuckles to her mouth for a second. Her mother would have loved it here. Henry stepped in gingerly behind her, tapping his toe on one board, then another, then bouncing with all his weight as if he expected to go through the floor. "Seems safe enough," he said, giving up on the floors and rapping on the walls.

"Why wouldn't it be?"

"It's a hundred years old."

"It's probably more solid for that," she said. "They built things to last back then."

"My grandfather salvaged the floorboards from a shipwreck," he said, going through into the parlor. "Some of the boards upstairs came from the old salt mill; they repel water—he couldn't paint them. Half the stuff in here he brought back from one port or another." He put the cat carrier down on the rug and Bunbury stepped out, giving them a malevolent squint before he set off on a sniffing tour of the room. Time seemed to have stopped here, maybe when Henry's grandfather had died, so that along with the shelves full of leather-bound books (Dickens, Trollope, *The Life of Sir Walter Scott* in ten volumes), the paintings (*Women Waiting on the Pier*, Genoa, 1865), the things (a brass gong, a collection of jade and ebony elephants marching along the mantelpiece), the sense of another era remained. Charlotte shivered with it, the idea of a man who had read the life of Sir Walter Scott, all ten volumes, in his chair beside the bay window, who had walked through the port of Shanghai in a time when no culture was diluted yet by any other and distant places were still unimaginably strange.

There was an antique music box—sandalwood, inlaid with ivory and mother-of-pearl. Henry read from a scrap of paper attached: "'Eighteen seventy-seven . . . dragonfly hammers'? Can you read this?"

Charlotte held the scrap up to the light. It was a corner torn from a newspaper page: the *Wellfleet Oracle*, June 17, 1972. So, when Henry's mother scrawled this note in her lax, loopy script, trying to keep something of the past vivid for her son, Charlotte had been eleven years old. It didn't seem long ago at all, but the paper was brittle and yellowed, as if it had come down from an ancient time.

"Yup, that's what it says, all right. 'Dragonfly hammers.'"

Henry sighed. "Mother was so . . ." But as he searched for the right word, Charlotte lifted the lid, to see the brass hammers fashioned as bees and dragonflies, and bells like the skirts of dancing ladies.

"Loot," Henry said, looking away in distaste. "From the colonies. Very quaint. *Quaint* was my mother's word for everything."

"Nobody got to go to China back then, except on a sailing ship,"

Charlotte said. She felt a great community with anyone Henry criti
cized. "I envy your grandfather. Can you imagine what it would have
been like to sail to someplace so very different, a place you'd never
even seen in a picture before?"

"Don't make a romance out of it. They were the truck drivers of
their time."

Above the bookshelves hung a pale, shimmering watercolor of
Isaiah Tradescome's last clipper ship, *Kingfisher*, painted with sails bil-
lowing, quayside in Brindisi. In the stairwell a black-and-white photograph of the same ship showed it too tall for its width, ungainly and
alone on a sea of towering waves. A haunted life Isaiah must have
lived beneath that mast, with no family, not even a tree to tell the seasons by. The bay out their window must have seemed like a saucer of
milk to him.

"Think, a little girl like you would have carried a candle up these
stairs to bed," Charlotte told Fiona, who was scrambling up the staircase on all fours. The cobwebs they'd run into six months ago were
gone—someone had cleared them away, in addition to getting the
water running and the shutters down. Fiona raced along the narrow
hallway, throwing the doors open to inspect each room as if she expected to find real lives happening in them, travelers opening their
steamer trunks to set out bathing dresses for the next day. Two bed-
rooms faced south on the bay; the third, on the north side, had a window seat built into the gable. The mattresses on the iron bedsteads
sagged almost to the floor. The wallpaper, stained and peeling,
showed full-blown peonies and roses in the big room, sprigs of violet
and forget-me-not in the others. You could imagine a woman's delicate hand drawing the curtain back to look across the bay to Try
Point, where there'd been a tryworks back in whaling days—a huge
kettle, really, in which blubber was boiled down for oil.

"It's like they're still here," Charlotte said, nearly whispering so as not to break the spell. There was a washstand in each room, with a pitcher and basin, though a little bathroom had been fitted in at the end of the hall. The tub was against the back wall so you could look out the window while you were washing and see the whitecaps at the end of the point. Only one red band of sunset was left burning at the horizon, and against the dark water she could see the green light of the channel marker slowly blinking.

"Mom!" Fiona said. She'd found a door no taller than she was, and pulled it open. A linen closet stuffed with the thickest sheets, and towels with . . . Henry's monogram? Charlotte laughed out loud. The house was like a secret he'd been keeping all those years under the bare bulb on Sullivan Street—a whole life that he'd disavowed. Some women discovered their husbands were escaped prisoners; Henry was an escaped patrician. Fiona saw the edge of something pink and pulled out a bunch of hankies, each embroidered with a different flower. They'd been wrapped around a little bottle of lilac water.

"Daddy, Daddy!" Fiona ran back down the stairs to tell him all they'd found. Charlotte came behind her to find her talking a mile a minute, with Henry seeming to brace himself against the mantelpiece, beside a portrait of a woman with his own piercing gaze, her chin outthrust and lower lip tightly gathered as if she were about to smack someone with a wooden spoon, and for a very good reason, too.

"*What* is that?" Charlotte asked. "I mean, who is that?"

The corners of Henry's mouth turned up happily. "That's my great-aunt Vestina, the temperance crusader."

"If I looked like that I wouldn't have my portrait painted."

"If you looked like that you'd think beauty was a sin."

"Well, she's coming down." Charlotte took the frame by its corners and lifted it away from the wall, pulling apart a spider's sac that was spun behind. . . . Hundreds of frantic little spiders poured out, scrambling crazily in every direction.

She shrieked and dropped the painting, whose thick gold frame smashed into pieces. Charlotte had always been careful to keep calm around spiders, so Fiona wouldn't catch her horror, and now of course Fiona started screaming—nothing was more frightening than seeing her mother afraid. Henry took off his shoe and smacked at them with it, without killing more than a few.

"Might as well try to sweep all the sand off the beach," he said, with a spectral chuckle. "This place is going to take a lot of work." He sounded as dire as when he talked about getting out of Iraq, and Fiona clung to Charlotte's leg.

"We will manage it," Charlotte said firmly, because Fiona had to see this.

"That's clear," Henry said dryly. Charlotte could fix a run with nail polish, and had once triumphantly unscrewed the drain cover in their apartment shower, fishing up a sludgy mess of hair, but this was the extent of her mechanical skill. He went into the kitchen and came back with a broom and a tin dustpan that must have been exactly where he saw them last, years ago. He picked Vestina up by the top of her frame, the one place where the canvas was still attached.

"Here, Mother labeled it," he said. "'Vestina Beasley, 1873 . . . painted by . . .' I can't read it." Every object in the house seemed to have a scrap of paper attached, with a date scrawled on it, and something else as inscrutable as *dragonfly hammers*—the name of the uncle who had left it to her, maybe, or the ship it had come back on. Everything in the house, everything Henry reviled, had been part of a story his mother was trying to pass on to him.

"A bibleface, that was the term, I believe," he said.

Charlotte shuddered, at the spiders and Vestina both. "Put it out on the porch," she said. "We'll deal with it tomorrow."

"With pleasure. Believe me, it's just lucky I never took a baseball bat to this stuff," he said, waving toward a corner china cabinet filled with porcelain teacups. Everything that made him: upright Protestant arrogance and the rage at upright Protestant arrogance, wealth and disgust at wealth, polio, loneliness, a longing so fully stifled that it had finally barricaded its own door—all of it was right here in this house; you could breathe it in with the mildew and the faint stink of mouse.

Charlotte sat on the edge of the sofa, which seemed to have absorbed years of cold.

"Where's the thermostat?" she asked.

"The heat's on," he said, touching the radiator. He pressed his hand against the wall. "I don't suppose you can make it any warmer."

"Oh, Henry." When Henry was cold it meant the world must be turning to ice. A heat wave was another sign that they were hurtling toward the sun. He'd never attended to science at school; it had interfered with his reading. A thermostat was no more use than a sextant against his general sense that things were getting worse by the day.

"I suppose they put it on low when they opened up the house," she said. "Just to keep the chill off. Here's the thermostat, behind the door. See, it's set at fifty. I'll turn it up."

He acceded to this with a shrug, indulging her in her superstition.

Headlights swept through the room—one after another, the trucks were coming up from the beach through their driveway. Charlotte went to turn on the lamp, but the bulb was out. Of course, it had been years since there was a light in this house. As she tried the switch in the kitchen a mouse poked its head up out of the stove burner and gave her an imperious stare. It was used to being master here. Bunbury leaped through the door and onto the stove in one motion, and the mouse dived to safety behind the refrigerator, leaving Bunbury crouched on the counter, teeth chattering in spasms at the lost opportunity.

Even the refrigerator bulb was out. It was cold—but empty. Charlotte had packed so carefully, making sure they had enough of everything they would need till the moving van arrived . . . except lightbulbs and food.

"Can we call Lotus Flower?" Fiona asked. Lotus Flower was the Chinese restaurant down the street in New York.

"No Lotus Flower here, honey."

"Mommy, no!"

"Let's go back to that little gas station and see what we can find."

Henry looked so bleak at this prospect, she expected him to bring up the Donner party.

"I will forgo that opportunity," he said, but Fiona couldn't get into her coat fast enough, proudly pushing its big round buttons through the holes—her newest skill. For the moment, the SixMart was as alluring as the Taj Mahal.

Outside, they realized it wasn't dark at all yet· The sky was a vivid lavender that shed mystery over everything, and there was a sharp, astringent breeze off the water.

"Blustery!" Charlotte said.

Fiona ran into the wind with her arms out. "Everything's blustery here!" she said, twirling.

"That is exactly the word," Charlotte said. Awake, aware, alive in the wind. Even the barren front of the Mermaid looked seductive as they drove by, the neon Budweiser sign glowing in the one window. There were secrets to be discovered there, and Charlotte wanted to know them. The truck that had just driven past the house was parked at the SixMart, among others with mud caked tires, and inside, the men who'd just come off the flats were standing around the coffee machine, big, restless guys like a team of oxen.

"You're going to lose flow that way, if you cram too many in a bag," one was saying, in a voice that would have carried easily across the windy flats, and another answered that he'd kept his numbers way down last season and felt they'd grown appreciably faster.

"It's your spot," a third said. Charlotte could feel them respond to her, the slightest change of voice, of stance, in recognition of a woman, an outsider. She was conscious of Fiona's coat suddenly—it had come from the chic baby store on Sullivan Street and it seemed to scream that they were precious city people who didn't belong here. "You get better tides for working but it can stagnate; there's not the volume of water passing through. . . . Darryl and Tim have the creek washin' nutrients day and night through their herds."

"And toxins," said one, glancing over at her.

"Darryl, right?" she said.

"That's me." The men were all broad shouldered from work, and dressed alike, in rubber boots and heavy sweatshirts from the same lumber company, but he stepped apart from the others with the same suddenness she'd seen that first day, quick movements and thoughts flashing over his face.

Then he hesitated. "You're Charlotte," he said gravely, wiping his hand on his coat before extending it to her. It was so thick with muscle and hard with callus, she felt she ought to take it in both of hers.

"I am."

He glanced over her shoulder and, seeing the others absorbed in their talk, took a step back, behind the postcard rack.

"Listen," he said, "I've wanted to say I'm sorry."

"Why?" He'd spoken so earnestly she expected some terrible secret.

"*You* know. . . ." He looked into her face with a frank, open gaze, as if he wanted to be sure she could read his thoughts. "For the way I was when you were here last fall."

"Oh, I'd forgotten. . . ." At least, she'd meant to forget; she was sure most people would have brushed it off, but his unfriendliness had stuck with her, a sort of warning: *Keep away; we don't want you here.* She'd just put him on the list of people whose sharp edges she had to watch out for. It was a long list; one more name hardly mattered.

"No, I regretted it as soon as I left. I just . . . jumped to conclusions about you, and it wasn't fair. I've been watching over that house as long as I've been back, and it's kind of an attractive nuisance; people think it's abandoned. There're so many tourists and it's amazing what they'll do sometimes. People broke in one summer—not kids, or homeless people, some guy in a Land Rover and his wife. They jimmied the lock so they could 'look around.' They acted like they owned the place too."

"You were looking out for my interests. . . . It's human nature to be . . . proprietary like that."

He smiled, with rue. "Yeah, human nature, I know it well. It'll be nice to have real people living in the house, after all this time."

"I don't know if we quite count as real people—we're pretty much tourists ourselves."

"Nah, you're washashores now."

"What?"

"Washashores! Tourists come and go, but you washed up on the beach, right at our feet. Like stranded whales, either we've gotta push you back out to sea or you're here for the duration."

"What a lovely image," Charlotte said, and he smiled so widely at this that she did too.

"Everything okay in the house? I tried to clear some of the dust out and such."

"It's amazing," she said. "It must have been quite a job."

"Couple hours," he said. "Nothing, really." Then, bending down to speak to Fiona—"How do you like your new house?"

Charlotte gathered Fiona up onto her hip so she'd be at eye level, but she was too shy and ducked her head into her mother's shoulder. Darryl waited, a smile playing, until she gave in and peeked up at him.

"I climbed the tree," she said, and hid her face again.

"You did? All by yourself?"

She nodded vigorously against Charlotte's shoulder.

"She's a little shy," Charlotte explained.

"But a good climber."

Fiona looked up with perplexed delight. "Mo-o-om," she said. "He's a nice man."

"He is," Charlotte said, feeling shy herself. "I didn't think to bring lightbulbs with me," she explained. "Or dinner."

"I should have checked the bulbs," he said. In fact, they were on the shelf right behind him, beside paper towels and other sundries. To get them she would have to reach past him.

"You did more than enough," she said.

He smiled and shrugged, but otherwise didn't move.

"Do you . . . Could I . . . Um, the lightbulbs are behind you, I think. . . ."

"Oh, oh, sorry. Sixty-watt okay?" It was strange to see something as fragile as a package of lightbulbs held delicately in that huge hand.

"Are there any hundreds?" Henry liked one-fifty if possible.

He looked, and shook his head. "You might have to go to Orleans for that."

A small, rabbitlike old man came around from the back of the store, wearing a satin-lined cloak and carrying two bottles of red wine.

"Orson," Darryl said. "I didn't know you were here."

"And yet," Orson replied, in a surprisingly deep, resonant voice, "I can always sense *your* presence. I'm going up to Provincetown to see *Cat on a Hot Tin Roof*; would you care to join me?"

Darryl's smile was fond, forbearing. "I have to build gear tonight," he said. "But have fun."

"Fun? I expect I shall be eviscerated," he said, counting out exact change for the wine. "As Williams intended. Oh, hello!" he said, seeing Charlotte. "I don't believe I've had the pleasure." He extended a soft, white hand.

"I'm Charlotte Tradescome."

"Of Tradescome Point?"

She nodded, then felt as if she weren't quite being truthful. "My husband is a Tradescome. It's my married name."

"Henry Tradescome?"

"Yes," she said, surprised. "Did you know him when he lived here?"

"I know his work. A fine sensibility he has. A pure flame of rage."

"Thank you."

"I'm Orson DesRoches; please give him my regards. Oh, there's my cab. I must away...."

An old green Mercedes was idling outside, and Orson hastened out, gathering his cape around him, and slid into the backseat.

"'I must away...'?" Charlotte asked.

"He has a dramatic streak."

"So I see."

That was all. Charlotte got a can of chicken noodle soup and a can of beets, vinegar for the beets, milk with a good date, the light-bulbs, soap, and a package of little cereal boxes that made Fiona gasp with joy. Some Rolling Rock, and the *Cape Cod Times*, whose headline read, "Global Cod Catch Declines Again." Darryl gave a low wave as he went out, and she waited behind one of the other guys, who had bought ten lottery tickets and was scratching them off, to the cashier's apparent fascination. He won five dollars and bought five more tickets. One of these yielded ten dollars, which instantly translated into ten tickets.

"Excuse me?" Charlotte said, fearful he'd win the big thousand-dollar payoff and she'd never get home. The cashier, a weathered, sinewy woman with a long braid down her back, sighed as if Charlotte's outrageous demands would kill her, and held her twenty up to the light in case it was counterfeit. Seeing it wasn't, she completed the sale and turned back to the lottery scratcher.

"Do you have a bag?"

The cashier's shoulders slumped, as if this were the kind of un-reasonable demand she might have expected from such a person as Charlotte, but she pulled out a paper bag, dumped the purchases into it, pushed it across the counter.

"Anything?" the clerk asked the lottery scratcher. Her point was clear enough: Charlotte was wearing a pair of loose-fitting, dull red corduroys and a striped shirt, and driving a new Volvo station wagon with New York plates. And the coat on the little girl—to spend like that on something that would be outgrown before the next winter! No, Charlotte was here because she could afford to be here. The clerk was here because she couldn't afford to leave. Charlotte wouldn't be getting one thing from her, not so much as a paper bag or a smile.

5

RICH

The cashier had been right: They had become rich. And almost without blinking an eye. By selling a single acre of land on the point, they had made enough to live on for years.

They closed on the lot in May, not long after they moved into the house. The town's pulse had quickened; the boards came off the windows on the Lemon Pie Cottages along Route 6A, and yellow shutters went up. Hammers rang and saws whined from morning till night, and the smell of fresh paint filled the cold air, but the sun that bred lilacs on the mainland produced only fog in Wellfleet; if that fog thinned and turned gold in the late afternoon, you had to count it as a nice day. Charlotte and Henry stood before their furnace, a wheezing behemoth, in prayerful ignorance, with Fiona crying at the top of the stairs for fear it would eat them. How did one gain its favor? Charlotte put on another sweater; she would not admit Henry had been right about the heat.

Forty miles up the cape, where the land was wider and the water's influence weaker, the lilacs bent in lush, wet bloom outside the Registry of Deeds. The buyer was a man named Jeb Narville, who'd made millions "in asphalt," however one did that. Somehow Charlotte knew it was him standing on the lawn beside the flagpole, a short, powerfully built man whose red face was crushed in around an avid, avaricious squint. She'd bumped up against such a person once before—the salesman who sold her the Volvo. She had bought the car just to get away.

"Mr. Narville?"

"Are you the seller or the attorney?" he asked, looking her up and down in a way that reminded her of every single flaw she had. She hadn't dyed her hair since they got to Wellfleet, so there were two inches of mouse brown roots before the mahogany color she'd thought so Brontë-esque, and she was wearing a flowered dress that had looked girlish and sweet on its hanger. But she was no longer a girl, and the uncertainty, the yearning on her face had become embarrassing: She ought to have figured things out by now.

"The seller," she apologized, and saw all interest leave Narville's eyes. "Your new neighbors," she added, extending her hand, smiling. Her smile showed the best things about her—her general tenderness and curiosity, her true concern. It made her beautiful and persuasive, and she relied on this without really understanding it. Jeb Narville did not attend to smiles, though—he kept his eye on the bottom line.

"The attorney will be here in a minute," Charlotte offered quickly, wanting, as always, to please. Henry was hovering behind her, here to sign his name but doing his best to stay invisible. He might have been mistaken for her servant. A bumblebee was flying low around them, trying out the clover blossoms in the grass, but every flower the fat thing settled on bent to the ground under its weight.

"Here's Skip now," Charlotte said. He was coming up from the parking lot and, seeing him, Narville relaxed, reassured by his stride, or his grooming—his hair was blown dry, his fingernails neat, his wingtips newly shined. The bumblebee had found itself a sturdy clover top just in front of them, and without thinking Narville ground the life out of it with his toe.

"Let's roll," he said, invigorated. They started up the marble steps, Skip pulling the registry door open and ushering them grandly through the metal detector. For the next half hour they bent over their papers, signing and signing, no one looking anyone in the eye. Then Jeb said he had a plane to catch.

"You're not going up to Wellfleet?"

"Gotta get back to work," he said. "A lost hour is a lost opportunity. Speaking of which, Skip, let me ask you something...."

They were out the door before Charlotte could say good-bye. It felt wrong, but then all business felt cold and dissonant to her. The cop at the metal detector directed her to the ladies' room, where she sat with head in hands until her nausea passed, repeating to herself: "We're millionaires, we're millionaires." It had to be a good thing.

All the way home, Henry glowered until she saw his resemblance to Great-aunt Vestina. "We'll put it in the bank, obviously," he said.

"Oh, I'd been thinking of building a gold fairy castle for Fiona. And a replica of the Trevi Fountain to replace the old well." He was the most dour and forbidding man on earth, and the only one she dared contradict. "Actually, apart from fixing up the bathroom, and maybe getting some mattresses that are younger than I am, I was thinking we ought to invest it."

"Now you're an authority on the stock market?" he asked.

"No, I'm going to try to find one."

"Where would you begin to look?"

Natalie's brother suggested a place in Boston, where men pallid as mushrooms dog eared folders in a back room, while in the front a person named Richmond Chase—"Call me Rich," he said without irony—took them out to a lunch of Belon oysters and seared tuna, showing them different pie charts and talking in a voice of plummy self-assurance about the outlook for Standard & Poor's. Charlotte, hearing the words *wealth* and *investment* over and over like this, remembered her parents sitting at the kitchen table, drinking wine and dreaming about what things would be like when they got out of debt. They'd had a few happy evenings that way. Henry looked claustrophobic, locked in a bank vault with his parents' money and no reading lamp. Rich, sensing their anxiousness, tried an analogy.

"It's a bit like raising a sail," he said. "You leave your sheets loose, or they'd fill before you were steady on your course. We want to take you in easy. . . ." The room was too hot. Words like *luff*, *leech*, and *boom* drifted past, shifting form like clouds. Charlotte looked at her watch: They'd left Fiona with Skip Godwin's wife, as the Godwins had a daughter about the same age. It was hard to be away from her, almost physically hard—she'd need something, she'd look for her mother, she was too young to understand time, and she'd start to feel frightened and alone. Charlotte tried to catch Henry's eye, but he was staring out the window like a schoolboy in June.

"Do you golf?" Rich was asking, sensing he'd lost them. Charlotte touched her toe to Henry's under the table. She had remembered their beginnings—the way she'd peered in through his curmudgeon's scowl and seen the lost child back there, timid but fascinated with life, watching it avidly from the safe spot behind his desk. Someone not unlike herself, not at all.

6

THE SEAWALL

Impossible to get away from Rich Chase's office without running the gauntlet of beggars set up along the sidewalks nearby. A dollar in the cup did nothing to assuage Charlotte's guilt; nor did it satisfy the woman she'd given it to, who shot her a hard look—why not twenty? Why not a hundred? Trudging up the ramp of the parking garage, Charlotte realized she had no idea where she'd left the car. They circled up and down through the industrial labyrinth, like ants in a machine. "It was right here," Charlotte kept insisting, standing in a particular corner. But all the corners were the same. A familiar dread settled in her chest—she couldn't manage, the way everyone else seemed to. Education had only shown her how little on earth was certain; marriage seemed a kind of structured loneliness, and the job—oh, thank God she had found a way to escape that job! To go up in the elevator, up and up until you could see over the whole city, and kick off your glamorous heels under a desk where you are paid to comb through photographs analyzing celebrity style trends! Of course, nothing you wanted to say could actually be printed: "So and so perfectly complements her own natural bovinity with this stunning cowhide vest." Oh, no.

And everyone, *everyone*, would say—"Oh, you write for *Celeb*," as if this meant you were a very accomplished person. Only Henry had the wit to sneer at it. Henry, whom everyone looked up to—she'd expected him to guide her. He was twenty years older; it was only fair. But Henry would never have taken time from his reading to buy a car and certainly would never have parked one in some immense garage.

"There it is," he said comfortably, pointing to something of a similar shape.

"Well, that one is blue, and ours is green. And it's a Saturn, where ours is a Volvo. It does have four wheels...." Perhaps she sounded too sharp. He was like some Darwinian insect who secreted an impenetrable shell made of politics and poetry, and reached a bony claw out only for an occasional morsel, or the necessary mating. Charlotte started to cry, causing him to withdraw more completely.

The search took nearly an hour, but as they drove back toward home the tint of meaning seeped into things again. There was still a bouquet fastened to the Sagamore Bridge in the same spot, but now it was full-blown peonies with a blue ribbon fluttering in the breeze. In Orleans the middle school was letting out; the buses passed by at the light, all of them named for their destinations: White Crest, Drummer Cove, Penniman's Landing. Every child went home to his singular spot, a place with its own history, noble or mundane. The Turnip Field bus went through the old farmland; Penniman's destination was the cluster of houses beside a town landing, once a stop on the Underground Railroad.

Fiona came bounding out the Godwins' door, full of news (they had played with the Godwins' hamster!), and, lifting her up, Charlotte knew the exact weight of grace. At home she clomped up the stairs and pulled off her suit, feeling like a cat that had clawed off its doll clothes and scratched and licked itself to retrieve its dignity. In the bathtub she poured pitcher after pitcher of water over her head, washing off the day. The bay was a satiny spring blue, as smooth as the future spread before them.

They were sitting at breakfast the next morning when the mason jars on the windowsill started clinking together; the living room chandelier swayed as it must have when it still hung in the *Kingfisher*'s salon.

"Tanks?" Henry asked brightly.

"That is what it sounds like," Charlotte said, "but . . ." There came another huge shudder and Fiona's building-block castle crashed to the floor.

"What's a tank?" she asked, clinging to Charlotte's leg.

"Something soldiers drive in a war, honey, but that's not what it is."

"Earthquake?" Henry tried, cheerful. "People underestimate the New England fault lines."

"They do," Charlotte said, "they do."

"*Orthquake?*" Fiona shrieked, her eyes huge, her teddy bear tight in the crook of her arm.

It was a bulldozer, biting off huge hunks of their beachfront— well, Narville's beachfront—followed by a convoy of dump trucks, each one loaded with boulders.

"Tanks would be better," Charlotte said as the bulldozer slammed its bucket into the earth and a piece of the shore crumbled forward. "What are they doing?" Charlotte asked.

A smile crept over Henry's face. "Developing real estate," he said. He'd warned her not to play with fire.

"Well, I'm going out to see," she said.

"No!" Fiona cried.

"It's safe, honey." The best view was from the kitchen door—Charlotte held Fiona up to see. "Look, there's a man driving it, just like a car."

"Cars stay on the street!" Fiona insisted, blotches breaking out on her cheeks and neck. Of course, in the city there was that magical barrier, the curb.

"Come with me," Charlotte said. "I'll keep you right on my hip."

"No!"

"Okay, then stay with Daddy and you can watch me out the window."

"*Nooooooo!*"

"Let Mother go," Henry said, glowering.

"Henry, she's frightened."

"There's nothing to be afraid of," he said. "She's got to learn not to bother you all the time."

"She's *not* bothering me! Why . . . ?"

Why couldn't he hold out his hand to his daughter? Why couldn't he say, "Stay here with me, because I'd like that"? The house shuddered as one of the dump trucks dropped its ton of rock, and Fiona screamed: "*Mommy*, don't go!"

"If someone doesn't discipline that child, I don't know what's going to become . . ." Henry said, going back down the stairs into the basement.

At the stroke of noon the thunder ceased, and the bulldozer operator stepped down and examined his work. "Now?" Charlotte asked. Fiona nodded bravely, and Charlotte lifted her up and ventured across the threadbare lawn. The lilacs were opening finally—she pulled down a branch so Fiona could smell the pure sweetness as they passed.

She shouldn't have been surprised when the bulldozer guy

turned out to be Darryl—everyone here worked two jobs if not more, and still ends rarely seemed to meet.

"Hey," she said.

"I figured I'd be seeing you," he said sheepishly.

"What are you doing?"

"Building a seawall. I mean, it's not my idea, just I was hired to do it, that's all."

"But . . ."

"I know," he said. "It makes no sense. It's not like we're exposed to open water. You don't get big waves in here except maybe in a hurricane. It's kind of . . . a fad, really. A lot of people over on Try Point have seawalls now, and then everyone starts to want one."

"Like designer shoes."

He laughed. "I suppose. Except designer shoes don't run counter to nature."

"Clearly you've never tried on a pair of designer shoes."

"No," he said, "that's true."

"This is kind of . . . cataclysmic," she said. The bulldozer had taken giant bites out of the shorefront and begun to fit boulders— from a pile ten feet high—together to make the wall. Everything else was so peaceful—the tide was low and still, about to turn, and way out a flock of white birds wheeled together and landed in perfect sync. There was a chill breeze off the water, but heat was rising from the ground. Darryl wiped his forehead with his sleeve.

"I don't disagree," he said. "I've got oysters out there, and everything you do here affects them. The seawalls change the tidal flow; it's bad for my herd, for everyone's. But it's gonna happen one way or another, and I need the work."

"Your 'herd'?"

"Of oysters . . ."

"Do they stampede at all?"

He smiled—this wasn't the first time he'd heard that joke. "They're pretty sedate."

"Phew. Glad to hear it. We sold them this land," she admitted suddenly. His apology at SixMart had been contagious somehow; she wanted to return it.

"Well, you gotta do what you gotta do," he said, rushing to exonerate her. The smallest act of generosity, of awareness. It felt as good as the spring air. "Believe me, if I owned this place . . ."

He stopped. No stepping into that morass. He lived back in the Driftwood Cabins like half the rest of the town. If you hadn't already owned a place before the buying frenzy in the mid-nineties, you were out of luck now. And there was no such thing as a year-round rental, not when a landlord could make more by the week in tourist season than by the month the rest of the year. Wellfleet was owned by wealthy city people . . . people like Charlotte. Locals—fishermen, carpenters, cooks, waiters, chambermaids—lived on the leftovers. And were proud of it. You had to be proud; otherwise you'd have to be ashamed. Some flicker of this showed on Darryl's face and Charlotte rushed in:

"In some ways you're more of an owner than I am," she said. "You work here every day." This attitude, like so many things, she had learned from Henry.

An involuntary smile spread over his face. "I do know it, very well."

"Maybe you'll show us the oysters—your herd?—sometime?" Charlotte said.

"My pleasure."

Fiona was sitting bolt upright on Charlotte's hip, watching as if she'd like to take notes. "Maybe *you'd* like a ride on the bulldozer?" Darryl asked.

She stiffened. "No!"

"Okay, I promise. No bulldozer rides. But I've got to take one myself now, get this done. The tide's going out and my herd needs me." He grabbed his water bottle from the cab and drank it down. Charlotte had rarely felt so physically aware of a man—in the city they all had the same muscles, created by the same gym equipment, but Darryl's had been made by work. His joints were huge; she could see the tendons glide over the bones—she had a guilty wish to see an X-ray of his shoulder. Still, he moved so quickly, he was back in the driver's seat before she could say a word.

Wait a sec, she mouthed to him over Fiona's head, and he nodded, waiting to start the bulldozer until they were back safely in the house. Fiona ran to the window to watch him drive away.

"Mom, we made a new friend!" she said.

"In New York, you'd have to get used to a new building that blocked off your whole view. A seawall, really it's rocks where there used to be grass," Charlotte said. She'd been addressing Henry, but he was buried in the *Times*, so she found herself talking to Fiona, who listened greedily, if without understanding. "It feels kind of suburban, that's what's sad, when what I love here is how wild it is. And the way the high tide slaps against it—it sounds so . . . contained. But we still have waves right out front, so we can't really complain."

A gleaming black pickup drove into the driveway, one she recognized from the nightly procession to the flats, though she didn't know the men who jumped out. She went to the door, figuring they were about to knock, but no, they had shovels—they were uprooting the lilacs.

"Wait, wait! Sir! Excuse me?" Charlotte ran out to them, but neither looked up. They were working energetically, angrily even, as if they knew they were making trouble and were glad to do it.

"Excuse me," she said again, sounding imperious by now, but at least that made them stop. The older one was wearing an eye patch, something she had never before seen in real life.

"What?" He took instant offense.

"Why are you digging up my lilacs?"

"Putting a fence here."

"What? Who? Are you working for the Narvilles?"

"Yup," he said, insolent—as if to say, *And there's nothing you can do about it.*

"Well, I don't believe these bushes belong to the Narvilles."

"He hired me to take 'em out."

"I think there's a misunderstanding," she said. "Not sure, but I guess we'd better slow down a minute and see what's what exactly."

The landscaper sliced his spade into the ground. "I'm hired to do this today," he said.

"Do I have to call the police?"

The guy shrugged and continued his work, daring her.

Charlotte called Skip Godwin, who said she could call the surveyor, but from what he understood the property line ran about three feet east of their driveway. Straddled by the lilacs.

"I didn't think," Charlotte said to Henry. "I didn't imagine. . . . Why would anyone take out a whole stand of lilacs, right in full bloom?"

"Didn't think," Henry echoed, giving her a significant look over the top of his glasses. His madcow-birdflu-globalwarming-Bush-administration look: Things go wrong, they always do, and if they had stayed in New York, they, and the lilacs, would have been kept from such harm.

"I guess it's better not to fight it?" she asked.

"I wouldn't."

She went back out. "You were right," she said, as graciously as she could manage. "I'm just wondering, do you have any plans for those bushes? Because I could probably replant them." Not that she had ever planted anything larger than a pot of basil.

"Using 'em on another job," he said, pleased to disappoint her. "Part of the deal."

The next day he came back and sank posts, and soon there was a white board fence, six feet tall, topped at intervals with carriage lamps. Charlotte stayed in the house, noticing from the window that his bumper sticker read, DON'T HASSLE ME, I'M A LOCAL.

"To put up a fence before you build the house, what do you suppose that means?" she asked Henry.

"Nothing very deep," Henry said.

"I don't think the Narvilles realize what they're doing," Charlotte said. "They've barely ever been here. I'm afraid they're not going to like it when they see how . . . out of place . . . it all looks."

"They don't care how it looks to you," he said. "It's their fence."

"It's cutting off the whole east side of the view."

"Look west."

"Well, I'm going to call them. Just . . . to get to know them a little."

She dialed in a righteous fury, and got Mrs. Narville—Andrea, or On-dray-uh.

"Oh, you're our neighbors up there," Andrea said, without enthusiasm. "Are you there right now?" she asked.

"Um, yes."

"Wow, how early do you usually go?"

"I . . . I guess I'm not sure what you're asking."

"It's kind of empty out there now, isn't it? Do you always go out before Memorial Day?"

"We just . . . live here," Charlotte said.

"Oh, wow." Andrea's voice was slow and husky, with a Southern accent but almost no inflection, so that a sentence like, "Oh, wow," took on a satirical cast. "Aren't you lucky. You don't go crazy in the winters?"

"Well, we haven't been through a winter yet." Charlotte laughed. "I guess we'll see."

"There's something I'd been wondering," Andrea said. "Where do you get your hair done? I mean, where are the high-end salons there, the salon-spa-type places? Is there a good one in Wellfleet, or do you have to go out of town?"

"I . . . I don't know. I'll try to find out for you."

"Thanks, honey, that's really good of you."

"Listen, Andrea, the reason I called is, they just put up your fence here, and . . . I'm not sure it's really what you want."

"Why, what's the matter? It's supposed to be the same as the one we have here at home."

"Well, maybe that's the thing. It's very wild out here and the fence feels more . . . like something that belongs somewhere else. It's so high, it's like . . . well, it felt as if everything was wide-open and natural out here, and now the seawall, and the fence, and . . ."

"You know, honey, Jeb deals with all those things. Honestly I don't even know what he ordered for fencing. Why don't you call back later, okay?"

She did, and got the machine, and when Jeb finally answered, the next evening, she realized her mistake.

"Good fences make good neighbors!" Jeb said. "Robert Frost, right?"

"He quoted that to debunk it," she said in a small voice.

"I'm not really a literary type," he answered, "but I'd guess you'd need to ask Mr. Frost to get the lowdown on that."

"It's six feet tall," Charlotte said. "Six-foot-one is a spite fence."

"A spite fence? I've never heard that term. I'd call it a privacy fence."

"But . . . there's nobody out here. It's private with or without a fence." Charlotte had taken down the kitchen curtains, intending to replace them, until she realized they were unnecessary. No one could look in the windows unless they were on a boat in the bay. "And they dug up those lilac bushes; they were eight feet high at least."

"Flowers. Another of my weak points, I'm afraid. Did you mind the lilacs, since they were so much taller?"

"Well, no . . ."

"And the fence is on my side of the property line?"

"Yes."

"I'm sure you know more about poetry and lilacs than I do, Mrs. Tradescome, but I feel pretty comfortable on the topic of real estate, and as far as my understanding goes, what I do with my property is my own business. Is there something I'm missing?"

"No." The tide was ebbing. The first of the oyster trucks jounced over the path toward the water, which was crosshatched with neon pinks and oranges, reflecting the sky.

"End of conversation, then, eh?" he said, genial. "Unless you'd like to get back on with Andrea."

"No thanks, just give her my best."

"I certainly will."

· · ·

The fence blocked their view of the road from the driveway, but who ever came down this road, except the occasional curious tourist, and the oystermen at low tide? Then Charlotte took Fiona for an after-dinner ice-cream cone and turned onto Point Road into the path of an oncoming truck. She braked hard, he braked hard, and they stopped sideways, inches apart. Fiona was in the back, in the car seat, and Charlotte saw her in the rearview mirror; her dark eyes were wide and watchful, but not frightened, not as long as she was with her mom.

The driver of the truck—eye-patch guy—leaped out and came toward Charlotte as if to pull her out of her seat through the window.

"What the *fuck* do you think you're doing . . . ?"

"I'm sorry," she said. He'd been on the wrong side of the road, but this was no time to argue the fine points. "I'm so sorry."

He clenched his fists. His arms were immense, and tattooed over every inch with an aquarium's worth of sea creatures, each drawn with such precision they could have illustrated a textbook. *This is the kind of thing you notice*, Charlotte thought, *when you're about to be strangled*. She watched for a long second as he wavered between reining in his anger and just killing her.

"Are you all right?" she asked. Because he was, which meant he had no excuse to hurt her. He looked down at her with a loathing that seemed to grow until he decided finally that she was not worthy of a beating. Another truck was coming along behind him, and he went back to his, spitting: "*Look both ways*," over his shoulder.

"Mom, was that a pirate?"

Charlotte laughed, though she was trembling all over. "He'd have made a good pirate, wouldn't he?" she said, as lightly as she could.

The next truck was Darryl's patchwork one, with ladder rails made of two-by-fours. He turned down the driveway beside her and rolled his window down.

"Was that Tim?"

"Is that his name? I thought he was going to kill me." The trembling seized her now that she wasn't alone.

Darryl reached out to her, then pulled his hand instinctively back.

"Tim is . . . he's had his troubles."

"Were any of them murders?"

"No." He laughed. "He's a good guy, really. You should see his claim—his oyster claim, you know—no one else is so scrupulous about it. He had a couple of animals with QPX—that's a parasite—last year, and he dug the whole thing out, every last ounce of sand, all the seed clams, trucked it all out of here—way beyond any requirements; it was painful to see it. He's driven, he's a perfectionist, he's got an anger problem, but really, he means well. . . ."

"Convinced yourself yet?"

He smiled and sighed. "He's my brother-in-law," he admitted. "I've gotta keep on his good side."

"What's with the eye patch?"

"Oh." Darryl winced. "Fishhook."

"In the eye?" Charlotte squinted hers shut, for fear he'd say that fishhooks sometimes blew into people's eyes on Cape Cod.

"It was back when he was scalloping," Darryl said. "Drink four days and fish three, you know."

She did not know, but nodded.

"So, you're okay?"

"Oh, I'm fine," she said, brushing it off. It surprised her to hear such honest concern in a man's voice.

7

TUNA SEASON

She was coming to know the place a little; the summer began and she learned to live according to the local rhythms, doing her errands in the early morning before the tourists were awake, or at noon on a hot day when they were all at the beach. Summer rain constituted an emergency: Vacationers trying to escape their motel units would hop in their cars to creep, bumper-to-bumper, north toward Province-town or south to Orleans. Charlotte had learned to stay home. She knew the tides by smell—the rich brine and sulfur stench of the ebb, the fresh, sharp scent of a high-tide plankton bloom that gave a deep sense of well-being, as if the most primitive, waterborne part of her recognized it as plenty.

And the people: oystermen, artists, Trotskyites still reeling from the breakup of the Soviet Union, ecologists who revered the hognose snake and the spadefoot toad. The extended Mulligan clan, who'd met one another at Woodstock, recognized their natural affinity, and moved to Wellfleet to start a commune. That hadn't worked, but they'd married into one configuration and then another, the kids liv-ing back and forth between parents' and stepparents' houses until they were as homogeneous as a family, and each of them with his or her trade—plumbing, landscaping, sweeping the chimney. They weren't all Mulligans, but that was the name that stuck, and if you had termites or your well went dry people would say, "Isn't there a Mulligan for that?" Beyond the Mulligans, there were lobster divers, chambermaids, and, in the summer, professors and editors who found the lobster divers and chambermaids irresistibly attractive. There were Freudian analysts, Jungian analysts, and a stray Kleinian analyst who was furious at both groups. There was Sklew Margison, who had a Nobel Prize in physics, for discovering something no one could explain. And Reggie the glass eater, who was said once to have swallowed a shot glass right along with the bourbon in it, and shown no ill effects. Reggie got around on a bicycle, calling out, "Telegram!" as he passed. Those in the know replied with a cheerful: "Rhode Island Red!"

And Ada Town, the old woman who walked to the end of the point every morning regardless of the weather, dressed in a neat skirt and blouse and always with lively interest in her face. She'd been found on the church steps as an infant, rowed in from a passing ship, people said. Someone had seen a light on the water, heard the quiet splash of an oar. This scene, like so much of the town's history, remained vivid in every imagination—the streets were still narrow, angling up from the harbor to the town center, where the Congregational Church stood at the highest point, its steeple stark against the sky. If you stood on the steps there, you could see exactly how a dory might have been pulled ashore for the minute it would take to run up the hill and set a baby safely at the church door. It was said she was found in a life preserver ring; it was said that some ship's captain had a child with a woman in another port, that he promised to keep the baby secret, but safe, to see it was raised with kindness. "A child not of one man and one woman, but of every man and woman in Wellfleet, our responsibility and our joy," the minister had said, christening her with the name of Town. Ada had been Henry's babysitter in the summers, when his father brought the family out to Wellfleet, "rattling around alone" in Boston during the week, arriving in the Buick on Friday evenings to take great, satisfied lungfuls of air on the front porch as if he were breathing in virtue itself.

This was how Charlotte pieced Henry's father together, from the scraps in Henry's memory, and the few photographs: the one they'd kept in his room at the nursing home and one of him with his pipe, looking the way some men did back then, truly, quietly confident of his place in the world. In the family portrait he looked only forbidding, and Henry's mother was blond, tailored, and in her face a stony misery that might be mistaken for haughtiness. Or maybe she'd been haughty. Whatever, Henry, who might have been four or five, stood between them, so intent on the model ship he was holding that he didn't seem aware of his parents' presence. "That was my nature," he said, when Charlotte asked him. "They were the most upright, honorable people, and they had to put up with me. It wasn't easy for them. It's not their fault I'm the way I am."

Singing Fiona her lullaby in the evening, looking out to see the tide pushing in through the spartina, until only the green tops showed, Charlotte felt that one part of this was true: that every child is born with something of his or her own, beyond DNA. Fiona's fierce little spirit, her purposeful goodness, seemed set solidly in her from the day she was born. Her cheeks flushed as she slept, as if that same ambition was still working. Falling asleep herself, Charlotte heard the tide, gentle at first, then, on a windy night, rushing and swirling up the serpentine paths of the river, straight into her dreams.

At five a.m. Fiona awoke, like a little general, ready to march into the day. If only she dared leave the safe island of her bed—but no, so she called for her mother until Charlotte stumbled down the hall in the bleak light.

"Yes, darlin', here's your mom." *Your deeply resentful mom.* Never once had Fiona called for Henry, who wouldn't anyway know a child's cry from a gull's. When Fiona was tiny Charlotte had assigned him the two a.m. feeding—he was usually still at his desk at that hour—but after a few nights in the crook of his bony arm, sucking on her bottle while he read *The Economist,* Fiona had given up and started sleeping through the night.

The little arms cinched around Charlotte's neck; the damp forehead rested on her shoulder. "Oh, Mama," Fiona said, "there's no place like you."

So then it was worth everything. It was a new moon; the trucks were parked on the flats with their headlights shining over the grants so the men could work. The best, lowest tides came at the new moon, just before dawn.

"Maybe you'll have an oyster farm when you grow up," Charlotte said. "You seem to like the hours." Fiona cuddled in deeper, rubbing her soft little earlobe between thumb and forefinger, "whispering my ear," as she called it, while Charlotte brewed coffee, heated milk for cocoa. The house smelled of old summers, shells and seaweed and sun-bleached bones, a boy's rank treasures. It was as if the ghost of Henry as a child still lived here, slamming the screen door, racing down the lawn to the bay. A boy all alone, without siblings or cousins or even aunts and uncles—just the parents, those models of rectitude, his grandfather the ancient mariner, and Great-aunt Vestina on the wall.

Once Vestina's frame broke, the paint began to flake off the canvas and the mean face turned pathetic. Charlotte put her in the attic with the other things they couldn't bear to throw away. Up there, where the wiring ran between porcelain knobs, and a thick spiderweb was spun in the corner of the one small window, history felt less romantic and more cruel. There were two steamer trunks full of old papers—ships' logs, mostly, cargo all neatly detailed: wheat, lard and whalebone, tallow, boots, and staves. Or maybe slaves. The paper was brittle and sooty—it had been through a fire. Fires on shipboard, like smallpox and gangrene and all manner of other terrors, had been common back then, and you could smell this somehow when one of those trunks was opened. Henry had wanted to sell them, with everything else, to an antique dealer up-cape; Charlotte wanted to go through them, try to find something out. Or so she said. In fact she was afraid of the spiders and the old wiring and the papers that told the story of the dangers people faced, the dark, cold lives they had lived then. The antique dealer, a short and wide woman who was named Grace, though Charlotte thought Avarice would have been just as pretty and more apt, insisted it was foolish to keep the trunks, that they would draw in buyers who would drive up all the prices, but Charlotte couldn't let them go. Instead, anxious to please this woman she'd never met before and would never see again, she gave up the crystalline gouaches on the living room wall.

"Out with it, all of it," Henry had said, shuddering. He'd have given up the painting of the *Kingfisher*, but this Charlotte had the courage to hold on to. "Your great-grandfather built it. Your grandfather sailed it. Surely it has some sentimental value?" she asked. The most ordinary things—a scorched glass pie dish, the sight of a horse standing in a field—would trip her into grief suddenly. Her mother had been such a soft, defenseless creature, and Charlotte couldn't help picturing her wandering alone out there in the empty space between the stars, with no one to protect her. When Charlotte buttered a piece of toast for Fiona in the morning, she felt as if it might keep her mother from feeling so lonely. She knew it was silly, but she did. "I'm not a sentimentalist," Henry said, irritated, dying to get back downstairs to his reading. "Keep the painting if you like; it's no business of mine."

She did, and bought a big pillowy sofa to replace the stiff velvet one. She set it to face the window. Snuggled into it in the morning, with Fiona on her lap, she felt safer than she ever had before.

The sky grew pale, blurred with fog, but the terns sparkled in the midst of it, their wings catching flashes of sun. The tide was ebbing; the first trucks turned down toward the flats. They'd see to the oysters and be at work on land by nine o'clock—Darryl and some of the others were building the Narville house, which rose with mighty pretension on the other side of the fence. Charlotte tried to ignore it, which wasn't easy, given its lighthouse-shaped tower, and the delivery-by-crane of a stainless-steel hot tub said to have been made to Andrea Narville's measure, with the jets placed just so—at a cost of twenty thousand dollars. Every day the Narvilles dreamed up some new flourish—the latest a fishpond stocked with exotic Asian breeds: koi, comets, shubunkins, and a meditation platform shaped like a lily pad in the center: Andrea was very serious about her yoga.

Darryl and Charlotte had laughed over this in the hardware store the day before. He was ordering more shingles; she was renting a tank of wallpaper remover. The living room wallpaper, a print of brown and purple feathers, was waterstained in the corners from some leak long ago, peeling off as the wall crumbled away behind it.

"It's fine," Henry said. "I've barely noticed it. What can't be cured must be endured, as Mother used to say."

"But it can be cured."

"If you say so," he said, retreating to his study. Charlotte had marched off to rent the equipment, just to show him a thing or two. She felt ridiculous, lugging the heavy tank of paper remover up the front steps. What did she know about real estate development, or home renovation, or anything? Henry at least had the sense to stay safe behind his book.

But it was easy! You sprayed, you waited; then you pulled the sheet of wallpaper away, using the scraper to unstick the stubborn bits. It didn't smell bad, it didn't leak, it didn't burn. It was easy and Charlotte was competent. She imagined herself on one of those home-improvement shows, demonstrating the right technique, spraying until each sheet of wallpaper was thoroughly wet, waiting, using the scraper to unstick the stubborn bits as she pulled it away. By dinner she'd nearly finished. She stood in the doorway admiring her work, dirty and tired and as satisfied as if she'd just painted a masterpiece. The room seemed bigger, and the bay seemed closer somehow. She had poured herself a glass of wine and toasted her reflection in the china cupboard.

Now, in the morning sunlight, she saw something was peculiar. The paper had come off but the surface beneath was porous and chalky—it looked as if it would absorb paint like a sponge. She scratched her fingernail across it, making a deep mark.

"What . . . ?" She tugged at the edge of one of the scraps of wallpaper that was left. . . . It had bonded completely with the paper covering of the drywall beneath—she hadn't been stripping wallpaper; she'd been pulling the walls apart.

"Henry!" But he was still asleep.

"Oh, Fiona," she said. "What have I done?"

"It's okay, Mama," Fiona said, kissing her forehead just as Charlotte would have done if she herself had been upset.

Darryl's truck turned down the driveway toward the flats. She rushed out to the porch, pulling her bathrobe around her, waving an SOS.

"What's up?"

"I don't know. I was stripping the wallpaper, and it's like I've turned the house to mush."

"What do you mean?"

"I don't know; it seems like the wallboard is all crumbling. I got it too wet, or . . . I don't know." She could hardly bear to look at it; it was like the time she'd cut one of Fiona's little toenails too short and it started to bleed.

"The tide," he said, anxious, looking out at the water and back to her face. "Well, I'll come take a quick look."

He took off his rubber boots on the porch and came in in his socks, to pick at the edge of the last bit of paper. "No sizing," he said. "They cut corners on the job; they pasted the wallpaper straight to the drywall. Or . . . this stuff is old . . . maybe drywall was such a new thing they didn't know they had to size it. God, what a mess."

"Thanks."

"Looks like you made a big effort here," he said, consoling.

"Yeah, it's hard work, ruining a place like this."

"I *think* you can coat it with mud . . . you know, like plaster. I'm not sure, but you could try."

Charlotte sat back on the arm of the couch. "I was so proud of it," she said, as lightly as she could. Truly, the mistake seemed a sign of how wrong she'd been to think she could manage this house, this new life.

"It's okay," he said. "It's the kind of thing that happens with an old house. Believe me, I've done enough renovations to know it's always one step forward and two back."

"What do I do?"

"Let's see . . . get some lightweight joint compound, a plasterer's trowel. . . . Do you have a belt sander?"

This made Charlotte laugh.

"I can help you," he said, and meant it, but his shoulders sank slightly, from the new little weight.

"No, you've got the oysters, and the monstrosity. . . ." She nodded toward the Narville house, and he laughed.

"That's a good name for it, and they're lookin' for a name. They've got someone making a family crest to put up on the turret, and it has a ribbon running along the top that's supposed to have the name of the place painted on it. . . . He wants to call it Bootstraps, but she wants Navasana; I guess it means *boat* in Sanskrit. So I've got to wait until they decide before I can do siding on the turret."

"See, you've got enough to worry about."

The stairs creaked and Henry appeared, looking like an owl that had fallen out of its nest.

"What's this?"

"I kind of . . . poached the walls . . ." Charlotte said.

Henry giggled and Charlotte gave him a crooked smile. He just assumed everything would go wrong; it would never occur to him to blame her.

"How about a trade?" Darryl asked. "It's tuna season; I'm short on help. You help me on the flats and I'll get you started on the drywall."

"Really? But I don't know what to do. . . ."

"I'll tell you. Here, put on some clothes and hop in the truck. I've got about thirty bags in the back and you can help me set 'em out while the tide's low. . . ."

"Can I bring Fiona?" It was wrong to ask, but she was greedy for experiences for Fiona; she had to snatch every one that passed.

"Okay, but we gotta get down there."

They were dressed in two minutes and Darryl was throwing the old soda bottles and oily rags out the back window into the truck bed to make room for them. Fiona snuggled between them, her little hand tight in Charlotte's, her eyes wide, ready for adventure as they bumped down the driveway and turned onto the beach across the wet sand. The wide view made the distances seem shorter than they were; Charlotte hadn't guessed they would need to drive so far. The individual grants, each one a small farm, were laid out on a rough grid, maybe a thousand square feet apiece, marked by buoys at the corners, and Darryl's claim was at the farthest reach, what seemed like the middle of the bay.

"You don't get a lot of time when you're out this deep," he said. "I've gotta get in and out faster than some of the others. But the animals are underwater longer here, more time to grow." He got out and went to retrieve a bag of oysters that had broken loose from the rack, and Fiona jumped out behind him, running across the flats, frightening the gulls into flight as she splashed through the little streams of tide.

"Blustery," Charlotte said to herself, happy.

"What?" Darryl asked.

"Oh, nothing . . . We sort of use that word to mean . . . fresh and exciting, or something."

"It means windy, right?"

"I think so. . . ." An awkwardness came over them. Charlotte's hands hung useless there at the end of her arms. What did one do out here? How?

He walked down between the racks, shaking the bags, considering. Most of the oysters were in bags of plastic-coated mesh, pinned to the rebar racks that stood maybe a foot off the ground. Others hung in wire baskets from long rails of PVC pipe anchored in the wet sand.

"The baskets swing back and forth with the waves," he told her. "The oysters grow faster when you've got more water passing through them, and the pipe breaks the surf if it gets rough. I don't know why Tim and the others don't try this. I'm hoping to do 'em all in the baskets by next year." He picked a silver-dollar-size oyster, the green-brown color of the sea bottom, out of one basket and set it in Fiona's palm. "Feel how heavy that is?" Fiona nodded gravely, thrilled to be included, determined to act grown-up.

"These are real Westsiders, nice deep cup; these are going to sell. Now, see over here?"

He pointed and Charlotte saw a square of mud covered with netting. "Here, step on it. . . ."

She did—it felt like cobblestones, and Fiona, after a first gentle step, began jumping up and down. "Is it paved?"

"No, those are clams. They dig themselves down into the sand and they just grow. You don't even have to take them out in the winter."

"You have to take the oysters out in the winter?"

He laughed. "You'll see, but yes, we take them all out and put them, you know, in a basement or a root cellar. Otherwise they freeze into the ice and when it breaks up in March they go right out to sea with it. The clams can stay, though—they're deep in the mud; they're not going anywhere. . . ."

"I had no idea. . . ."

He smiled. "I grew up here; my father was a fisherman, and I barely knew anything about aquaculture until I came back."

"You went somewhere?" This question burst out embarrassingly.

She was ravenous to know the answer, for some reason. "I mean, I guess . . . it's so beautiful here, it must have been hard to leave."

"Yeah," he said. "But there're more chances out there, more possibilities. At some point you gotta go over the bridge." He sounded more resigned than pleased, picking up a shell and tossing it into a pile of refuse at the side of the claim. "You've gotta keep it neat out here, or it gets away from you," he said. "I mean, look at this . . . what a wreck." Now that Charlotte looked at it, the claim beside his did seem haphazard and unkempt, bags heaped on algae-covered bags, oysters growing like limpets over every surface. "It's Bud's; he's trying to do too much. . . . Everyone's flat out, working carpentry and oystering and tuna season and whatever else."

He glanced up at the Narville house, which looked, if possible, more imposing from this side.

"Anyway, we gotta get to work here. . . ." He got a pair of rubber-coated gloves out of the truck. "Wear these; the oysters have sharp edges." Opening the tailgate, he lifted a bag of oysters into Charlotte's arms. It weighed more than Fiona. "What you need to do is carry these over to that rack; do you see?" She nodded. "Set them side by side, all the way along; then we'll pin them. Then we'll take in the bags on the far rack and I'll cull them tonight."

"What's *cull*?"

"You know, go through 'em. Chisel 'em apart so they have room to grow. Pry the seed oysters off the big ones, chip away at the edges so they fatten up all around, wash 'em, sort out the ones that are ready to sell, put the others back to grow—you know."

"Can you carry the pins for us?" Darryl asked Fiona, who was standing there like a little soldier. "That's an important job." She nodded solemnly, and took the rusted box of pins as if it contained a medal of honor.

Charlotte's arms would ache the next day, but like Fiona, she was grateful to be trusted with the work. And determined not to seem like a weakling, a city girl.

"What does it mean, tuna season?" she asked.

"You've heard of tuna. Like . . . the fish? Did you think they picked it off trees in little cans?"

Even Fiona laughed.

"No, but I didn't know it interfered with oyster farming . . . though it's also true I didn't know oysters came from farms. . . ."

He looked happy, setting off on his explanation.

"Do you know what you make for a tuna? Up to ten thousand dollars a fish. Three months' pay in an afternoon. And the season is ten days long, so everybody takes off after them. Tim got three last year; that's how he bought the truck." The truck, the instrument and emblem of his menace, gleaming black with high wheels and tinted windows and the I'M A LOCAL bumper sticker that meant, *I'm above the law.*

"It's three months' pay in an afternoon," Darryl repeated, almost to himself.

"But you don't go?"

His eyes flicked away and she knew she'd tripped a wire somewhere. "I don't have a boat," he said. "It's . . . Fishing's a good job for a gambler. You follow your instincts, and maybe you strike it rich, maybe you come up empty, maybe . . ."

He looked out to the mouth of the bay: a perfect watercolor with two yellow kayaks crossing. "My father was pulling in a purse seine, out on Georges Bank. He lost his footing and slipped into the net. They cut the line but it was too late. There was nothing anyone could have done."

He spoke the last sentence by rote; he'd heard it over and over, of course. What else could anyone have said to the men who'd had to come back with the story?

"How old were you?"

"Sixteen. It was summer, not a cloud . . . like today. . . ."

The tide was creeping up, licking around the edge of a shoal until it disappeared. The water had a soft sheen now that the fog had burned off, and they watched the reflection as a gull flew in great slow flaps just above the surface.

"Darryl . . . I . . ." It seemed an honor that he had trusted her enough to say this, and she wanted to live up to it, to say something truly consoling. Except that, like so many things, it was so terrible, she could think of no consolation.

"That's appalling," she said finally. "Out of a nightmare."

"I do have nightmares," he said.

"I expect I will too."

She felt this strike him more deeply than she'd meant. He glanced quickly into her face, and away just as quickly, but it seemed the light had been at just the right slant; Charlotte caught a glimpse beneath the surface, sensed the way things moved there, and everything in her leaped to meet it. She would take a corner of his trouble, help him bear it. She'd be glad to.

They'd laid all the bags out along the racks, and he took the pins from Fiona's hand and went down the row, fastening each one tight to the bar as he continued the story.

"I took over his building jobs, but fishing—forget it. I don't like being out on the water, and working on a dragger, you go down to the pier in the morning and there's your mate with a spike in his arm . . . you know what I mean."

"No, I don't!" she said, laughing now. "I mean, unless you count getting stuck in an elevator, or being yelled at by a pumpkin farmer, I've never had a dangerous job."

"It's worse in New Bedford," he said. "The stuff that happens there, you wouldn't believe it. Anyway, I'm just better with the shellfish. You're still at the mercy of nature, but you try to work with it, not against. It's just patience, daily labor, bit by bit." His voice, his bearing, were full of pride—and why not, when he was standing on a firmament of his own making? "The fish are disappearing; guys can't make a living on a boat now anyway. The town gave people like Bud shellfish grants, to keep their families from starving. But they're not farmers, they're . . ."

"Pirates!" Charlotte said, glancing over to see Fiona, who was on her hands and knees in the mud.

"Something like that," he agreed. "You can't do aquaculture that way. And you can't say, 'It's too cold; I'll go out tomorrow'—the bay'll freeze over and you lose half your herd." Then: "What is your line of work, anyway? Who gets yelled at by a pumpkin farmer?"

"Journalists. That was before I started writing about fashion. Then I went to *Celeb* and got yelled at by handbag designers." The job at *Celeb* might have been a cheap, ill-fitting costume, but she was naked without it.

"Wow, you worked for *Celeb*?" Right, he was impressed. Despicable.

"It was awful. Though I'm sure it's worse in New Bedford. . . ."

"Why are you two laughing?" Fiona had come running toward them, her arms muddied to the elbows, a long sea worm closed in her fist. She dropped it so as to set hands on hips and scold, exactly as her mother did when Fiona had some mischief going. She knew she'd caught them, without understanding what she'd caught them at, but hearing her, Charlotte felt it and her cheeks blazed.

"Who put you in charge, anyway?" Darryl asked Fiona, taking her hands and swinging her around full circle.

"More, more, do it again!"

"We can't," he said. "The tide's coming to get us, look!" He put her over his shoulder and leaped back toward the truck, asking, "Why are *you* laughing?"

"'Cause I'm happy!"

The sun was already high as they ran up from the water, and the house with the hollyhocks straggling by the front porch looked as if some happy family lived a good, simple life there. Charlotte got Fiona out of her wet overalls and rinsed her feet with the hose and they came in laughing, but somehow the house seemed to insist on quiet: Henry was working.

"Hello!" Charlotte called from the top step. She didn't like to go down there. The windows were painted shut and Henry had no interest in opening them, nor in clearing the spiderwebs—so thickly spun they had real entrances where the spiders sat like shopkeepers all day. He was working in a kind of panic—whenever he sat down at his desk he faced a tribunal: Other men had surpassed him, shaping the popular thought with their work, while he seemed to labor against a granite cliff face with a diamond cutter's tools. The book that rescued him would have to be so big, so important that his whole being must be dedicated to it, entirely.

Whiskey was his best respite, and Charlotte had wondered what he would do without McClellan's Tap when they left the city, but it turned out the Mermaid was two miles up the road, the perfect length for an evening constitutional. Every night she would hear his solitary footsteps as he set off along the dark road. The men who drank at the Mermaid were a very distinguished lot, he said—one was a former Moscow correspondent, and another, rough though he might appear, had trained as a classical pianist before liquor got hold of him. And there was Orson, the Tennessee Williams enthusiast Charlotte had met in the SixMart that first evening. Orson had been an attorney in New York, but had given up corporate life and moved to Wellfleet to devote his full attention to art and debauchery (not necessarily in that order). Provincetown was only a few miles away, and the variety of men available there was as wide as, well, the array of cinquecento painting on view in Venice, or pastries in the window of some sublime Parisian *boulangerie*. And now it turned out that not only was he treading on the same sandy soil as Thoreau, gazing over the same vista as Eugene O'Neill, but drinking elbow-to-elbow with Henry Tradescome, a living author. . . . Orson could not have asked for more.

"He's read everything," Henry said. "He can quote Cavafy, Ovid. . . ."

"Invite him for dinner," Charlotte said.

Henry looked confused, as if he doubted such a thing were possible. The Mermaid was a sanctuary, another planet down the road. It closed at one, and at one thirty Charlotte would hear Henry's footsteps, quick and certain, returning home. In their early days, when she'd expected physical intimacies would lead to emotional ones, she'd turned to him in sleepy compliance when he came to bed, stretching out to meet him, fold him in. Now she feigned sleep, and felt him slip quickly under the covers on the other side of the bed, careful not to brush his foot against hers.

8

TELL ME

"*What* is that smell?"

Charlotte was leaning against one of the columns on the Narvilles' expansive porch, watching Fiona concoct a stew from rose hips and sawdust and seawater, the materials available in the yard. Tim Cloutier had just driven up from the beach, and a second after his truck passed, a profound stench hit them.

"Tuna," Darryl said from the doorway. His table saw was set up just inside, and his goggles were up on his head. "He got two. And now he needs to wash that truck."

"Where's he going at this hour?" The tide was rising—playfully, little waves racing to butt one another head-on. There was no way to do anything out on the claims.

"He left a few bushels down on the beach," Darryl said. "He was way behind on orders. He'll be back at work here tomorrow, though, so . . ."

"I should look busy?"

"Something like that," he said, glancing away so she caught only the corner of his smile. All week it had been just the two of them . . .

or, really, the three of them: Fiona playing at the edge of the conversation, making her stews or trying to entice the seagulls with bits of bread. The morning after Charlotte had helped Darryl out on the flats, he'd arrived with three tubs of joint compound, a ladder, and two plasterer's trowels, which he showed Charlotte how to use. They'd rolled up the rug and covered the furniture with some of the monogrammed sheets from the linen closet, and, with Darryl on the stepladder and Charlotte beneath, coated the walls and sanded them until they were smooth as new. Charlotte was going to paint them a soft yellow, but for the ten days of tuna season she did what she could to help Darryl at the Narville house—sweeping up the sawdust, the tile dust, the plaster dust, running to the hardware store for bits of metal or new blades for the tile saw—whatever would make the job run smoother. Even when they were working in different parts of the house, they were happily aware of each other. Charlotte would be singing, without realizing it, and she'd hear him pick up the next line on the other side of the wall. Nine fifteen was break time; she'd roll up the blueprints and set the coffeemaker on the sawhorse table, and they'd take their cups out into the sun and continue their conversation.

It had begun . . . well, really it had begun the day he found them on the beach, the first time she saw the house. Bits of life like this stuck in Charlotte's heart and mind; she would remember a disapproving glance or a perplexed look, would turn these moments over and over in an attempt to understand them, while for Henry (for almost everyone else, it seemed), they were just rinsed away, forgotten. So, when she met Darryl in the SixMart, months after their first awkward meeting, and it was clear it had stayed with him too, and he'd wanted to continue the conversation . . . it was new to her, to think that someone else might attend to such things in the same way she did. And then there were the drop cloths—yes, the real linen sheets left from other lives, but they didn't have enough, so Darryl had gone home and returned with a sail he'd salvaged after a heavy storm, and a bedspread, pea soup green with darker stains.

"It was on my bed in the halfway house," he said, throwing it over the Chippendale sideboard, then turning to see her reaction.

"You lived in a halfway house?" she asked, cautious. He was trusting her, suddenly, with something precious; she handled it with care. "Where were you halfway from?"

"Rehab, where else?" The floor dropped out from under his voice: The story was raging to be told, confessed, stabbed into a vein, suffered in revulsion, in ecstasy. Through the telling it might be transcended. Or relived, maybe that was all he wanted. Whichever, he was offering to share a raw secret because he'd caught some reflection in her eyes.

"Where else?" she echoed lightly, sitting down on the wretched bedspread, hungry as a hatchling, heart wide, wide open now for the drop of real human substance he offered. "So, how'd that happen?"

"Eh, how it always happens," he said. Of course, this was true— life kicks you in the teeth, you grab at what you can. It was worse in New Bedford: The poverty was deeper there; possibility a distant star. "My counselor said . . . well, he was sympathetic, you know; that's what they get paid for. The fact is, I'm an addict by nature; it's like . . . my inheritance. My mother gave me a joint for my thirteenth birthday."

"Really?"

"It was 1974," he said. "The card read, 'Feed your head.'"

"That's perverse."

"Perversity was in fashion. She's . . . she's got a lot of shame now;

she joined AA, got involved with the church—that makes her feel better."

Charlotte shuddered. "The seventies, blech."

He laughed. "Yeah, and then my father died, and man, I wanted to get as far away as I could, so I moved to L.A. and got work in the music business, which is the most fertile ground you can imagine for an addiction. God knows why I'm still alive after all the stupid-ass shit I did. But here I am, starting back at the beginning, and we'll see how it goes from here."

She had a billion questions, none of which were polite to ask. "What'd you do in the music business?"

"Besides shooting up? Tech, to begin with, but I was good at it, and very reliable, for a junkie. I ended up working at Paramount, mixing, editing . . . my last gig, before . . . well . . . before . . ." Before the disaster, whatever it had been. She nodded quickly, to save him embarrassment. Though as much as he wanted to tell, she wanted to hear, as if she were coming to possess him detail by detail.

"Anyway, it was the movie *Heaven in Winter*; did you see it?"

She'd seen maybe two movies in the last eight years. Henry despised them, their false glamour, their happy endings. Background music seemed pernicious to him, those violins strong-arming the hapless viewer into melancholy or tenderness against his will. The few times she'd dragged him he'd inveighed so loudly against so many things (the popcorn with God knew what poured over it and the monstrously obese people waiting in line to buy it; the waxen beauty of the generic actresses; the heroic gun battles when the fighters in real gun battles were always terrified) that she had decided not to repeat the exercise.

"Have you never heard of the suspension of disbelief?" she'd tried, after a scene of a family dinner that had provoked him to call the director a "lying scum," loudly enough that the people behind them had switched rows.

"The *willing* suspension of disbelief," he'd corrected. Willing, Henry had never been.

"No, I never saw *Heaven in Winter*," she said to Darryl. "It did pretty well, though, right?"

"What would I know?" he said. "I was in rehab by the time it came out. So, I got out of the halfway house, I had bus fare back here, and that was about it. The bus stops at the SixMart, so, you know, you can see the movie screen at the drive-in."

Yes, it loomed there, an extra square of gray sky in winter. In summer you'd see the top half of a movie as you drove past—the wide, liquid eyes of a beautiful woman or the halo of flame around an exploding car.

"I was waiting there for my mother to come pick me up. . . ."

The way he said this she could feel what it might be to be pushing forty, standing beside the highway with all your possessions in a duffel bag, waiting for your mother to come get you because you had nowhere else to go.

"And I looked over and saw snow falling—it was *Heaven in Winter*. Of course, I couldn't hear anything . . . you can't imagine how I'd worked to get the exact sound, or not the sound, but you know, the feeling of snow falling—that absolute silence, or the way it seems so silent because the sound is soft enough to mask everything else without really being heard."

"I do—now that you mention it. Though I'd never thought it out like that."

"It was the strangest thing. It was like I'd disappeared and every trace of what I'd done had been erased, from the movie, from the world." He'd laughed, as if he were reporting this only as an interesting phenomenon, and then Henry had come up the stairs and they'd remembered they were supposed to be working.

The tide was well up; light sparkled on every little wave. Small boats were anchored out in the middle where the bass had been feeding at the surface, and striped umbrellas tilted along the sand across the way at Try Point beach. Fiona whispered her little recipe happily to herself as she picked the clover tops for her stew. Charlotte and Darryl's conversation had wound through the days, growing tendril by tendril, story by story: He'd been walking down a street in Los Angeles, seen a woman in a phone booth, a man pushing boxes along on a dolly . . . a second later the gas main exploded and it all turned to flames. The *Challenger* blew up on the anniversary of her mother's death; the pattern it made, an emblem of frightful chaos, was always in her mind. When his best friend died in a car wreck, he'd been too stoned to care. His confessions inspired her and she found herself telling him things she usually tried to forget—that there had been times when she just wished her mother would die, so she could go on living. That she'd always slept with the loneliest, oddest boys, because she felt so odd and lonely herself. That nevertheless they had managed to betray her.

"You're brave to keep trying," he'd said. "I wish I was so brave."

"To start all over? Make a whole new life?" she'd asked. "You don't call that brave?" And she saw this affect him, all over. He looked as if he were seeing an angel. It was the height of summer; everything was bubbly and sparkly and bright.

"So, did you ever go see that movie—*Heaven in Winter*?"

"It was another life," he said, his hands tense around his coffee cup as if he were watching everything slip through his fingers again.

"It's something you accomplished," Charlotte said. "It might be good; you might be proud of it. It can't be erased."

"I'm not sure you can lose the   well, I won't say sins, but the wrongs you've done. It's not really fair to forget those and keep all the good stuff."

"Darryl!" she said. "No!" Thinking for a second she added: "You don't seem to have forgotten the wrongs, anyway."

"No," he said, checking his watch and getting up, ready to go back to work. "I think about them every day."

He stood there like an old horse: strong, patient, aware that the next stop was the glue factory. But his eyes were bright and searching, he believed there was something to hope for . . . some kind of redemption.

"First thing I did when I moved back to Wellfleet," he said, "I planted seed clams—eighty thousand of 'em. *Seed* was the right word—they were smaller than sunflower seeds, about a hundred in a handful. I started them in grow-out trays—I went down to see them every day; I never missed a tide . . . then, when they were big enough—like marbles, maybe   I raked out a bed for them on the seafloor. I was so careful. It seemed like, if I didn't get it right, it was a sign that I was just a natural fuckup and I might as well go back to shooting dope. I dug way deeper than you have to, just to be sure all the moon snails were out. So I spent the whole tide raking; the water was at my heels before half the clams were in. I couldn't get the net down, and if I'd left them out overnight the bed would have been full of snails by morning. So I had to dig them all out and do the whole thing over the next day, with Tim laughing at me, of course, saying I'd staked my net like an old lady knitting a doily."

"And so," she said, "there they are, solid as a rock, literally."

"Yeah, it's a good feeling. There'll be a ton, really, two thousand pounds, when they're ready next summer. And I've started more, so it should be a pretty steady income, once it's going."

"So there's your example. Good is something you can build with—brick by brick. The rest—the wrongs, the stupidities—they do real damage, but you can transcend them; you've got that solid foundation of good to stand on."

She sounded so encouraging, inspirational even, as if she actually knew something. She could have kicked herself for acting as if she were better than he, though her own life had been a series of desperate acts too.

"Maybe," he said, smiling. "I suppose. God, when I first got back, the work was like an outrage—get up in the freezing dark; the wind was so raw, my boots would leak, and if I went in to get another pair I'd lose the tide. . . . But in summer, you're out there at dawn. . . . I saw an egret last week; it landed not ten feet away from me. It was so white, it reflected the colors of the sunrise just the way the water does. It feels good to be out there working. And I got out of my mother's place. I can probably pay her back some of what I owe her. I feel pretty lucky now."

A seagull with a clam in its beak was rising on an updraft in front of them, higher and higher, until thirty feet up it dropped the clam, which smashed on Narville's seawall, the gull floating down to pick out the meat. They stood watching together, hating to break the moment. Through the rippled old windows at her own house, the bay showed infinite moody variations: Sometimes you seemed to have a direct glimpse into history, so a whale ship might round the point at any minute; sometimes the water brimmed up to the tips of the spartina, cool and pure; sometimes the bay was so hard and gray you'd think of the men who had drowned there. Framed by the columns of Narville's porch, though, the sea was simply a luxury, a bowl of gold.

"Gotta get back to work," he said, and she went to clear off the table, put the coffee things away.

"We're running out of filters."

"I'll pick some up tonight. Do we need coffee?"

"Wouldn't be a bad idea," she said, taking the pot to the sink to rinse it.

"Okay, I'll put it on the list." He looked over his shoulder at her and smiled. "We sound like an old married couple," he said.

"I know." She tried not to sound too pleased.

"Mama, Darryl, look!" Fiona ran up the hill with her cup of stew.

"Looks healthy," Darryl said with a grimace, taking the cup from her and peering in. "What's in it?"

"Clovers," she said, looking up at him, surprised by his attention, drinking it in. "The rabbits like them."

"Are you friends with the rabbits?" He glanced at Charlotte, and back to Fiona, his eyes crinkling warmly at the corners, sympathy and humor playing over his face.

"The rabbits . . . and the baby bunnies too!" she said, her voice musical, flirtatious, daring him to contradict her.

"If I was a rabbit I'd want to be friends with you," he said. "You're such a good cook." He lifted the cup and pretended to sip. "Tastes delicious. Though you know what I think it needs? A scallop shell. They have a very delicate flavor. Good with clovers."

"I'll get some," she said, and skipped off with such confident purpose it was almost painful to see. She wanted so much to be good, and as she was four years old she was sure this was a simple matter.

"So, would you go back to that other life someday? I mean, not all of it, obviously, but the work—maybe working for a recording company, or . . ."

"Oh, no. No, it's the worst place for a . . . drug addict." He forced himself to say this, though not without an abject, confessional pleasure. Then he squared his shoulders and picked up a bundle of shingles to go back to work.

"I'm stayin' here, get my general contractor's license, grow the oyster business, settle down." He thought a minute, then spoke harshly. "Life, plain life, that's what I want. Health insurance. Buy some land, build my own place, start a family . . . go to bed every night feeling like I've accomplished a little something. Just a real life, you know, like yours."

He started around to the side with the shingles, but turned back. "Yours and Henry's, I mean," he said soberly, and in a minute she heard the nail gun firing steadily: *Bang. Bang. Bang.* She'd been finishing the doors for the upstairs closets, and she opened the polyurethane again and stirred it, watching Fiona out the front window as she started back to work.

"Clouds so swift the rain's falling in," she sang, hardly realizing it until she heard Darryl's voice, outside, coming in with the next line.

The stench of rotten fish hit her again, and she turned to see Tim at the back door, with mirrored sunglasses covering the eye patch.

"'Lo," he said suggestively, as if he'd caught her at something.

"Hi," she said. "Darryl's outside." But he'd seen Tim come in and was standing behind her at the French doors. Some kind of pride bounced between them at being found together like this.

"Hey, man," Darryl said. "Had a good week, I hear."

"Sashimi heaven," Tim said, looking hard at them from behind the sunglasses.

"You here to work?" Darryl asked. "Because if you are, the whole east side is ready to be shingled."

"Tomorrow," Tim said, turning his head to show, at the base of his neck, a bare patch among his tattoos. "I'm gettin' a stingray here." Then he lifted the sunglasses so she could see his eye narrow. "Anyway, looks like you've got help for today."

"Am I . . . not supposed to be here?" she asked after he left.

"No, you've been terrific," Darryl said. "I mean, thank you, you've done so much. But . . . tomorrow the guys'll be back; it might be distracting. . . ."

"But . . ." she began. They couldn't just stop the conversation.

"I did one quick favor for you; it's not like you have to work for me forever now." He caught her eye with a half-pleading, half-consoling look, but Charlotte, wounded and ashamed of her silliness, shook her head and laughed, saying she had to get Fiona home for her nap anyway.

9

FLOATING

Henry came up from his office in the late afternoon, grimacing in the bright sunlight. Charlotte was keeping Fiona out on the beach so he could get some peace to work—they had built a little village of wet sand and shells.

"Daddy! We made a whole town!" Fiona cried, running up the lawn toward him. She was wearing a flower-girl dress they'd found at the church thrift shop—white lace with little rosebuds stitched in. Clothing made no sense to her: She only liked to be naked or in costume. Stepping out the door, Henry looked down over the water like a man surveying the battlefield at Guernica, half bent so Charlotte thought he was about to double over with some internal pain. Fiona tried to grab his hand but he let it go limp and slip away. She solved this problem by taking his wrist tight in her two hands and began to pull him down the lawn. He followed so unwillingly it did look as if she were dragging him.

"Nice," he said, not seeing it.

Charlotte wrinkled her nose at him.

"It's a few lumps of sand," he said between his teeth. "I can't say what I don't feel."

"Yes, that puts it quite truly."

"So don't expect . . ." It was a warning.

"Believe me, I expect nothing."

"Mama!" Fiona jumped up in fear; Henry's anger was as familiar as a gray sky, but Charlotte's was a thunderbolt.

"Never mind, never mind, sweetheart, let's go in the water," Charlotte said, and Fiona brightened instantly, running in without a thought for the dress. Charlotte lifted her hand and twirled her around, and the petticoats swirled over the surface.

"Henry, come in," she said. She didn't want to be angry, and she let sympathy fray the edges—she'd known fatherhood wasn't natural to Henry, she'd married him and had Fiona nevertheless, and she probably did expect too much. If only she could find some route for him, some way toward comfort and happiness. If they could be something like the family Darryl imagined . . .

Henry waded in up to his ankles and stood rooted, stiff as if he thought the water might erode him, squinting across the bay. "That's where Billingsgate Light used to be—out there," he said.

"Where is it now?"

"The sea came up, bit by bit, year by year—there was a settlement out there at one time. They floated the houses in to the mainland when the ocean started rising. Finally it was just the lighthouse, and one winter night in 1915 the waves smashed it up, and that was the end."

"The end," Charlotte echoed. She knelt in the water as if she could wash off Henry's gloom, leaning back to wet her hair, sucking the salt water from her fingers. Fiona jumped and splashed beside her.

"Fiona looks like a water lily, with her skirt all spread out, don't you think?"

Fiona was looking up at him, intently hopeful, and he looked down at her, intently irritated. Why did Charlotte insist on asking impossible things of him? What could it matter whether the child looked like a water lily?

"It's good that you like the water," he managed.

"I *love* the water!" Fiona said, shaking her head so drops flew from her curls.

"Will you watch her for a minute?" Charlotte asked. "So I can take a quick swim?"

"Certainly, take your time." That much he could do, give his wife a moment's respite from the endless duties of mothering.

Charlotte swam away in bold strokes. She'd forgotten her own strength, and feeling it now as she sliced through the water she suddenly wanted to flee, to swim until she'd escaped from Henry and even Fiona, until she was fifteen again, with those long white arms, and her mother was dead, and she was free. The feeling itself frightened her and she stopped, well out, and looked back to see Henry standing right where he'd been, gazing out toward the mouth of the bay. Alone.

"Henry!" He didn't hear her. The distance seemed immense suddenly, she raced back across it, her heart pounding so she thought it would burst.

Fiona's skirt billowed under the water; she wasn't moving. Charlotte grabbed her by the waist; her eyes opened like a doll's and she took a terrible drowning breath. She coughed. She was alive.

And in a fury. She had seen her mother swim off and had followed her, assuming she would be able to swim as naturally as she walked. She didn't know about drowning; she didn't know about death.

"I can't swim!" she cried, fighting her way out of Charlotte's arms to slap at the water. It had failed her, insulted her. "You can read and I can't; you can swim and I can't. . . ."

Charlotte lifted her up again, holding the tense little body tight against her.

"I was *thinking*," Henry said, defending himself. "I just looked away for a minute. She's fine; she swallowed a little water. Don't make it into a big deal."

"Don't make it into a big deal?"

He turned around and walked back up toward the house. He'd been asking himself some terribly important question, about Cambodia probably—that was the chapter he was on. And Fiona had done what she always did and followed her mother. Charlotte's heart slammed in her ears. "It's all right, it's all right," she murmured into Fiona's hair.

"It's not all right! I want to swim!"

"I didn't know how to swim when I was your age, either," she said to Fiona.

"You didn't?" Fiona relaxed entirely, laid her head against her mother's neck.

"Of course not, silly. Someone had to teach me. And now I can teach you."

"I don't want you to teach me! I want to know."

"I can't say I blame you," Charlotte said. "But since I can't think of any other way . . . let's try it." She pulled the dress gently over Fiona's head. Her little shoulders, her bottom . . . thirty seconds more, another minute, and . . . the world would have turned to ash and blown away.

"Here, we'll wade in together; hold my hand."

Charlotte knelt in the water and held out her arms. "Lie back;

look up at the sky," she said, serene as a mesmerist. Fiona lay back across her arms.

"Now take a deep breath. I'm holding you. Do you see that one little cloud moving?" She dropped her arms an inch, then another, and after a few tries she was able to lift her hands out of the water. "See, you're floating!"

Fiona lost her composure and sank.

"Try it again."

"No, I can't do it!"

"You just did do it."

"No! I didn't float; I sank!"

Charlotte said nothing, waiting for Fiona to consider this on her own. A yellow kayak issued from between the reeds in the boat meadow, heading toward Try Point along the shore.

"Go behind me," Fiona said suddenly.

"Why?"

"Because . . . because I'll be able to bend backward if I can see you there."

And suddenly it was second nature. Fiona fell back on the water, arms outstretched, and kicked along in a blissed-out circle, her hair feathered into a wide halo.

"Do it again," she said.

"I'm not doing anything!" Charlotte laughed.

"No," Fiona said. "You did. Do it again!" Much as she wanted to be free, she'd rather believe herself buoyed by her mother's magic. So she leaned back and Charlotte raised her heels in her palms, and Fiona floated away through the sparkles, saying, "Mom, look, look at me!"

As if Charlotte could have torn her eyes away. It *was* magic to know just how to let go so the last thing a child feels before the cool rush of freedom is the fit of her heel to her mother's palm.

. . .

They came up the lawn to find Henry reading on the porch, Bunbury curled on his lap. Charlotte wrenched herself toward forgiveness. Back in the city, rushing to catch a walk light, she'd pushed the stroller so harshly over the curb that it tipped and Fiona nearly fell into the street. It was the same thing, a moment's lapse. Henry wouldn't have imagined Fiona would try to swim after her, that she was connected to Charlotte by a filament as weightless and strong as spiderweb, was drawn through life by it, following her every thought, feeling, and move.

"We had a swimming lesson," she said, bending down to scratch Bunbury behind the ears.

"Daddy," Fiona called. "I learned to swim!"

"That's good, very nice," he said, barely lifting his eyes from the page.

"I can swim!" she repeated, jumping up and down to get his attention, so water sprayed over him.

"Stop it!" he said, shielding the book, taking off his glasses to wipe them.

Fiona hung her dripping head.

"It takes time to learn to swim," he lectured.

"How's your swimming, Henry?" Charlotte asked, and he gave her a small, ironic smile, pulling his bad arm in against his side. He had accepted his limitations; maybe one day Charlotte would accept hers.

"So you see, honey, Daddy doesn't know much about swimming," she said lightly. Henry continued reading.

"He hates me," Fiona said, provoking no response.

"No, no, he doesn't," Charlotte said. Could Henry even hear them? He gave no sign. She lifted Fiona and carried her inside.

"He loves you," Charlotte told Fiona, wrapping her in a towel, rubbing her hair dry so it stuck up all over. "He loves you very, very much, but he has no idea how to show that."

Fiona looked more skeptical than a four-year-old ought to be able to manage. It was wrong to ask her to understand so much, but it was the best Charlotte could think to do. She sat on the edge of the bathtub, rocking Fiona on her lap.

"Listen, you accomplished a lot out there, and you will do better every time you try; do you understand? No one just jumps in the water and swims; everyone learns it bit by bit. Daddy's arm doesn't work so well, and it makes swimming hard for him, so he doesn't really know much about it." The little head nodded solemnly against her neck.

"The learning itself ought to be her satisfaction," Henry said later, defending himself. "You praise her for every little thing. She has no sense of reality."

"You never minded it when I treated you that way," she said. "You don't notice when she's drowning, but one drop of water on your goddamned book and you're in a fury. This has nothing to do with swimming; it has to do with a little girl who wants her father's love."

They were on the porch, with Fiona just inside. Looking in through the window Charlotte saw Fiona had balled up the lint from the dryer screen and was holding it to her chest, petting it softly, whispering to it as if, being so warm and soft, it must be alive. Oh, she was so absolutely, entirely human: noisy, dirty, boastful, grasping, jealous, recklessly curious, full of love and tenderness.... Henry was so old and august he had overcome every single one of these qualities.

"I will try to do better," he said between his teeth. He had given her those beautiful, grave poems to read: "and the seas of pity lie / locked and frozen in each eye." He had seemed to know more of the depth of life and feeling than anyone she'd known. She remembered how angry he had been at her when she was new on the job and used a cliché to describe the death of a child. Now she saw that the phrase had mattered more to him than the life.

"You're a fraud, Henry."

He snarled, like a cornered animal, and reflexively covered his weak hand. He was wrong, though; the hand was nothing to be ashamed of. The pity was his blinded heart, tap-tapping its grim path through the gorgeous world.

And she had followed along behind him, though she was a see-ing woman and ought long since to have found a better path. Well, Fiona was not going to suffer for her idiocy. Charlotte almost felt the little snap in her chest, as the marriage gave way.

10

MOTHER NATURE

Later that evening she opened the freezer door to find two martinis standing together, upright as sentinels, inside. She shut the door immediately; she didn't want to think how Henry would have come up from the beach in a fury, cursing her and everything that distracted him from his work, then looked back down to see them—his wife, his little girl!—whom he had nearly lost in one careless moment. The anger would have swung around then, struck him straight on, and with it the great sympathy he could feel when he had a little distance from things. Tender, sorry, he had imagined a reconciliation, getting the martini glasses out of the china cabinet as his father would have done, mixing the drinks with the same care he used to take getting Fiona's hot water bottle just right.

Then, of course, Charlotte and Fiona had come running up the lawn, laughing, dripping, boasting, wearing on every nerve. He'd snarled at them, or at himself, and had stalked off toward the Mermaid while Charlotte made pancakes for Fiona, who fell asleep as soon as she'd eaten her last bite and had to be carried up to bed. It was high tide; the bridge was submerged; Henry would be gone at least another hour. Another woman might have used this hour to pack a little suitcase of essentials, so that she could take her daughter and get out, as soon as the getting was good. Charlotte took the tide as a sign that the getting would never be good, that Henry was Fiona's father and Fiona would need him no matter what. There was an unbearable poignancy in those martinis, as in the wilted rose he found for her somehow, at three in the morning after Fiona was born. Another woman would have known when to cut her losses, get a divorce, and Charlotte wished she had that woman's conviction, but she had never been blessed with such certainty. She was porous, soluble; other threads got woven in with her own substance and became a part of her. Divorce was not the thing for Charlotte and Henry. They needed an operation, the kind where seven specialized surgeons worked for hours, teasing apart the nerves inch by inch, disentangling all the veins.

Natalie, on the phone from New York, put it differently: "Well, you're not going to give up that house, are you?"

No, she was not. Day by day, job by job, she had claimed it for herself. The portrait of Vestina over the mantel had been replaced with a painting she'd found in the attic, of Billingsgate Light, around the turn of the century, before it washed away—the square tower of whitewashed brick with the lightkeeper's house attached, clumps of beach rose at the back door, and then the whitecaps of a pale summer sea. This, and the freshly painted living room, the scrolls of new trim on the porch that exactly matched the old, the morning glories spiraling with berserk genius over the balusters, these things raised a fierce will of love in her, and she was going to stay.

So, on September first, she was sitting at breakfast just like always, cutting a peach over Fiona's cereal while Henry replenished his outrage from the bottomless well of possibilities in the *Times*.

Way out on the flats the men were working: She recognized the motions as they angled their bull rakes into the mud, rocking them back and forth, then jerking back hard to wrench up the clams. Tim Cloutier had driven right out to the edge of the water beside his claim. It was the new moon and the tide had ebbed so far it looked as if you could walk all the way across to Try Point, though Charlotte had tried this once and knew that what looked like a few shallow rivulets from here were really as wide as rivers and three feet deep, with a bottom so soft you could sink up to your hip on a wrong step. September was a month with an R in it; Labor Day was coming—prices were good; they'd harvest as much as they could today.

A red fox stepped around the corner of the house with a live squirrel held lightly between its jaws. It stopped to look in through the window at them, curious and unafraid.

"Henry, look. . . ."

Ordinarily he'd have refused to turn his head. Today, though, he knew he had lost his wife's sympathy, and he had to reclaim it somehow, so he lowered the paper and found himself face-to-face with this fox, who kept still, his ears pricked and foreleg proudly raised. The squirrel hung limp from the fox's mouth, but its large wet eyes seemed to be looking straight into Charlotte's.

"Mama, him's going to eat that squirrel!" Fiona said, jumping off her chair, breaking the trance, so the fox bounded off up the driveway. "Mama, go after him; don't let him!"

Henry flinched and lifted the paper again, protecting himself from the noise.

"He has to bring some supper home to his family," Charlotte tried.

"Him's could eat his vegetables!" Fiona replied, sounding just like her father.

"Speaking of which, how about a bite of cereal?"

Fiona ate, and seemed to forget. The squirrel had been torn to pieces by now. The tide was streaming in—Charlotte could pick out Darryl by the red canoe he used to tow his oysters in. Tim heaved bushel after bushel into his truck bed, until as he turned to grab another load, the truck listed, the back tire sinking into the mud. Tim stepped back, knelt beside the wheel, and started digging with both hands.

"What's he doing out there?" Charlotte asked.

"Who knows?" Henry said, going downstairs to his desk.

Fiona knelt on her bed while Charlotte combed her hair into ponytails. Tim's truck was marooned on its own little island, the tide cutting around it in two streams. Darryl, Bud, all of them had gathered around it, shoveling, but they seemed only to dig it deeper. Darryl ran up to the Narvilles' and came back with a sheet of plywood, which he wedged under the back wheels, but as Tim tried to back up on it, the front sank in deeper.

"It's stuck," Fiona said.

"They must know what to do when something like this happens," Charlotte said. "They're out there every day." She had the wisp of memory, though, of a child's sense that her parents always knew just what to do. The late-summer air seemed full of gold dust, the bay so still it was hard to believe the tide was rising. But it had closed over the island so the truck looked to be floating. And then it was halfway up the tires. "They've been farming out there for years," she went on calmly, twisting a curl between her fingers.

"They look all confused," Fiona said.

"Well," Charlotte had to admit, "that's true." As she said this the truck lurched to a tilt, and the plywood shot out from under it. The men jumped back and stood shaking their heads, rubbing their beards. A backhoe came chugging around the end of the point and down the beach toward them, stopping at the edge of the water. Tim ran across to it in three splashing jumps, explaining something to the operator, hands out as if to shake him, so that Darryl went over and set a quieting hand on Tim's back. Tim shook him off, pushed the backhoe guy away, and jumped onto the backhoe himself, starting out through the water toward the truck, and Charlotte and Fiona watched as the treads sank into the mire. There was a terrible grinding sound and the smell of burning rubber and everything stopped.

Tim jumped off the backhoe and got into the truck as if he meant to go down with the ship. By the time he gave up, he couldn't open the door against the water. He pushed, and the others pulled, but they were helpless, and as the water reached the door handle, Tim rolled down the window, pulled himself out through it onto the roof, and floundered ashore to watch in silent homage as the water rose, as if watching a coffin lowered.

"Daddy, Daddy, the oyster truck got stuck!" Fiona raced down to tell Henry, who came up and looked out, though only the roof of the truck's cab and the yellow bucket of the tipped backhoe were showing. He shook his head—all his predictions had come true; everything was revealed to be just as skewed and dangerous as he had said all along. It felt like a holiday: Misfortune Day, when everyone would take a break from all their constructive, orderly efforts, and stumble drunken into the streets, howling at the moon.

"Do you suppose that once it's totally high tide, a boat will come by and the rudder will snag on the backhoe bucket and the boat will capsize?" Charlotte asked.

"We can hope," Henry said, with a thin smile. "I wonder what a day submerged in salt water will do for a truck." He doubled over, laughing and groaning at once.

"A day underwater?" Charlotte asked. "That truck will be there for the rest of our lives."

11

SALT

As soon as the last truck—Bud Rivette's, with Tim in the passenger seat looking straight ahead—turned away up Point Road, Charlotte ran down and squeaked around the end of the fence on the seawall. The bay was brimming. Beneath its little dancing waves was a huge new pickup truck with a V-8 engine, four-wheel drive, a W '04 sticker, and an eel in the carburetor.

Stepping over onto the Narvilles' side of the fence, Charlotte seemed to have stepped into a foreign land. The house, finished in all but the last details, was as solid as a fortress; even the windows were not only wide and high, but also gleamingly thick, as if made of some special kind of glass. The tower had a copper roof surmounted by a weather vane that depicted a dragon rampant. Mahogany chaise longues were set in a row between the porch columns; she could hear the delicate plash of the fountain in the koi pond, stroke the soft fronds of the high-end bulrushes planted at the edge. Darryl was bending over the kitchen's central island, polishing the marble countertop. About to knock on the French door, Charlotte hesitated, pierced by a sudden qualm, heard a robin hit the glass above her, and looked up to see it fly off crookedly in the wind.

Darryl looked up and blinked to see her, pulled off his goggles and came to the door.

"You came," he said. "I didn't expect . . ." He seemed as surprised as if she'd finally tracked him down in Istanbul, where he was living under an assumed name. And as glad as if they'd been lovers separated by a war. The room filled up with light, or it seemed to.

"Because of the truck . . . that got stuck on the flats . . ." Excuses, as if she had in fact crossed oceans to find him.

"Tim parked on the soft spot," he said. "We knew it was there; I sank into it over my knee the other day. Put a chair out to mark it, but the tide must have pulled it up last night. Brand-new truck."

"Now what?" she asked, trying to sound sensible, though she was electrified and barely knew what they were saying. He'd missed her.

"Oh, it's total," he said. "Total loss. About the only thing that might help now is if he drove it into a pond."

"What?"

"To rinse the salt out, stop the corrosion. You'd be amazed at the power of salt. When I first started oystering I used to drive through the shallows . . . until the chassis just crumbled out from under the truck. Pieces of steel came right off in my hand."

He held out this imaginary hunk of metal, his thick hand gripped around the space so she could see it exactly.

"Gas tanks are porous; did you know that?" he asked, lighting up. It was a gift he could give her, this scrap of information.

"I didn't," she said, dazzled.

"It's a stupid-ass mistake; the thing's going to leak all day, and that oil's going to hit someone's herd," he went on. He shook his head, disapproving, but then shrugged it off. "It happens on a spring tide," he said. "It could happen to anyone."

A spring tide was the extreme low; it came twice monthly, on the new and full moons. Knowing this pleased Charlotte as if she were back in third grade again and had the right answer. She was coming to know the language of the place. She stretched in the sunlight that flooded through the Narvilles' window, looking out to see a speck come around the point and up the bay toward them. It was a little old dragger with three guys crowded into the wheelhouse and a black dog sitting up front. It slowed, weaving across and back—of course, it was Tim, returning to the scene. Who could have kept away? Thirty thousand dollars' worth of truck and a whole continent of pride were submerged there. They cut the engine; they'd found it. Then they circled, agonizingly slowly, over and over it, all of them, even the dog, a quizzical figurehead, peering down over the bow.

Yes, Charlotte knew it well, the circling, circling, over what's been lost, so close you can see it, even touch it, though even as you watch it's being corrupted; time and nature are wearing it away. And all through your own fault, too, your own idiot misreading of the signs. No one but yourself to blame.

"So, the house is nearly done," she said.

"Ready for its close-up. The owners are coming for the weekend. They haven't been here since we started building."

"I hope they like it."

Darryl looked around the room. "It's just what they wanted," he said with a sigh. "Look at this. . . ." It was the bill for the exotic fish in the koi pond: thirty-five fish, at seventy dollars apiece.

Charlotte laughed. "I'm surprised they didn't have you wallpaper it with hundred-dollar bills."

"Well, don't suggest it!" he said. "It's too bad. With this spot, the simplest thing would be amazing."

"I know. Just a shingled cottage with a screen porch so you could sit out late on a summer night . . ."

". . . and you'd put the bedroom on the east side, so you'd wake up in the morning sun. . . ."

"And you'd have the kitchen open, like this, but on the west side, so when you were cooking dinner you'd have the light, and Fiona would be playing on the rug there, and I'd have an herb garden outside the kitchen door so I could just step out and pick some rosemary."

"You would, would you? What about me?"

"You . . ." He'd caught her by the corner of a thought. He was right there, in the scene she had imagined. "You'd be on the flats, just getting the last bags in."

He kept it up, daring her. "Are the bluefish running?"

"Oh, yeah, you're going to catch a couple for supper. I saw you get the fishing pole, so I went out for the rosemary."

"I love bluefish," he said. Her throat closed suddenly had he mentioned hunger? She looked down to avoid his eyes.

"We'd have a woodstove," he said. "We've got a southern exposure—we wouldn't need much oil. I've been heating with wood since I got back, and I haven't bought a stick. I go out in the National Seashore forest, early morning, with my chain saw, and cut up the fallen trees."

"They allow that?"

"Well . . . no . . . but my father did it and his father before him—that was way before it was National Seashore. It used to be woodlots, you know, back before oil."

"So, I could pick the beach plums and make jelly?" There were hundreds of them, dusky red and purple, on the low, rough-leaved bushes along the Seashore Road.

"Sure! I mean, I'd bail you out if the park rangers got you." He laughed so sweetly.

"And you'd build a swing for Fiona?" Tears sprang up and she wiped her eyes with the back of her hand, but it was a sign that they'd strayed too far.

"Anyway," he said, "I'd be lucky to afford a tenth of an acre with a view north over the landfill. I'd better get this finished. I gotta help get that truck out of the sand next tide."

"Drink?" Henry had come up next to her while she stood at the window watching the tide recede. It pulled a long iridescent thread behind it—the gas from the truck's tank, which would have filled with salt water by now, like the glove compartment, the six CD slots, the heated leather seats. The electrical system would have shorted out, setting off the wipers and flashing the headlights until the battery died. Crabs were investigating, barnacles settling in. That was the day's progress, underwater. She could see the backhoe's bucket sticking out of the water at a crazy angle, and there was a still spot in the water beside it, the roof of the truck's cab.

"Is there any wine? Look, here comes the radio antenna."

Henry looked out, his mouth twitching toward a smile.

"One drives into mires," he said companionably, and went off on light feet to the kitchen, glad to be of service. Charlotte would relive an argument line by line, trying to pull some true thread out of the tangle, but Henry's encompassing regret swallowed the particulars. Surely he need not examine his faults one by one? He was infinitely blameworthy and must work to redeem himself; wasn't that every man's story? He returned with two glasses, and a sippy cup of orange juice for Fiona.

"Perfect timing!" Charlotte said. A bulldozer was coming around the point. "A toast! To the power of salt!" Talking to Darryl had cast everything in a golden light, and as Henry handed her the wineglass she saw him sculpted in relief, half man, half stone, reaching out to her, hoping she could free him. She clicked her glass to his, and to Fiona's, and drank. A fumé blanc—she'd liked a fumé blanc once and he never passed a package store now without looking for a bottle.

They watched as Darryl's truck turned onto the beach and headed out along the wrack line toward the spot where the others stood conferring. Even at this distance you could guess his life from his stance—he was strong, he'd been defeated, and he was carrying on. He waved to the tow truck that was backing along the wet sand, motioning it closer, then splaying both hands: Stop. The tow guy— one of the Mulligans, with blond dreadlocks and a gold earring that caught the sun—put his head out the window and laughed: The flats looked like a sandbox full of some child's abandoned toys.

Charlotte was barely aware of the other story that was bumping along the road toward them, in a brand new Hummer. The Narvilles had driven from Alpharetta, stopping in Charleston, Cape May, Old Lyme, and finally Newport, to soak in the seaside ambience . . . "pick up a sense of the decor," Andrea later explained. She taught yoga at the gym where Jeb Narville had worked out obsessively after the end of his first marriage, and by moving to Wellfleet she meant to flee a dictatorship ruled by Vonda, his first wife, into a land of inspiration and balance where the pull of gravity was felt not as a force to be resisted, but a firm embrace. She had a lifetime subscription to *Architectural Digest*, and a gold bracelet the spelled out, *Luxe, calme, volupté*.

Near Newport they had picked up their new catboat, a twenty-two-footer with brass rails, mahogany trim, and a forty-horsepower Yanmar engine that would allow for the occasional burst of yeehaw speed. As the tide withdrew, Jeb piloted the Hummer, towing the catboat, down Point Road, past the Mermaid and the Masonic lodge, the vine-choked woods, the Driftwood Cabins sign overgrown by blackberry bushes.

"I pictured it more ... upscale...." Andrea said. That was the way Jeb had described it, but he'd been there only the one time, and the various coves had run together in his mind. He'd looked at three lots in Olde Harbour Estates, where each house was bigger and more important than the last, but the choicest properties there were already gone. The land on Tradescome Point sloped gently south over a bay frothy with whitecaps like a meringue pie. One hundred feet of frontage, electricity already in place—and he could sink a mooring right out in front of the house. The purchase price had seemed ludicrous at the time, but it would have doubled by now. He had a sixth sense where money was concerned. Women, on the other hand . . . He glanced over at Andrea, who was making a little kiss in the mirror to perfect her lipstick. Could she not be satisfied that he'd just built her a million-dollar house?

Then a reassuring sight: their fence, tall, solid, white, with the carriage lamps spaced along just as they were at home, and the tower rising. The place made its statement. They turned off the broken pavement of Point Road into their cobblestone driveway, followed its curve into the porte cochere. Yes, everything was ready; they were home.

Charlotte heard the car turn in, the doors open and shut. The sun was red and enormous, settling into the western haze, and this pleased

her as if the scene belonged to her and she was generously sharing it
with her new neighbors. She imagined Jeb pulling his wife against
him, arms around her waist, affected together by the beauty of the
place, having a little moment of renewal together in their new home.
They would walk through the rooms, feeling all the care Darryl had
given that building, the perfect joints, the smooth sills; they'd look
out every window; they'd push open the glass doors and see the bay
spread before them like a banquet. The tide was well out by now. Tim
was hooking a chain under the truck's hood so they could winch it
out of its mire.

"*What the hell?*" A great bellow came from the other side of the
fence. "What the hell is going on?" And a figure—Jeb Narville, Charlotte realized, squat and ungainly in his khaki shorts, like a gorilla
with arms loose at his sides—came running down the lawn to the
seawall, brandishing a fist in Tim's direction.

"What's happened, what is it?" Charlotte ran out onto the lawn,
thinking he'd found the house full of snakes, or a ceiling collapsed,
or . . .

"What is *that?*" he asked her. His face, which had been ruddy
when she met him at the registry, was so red now it outdid the
salmon-colored shirt he was wearing.

"What . . . what do you mean?"

"You know what the hell I mean," he said, hulking closer.

"You mean the truck?"

"Bayfront. That's what I bought. Bays have water in them, Mrs.
Tradescome."

"Oh! You . . . You . . ." He'd seen the place only the day he bought
it. He'd been feasting all this time on the photographs the realtor
took—on a perfect summer day, in the golden late-afternoon light, at
the exact crest of the high tide.

"Mr. Narville," she said, expecting the federal truth-in-advertising board to descend from the clouds and take her away, "the tide's ebbing, that's all."

"I've seen low tide before, Mrs. Tradescome. I've seen junkyards too."

"It's different, different places," she said, going toward him, telling herself he was a civilized man and would not hit her. Also remembering that he had assumed she knew nothing but poetry and lilacs. "We have a pretty dramatic tidal range here—twelve feet. That's one reason it's so good for oysters. See, that's Tim, and Darryl, and Bud; they raise oysters out there. The tide's still on the way out. . . ."

He looked at her as if she had, impossibly, given him more bad news, and she hurried on. "You can get a shellfishing license; you can go out and gather your own dinner; it's wonderful. . . ."

"I don't want to gather my own dinner," he roared, as if this would involve rooting in garbage cans. "This is Cape Cod; you go sailing. I've got a hundred-thousand-dollar sailboat here. I paid for waterfront property, not for . . ." He shook his head, as if there were no words awful enough to describe this view.

Charlotte heard Henry's dry laugh and turned to see him behind her.

"You did indeed, sir," he said, absolutely jovial. "And that's what you got, waterfront—tidal—property. You'll have water brimming in about . . ." He squinted out over their heads. The rank scent of exposed seaweed reached them—the tide was near its low, exposing the seaweed, and the oyster racks, and, of course, the mired trucks. "Six hours."

"This is fraud," Narville insisted.

"No, no, no," Henry replied. "A misunderstanding." She knew

what he was thinking. "Unfortunate about the heavy equipment, of course." He laughed in sympathetic pain. "Believe me, it's worse for him than it is for you. Meanwhile, welcome, neighbor." He lifted his glass toward the sun, which seemed to have liquefied and spilled into the western sea. "Come on in and let's have a short one."

This was the Henry she'd fallen in love with, who had pulled her by the hand through the Fulton Fish Market at five a.m. one morning, so she could see the men slinging sea bass to one another across the counters, warming themselves at their trash-can fires . . . living their secret life while the rest of the city was asleep. Henry didn't get close to people, never *identified* with anyone (idiotic concept, he'd say), didn't suffer their troubles or feel obligated or try to understand. And so he went among them with ease, while Charlotte tried to comfort and encourage, got hurt, felt guilty, admired and disparaged, and could hardly bear to walk down the street sometimes for fear of all the crosscurrents she would feel emanating from every other pedestrian.

Narville gaped at Henry. Andrea, small and taut, with her blond hair pulled into a high ponytail, had come up on soft steps behind him, and smiled with polite incomprehension, as if she'd been offered a glass of motor oil.

"Who did you say those people are?" Narville asked, turning back from a few steps away, sweeping a hand out toward Darryl and the others.

"Aquaculturists," Charlotte croaked. "Oystermen. Like, you know, farmers."

Her voice was drowned out by the deep groan as the bulldozer strained up the beach, pulling the truck by a cable looped around the axle. For a long minute the truck didn't budge, but suddenly the mire disgorged it with a great farting sound, and among the men gathered on the flats an ironic cheer went up. Darryl shook his head and started off toward his grant. Tim hawked and spit over his shoulder.

"Well," Narville said, "they're farming on my land." He took Andrea's hand and pulled her away—she gave Charlotte a dazed glance over her shoulder, a church-tea smile twisted between suspicion and apology—and a few minutes later they heard the Hummer start and tear off up the road.

When they came back, Tim was the only one left on the flats. He'd lost three tides; he had to catch up, taking in three times as many oysters as usual, chiseling them apart, scrubbing the ones that were big enough and taking them up cape to the wholesaler, sorting the rest and getting them back underwater where they could grow. Charlotte, feeding Fiona her pastina in chicken broth at the picnic table on the screened porch, watched him work, a dark shape blending into the dusk. Fiona could not keep her mind on the food—she wanted to tell Charlotte the story of the exciting day over and over. By the time she'd eaten a little, Tim was visible only by the beam from his miner's lamp, and moths gathered thick on the screen outside.

They heard the Hummer pull into the driveway and Charlotte shuddered. Her persistent sense of wrongness, the thing that had made her sick after she sold the lot to the Narvilles, was confirmed now—she had put her hand out and tried to change something in the world, and now everything had swung wild and it was all her fault.

"Maybe they had a good supper and they feel cheered up," she said, and Fiona, ignoring the spoon Charlotte was trying to sneak into her mouth, held her mother's hand and said, "They'll feel better after a good supper," in exactly Charlotte's comforting tone, so that she laughed and gave up on the pastina.

A shadow darted down the Narvilles' front lawn and jumped clumsily from the seawall, heading out along the beach.

"Fiona," Charlotte whispered, switching off the light, "let's go sit on the step and listen to the crickets." They went out, closing the screen door so carefully you could barely hear the snap. The crickets were pulsing in their slow, end-of-summer rhythm—school was starting soon and on the beach across the way kids were gathered around a bonfire. The shadow floundered with comic effort over a stream that Darryl would have crossed in one unthinking stride, and bent down between Tim Cloutier's racks, grabbing one of the grow-out trays, trying to tear it away from the rack.

"Hey! What the hell?" Whether Tim was as immense as he seemed, or that was a trick of perspective, Charlotte wasn't sure. What was clear was his stance, which reminded her he'd been a marine sergeant some years back.

"I'm *gathering my dinner,*" Jeb Narville sneered.

Tim overtook him in a half second, but as Jeb was a foot shorter and twenty years older than he was, he hesitated. Narville's chest puffed as if he had the advantage.

"Get off my claim, little man," Tim said.

"This land belongs to me," Narville said. "I suppose we might work out some kind of rental agreement. Until then, you can get off of my land."

"Call the cops," Tim said, turning back to his work.

"You listen to me, boy . . ." Narville said. "I've just come from my lawyer this last hour, and it's very clear that I own this land. I suggest you go and consult your own attorney and we can take it from there. Meanwhile . . . I'm hungry." Narville, who would have guessed that, though Tim might have a public defender, he could never afford an attorney, reached for Tim's oysters again, and Tim shoved him away. Narville fell back in the low water, struggling like a beetle on its back.

"Jeb, Jeb!" It was Andrea, calling from the porch.

"I'm fine," Narville called back to her, struggling to stand. "Better than I was. That's assault, by the way," he said over his shoulder to Tim as he fled back to the house. He tried to lift himself onto the seawall, but couldn't, and had to go around over Charlotte's lawn.

12

CAPE COD GIRLS

Fiona started preschool two days after Labor Day. In New York, there would have been hair tearing, and perhaps hair pulling, as Charlotte investigated twenty places, waving Fiona under the admissions directors' noses to be sniffed like a wine, in hopes she might be considered worthy to finger paint alongside the best and brightest. In Wellfleet, everyone went to Mrs. Carroll's, a plain square house on Valley Road where the pines seemed to shed a darkness as intense as the sun's light. Mrs. Carroll's living room was entirely given over to the school, with dress-up clothes on hooks all around, shelves of books and art supplies, a train set on a low table, a hamster, a parrot, and an aquarium. Then there was the little kitchen with the bathroom off the back, and the Carrolls' bedroom, and that was all. Mr. Carroll worked for the Department of Public Works, and of course he had an oyster claim, so there was plenty of time for Mrs. Carroll to clean the papier-mâché off the dinner table before he got home.

Most of the other mothers averted their eyes from Charlotte and Fiona. They'd known one another all their lives and didn't feel up to bothering with a newcomer. It was a relief to see Betsy Godwin and her daughter, Alexis. Betsy smiled warmly, and Charlotte started toward her, but Alexis, with her hair pulled into four small ponytails fixed with fat round beads, regarded Fiona coldly. Alexis clearly understood that she was the standard by which other little girls must be judged, and felt for those who were about to be found wanting. Fiona headed in the opposite direction and sat down beside a small dark girl with a very large snarl in her hair.

"Hi, I'm Fiona Tradescome."

The girl stared at her as if she had just done something utterly bizarre. Fiona looked up at Charlotte as if to say, *I always knew everything you taught me was wrong*. But Charlotte smiled back encouragingly and Fiona tried again.

"What's your name?"

"Crystal!" the little girl said, as if Fiona must be an imbecile. "Everybody knows that!" There was a loud tap on the window—a round, hairy man whose T-shirt depicted a slavering hound. She waved to him and turned delightedly back to Fiona. "That's my dad," she said. "He picks up garbage on the end of a pole."

"Really?" Fiona said, with a baleful glance at her mother—why couldn't *she* have married someone interesting?

The girl nodded. "Once, he got a whole turkey sandwich, still wrapped up."

"*Really?*"

Charlotte kissed the top of Fiona's head, and began to tiptoe backward, bumping into Carrie, the clerk from SixMart, as grim as a jailer, her hand tight around the wrist of a little boy whose face was contorted with tears.

"Do you want to be the only one who has to have his mother here? Is that what you want, for everyone to think you're a little

THE HOUSE ON OYSTER CREEK · 125

wuss?" she said. He cried harder, of course, and she had raised her hand, apparently to hit him, when Mrs. Carroll intervened.

"Is this Tim Junior?" she asked, crouching down to his eye level. "Tim, I'm Mrs. Carroll; I've been looking forward to having you in class! Mrs. Cloutier, why don't you stay for a few minutes?"

"I'm late to work already," she said, with a poison look for her son, and a truly murderous one for Charlotte, who had turned back toward her, because if she was Tim's wife she must be Darryl's sister. You'd never know it—he was glowing, expansive, ready to listen to any story, take on any job; this woman's whole being seemed clenched against the world, her dark hair pulled into a squaw's braid, her stance pugnacious, and her eyes sharp, as if she never knew where the next blow would come from. "It's not like I can afford to lose a day's pay," she said bitterly, shaking her son's hand out of hers and stalking out the door.

The boy's wailing set off a panic among the other children— Fiona ran weeping to Charlotte, Alexis called "Crybaby, crybaby," from the door, two boys who had been involved in a quiet game began hitting each other with the toy trucks they'd been maneuvering

Mrs. Carroll sat little Tim in her lap and rocked him back and forth while he tried to escape. "The dad's in prison," Betsy explained to Charlotte, sotto voce. So that was why she'd been seeing Carrie out on Tim's claim. Darryl had said Tim was on parole, and the fight with Narville must have tripped the wire that sent him back to jail.

"You know, Fiona," Charlotte said, "he misses his mom. Do you think you could help cheer him up?"

Fiona jumped off her lap and threw her arms around the boy, who said, "Bitch, get your hands off me."

By the time Charlotte escaped it was ten o'clock, and she had to be back by noon. At home, she poured a cup of coffee and sat on the porch step in the sunlight, watching a fishing boat cross the mouth of the bay. She could hear Henry typing with one-handed fury below. He had learned on a manual, with his good hand, and though he used a computer now, he still hit every key with a vengeance. And that was all the sound there was: The Narville house was finished; there were no air compressors, no nail guns. Darryl had gone to work on Try Point for two guys who were building a place "in the Provençal style." The Narvilles had stayed in their house all of four days, then headed back to Georgia before Charlotte could get up the nerve to pay a call.

There was a soft sound—the first wave folding over on itself as the tide came up the beach. It used to be this quiet while her mother was sleeping off a round of chemo—the hours passing, a plane droning overhead. She'd had to get out of there—with one of the boys. . . . There had always been one or another, a boy whose suffering she felt more keenly than she'd ever felt her own, and she'd keep her arms so tight around him, her cheek against his back, willing him comfort as he gunned the motorcycle engine and they flew along the back roads. Oh, if only they would get somewhere! But no, there was just the graveyard, the privacy in back of the headstones to pull off each other's clothes, gently, like bandages. . . . *Let me see; let me heal you.*

She called down to Henry that she was taking a walk and set off, looking for Darryl without admitting such a thing to herself, sticking her hands into her jeans pockets, then pulling them out again, not sure what to do with them. Ada was just coming up the road, having walked to the end of the point and turned back, and was talking to herself in a bright, thoughtful voice. . . . "So naturally he would have . . ." Charlotte heard her say, as if she were puzzling out some conundrum she'd been brooding over for years. Seeing Charlotte, she smiled and continued on, but Charlotte put her hand out.

"Mrs. Town?"

"Yes, that's me." She was older than Charlotte had realized, her face so lined it could have been a sketch, showing the tender resignation of a woman who'd made her peace with life.

"I'm Charlotte Tradescome. I keep seeing you and I wanted to introduce myself."

"Charlotte Tradescome? Oh, my . . . yes, I know Henry has moved back to Wellfleet. It's nice to see the lights on in the old house. I knew your grandfather, you know."

Charlotte tried to imagine this. She had not known either of her grandfathers herself. "On the Pelletier side, or Doyle?"

Ada gave her a sharp look. "Tradescome, of course," she said. "Henry Senior. In fact, I was his secretary for many years."

"Oh!" Charlotte said. "Oh! You mean Henry's father. I grew up in New Hampshire."

"You—you're not Henry's daughter?"

"No, no, I'm his wife!" Charlotte explained, enjoying her surprise.

"You married him." Ada peered at her, puzzled, concerned. The experience of her years shaded her voice with more nuance than Charlotte could absorb.

"I did," she said, rather proudly, as if marrying Henry were some ridiculous trick she'd pulled off, like jumping twenty trucks on a Harley-Davidson.

"I used to babysit for him," Ada said. "Weeks at a time, when his parents went back to the city. He lived in his own little world." Looking out over the bay, she said, almost to herself, "They weren't bad people. They just didn't know what a child was, that's all."

"What do you mean?" Charlotte asked, too quickly, so Ada came back up to the social surface and returned to pleasantry.

"Isaiah Tradescome, Henry's grandfather, was born on his father's ship, in Calcutta Harbor. Did you know that?"

"No. No, I didn't. But I guess there's a lot I don't know. Why do you say that about Henry's parents—that they didn't know what a child was?"

"They didn't know quite what to do with one, that's all," Ada said. "But I don't suppose . . . Say, Priscilla Tradescome had the loveliest china collection. She loved delicate things. She didn't come from seafaring people; she never knew quite what to do with herself at the shore. She'd say, 'Terra firma for me, Ada,' when she was on her way back home, as if she felt stranded out here."

Natalie would have inquired further, but Charlotte was too timid. "Yes, there's beautiful china in the cabinet—I wouldn't dare eat from it," she said.

Ada didn't answer. They were stuck with each other for another half mile at least. Charlotte searched around for a good subject. A blue butterfly floated ahead of them, lighting on the goldenrod around the entrance to the Driftwood Cabins, catching up with them again. Charlotte looked up the dirt road, trying to guess which cottage might be Darryl's.

"This place has seen better days, hasn't it?" she said.

"It used to be an asparagus farm," Ada said. "Just a wide, sunny field. There were farms all along the highway—turnips, lavender—everything grows well here. The sea breeze keeps the climate mild. Then those tourist cabins, and now look." She shook her head, talking to herself again. "Birth by neglect, death by neglect, and very little in between."

"Excuse me, Mrs. Town?"

"Nothing, dear, talking to myself, as an old woman will. And I'm Miss Town, not Mrs.—I never married."

"Oh, I'm sorry."

"Not at all, it's a natural mistake."

They were crossing the low bridge; the tide streamed out beneath their feet. A dirt road cut into the trees on the other side, leading to a long row of big new houses at the edge of the marsh. Charlotte didn't know the owners, though she had probably waited with them in Six-Mart or eaten a clam roll at the next picnic table at PJ's. Her eye would have skipped them, in their khaki shorts, beach coverups, and sunglasses, as it searched out the people she was curious about, the local people. A cloud of grackles ascended from one oak tree to settle in another, cawing back and forth to one another as they plucked every acorn from every twig.

"Aren't they having the time of their lives," Ada said. "The Ecological Life League says the shellfish farms are affecting the migrations. I'd hate to lose our birds."

They cut through the Mermaid parking lot, passing Reggie the glass eater on his bicycle with a wire basket of clams over the handlebar.

"Telegram," he called.

"Rhode Island Red," Ada answered, crisply polite. Her driveway turned directly off the highway—it would have been a cartway when the house was built. Back then people traveled by water, and the sheltered spot at the head of Mackerel Bay would have been perfect. As they reached it Ada stopped and asked, "How is Henry? We always wondered.... after..."

"I think he's good," Charlotte said. "We have a daughter, you know, and . . ." She was thinking that she did not really know how Henry was. He was obsessed with the government, the war, global warming, bird flu . . . working to prepare a Kissinger obituary that laid the truth bare finally, stuffing himself with tales of horror from the barbarians to Guantánamo. He was disgusted with her frivolity, furious with himself for giving in to it and moving here . . . and underneath that? Bereft. Disappointed, ashamed, and alone.

"Yes, I'd seen you with a child." Ada looked at her questioningly. She pointed to the top of the telephone pole beside them, and Charlotte looked up to see an immense bird's nest made of seaweed and salt hay balanced on top. "Have you noticed the osprey? Can you imagine nesting in a spot like that? Good-bye, dear, I'm glad we met."

Charlotte suspected that Ada was not particularly glad, that she preferred her own company, her own thoughts and memories. Her step was light as she turned down the grassy little drive toward her home, picking up her conversation with herself again, stopping to pull a ragweed out from among the asters in bloom around her front door.

"Cape Cod girls, they have no combs, they comb their hair with codfish bones."

The girls were jumping rope in the schoolyard, or trying to. Charlotte had assumed that all four-year-olds tended to walk into walls, but Mrs. Carroll said that wasn't so, that Fiona was deficient in "motor planning."

"Her dad can throw her up in the air, tickle her . . . you know, just ordinary roughhousing," she said. "It helps them learn how to move." Charlotte had imagined Henry throwing Fiona into the air, Henry becoming distracted by a Very Important Thought, Fiona going splat on the pavement.

"Is there anything else that would help?" she asked. So out had come the jump ropes, and here Fiona was, watching plump little Alexis bounce and sing, with an expression of murderous envy.

When Fiona tried it, she would jump as she turned the rope, then stare dumbly as it hit her shoes.

"Try it again," Charlotte told her. "You'll pick it up if you give yourself a little time."

"Cape Cod boys, they have no sleds, they slide downhill on codfish heads," Alexis chanted, jumping.

"Cape Cod boys . . ." Fiona began, turning the rope perfectly, but forgetting to jump at all.

"Cape Cod cats, they have no tails," Alexis continued, seeming to taunt her. "They all blew off in Cape Cod gales!"

"Cape Cod . . ." Fiona tripped herself and fell down. "I hate jump rope!" She threw the rope on the ground and tried to kick it. Even there she missed.

"You shouldn't do that," Alexis observed, picking the rope up and skipping easily, glancing over to be sure her point had been made.

"And I hate you!" Fiona said.

"Fiona?" Fiona tumbled into Charlotte's lap, butting her little head against her mother's chest. "Can you tell Alexis you're sorry?" She felt the head shaking an absolute no. Alexis skipped along, counting—one hundred five, one hundred six. . . . Charlotte rather hated her too.

"Can I have a turn?" Charlotte asked. Alexis handed the rope over and Charlotte skipped twice before stumbling. "This is hard!" she said.

"You can do it better than that," Alexis said disdainfully, but Fiona started laughing, watching her mother fumble.

"Not that way, Mom," she said. "I'll show you." She took the rope and tried again.

They were the last two kids in Mrs. Carroll's yard. Charlotte watched the road, wishing Darryl would drive by, but it didn't lead anywhere except back to the highway through the pines.

"Mom!" Fiona said. "I *did* it!" And she had, sort of—swung the rope over her head and jumped once before dropping it in exultation. "I did it!" she said.

"Not really," Alexis said.

"She's on her way," Charlotte said. "You've helped her learn to-day." It was the best she could manage; she could only hope her smile looked real.

Betsy arrived, breathless with apology, to pick Alexis up. She was so simply, easily pretty—small and slender with her blond hair pulled back loose—it was always good to see her, the way it's good to see an apple tree in bloom.

"I had to pick up Skip's stationery," she said. "He's starting his own practice, did Alexis say?"

"That's exciting,"

"Nerve-racking, a little," Betsy said. "But it's what he's dreamed of, so here we go. We've bought the old Hooper place, on Main Street? Skip'll take the office in front, and I'll have my jewelry store in the an-nex, and the upstairs apartment looks over the harbor in back; it's amazing."

"Congratulations! That's wonderful!"

"You girls will have to come for tea, once we get settled."

"Of course," Charlotte said. Of all the women she'd met so far, Betsy was the most likely friend. She was from upstate New York, had come out to waitress one college summer and met Skip, whose parents had a summer place. "What's to become of Speck and Nittle, though, without Skip?"

"Well, Speck passed away right after Skip joined the firm," Betsy said. "And Ralph Nittle . . . he'll do fine; he's been everyone's attorney for the last hundred years. It's Skip I'm nervous about! He's my bread and butter."

"He's so sharp," Charlotte said. "I'm sure this will be a great thing for you two."

"I don't know," Betsy said, biting her lovely lip. She used her beauty as artfully as a sculptor, without realizing it. "He only has one client." She shook her head as if she were nervous, covering her pride.

"Someone with deep pockets, I hope."

Betsy made wide, confiding eyes. "I wish I could tell," she said.

"But I'll be seeing you cruise by in a yacht one of these days?"

"Wouldn't that be fabulous? Like, with crystal chandeliers and a steward to bring the champagne? Oooh! Alexis, honey, come on, Daddy'll be home soon."

It was maybe two days later that Charlotte went to the post office and found Darryl standing stock-still in the lobby, staring at a letter he'd just ripped open.

"Hello!" Charlotte said, and he looked up and blinked. "What is it? What's the matter?"

"I . . ." he said. "I . . . look at this." A fine piece of letterhead it was too—heavy paper, cream colored, with SCHUYLER GODWIN, AT-TORNEY-AT-LAW embossed in a subtly modern font. It announced that Jeb Narville was suing Darryl, and Tim and Carrie, and Bud Rivette, and all the shellfish farmers off Tradescome Point. He contended that he owned to the extreme-low-tide line, that any bit of the bay that was not underwater twenty-four hours a day belonged to him. And he wanted them off the flats.

"Do you know what this means?" Darryl asked, his voice almost breaking. "Do you have any idea what I—what we all—have put into this? This is my best hope. It might be my only chance to . . ."

To get out of the Driftwood Cabins, to have a place of his own, a wife, a family. His chance at redemption, no less.

"It can't be right," Charlotte said. "The town granted you permission to use that land, didn't they? That's why they call them shellfish grants."

"Yeah."

"So how can he sue you? You've never claimed to own it—you're just working it. He could—I guess he could sue the town?"

"I suppose," Darryl said, "except he's sued me, and I can't afford a lawyer. None of us can."

"You've all been out there for years and years," Charlotte said. "This doesn't make any more sense than if he were insisting he owned town hall."

"It's . . ." He started to explain, but she could see in his face that there was way too much of it to tell. "It's complicated."

"But the land beyond the wrack line is public; no one can own it."

The frustration on Darryl's face reminded her of the look on Henry's when he needed to use both hands.

"I don't have time to explain this," Darryl said angrily, turning to leave. "I can't lose the tide."

13

THE KING'S LAW

"There's no possibility that they do own the flats, is there, Henry?" Charlotte asked. She was scrubbing littlenecks for clam sauce; just after low tide she had answered the door to find Darryl there in his hip waders, holding out a bag of clams for them, and one of pasta seashells for Fiona the picky eater.

"I've got more than I can sell right now," he said, shrugging off their thanks, but she guessed he was trying to say he didn't blame them for his troubles. Which was nice, because Charlotte had dreamed she'd committed a murder, that she was carrying a severed head around, frantically looking for a place to hide it before the police—or the devil—found her out. If she hadn't barged in here, blithely selling off the property, Henry would still be at the *Mirror*, Darryl would be working the flats, and everything would go on as it had for generations. Henry had invited Darryl in for commiseration, but he had lifted a muddy boot, declining, smiling into Charlotte's eyes with an understanding that was way beyond forgiveness.

"We don't mind a little mud," Henry said heartily. "Stay for a beer at least. Your father never turned one down."

"No, I'm sure he didn't," Darryl said, with a quick, laughing glance at Charlotte. "I've got a meeting, though—this lawsuit. . . ."

With that they all became wretchedly uncomfortable, making various gestures of worry and absolution mixed with bright, conventional thank-yous. Darryl went back into the wet evening, leaving a trail of muddy footsteps behind him.

"I mean, we own to the high-water mark, right?" she asked. "Everyone does."

Henry looked as if she'd asked whether the universe would end by explosion or implosion, and said nothing.

"It belongs to someone. It's not just floating in limbo," she said.

"If you say so." Physical reality—boundaries, tide lines, weights and measures—didn't fit into Henry's mind. He couldn't help feeling that Charlotte only affected to understand such things, and he detested affectation.

The pasta boiled, the wine and tomatoes were absorbed in the oil, Charlotte dumped the clams into the skillet, covered it, and turned up the flame. The smell charged the atmosphere—made it feel holy, dinner a ritual that reaffirmed the hope Charlotte had begun with—that she and Henry, two strange, lonely people, could make a home together where they'd be safe enough that they could be doubly brave in the outer world. If only . . .

Henry softened, trying to give her an answer.

"The oystermen have been out there all my life. They were granted that land by the town. Amos Stead used to bring Father a barrel of oysters every Thanksgiving. They'd keep in the mudroom all winter long. Father loved oysters. . . ."

He smiled, sad. Now that his father was dead, and Henry didn't have to fight him, tenderness was seeping into the wells of rage.

The clams burst open one by one; Charlotte lifted the lid and steam covered the windows.

"Some people used to say we owned to low tide," Henry said, "but I never attended. Who would want to own a piece of tide bottom?" He shook his head. "Of course, I never even wanted to own *dry* land. When I drive home down Point Road now, though, I . . ."

Charlotte had never seen him nostalgic, except maybe for Watergate. She smiled; he avoided her eyes.

"The deed says, 'by the waters of Mackerel Bay.'"

"Whose deed?"

"Theirs is based on ours. The language is the same; the only thing different is the line between the two properties. I mean, if you took it literally, 'by the waters' would mean a different thing every minute."

"Special for me?" Fiona asked. Charlotte had cooked the pasta seashells separately and served them in Fiona's plastic Tigger bowl.

"That's why Darryl brought them," she said.

"I'm sure it has some particular legal meaning," Henry said irritably. He thought she was crazy to imagine she could have any effect in these matters. If she hadn't rushed in where angels feared to tread, they wouldn't have gotten sucked into this mire—surely she wasn't going to wade in farther?

Ada Town minded the church thrift shop on Tuesdays, so down Charlotte went into the airless church basement. Like all thrift shops it smelled of old sweat and smoke and perfume; but the book section always had something interesting, and when the summer people left, the place became a gold mine for a few weeks. Charlotte had found a stuffed tiger twice Fiona's size, with the price tag, three hundred dollars, still on. A gift from some estranged father? Who knew? The thrift shop price was ten dollars, and Fiona named it Pussywussy and pulled it around the house on a makeshift leash. This week there was a Kate Spade handbag, Seven jeans, and a thick cashmere sweater in an amazing shade of teal with sweat stains that would probably never come out. And one thing Charlotte badly wanted: a canvas coat just like Darryl's—Carhartt. And a tartan shawl.

"Isn't that funny, dear," Ada said. "I brought that piece in myself. I love these Scottish woolens. My father—Pastor Stewart, I mean—was a Scot. I guess it's in my blood." She said this simply, and Charlotte thought she was perfectly right, even though Pastor Stewart wasn't her natural father.

"It's so nice and cozy, and I love the colors," Charlotte said, wrapping the shawl around her shoulders. "Is it a Stewart tartan?"

"Hardly, dear. Braemar. I wouldn't let a Stewart go."

"Do you know them all?" She wanted Ada's trust, so she could find out more about Henry, and about Wellfleet.

"I made a study of them when I was younger. I loved thinking about Scotland," she said, smiling into the distance.

"Miss Town, you said the shellfish farms were bad for the birds?"

"Apparently so," Ada said. "That's what Preston Withers tells me, and he's the director of the Ecological Life League. Those boys don't seem to care what harm they do. Not that they're boys anymore. . . . Now they have boys of their own. They don't respect any law, except that might makes right." She sounded only sad. "Their fathers and grandfathers went to sea, and that's a vicious way of life. They can't get themselves over the bridge, but they feel big and important here."

"But that's what Wellfleet is, a fishing town."

Ada smiled to herself, tucking a sheet of tissue neatly in as she folded the shawl. "In the eighteen hundreds, fishermen here brought in millions of pounds of cod every year. Can you imagine? But as the fish dwindled, the more able people found ways to leave. Only the roughest stayed. Replaced by washashores—fishing sounds romantic to them!" She laughed at the thought. "I don't blame your neighbor for wanting Tim off his beach," she admitted.

"You know about the lawsuit."

"Skip is the church deacon," she said.

"But . . ."

"We do own to the low-tide mark here," Ada said quietly. "It's one of the King's Laws . . . from the sixteen hundreds. Everyone traveled by sea then, and no one would build a wharf on land they didn't own."

"So no one could go on the beach except people who lived right there?"

"People didn't hold beach parties in 1650," Ada said. "You're allowed to use the beach for 'fishing, fowling, or hunting' . . . which was what they needed it for. Oysters were so plentiful . . . no one would have thought to farm them. Through the Depression, they were almost all we had—I swore I'd never eat another one if I didn't have to. Now the summer people come and I hear them talking about the oysters. One has a brinier taste; one is more metallic. . . . well, it makes me laugh! I'd take bread and butter any day."

"Times have changed."

"Yes, they have," Ada said. "There's barely a mackerel left in Mackerel Bay . . . in fact, the bay was nearly fished out before I was born. The Portland Gale swept the old wharves off their pilings—there was no reason to rebuild. We had the railroad, then the state highway. No, the laws are about all that's left of the past now."

"And that, oh, my best beloved, is the story of how the oystermen came to carry guns," Charlotte told Fiona in the same folk-wise voice she used to read Kipling aloud. (Yes, Kipling, with Henry's clipper ship bookplate still affixed inside the cover.) They all had fishing rods in their trucks now—as long as they could say they were fishing, they wouldn't be trespassing. Some kept guns instead—for *fowling*—really to remind everyone who was boss as long as he had a gun in the back of his truck. Fiona had made a thank-you card for Darryl, with cutout snowflakes and pasta shapes smashed onto it in smears of glue, and they ran out to meet him as he drove down to the water.

His face, when he saw them! He got out of the truck and came up around toward them, looking if they were his family.

"We wanted to say thank-you for the clams," Charlotte explained, awkward now that they were standing together.

"You haven't said, 'How beautiful,'" Fiona said. "You always say, 'How beautiful, how beautiful,' when the sun goes down."

"How beautiful," Charlotte said, laughing, and they all said together, "How beautiful."

Fiona handed the card to Darryl. "How beautiful!" he said. "Did you make this yourself?"

Fiona explained in detail how she had folded and cut the snowflakes; it seemed like she'd talk for as long as Darryl would listen, and he listened a long time, while Charlotte drank him in. His nose was bent as if it had once been broken, there were laugh lines at the corners of his eyes, his hair was cut very short but still it was beginning to curl. Charlotte was like a shoplifter, secretly pocketing these details. She lifted Fiona onto her hip so she too could see into his honest eyes.

"I'm glad to get a card, because you know what? Today's my birthday. I'm forty-three today."

"Mom!" Fiona said, looking, of all things, accusatory, so that

Charlotte laughed, thinking she'd say they should have made him a cake or . . .

"What?"

"You're the same age as Darryl! You could have married him!"

"I . . ." Charlotte said. "I . . ." She couldn't speak, and the silence stretched on, a soft silence that seemed to envelop them all in a dream. Darryl reached out and tucked an escaped strand of hair behind Fiona's ear.

"That would have been so nice," Charlotte said finally, letting all she felt pour into it. They seemed to have made a pact so secret that they didn't mention it even to each other, that they would always show their hearts fully to each other, no matter the risk. She had to honor it, and then, because she had a pact with herself to keep Fiona's world whole and safe—"But I'm already married, silly! And we'd miss Daddy, don't you think?"

Fiona turned her sweet, rosy, ringlet-haloed face to her mother, and gazed at her with a cool, sidelong smile that would have seemed more appropriate from a very well-read and sophisticated sixty-year-old man.

14

SQUID

" ' Cupid and Bacchus my saints are, may drink and love still reign, with wine I wash away my cares and then, to *cunt* again,' " said Henry, deeply stirred, gazing at the wine list as if it were his bible. He'd meant to entertain the waiter, who stood frozen, his pencil poised above the pad. Henry assumed all men had this in common, a connoisseur's enjoyment of wine and women, a pleasure in comparing and contrasting the various vintages and ethnicities, full-bodied or light and sweet, with a slight smoky finish, hints of melon and pear. . . .

"Did you want the merlot?" the waiter asked in mortification.

"I guess he hasn't read Lord Rochester," Henry said, once the man had fled to the kitchen.

"Another philistine." Charlotte shook her head.

"It's shocking how little people read," Henry said. "You look in people's windows at night and you don't see a single bookshelf, just a big television." Charlotte had sworn that if she heard this lament one more time she would buy a forty-foot plasma TV and keep it tuned to the Cartoon Channel twenty-four hours a day.

"It's true: print is dead," she said, running him through with his own sword. The waiter returned with the wine.

"A devout Catholic, Lord Rochester," Henry said somberly, trying to get back in the man's good graces, but once he'd approved the bottle and the man went on to the next table, he added: ". . . *on his deathbed*," and began to laugh, silently at first, holding it in until he wheezed and sputtered. "I'll admit he was a bit spermy earlier on."

"To Lord Rochester," Charlotte said. It was their wedding anniversary, though Henry didn't remember and she had no intention of bringing it up. It was also the day after Columbus Day weekend, the last gasp of Wellfleet's tourist season, so they'd come out for half-price day at the Wharf Grill. The tide was rising under the floorboards: The grill had once been a fish shed. It was dark and low, with nets and buoys hanging in the corners and small-paned windows looking onto the harbor. There was a stack of plywood by the entranceway—tomorrow the place would be shuttered for winter, but tonight everything was half-price and everyone in town was here. The paint man from the hardware store was at the next table with the lady from the post office. She, a heavy woman with a harsh face and two inches of straight gray hair, still looked almost pretty in the candlelight, and seeing Charlotte, she broke into a broad smile. "Twin lobstah, ten ninety-nine!" she said, and Charlotte lifted a glass, and would have hugged her, she was so grateful to be included, to have a little part in the life of the town.

Charlotte and Henry were seated beside the window, a dark mirror now that the sun was down. In it Charlotte could see Ada come in, with a man who might be one of Henry's ancestors, an ancient mariner. Half the faces in town had that sharp, weathered, British look. Portuguese fisherman had filtered in, and French Canadians (being French Canadian herself, Charlotte was deeply suspicious of

French Canadians) and otherwise most seemed to be Irish, ruddy and welcoming.

"Twin lobster," Henry said, watching the post office lady tie on her bib. "How Americans eat!"

"They're followers of Lord Rochester," Charlotte said, without turning from the window. Alone in the opposite corner, Orson was sitting with a glass of cognac and an open copy of *Cities of the Plain*, which he was using as a sort of duck blind from which to survey the room. Henry tried another tack.

"I don't ever remember an October as warm as this," he said.

"You haven't *been* here for twenty years."

He looked as if he'd been bitten by a shrew.

"I just can't talk about global warming right now," she said.

"I wasn't talking about global warming. I was saying we've been having some nice weather."

Ugh, this was probably true. Henry tried again, a smile brewing up amidst the fierce lines of his face. "Fiona seems to like this preschool."

Six weeks she'd been in preschool and he had managed this deduction. Excellent. Was she growing needlelike teeth like a shrew? Probably. She pressed her forehead to the window so she could see out to the fishing boats moored at the end of the pier.

"Nah, anywhere's fine." Darryl's voice. Charlotte knew it by the wave of feeling that washed through her. She found his reflection in the window—his and his date's. She started to study the menu as if she were supposed to memorize it.

Henry, however, jumped to his feet, becoming loud and good-humored, his way with men. "Darryl! How're ya doing?"

"Very well," Darryl responded, in the same hearty tone. "And yourself?"

"Good. Or as good as a man can be under the circumstances..."

"Circumstances?"

"The White House?" Henry said.

"Oh, *him*," Darryl said with a sigh. Then, quickly—"This is Nikki.
Her brother's in the service."

Nikki. Tall, and thin in a wiry, masculine way, with long, loose
sun-blond hair and big expressionless eyes softly blinking. A worker-
mermaid.

"You of all people must be tormented," Henry said to her. "Bil-
lions a day, thousands dead, by presidential inanition. Impeachment
would be a start, but why not prosecution?" Henry would never insult a person by assuming he or she might vote Republican. He didn't
sit with the other parents in Mrs. Carroll's parking lot. He didn't
imagine there were people who, if they didn't see themselves as he-
roes fighting for the American way, would have to see themselves as
failures. He'd never noticed they always had FOX News playing on
the SixMart TV.

"I'm pleased to meet you," Nikki said, looking past him.

"Nikki works for Pembroke and Sons, you know, the crane guys?"
Darryl said. "So I know her from work." He seemed to be trying to
explain himself to Charlotte, as if he'd bumped into his wife when he
was out with his mistress. "We couldn't resist half-price night."

"No, neither could we," she said. "It wouldn't be economical not
to eat out on half-price night." They stood there in magnetic paraly-
sis a minute longer before she managed to speak. "You'd better sit
down and order. I was going to get the calamari but look, he just
crossed it off the blackboard; they're already out."

"My God, he's handsome," Henry said once they left. "His father
and I used to drink together—that was before the Mermaid, back in

the Mooncusser days. Amos Stead was a good man, and oh, the things he knew! He could tell you the story of every ship that was ever wrecked on the back shore. He'd started college, but Marlene fell pregnant and he had to come home and go to work fishing. It was a grim day when Amos Stead died. I saw old Bart Speck coming down the street like a horse pulling a hobble, and my heart dropped to my feet.

"But what a son," he continued, with thunderous approbation. "A fine specimen of American manhood."

Charlotte looked out the window for fear she was blushing, and seemed to see a small ghost ascending—a very large moth, maybe.

"He's the kind of man we need in Iraq," Henry said stoutly.

Charlotte gasped. "I thought you were against the war!"

"If we're there, we might as well win."

It was one of those conversations—all conversations—driven entirely by intuition. Henry was no less sensitive than his wife but, having been born into a family that would have been appalled to see their son peering into the hearts and minds of others, had covered himself with layer after hard cerebral layer: A critic was born. A part of him recognized every nuance of Charlotte's feeling, and another part recoiled from such knowledge, preferring to ship any threats directly to Fallujah.

"They're calling up the National Guard," he said, with a torturer's little smile.

"Henry!"

"Write your representative." He shrugged.

Skip and Betsy Godwin had just come in, looking flush with Jeb Narville's money, in command and therefore out of place; you didn't really belong here until life had beaten you down a little.

"We've got to get Fiona over for a playdate soon!" Betsy said as they passed, and Skip told her to go ahead and order their drinks; he wanted to have a word with Henry.

"I've been meaning to get over and see you," he said. "You grew up here, Henry; you know what we're dealing with, out on the flats."

He was appealing to the deepest arrogance—the pride of truly belonging to the town. The essential thing in Wellfleet was how long you'd lived here, how many generations your family held on. You might have dazzled the New York art world, or won the Tour de France, but alas, these achievements were the positive proof you'd come from away, and the grocery clerk whose brother went down on the *Mary Belle* in 1973 was your superior. Skip had guessed that the way to attract people to his cause was to appeal to this sense of entitlement by history, but if he'd looked a little closer at Henry, who was wearing a sweatshirt that had washed up on the beach the other morning, he might have thought again.

"I came summers," Henry said. "Stead, Rivette, Cloutier, those are the old names here." Skip stiffened; these were names from the police blotter. Another . . . ghost? . . . flew up outside the window. Otherwise Charlotte could see only the quiet harbor with the lighted masts of summer's last sailboats swaying.

"They think they own this town," Skip said. "'By the waters' means 'to the mean low tide.' That's the law."

"The King's Law," Henry said. "We're still living by the King's Law, in the twenty-first century? They've been working that land for generations," he said. "And they're not doing anything to trouble the rest of us."

"You're a Tradescome, from Tradescome Point. If you don't defend your rights, next thing you know you'll have lost them."

"Tradescome Point, beside Oyster Creek. The oysters make it the place it is."

Charlotte saw Darryl glance toward her; she hated for him to see her talking to Skip and concentrated all her attention out the window, so he'd see she wasn't going along. Two more apparitions flicked up from the water.

"Do we have giant moths out here?" she asked, and, having caught Skip's attention, took a deep breath and proceeded. "Skip, why didn't you mention any of this when you drew up the subdivision documents?"

"Didn't come up," he said. "Why should it? But now there's a case; I took it. It's purely a business matter."

"We're not joining the suit, Skip," Henry said, with that steely decency that was the first thing she'd loved in him. He was not interested in joining the upper class in their attempt to pull the shore out from under the lower.

"You'll be the only ones," Skip replied. "I've talked to nearly every upland owner on Try Point—they're delighted. They've had it up to here with these guys."

Their oysters were served. "Another round?" the waiter asked.

"Please."

"Think about it," Skip said, leaving.

"'Purely a business matter,'" Charlotte mocked. "I'll never understand how people can say that, as if you're supposed to assume that business and ethics never cross paths at all."

"Calmness, calmness. This too will pass," said Henry, who, having once been a Marxist, was in a position to know. "Have an oyster. They transcend description."

Skip had joined Ada and her friend across the room, and they were listening intently.

"Henry, don't you want to say hi to Ada?"

"Hi?" he said, dubious.

"Well, you know, 'Good day, Miss Town,' or whatever Trades-comes say."

"She's talking to Skip. And Preston Withers."

"Maybe later, after Skip's done. She's kind of the last thread between you and your family, and we've lived here for months now without a visit."

"It's unconscionable," he said, with an expression of vile loathing such as he felt only toward himself. "But not here, not now."

"That's Preston Withers? He looks a little like you." The hard squint, the outthrust jaw: They'd have been clergymen in an earlier generation.

Henry gave a little snarl at this idea, and Charlotte shuddered.

"Are you getting a draft? Do you want my sweater?"

"No, no, thanks, honey, I'm fine."

"Aaahh, it was one of those *inner* drafts, the breath of the grave," he said, laughing. "I know them well."

Orson had paid his tab, stopped by Darryl's table to say hello, and arrived beside them.

"Mr. Tradescome!" he said.

"Captain!" Henry said, perhaps because Orson was wearing a Greek fisherman's cap, or because he was three sheets to the wind. "Join us! Please sit down!"

He motioned to the waiter, who seemed not to see him.

"He's been quoting Lord Rochester. The waiter's afraid of him," Charlotte explained.

Orson looked over his shoulder and caught the man's eye, making an undulant cognac-sniffing motion—apparently a universal signal, as the waiter held up a finger and went to the bar.

"Lord Rochester, an excellent fellow," Orson said. "A man truly open to *all* the pleasures of the world. Your husband is an uncommonly learned man, my dear, but then I'm sure you know that. I'll never forget reading *Dread and the Common Man.* You were prescient, Henry; it's awful to realize how far you saw."

Henry looked mortally pained; praise appalled him, but Orson was just warming up.

"In fact, you'd studied the past so thoroughly you were able to see into the future...."

Henry writhed, but the drunken oration continued, Orson rolling each new compliment over his tongue with a nearly obscene pleasure.

"Vietnam," Henry said. "That raging energy—you could feel it in the streets, everywhere. Everyone went dancing every night; the women were ablaze with it.... My God, they were beautiful."

He gave Charlotte a hard glance—she had disappointed him by aging.

"I used to roar at my father, after he voted to reelect Nixon," Henry said. "Oh, the house shook...." He laughed. "I can see him shouting up the stairs at me—'You should see a psychiatrist!' He thought I was a traitor—you understand."

Orson nodded dolefully. "My father forced me take up law," he said. "He thought it would make a man of me."

"Do you still practice law, or have you retired?" Charlotte asked. "What do you think about Jeb Narville's lawsuit?"

"Wills and trusts, my dear, wills and trusts..."

"Still, you must have some sense...."

"I've long since despaired of penetrating the popular—or, for that matter, the judicial—mind. It's not going to be about what's best for the town, or the people, or what's most ethical and fair. It will be about the way the judge interprets what's written as law. A very similar lawsuit shut down the aquaculture in Truro ten years ago, so precedent would seem to be on Narville's side. Tim Cloutier is not what you'd call a charismatic fellow, and you've got twenty people signed on as plaintiffs already. They have the money, so they have the lawyers. We shall see."

"Orson, why are we living under the King's Law all these centuries later?"Charlotte asked.

Orson leaned back in his chair. "Wealthy people own the beachfront and, coincidentally, the government. They have no incentive to change a law that works to their own benefit."

Here was Orson's cognac, and for Charlotte, a plate piled with calamari.

"I didn't order this," she said to the waiter. "I mean, they erased it off the board; I thought you said you were out?"

The waiter looked over at Darryl, who was laughing as if he'd pulled off a great joke. Charlotte turned up her palms, mouthing, *What? How?* and he stood up, stiffly, and came over to explain.

"They're running. It's easier to catch them than not. My cousin works in the kitchen—he ran a line out the upstairs window."

Back at his table, Nikki tapped a cigarette out of her pack, smelled it, fitted it back in again. Charlotte couldn't quite speak.

"They're just squid; the sea's full of 'em," Darryl insisted, but there was such light in his face, as if the rest of this sentence, unspoken, were . . . *And I own the sea, so I got it for you.*

"Oh, of course, squid. Now I see." She laughed; she felt she would cry. "You . . ."

"It's nothing," he said, going back to Nikki. Maybe that was true. It didn't feel that way. It felt as if he had blown, gently, on the last ember of an old, old fire, and it had whooshed to life with the force of a blowtorch.

Orson and Henry, civilized creatures, had been attending to their drinks; Orson was warming his glass in his palm and opining that Columbus was the only mass murderer ever to have a holiday named in his honor.

"People ask how we can say he discovered America," Henry was saying. "It's simple enough . . . he was able, he had that kind of imagination. The Native Americans didn't guess there was a land beyond this one—or they might have *discovered* Europe."

"It's so," Orson said. "It's so."

"Of course," Henry said, "he was reprehensible. . . ."

"People who *do* things always are," Charlotte said. "They're trying to get somewhere—to the New World, or to the root of some problem—they focus on that; they forget the other stuff. The rest of us worry about what might go wrong, who we might hurt, and we don't get anything done."

"There's a grain of truth in that," Henry said, surprised.

"Have some calamari," Charlotte said with her mouth full. "Here, have a tentacle. They're *so* good." The faces, the candlelight, the conversations around them; everything was spinning gorgeously together. "I love this town," she said.

"It's quite a place," Orson agreed.

"I think this is the best wedding anniversary we've ever had," she said, giddy.

"Is this our wedding anniversary?"

"It is."

"How long since we were married?"

"Forever!"

Henry smiled at her, crookedly, sweetly. "That sounds about right."

She drank the wine down, hearing the boats bump against the pilings, the foghorn, the name *Wolfowitz* repeated like a soft wind through the trees. The nation was lurching over a precipice—"A superpower on the skids," Henry said, and he and Orson shook their heads in grave agreement. . . . Yes, they'd been right all along. Skip had left Ada's table and gone back to Betsy to give a report. Darryl was explaining something to Nikki—with an intensity that made Charlotte guess he was telling her about rehab. Rehab had saved him, given him hope that he wanted to share with everyone he met, but Nikki looked as if it were an old story she'd heard once too often.

The two girls who were clearing the tables were the ones Charlotte had seen standing at the side of the road that first day. They were Carrie's daughters, Desiree and Jelissa. They went to the high school in Eastham; Charlotte would see them getting off the bus at the Driftwood Cottages in the afternoon. They moved smoothly among the tables, proud to be grown-up and working, sashaying a little to show off their hips, wiping each table with one efficient sweep of the rag.

At home, Henry paid the babysitter and bade Charlotte a formal good-night at the bottom of the stairs; as she fell asleep she heard his footsteps on the shells in the driveway as he set off for the Mermaid.

15

THEY

Charlotte had never been a woman who could assume love was her due. She was pretty sometimes, with the dark hair and the blush coming up in her cheeks, but any lapse of confidence and it all fell apart—she became awkward, anxious, with eyes narrowed, a raw need in her face no one would like to see. That Darryl had seemed . . . well, *seemed* was the word, wasn't it? He was a natural: He could hear the qualities of different silences and his eyes reflected every sparkle they saw. It would be easy to mistake his intention. Still, Charlotte felt as if a knot in her chest had hatched and was stretching its shimmering wings.

She hadn't guessed what fall would be like here; they'd had a light frost that shriveled the morning glories, but the roses were still blooming. The bay was a dark, bottomless blue; the oak leaves, last to turn, made a tapestry of deep colors like a Persian rug, the marsh grass thick and gold. Every afternoon Charlotte and Fiona scuffed through the woods, imagining how souls must sneak from tree to tree around them, shivering cozily. Fiona, Alexis, and Crystal went trick-or-treating together in the town center, each holding tight to her mom's hand. Fiona had never been outside after dark before. In every doorway an old woman hovered, offering candy in exchange for a glimpse of the children's excitement. Alexis and Crystal were Disney princesses, but Fiona went as a witch.

"You look so beautiful," Ada Town said, and Fiona stamped her foot and cried," I don't! I don't! I look ugly! Like a witch!"

"I'm sorry, dear, you're quite right," Ada said. "I was wearing the wrong glasses."

Along with the mini-Snickers and Tootsie Pops in Fiona's bag, Charlotte found a "Preserve Our Boat Meadow" pamphlet. The picture on the front showed Oyster Creek at sunset, so still, so beautiful with the pink clouds reflected and the grasses turning red at the tops, that Charlotte felt a pull of homesickness, as if it were a place she'd loved and lost already. Inside was a photo of Bud Rivette's claim, with Darryl's truck parked at the side—it reminded her that Jeb Narville had called it a junkyard. There was a bulleted list of the perils of aquaculture: damage to the eelgrass beds; danger to shorebirds, turtles, and horseshoe crabs; the "voluminous waste produced by oysters and the consequent increase of sedimentation," whatever that was. "For our children's sake," it read, "let's stand together against the desecration of our most precious resource, before it's too late."

Charlotte's heart might be swelling, but others' were closing up tight. Winter was coming, the tourists had gone and taken all the money with them, no one would buy oysters until Thanksgiving. Tim being away, Darryl was helping Carrie with her grant as well as working his own. The two of them would be out on the flats by the light of Darryl's miner's lamp before the sun was up, the raw wind rattling Charlotte's windows. Cars were parked at the end of every other driveway, apparently poised to turn, with FOR SALE, RUNS GOOD, $6880 OR B.O. signs in their windows. On the fences, signs advertised firewood for sale, snowplowing, handyman services, brush clearing . . . anything that might inch a family a few days farther through the winter. Dramas that played out crisply in sleek Manhattan living rooms were ragged here, like the wounds of a blunt knife, festering, scarring, slow to heal. At the hardware store, Charlotte's credit card wouldn't go through, and the cashier was so kind ("The fourth one today," he said. "I know mine's at the limit. Gonna be a lean Christmas") that she put all her purchases back rather than use another card and let him know she wasn't in his predicament.

"Truck's floor rusted through," someone was saying in the next aisle, as Charlotte tried to fit the weather stripping back into its spot. "Won't pass inspection, and when I tried to take out a loan for a new one, Joe Silva at the bank said he didn't want to stick me with a debt I wouldn't be able to pay if I lost my grant."

"If they win, I'm going south," said another. "Get a little place in Mississippi and raise catfish."

"How ya going to do that?"

"Sell my place!"

It was Bud Rivette—Charlotte recognized his laugh as it turned into a deep smoker's cough. Bud's place looked likely to fall down any day, but no matter—it was on a wooded hillside, less than a mile from the bay, and whoever bought it would tear it down, top some trees, and build an upside-down house with a water view.

"Meanwhile I gotta build gear, and the mesh is three hundred dollars a roll."

"Charge it," someone said, with a laugh that was more like a groan.

"I've got a buddy in North Carolina, grows geraniums."

"Geraniums?"

"Yeah, geraniums. You plant 'em, you water 'em, they grow.

When they're big enough you sell 'em. Everyone loves geraniums. No one's ever gotten sick from one. No one ever moves in next to a geranium farm and complains it's ruining their view."

"They . . ." someone began. Charlotte wanted to go around the aisle and make it clear she wasn't a member of "they," that she loved this town because you could still touch the earth here; everything hadn't been buttered over with wealth, crusted with high-end beauty salon/spas, surfaced with the finest Italian marble. . . . The rooms hadn't gotten bigger and bigger until they looked like hotel lobbies; they were still rooms where people lived and children built block castles on the floor. Up on the back shore there were miles of rough scrub plants grown low and thick under the wind, and the Atlantic Ocean looked as vast and blank as a desert. You looked at life from a different perspective when you saw this and remembered these lighthouses had been built to warn ships away, because if they ran aground in a storm, the waves would batter the ships to splinters, and their men to death.

These thoughts didn't matter; nor did it matter that she hadn't joined the lawsuit, that she was repulsed by Jeb Narville and admired Darryl and the others, with their lives of methodical effort and small gain. She hadn't been born here, gone to school here, been disillusioned by love or crushed by debt here. None of her relations had been lost at sea, or to an overdose, or the kind of car crash that came from gunning an engine in a drunken rage with the momentary illusion that you *will* escape, because you have that spark of imagination even though no one ever noticed; you'll get out of this town and make something happen in the world. A boy she knew back in New Hampshire had died like that, a week before their graduation. They'd given him a hero's funeral, saying that he'd lived every moment to the fullest, lived his life on the edge; he was always a risk taker—it ran in the family. It would have been too sad to say that he had been careless with his life, because it didn't seem to be worth very much.

The name Cloutier had proud meaning in town—Tim's uncle went down on the *Sola Mara* when it was pulled under by the enormous weight of scallops it was trying to bring back from Georges Bank; his cousin OD'd on a January night and was left by his frightened companions to freeze on the roadside. Tim's father had worked for the Department of Public Works all his life, pocketing a percentage of the dump fees year after year. When he was discovered, the town manager took the blame for subjecting him to temptation. They gave him a job where he wouldn't come in contact with money and the matter was closed. The Cloutiers had suffered, had been brought low—they belonged.

"*Our* boat meadow?" Charlotte asked Betsy Godwin, as they waited at Mrs. Carroll's for pickup time. "Who's 'our'? Did you get one of these things in Alexis's Halloween bag?" There was no name, no phone number on the pamphlet, but reading it aloud Charlotte couldn't help mimicking Preston Withers's Yankee accent.

"Oh, I'm sure it's just meant to get people thinking," Betsy said. "Bring the issue out into the open, you know."

"Is there really a shortage of eelgrass?" Charlotte asked. "Is crabgrass endangered too? And do oysters produce voluminous waste? I thought they helped clean the water—filter feeders, you know. . . ."

"I don't know!" Betsy laughed. "I'm in retail. How do you like my new wheels?"

She was driving a brand-new BMW, a bulbous SUV. She'd parked next to Carrie, whose tailgate was tied shut by means of a rope pulled through a rust hole.

"Spiffy," Charlotte said.

"I've got room to drive the whole Saturday gymnastics gang

now," Betsy went on; then she smiled at Carrie and added, "Though who needs another monthly payment, huh?"

Charlotte hardly dared look at Carrie—she was too hungry to know every single thing about her. How could it be that Darryl's goodness was evident in every move, while his sister had that renegade's gleam—the tough, pocked face, the eyes flashing with shrewd judgment? Carrie glanced at Betsy and away, as if, due to an unfortunate blind spot, she could not see BMWs.

Mrs. Carroll had taken the kids on a field trip and they weren't back yet, so there they all were together, the moms—Lisa Gonsalves of the bait-shop Gonsalveses, Pam Powers the liquor store cashier, Geneva Mulligan of Mulligan Electric and Stell Mulligan of Mulligan Chimney Sweep, Stephie Brown whose husband dove for lobsters and Lolly Soule who was married to the Soule Propane guy. Lisa and Steph and Lolly, who had been in the same class at Wellfleet Elementary and then Provincetown High, stood together, backs to the others. They'd married their high school sweethearts; this had determined their fates. Lolly had a bright, kind face, and it was easy to imagine her winning Matty Soule, a shy, pudgy man who had inherited the gas company from his father, knew everything about gas stoves and bass fishing, and if you brought up any other subject would smile helplessly and cast his eyes to the ground. Lolly's house was paid off; they owned an enormous boat and a Florida time-share, while Steph and Lisa were just getting by. Pam was twenty; she'd had her older son the night of her junior prom, then Crystal, the girl with the tangled hair whom Fiona had befriended the first day. The others kept a motherly watch over her. They opened their circle to Betsy too—Betsy with her jewelry shop and her husband's Main Street office had a clear place in town. Charlotte might have been a CIA agent, or witness protection client, for all anyone knew.

Pam was so bowed down, her eyes so dull and her voice so weary, it seemed as if she'd carried those children until she began to droop to the ground. The boy was with her now, complaining in a high, thin voice while she repeated, eyes closed: "I don't care, I don't care." Charlotte was glad to see her, though. Pam was the only one who would really talk to her.

"You look tired."

Pam sighed and rolled her eyes. "What Freddy Low expects for ten dollars an hour," she said. Freddy Low managed the liquor store. "Not that I give a damn. I'm over it, I can tell you."

"I wonder why they're late," Charlotte said. A stiff wind had come up and the pine trees were shaking their shaggy boughs. Everyone pulled their sweaters tighter. Charlotte realized she still had the "Preserve our Boat Meadow" brochure in her hand, and folded it into her back pocket in hopes no one would see. There was a hoot of laughter from the circle of other moms at some story Betsy was telling.

Steph and Lisa had sat down together on Mrs. Carroll's front step, talking about the tides. Both their husbands had oyster grants, though Steph's was off Egg Island and wasn't affected by the suit. They glanced over toward Betsy, worried she'd overhear them. "He's a lawyer," Lisa said with a shrug. "That's what they do."

Carrie, who'd been sitting in her truck the whole time, gunned her engine suddenly and drove away, tires squealing.

"Jesus," Lisa said, "is she using again? She's out of control."

A flurry of looks passed among the moms. They'd jumped at the roaring engine the way seagulls flap up in a scare, and now they settled themselves back into one group. Betsy made sympathetic puppy-dog eyes, shaking her head, and the others looked grim, censorious, and also proprietary.

"She's my cousin," Pam told Charlotte. This was a quiet boast, the way Charlotte might have mentioned that she had a friend who wrote for the *Times*. "We used to call her the Stump Grinder."

"It must be hard on her," Betsy said, "having her husband . . ."

"Up the river," Charlotte finished darkly, just as Betsy said politely, ". . . away."

"Why would anyone marry that guy?" Charlotte asked, though what she wanted to ask was whether Betsy understood that her new BMW had come at Carrie's expense.

"I guess love's always a mystery," Betsy said, in a sentimental singsong.

Pam said, "Boy, you can say that again," and there was a flurry of sighs among the women.

"Mysterious as quantum mechanics," Charlotte said, and they gave her that *What kind of freak are you?* look she remembered from high school.

"I mean, it works by the most complicated, convoluted laws," she said, "but they're laws just the same."

Pam stepped away, but Betsy giggled. "Skip and I were one of those love-at-first-sight things; we just couldn't keep our hands off each other."

Charlotte and Henry had been a love-at-first-sight thing too—they'd set off a burst of static in each other, a distracting, unreadable signal that neither of them could escape. With Darryl . . . Charlotte looked up the road, wishing to see him, at least catch a glimpse of his truck in passing. She'd come to think of it as the Very Honorable Truck—its patchwork pieces, its ladder rails built of two-by-fours—there wasn't much left of it, but it did what it needed to, every day, and when she saw it on the beach, or getting gas at SixMart, or waiting behind the school bus as the first graders tumbled into their mothers' arms, she felt a little safer, as if the truck itself were proof of a steadfast goodness woven through her life. She attended to Darryl's movements like a sunflower turning its face upward, east to west all day. From a distance, always. If she saw him getting gas at SixMart, she'd go to the Texaco in town. It was worth a few cents more per gallon to avoid him, out of fear there'd be no spark in his eye.

Mrs. Carroll's van came over the rise then, and she pulled into the driveway just as the sky began to redden behind the pines.

"Sorry, ladies, someone rolled his Jeep on suicide alley. We were detoured through Harwich and half of Orleans."

Fiona leaped out into Charlotte's arms, still talking a blue streak to Crystal, who gazed at her with fond amusement and something like pride. Then Alexis came out, stepping carefully in new shoes, and the others, and last of all the sturdy and pugnacious Timmy Junior, who looked around and said, "Yeah, I told ya my mom wouldn't be here."

"She was here a minute ago, honey," Charlotte said. "She probably just went to get some cigarettes."

"Or some dinner," Betsy rushed to say, to protect her from defamation.

"She's always outta cigarettes," Tim said.

"Tim, you come on with me," Pam said.

"Nah, I'm gonna walk home," he said, puffing out his chest. It was about four miles, but of course he was too small to have any idea of that.

"I'll take you home, honey," Charlotte said. They lived in the Driftwood Cabins; if Carrie wasn't there Charlotte could just keep him until she came home. But Pam and the others closed ranks as if they suspected the worst kind of things about Charlotte.

"That's all right; I'll take care of him," Pam said, taking him by the arm, but Timmy shook her off.

"I'm walkin'!" he insisted, setting off up the driveway with manly steps, only to turn and run back in terror.

Carrie pulled in with a squeal of tires. "I'm here, I'm here," she said. "Get in the truck. I said I'd be here and I'm right here."

"You *weren't* here," Tim said. His face started to crumple, and he made a fist and punched the truck door.

"Don't cry," Carrie said, leaning across to yank him up into the passenger seat by the arm. "Just don't, or I'm gonna *fuckin'* cry too."

16

FOG

December's full moon fell on the sixteenth, nearly Christmas, though there wasn't a proper chill. In spring, the cool wind off the water had kept the temperatures low. Now the water held its summer warmth long after frost had withered the green on the mainland. There were still a few little roses blooming on leafless canes outside the kitchen window: That morning as Charlotte stirred Fiona's oatmeal on the stove, she looked out to see each bud glazed with a perfect coat of ice, like Persian domes.

And beyond, the tide receding over the ridges of the flats, and one truck, Darryl's, parked at the water's edge. The men had been out every minute they could be the past few days—they were getting the oysters out of the water before the hard cold. The tides wouldn't be low enough again for two weeks, and by then the bay could be frozen over. Most of the grants were bare by now, and you'd see the rusted racks piled up against people's garages beside their stacks of lobster traps, or under the hulls of jacked-up boats. Darryl had helped Carrie clear her grant, but his own oysters were still on the racks.

Charlotte had put a load of laundry in the dryer when she first came downstairs, but an hour later it was still sopping. She got the stepladder and drove a nail into the soffit over the porch, tying a rope between it and one of the oak branches, feeling magnificently capable, a veritable frontierswoman. There was a bag of clothespins in the kitchen drawer, and the day was clear, though a fog bank loomed like a distant mountain range over the back shore. The laundry was mostly Fiona's—her overalls printed with teacups, her striped turtle-necks and footie pajamas—and Charlotte had to wring each piece out before she could hang it. She waved when she saw Darryl look up from his work, and when he had a full load and started driving up the beach, she stood her ground, methodically pinning Fiona's pink socks to the line.

He drove up and parked directly in front of her.

"You!" he said, jumping out of the truck as if his pleasure at seeing her were too great to be borne sitting down, coming to stand on the other side of the laundry basket, smiling and smiling.

"You!" she said, and every tender, furious, disappointed, prayerful atom in her heart was in it, the one syllable. It made him shy.

"How are you?" she asked, averting her eyes a little. He looked so substantial in orange waders and a thick sweatshirt. The most natural, appropriate thing to do would be to walk right into his arms.

"Good. Pretty good," he said, measured. If the gods were looking down, they wouldn't see anything suspicious, just an ordinary conversation. "Busy, I mean. Really busy. Between my grant and Carrie's, and trying to get the house on Try Point buttoned up tight before winter."

"That's nice of you," she said, "to be helping Carrie, I mean." Really she had no idea what she was saying, but it didn't matter. If they'd been reading the shellfish regulations aloud the message would still have been clear. "Can I help? I'd be happy to."

"Nah, I'm fine."

Then he thought again. "But . . . come down if you'd like, just to hang around. I . . ." He took a deep breath. "I've missed you."

Life became so beautiful at that moment that Charlotte could feel it glowing around her—every bit of it, the black ducks patrolling like old gossips at the water's edge, the weight of the waterlogged dish towel in her hand.

"I've missed you too," she managed, so softly she wasn't sure he could hear.

"You can wear my extra boots."

"I'll be right there."

She ran around the house and tapped on the basement window. "I'm going down to help Darryl on the oyster claim."

"You are?" Henry asked, looking up from his desk.

"Yes. So you'll answer the phone?"

"Certainly."

She hopped into Darryl's passenger seat, pushing his extra jacket, tide chart, pliers, gloves, and rags aside to make herself a spot.

"Wait." Foam stuffing was pushing out through a tear in the seat, and he tore off a length of duct tape to patch it. "There, that's better. We gotta take this load to Tim's mom's house. She has a root cellar. Then we'll go down and get the last load in."

"I guess this must be what it's like in heaven," Charlotte said, leaning back into her seat.

"Excuse me?"

"Nothing. Or, I guess . . . somehow this feels like driving to the hardware store with my father on a Saturday morning. Or . . . it's nice to see you."

A happy, secret grin flashed over his face and he glanced sideways at her. The truck bounced and squeaked at every little bump.

They turned onto the highway, then off into the woods, toward the back shore.

"Like wild picking," he said. "We'd go the first day of the season every year. My father knew every nook and cranny of all the little coves. We'd be up at the crack of dawn; he'd make me coffee full of milk and sugar...."

They'd turned down a sand road, and finally into the driveway of a sagging cape whose shingles were curling up with age. Set into the back hillside, behind a pile of lobster traps overgrown with vines, was a low wooden door such as might lead to a hobbit hole.

Darryl lifted each bag of oysters out of the truck bed and handed them to Charlotte, who set them in stacks beside the door. They barely spoke, picking up each other's rhythms, crouching low as they shifted the bags into the dark earthen room.

"Won't they crush each other?"

"Nah—see, the big ones are in the bottom bags; their shells can stand a ton of pressure. Literally. The little ones have thinner shells; they don't weigh much at all."

"Don't they need to breathe?"

"They're dormant; they don't need air, or water, or anything. If it gets too cold I'll run an extension cord out the kitchen window and turn on a lamp with a hundred-watt bulb in there. If it's too warm I go down to the rink in Orleans and get a load of ice from the Zamboni."

They heard a window open, and Tim's mother called to Darryl from above.

"Come around the back; I got somethin' for ya."

It took her some time to get to the back door . . . she was very small and old, and she avoided Charlotte's eyes—in fact, she seemed to avoid seeing Charlotte at all, as if out of some superstition. She opened the door just enough to hand Darryl a package wrapped in newspaper.

"Cod," she said. "Bud brought it over; I got it dryin up th' attic." This sentence had been constructed to fit within one shallow breath. A cough seized her as soon as she finished, and she bent into it, waving them away. Her hair was all wiry tufts with pink scalp visible.

"Wanna come take a ride with us out to the flats?" Darryl asked her, and the idea made her laugh until a new coughing fit started.

"I gotta wash the livin' room walls this afternoon," she said, shutting the door again.

"She never leaves the house," Darryl said as they drove away, the truck slipping sideways on the sandy hillside. Now they could see the ocean, its blue sameness stretching endlessly. "It happens to women around here; I don't know why. They're inside raising their kids and then the kids go off and they don't want to come out."

"They've got those walls to wash," Charlotte said. "If she never leaves that house, then she never sees all this, and it's a few minutes away." They were driving along the ridge of a dune: The whole spiral of the cape curved out before them.

"Yeah, it's a funny hollow down there."

"Everyone misses so much, because they don't quite dare to look. When I think . . ." She stopped, because what she was thinking was how big and powerful Henry had seemed once, how she'd imagined she could keep safe by marrying him.

"It's true," Darryl said, thoughtful, regretful. "I was married . . . before . . ." he said suddenly.

"Before what?"

"Before I got thinking I was going to be great big shot in the entertainment business." He checked the rearview mirror and veered down Point Road. "A notion fueled by huge amounts of cocaine, and ... Anyway, I used to be married. Six bleary months, and she still uses my name—Lisette Stead—why?"

"Maybe because she's proud of it. Maybe you're the nicest thing that ever happened to her."

"That's pretty far-fetched." He laughed, turning onto the sand. But he shot a glance at her to see if she meant the compliment.

"We should be able to get the last ones in," he said. "If not it'll have to wait till tomorrow, and that's going to be a lousy tide."

His old red canoe was tied to the nearest rack—by the time they'd settled the bags into it the tide would have come up and they could float it back to the beach. "Here, you go down the row and take out the pins; I'll throw 'em in the canoe."

It took some strength to work the pins but she was getting the hang of it.

"We gotta bring the racks in too," Darryl said. The rebar was crusted over with translucent young oysters clinging tight as limpets. Charlotte bent down to pull the corner of one rack up out of the mud.

"No, no, no!" he yelled, but it was too late. Charlotte yelped and grabbed her bloody thumb tight in her fist.

"They're sharp," he said. "Those new shells are like razors."

"So I see." She shuddered. She could still feel the oyster's edge against her flesh, like her knife slicing through a chicken breast in the kitchen.

"I've got Band-Aids in the truck. Stay there." He ran and leaped to the truck and back. "There, the blood's a good sign; it's cleaning the wound, but you'd better wash it—just swish it in the salt water; it's deeper over there."

She did, and dried it on her shirt, holding it out so he could put on the Band-Aid, but he hesitated, as if he were afraid even this little touch would be inappropriate, so she took the Band-Aid in her good hand and put it on herself.

"That's nothing, believe me," he said. "Tim cut himself last summer—I guess there's an artery at the base of your thumb? The blood came out in jets; it was unbelievable."

"That guy can't do anything right."

"You wanna know something about Tim?" Darryl said suddenly. "He's got a copy of *Chesapeake* on his bedside table—he loves it. He reads it over and over. I don't think he's ever read anything else. He's proud to be working the tides like he does; it means everything to him. I've known him most of my life. I'd *be* him, if . . ."

"If what?" They were back at work; a breeze had come up from the east, and the foghorn at the end of Try Point started—it sensed the damp even while the sun was still shining.

"If it weren't for dumb luck. I played football in high school; everyone looked up to me." He laughed—derisive. "Because I was good at football. Also I was a stoner and a heavy-metal fanatic, and for a while I made a pretty good living unloading bales of dope up in Bound Brook in the middle of the night. That's the national seashore; no one's there to see—all the guys with boats were bringing stuff in from Mexico and Colombia back then. It beat hell out of codfishing."

They worked along consistently, though Charlotte's thumb slowed her down.

"You certainly do sound like a lucky guy," she teased.

"No, I mean . . . I never got caught. My hearing was always really good—I just had a certain awareness, I knew when something wasn't quite right, I knew when to get out of there. Then it turned out that I could do stuff with sound—I had a knack for it. So I escaped. I mean, not that there's anything to escape from, but you know what I mean . . ."

"Darryl Stead, I do not know what you mean! You were talented, ambitious, you listened, you understood things, and you used that talent to get away from a dead-end life. Not . . . not that this is a dead-end life . . . but . . ."

"No, it's not; it's not a dead-end. It's good, solid work, in the most beautiful place in the world. You're exhausted at the end of the day, a good exhaustion."

"Exactly," she said stoutly.

"Except that when you're shellfishing, you're kind of running in place. No one gets wealthy; they just keep their heads above water, year after year."

"I'm seeing that," she admitted.

"Or even secure. You never know what's going to hit you next—red tide, parasites. . . . Have you ever seen a moonsnail?" He kicked over some shells on the seafloor until he found one that looked like someone had used a hole punch on it. "See that? Their tongues are like drills. They bore right through a clam shell and suck out the meat."

"So where do New York washashores fit in—are we parasites, or predators?"

He stood up, hands on hips, arching his back to stretch, and laughed. "It's not your fault. I know that. Tim is spoiling for a fight, always. The people who've signed on to the lawsuit, every one of 'em's had some kind of a run-in with him. He acts like he owns the town."

"What was he in prison for in the first place?"

"Oh, he bit off a piece of Rob Welch's ear." Rob Welch was the deputy police chief.

"That's just something a person should never do," Charlotte said. "Even the worst cop has the right to possess two whole ears." They laughed happily, naturally, a couple of old collectors admiring an excellent specimen of human folly.

"In Tim's defense," Darryl said, "I should say that Rob Welch was my partner in high school crime. We had a marijuana patch back in among the old woodlots; we did quite a business. When I see him in his uniform I always feel like there must be a real cop tied up in a closet somewhere. When we were kids, there was your house, and Ada's, and almost everything else was wild. We knew every inch of it; we picked oysters all through the inlet here, and blueberries in the summer. . . . It seemed like it all belonged to us. Then the real estate developers turned up, and one day there was an empty cul-de-sac out in the middle of nowhere, and then there were houses around it . . . and of course they tore up all the blueberry bushes and planted lawns. Tim never got used to it. He'll still walk right through someone's yard if he feels like it."

The tide had lifted the canoe, and the fog was drifting over them in thick wisps—it felt like you could reach up and pull off a piece. They couldn't see Try Point anymore, or Ada's red house at the head of the creek, and they worked along quickly, silently, in a kind of dream.

"I saw Henry the other night," Darryl said. "At the Mermaid . . . Does he . . . does he like it there?"

"He loves it there. He says he's been waiting all his life for a bar named the Mermaid. There was a Mermaid in London that was supposed to be Shakespeare's favorite. Were you there too?"

"No, oh, no! AA meets in the Masonic lodge, across the street. No, I've had my fill of the Mermaid."

"Henry loves a good bar," she said, seeing that Darryl was trying to understand what could be wrong between the two of them. Everything Charlotte did, the way she laughed with Darryl, the way she listened to him, showed there must be something amiss.

"It's not that . . ." Charlotte started to explain. "It's . . ." Henry didn't hit her; he had no other women; he wasn't, as Darryl hoped, a drunk. He took out the garbage; he swept the kitchen floor. All he had done was keep his distance from her, hold her in quiet disdain. Her throat closed—the story felt shameful; she couldn't let Darryl see.

"I didn't mean . . . I . . ."

"No, no, I know . . . it's just . . ." She took a deep breath, looking out over the grants. The water sloshed against the canoe now, and they piled on the last few bags, full of little ones, the size of quarters.

"How long do they have to grow before you sell them?" There, a safe subject.

"Three years, more or less. These'll be ready in two. It's like money in the bank. I mean, given decent weather conditions, and freedom from disease."

"And from lawsuits."

He smiled. "But assuming the best, these oysters will be the down payment on a house in a few more years."

"Who do you sell them to?"

"Aquaculture Central, down in Yarmouth. I mean, in the summer the Wharf Grill buys most of 'em, but winter, nothing's open; they truck 'em over the bridge to Boston."

"So . . . that's wholesale."

"Yah . . ."

"Could you sell them in Boston yourself?"

"Nah, you'd need a refrigerated truck for that."

"But if you had one, you could do better . . . maybe a lot better."

"I suppose. . . ."

"I wonder what I could do for work around here," Charlotte said, thinking aloud.

"You're a mom!"

"But if—you know, if I had to make money. I always wanted to be a reporter—to poke around and get to see all kinds of stuff, find out how everything works. I don't know how it turned into *journalism*— so serious and important. In fact, Henry seems to think that if something's interesting that means it isn't serious enough to bother with." It had been such fun to make real money at *Celeb*! At least at first— then somehow it would be a handbag she had to rave about to sweeten relations with an advertiser. Then a famous comedian's wife took up fashion design and Charlotte was required to gush in person and on paper. . . . Finally she could not find one thing to be proud of, and the money began to seem like ill-gotten gain.

"I wonder if I could get work at the *Oracle*."

"That'd cover your morning coffee," he said, laughing. Then, with a glance into her face to check for danger: "It doesn't look like there'll be any end of construction jobs, though. I'm getting my independent contractor's license. I'll be working for myself."

It was the future all laid out, stepping-stones to a dream—it seemed as if they'd been building a bridge to each other all these weeks, each working from his own side until here they were, face-to-face. . . .

"So we could buy out the Narville property," she said, "and raze that house!"

He looked up suddenly, as if she'd read his mind, then away. "We'd have to work a long time before we could do that." He jerked the last rack up out of the mud and laid it on top of the canoe.

"I think that's it. Except for that piece of net over there."

She looked where he was pointing and realized the fog had closed around them, so thick that even the far end of the canoe looked blurry.

"You could get lost out here," she said. She could see only the dim outline of the houses, hers dwarfed by the Narvilles', and the dark line of trees behind.

"Bud did, once," Darryl said. "I suppose he'd been drinking. But it comes in fast sometimes, and if the tide's real low every direction looks the same."

"It's eerie. It feels like we're alone . . . in . . ."

It was the word *alone*. . . . Some inflection crept into it so he knew everything; she saw it dawn in his eyes, and reached out by instinct, and her hand seemed to go through an invisible barrier. There he was, the real man; she was touching his cheek, and he turned his head to kiss her fingers, a half kiss, his arms at his sides, his eyes half-closed as if he were praying. Then he pulled her in tight, his hand pressing down her spine as if to seal them together so nothing could ever separate them, and she kissed his collarbone, his neck, his mouth.

They broke apart, flew back together, Charlotte pressing her face into his sweatshirt, breathing in the smell of woodsmoke. She'd been on an endless journey; now she was home.

"Darryl," she said, rapt.

"Henry . . ." he replied. "What about Henry?"

Bliss to consciousness: sixty seconds flat.

"It's . . . it's . . ." she said. "It's nothing." It was bad enough to kiss him—to let him see her in this state of hope and uncertainty, as Henry never had. She could not criticize Henry too.

"It's funny," he said. "I'd been thinking that someday I might be lucky enough to have a marriage like yours." He laughed bitterly.

"I'm sorry."

"Eh, you can never really see inside a marriage."

This was enough; Charlotte was crying. She had not cried . . . well, her mother's funeral was one of the many places she hadn't cried. Everyone had expected it; they'd watched her, afraid she'd come apart and they'd have nothing to offer. She spared them. Or spared herself. She couldn't have cried that day if you had run her through with a sword. Now she couldn't stop. A life's worth of sorrow came loose in her, sorrow so common it was usually hidden in plain sight; no one would notice it any more than they noticed the salt and pepper shakers on a kitchen table—everyone had some of their own.

"You must think I'm a terrible person."

"No, no . . . the opposite . . ." he insisted, but he was holding her loosely, uncertain now. Desire—he had thought of it as a synonym for lust.

"I'm sorry, I'm so sorry," she said, her forehead against him, the rubbery smell of his waders breathing up at her. Where was she?

"It's okay, it's okay," he was saying, openhearted. But it wasn't true. He was barely able to keep his own balance; her poise was the first thing he'd noticed about her, and now, the second he touched her, it dissolved. He was late getting the oysters in; he couldn't lose this tide. But they'd started building a little life together, like children playing, and . . .

"It's okay," he said, truly now. The tears were honest, as few things are. "When I was in detox," he said, "in the very beginning when it was . . . just . . . hell . . . I'd hear my roommate on the other side of the curtain repeating something over and over. At first I thought he was praying. I started to listen, try to figure it out. He'd say 'chicken,' 'almonds,' 'saffron,' and then 'sauté the onions in butter' . . . it was like a story I was listening to, and I couldn't give up because I had to know how it turned out."

"How did it turn out?" She'd stopped crying; she was just listening.

"It turned out to be a biryani, a chicken biryani. His mom came from India; that was her special dish. He always said that's how he made it through, remembering the recipe step by step. It was how I made it through too, at least that first part."

He was speaking into her hair so she could feel his voice as much as hear it.

"Someday let's make one," she said, and felt his shoulders drop. "You can call him up and get the exact recipe."

Darryl shook his head. "He relapsed."

Charlotte missed the point.

"He's dead. Three years clean; then his wife left and he went back to using. . . . Fell off a highway overpass, Christmas day. Or jumped, they couldn't tell. There's two of us left standing from that group that came in together."

As he said this he leaned into her so completely she nearly lost her balance—it was as if he thought she could bear his whole weight. Of course, he was desperate—who isn't? And she was looking to him for rescue. She stepped back, away. The tide was streaming in around their boot soles; God knew how long they'd been out here.

He went back to work, giving her one end of a length of rope he'd had attached to his belt, so they could tie it to the ends of the canoe. The work steadied them, and with the canoe between them they could begin to talk again.

"Do you remember when Fiona yelled at us for not getting married?" she asked him.

"How would I forget that?"

"We've been thinking about all the same stuff!" she said.

"I guess so. I thought . . . maybe . . . but then I thought I must be crazy. . . ."

"Maybe we could do something with Fiona sometime. She has this image of herself about riding on some man's shoulders. . . ."

"I don't know if that's such a good idea. . . ."

The tide was lapping over their feet and he started toward shore, floating the canoe behind him. Charlotte's boot had leaked full of water and she could barely keep up.

"Shit, we left that net," he said when they got back to the truck, and she turned to get it, but the water was already too high.

"Go on," Darryl said harshly. "Go home, get dry, this is a bad idea, forget it."

She stood stupidly for a minute, wounded, confused, then started up the beach away from him, head bowed.

"Charlotte!"

She was maybe ten paces away from him, far enough so he felt her loss. She turned and saw him there with one arm outstretched, his face radiant and guileless, as if his whole heart, his whole being were open to her.

"I do!" he said. "I do want to be with you . . . more than anything. . . ."

Now the bolt of fear struck her. "We can't! We can't," she said, running away toward the shadow in the fog that marked her home, trembling like a murderess, and weeping, and thrilled.

"'Lo!" Henry called up from downstairs.

The same life was sitting here waiting for her, just where she'd left it. Fiona's socks were still on the clothesline, sopping now, though they'd only been damp when Charlotte hung them out.

"Hi!" she called down to Henry. So her voice still worked; it didn't come out as a moan or caw or scream. "I'm going to pick Fiona up."

"Okay. We need milk. . . ."

"Okay." Milk. Socks. Charlotte moved electrified through the world of milk and socks, the roly-poly beetles in the stair corners, laundry on the bathroom floor. She seemed to be hovering over herself, watching as she changed into dry clothes. The bed was pulled apart, the sheet on her side and the quilt on Henry's, as if they'd spent all night in a tug-of-war. She made it up. She would have to call Mulligan Appliance and see if they could fix the dryer. Hearing Darryl's truck come up the beach, she stepped away from the window.

At Mrs. Carroll's door, Fiona jumped into her arms. "We're having a recital," she said. "We're singing 'Jingle Bells' and 'Piggy-Wig' and you can bring cupcakes."

"I don't think I know 'Piggy-Wig,'" Charlotte said, buckling her into the car seat.

"It's a *great* song," Fiona said, in a Henry-esque tone that suggested Charlotte must be a philistine if she didn't know "Piggy-Wig." Then she broke into heartfelt, tune-free song. Mrs. Carroll waved good-bye. No one noticed that Charlotte happened to be in flames. She got milk and a box of animal crackers from the SixMart, waited at the bridge while Bud Rivette crossed from the other side, took Fiona home and gave her the snack at the kitchen table, went out to get the socks off the line, laid them out on the radiator, where they gave off a wet, comfortable smell. Was this her life? Yes, yes, she could hardly believe her good luck!

Henry came up at five o'clock with a wooden ruler in his hand—the old-fashioned kind with a metal edge.

"Here's something for you," he said to Fiona, who was so unused to being spoken to by him that she didn't look up from her coloring book.

"Fiona, look," Charlotte said. "Daddy has something to show you."

"It's a ruler," Fiona said politely, going back to her work as Henry would have if she'd interrupted him. She had a ruler already, pink Lucite with dogwood blossoms, that Natalie had sent from Fayetteville when she was tracking down Bernie Kerik's secret first wife. This one was not nearly as cool.

Henry's shoulders sagged and he glanced over to see whether Charlotte had taken note: He was trying; it was Fiona who was at fault.

"Let me see," Charlotte said. "What did you find?"

It was printed with block letters advertising his father's business. HENRY F. TRADESCOME, INSURANCE. ACCIDENT AND INDEMNITY. TRUSTWORTHY, HARDWORKING, RELIABLE. 797 BEACON STREET, BOSTON, MA. MULBERRY-4-5202.

"My desk drawer got stuck, so I had to pull it all the way out and I found this caught in the back. 'Trustworthy, hardworking, reliable' . . . Can you imagine?"

"Now it would be 'hip, sexy . . .'"

"Edgy, that's the one I like," Henry said. "Apartment for rent—edgy."

"What's edgier than accident and indemnity insurance?" Charlotte asked with a laugh. The conversation skated along as always, over the cauldron of her feeling.

"It describes my father to a T," Henry said, smacking the ruler against his palm as if to test it. "A straight, straight arrow. Oh, what a disappointment I was to him!" He laughed as if this were a happy memory. "He liked everything done one certain way. Period. What was I to do?"

"Let's see, I suppose you could have moved to New York to start a newspaper that championed the opposite of every single thing he believed in?"

"Most amusing," he allowed. "I found this too." It was a Christmas card with a picture of Richard and Pat Nixon, a special thank-you to campaign contributors.

"Oh, my God . . . 1972. The year my mother got sick."

"When I told my father I'd never get married, he cried," Henry said, laughing again, a laugh crossed with a groan, as if he were talking about something he'd read, not lived. He kept things at arm's length, while Charlotte swallowed it all down.

"Look, this was your grandfather's ruler," she told Fiona. "Can you imagine, when Daddy was your age he would be coloring at this same table, just like you are now?"

"Did you like coloring, Daddy?" Fiona asked, but it was as if Henry's ear couldn't pick up the frequency of her voice.

"Henry, Fiona's asking you if you liked to color. . . ."

"I don't remember a thing, not a thing," he said.

The fog had gathered so thickly they could hear big drops dripping from the eaves. Charlotte was shot through with every kind of thought—she would get Fiona a better father, a man who could see her, hear her. Or, she would find the thread to connect Henry to Fiona. She would forget this day ever happened. Except . . . it had been the best day of her life.

"How was the oystering?" Henry asked.

"It's brutal work," she said, "but there's something about being out there, having to reckon with the wind and the mud and the tide . . .

it feels good—real." This was so easy. She had protected herself from Henry, letting him see less and less about her, talking to him cordially, intelligently, without saying a thing that mattered, as if she were sitting beside him on a bus.

"We lost a lot when we gave up the agrarian society," he said.

By the time she tucked Fiona into bed, the fog had blotted out the lights on Try Point, even the green buoy lantern that marked the channel. For all you could see they might have been floating alone through space. She opened the window an inch and sharp, wet air poured in—she felt it as fully as when she was sixteen and every sensation was new. She'd imagined then that love would overtake people two by two, like a storm they were caught in together. Silly girl. Or—silly woman, who had let that girl fade away. The front door closed quietly; Henry's quick step went up the driveway. She pulled the cover up and listened, listened—she had never been more awake. The tide was coming in, waves rushing together at the end of the point, flooding up the bay.

17

PERFECT CLARITY

The wind came up sometime after midnight, battering at the house, waking Charlotte, who had drifted off in spite of herself. The fog had blown away and sharp-edged clouds were racing across the moon. Henry was tight asleep, curled at the far side of the bed, with the sheet clutched in his hands as if it were the only shred of comfort in his life. Leaning over to close the window, Charlotte heard Fiona's feet hit the floor, then her definite little steps bounding down the hall. She vaulted over Charlotte to get cozy between her parents, kissing Charlotte's shoulder, then Henry's. His bony hand reached around back to pat her, reminding Charlotte of a hermit crab's claw.

"Mama, Daddy, me," Fiona said, with a tidy satisfaction: Her life was settled and cozy; everyone was in place. She kissed her bear on the top of his head and fell back asleep.

By morning the window was frosted in wild baroque plumes. The furnace could not keep up; Charlotte wore two pairs of socks and still felt the cold through the floor. She held a hot washcloth to the kitchen window so Fiona could see out—the bay had been thickened by the cold, the waves lifting and cresting in slow motion like oil, a sheen of ice forming instantly in the lee. A clump of black ducks bobbed together in a huddle, heads tucked down, into the wind. Looking southwest you could see all the way across to Plymouth, maybe forty miles.

"The perfect clarity of a winter day," Henry said in a distant voice. His father would have stood there and said that. And someday Fiona would say it, and hear the echo of her father's words.

The furnace huffed and wheezed. Charlotte drove down to Orleans to buy a pot roast so she could keep the oven on all afternoon, then tucked Fiona in beside her on the couch, reading *Little House on the Prairie* aloud. She'd felt stiff in the shoulders when she woke up, and by now every muscle ached. When she stretched her legs out she seemed to feel her knee bones rubbing against each other, and when she got up to take some Advil her back went into a spasm and she had to call Henry for help.

"What happened?" He held her around the waist as she let herself down, carefully, to lie flat on the floor.

"Oh, I was too eager to help with the oysters yesterday. I had to heave those bags like I'd been doing it all my life; I didn't want to look like a weakling." Henry laughed in sympathy.

"Are you warm enough?"

"No, it's freezing down here." Fiona jumped up and ran off wild-eyed, as if she'd been waiting years for this chance, returning with a blanket and her teddy bear, which she tucked in beside Charlotte, with a kiss for both. Bunbury circled her, sniffing, then jumped up and took her spot on the couch.

"Do you want a pillow?" Henry asked.

"No, I'm fine."

"A sandwich?"

"No, thanks."

"A hot water bottle? Tuck it under the small of your back; it would probably do the trick."

He stood over her worrying, his head crooked, his hair sticking out on both sides, glasses slipping down the bridge of his nose.

"Yes," she said, "a hot water bottle would be nice."

He went off with the light step of a man who knows just what to do, and Fiona lifted a corner of the blanket and nestled at her mother's side. Henry should have married an invalid. Emotions unnerved him, storms that blew out of the dark, wrought havoc on his orderly life, and disappeared. The physical you could see and understand. What a thrill he'd gotten from her placenta, the huge bloody jellyfish that slid out of Charlotte in Fiona's wake. "Look at that!" he'd said, with a cook's gusto. "What nourishment!"

He was back in a minute with the hot water bottle, and when she felt better he helped her onto the couch again, brought her a glass of wine, started setting the table. Charlotte went back to reading aloud. As the light faded Darryl's truck came along down the driveway, and stayed a long time at the water's edge. It felt like a cosmic test: If she turned her head to look at him she'd be vaporized instantly.

"'"Would a panther carry off a little girl, Pa?" Laura asked. "Yes," said Pa, "and kill her and eat her too."'" Fiona snuggled in tighter. Henry was whisking the salad dressing, after checking with Charlotte to be sure he had the right proportions. The truck turned and came back up the drive. Darryl would see the two heads bent in the lamplight; he would see a family that must be protected from harm. His taillights disappeared around the corner of Narville's fence.

"There's the question," Henry said at dinner, "of what Joyce would have written next, if he'd lived. People have speculated, of course— there are all kinds of answers. How could a man follow *Finnegan's Wake*?"

"Poor James Joyce," Charlotte said without thinking.

"What?"

"*Dubliners* . . ." she said. "He was writing about life, and people, and the feeling in a room, and . . . and then by *Finnegan's Wake* he'd lost the humanity; he was only arcane."

"Preposterous," said Henry, who was probably the last living being who could get away with using that word.

"It's like he had to keep proving how smart he was," she persisted, though she wanted to give in, "and his heart—his talent—kind of atrophied. . . ."

Henry laughed, incredulous. Did she really dare to question James Joyce? She who was an absolute nobody?

"I don't know." She shrugged. "It's just the way I feel."

This was deft—Henry had ceded the province of feeling to her. He started talking about modernism and postmodernism and how the Holocaust had smashed everything up and a broken literature might be the only way to respond and . . . Charlotte remembered Darryl's face, his eyes lowered, the way he had turned his head so his mouth just touched her fingers, as if that were as much as he dared.

Through the night she could hear the sharp cracks and dull blows as the bay froze, each successive wave pushing up under the crust of ice, lifting it over the last bit frozen. By morning it was a solid, jagged expanse and all she could hear was the wind.

18

QUAINT

"So, I'm up in New Hampshire and I see they're giving frost," Bud Rivette said, standing by the coffee counter at SixMart. "I gotta finish the job up there, and I'm thinking—'I got Danny's Ritalin; I can drive through the night and make the morning tide.' I lined up Carlos and Paul and Flyer; they met me there at five. . . ." Bud was small and stocky, probably Henry's age, his eyes hugely magnified by his thick glasses. Danny, his ten-year-old son, was one of a number of kids in town who owed their existence to the Mermaid. Danny's mom, a tired, all-forgiving woman and the best cashier at Stop & Shop, was just grateful to have a child and asked nothing of Bud—in fact, she shared what she had, Danny's Ritalin, with him. "And the whole thing was frozen all the way to Try Point. I've never seen it happen that fast."

"You won't be needing Ritalin to keep you awake the rest of the winter," Carrie said, grim. The other men at the coffee counter, Matty Soule and Jake Becker, laughed and agreed. Carrie counted out Bud's change with hands rough and strong as a man's. Oystering, mothering, forty hours at SixMart supplemented by as many as she could get at the fish market shucking oysters and clams, and in summer she did changeovers at the Lemon Pie Cottages, cleaning them all every Saturday between checkout in the morning and check-in in the afternoon. Now she was going up to see Tim in the House of Corrections every visiting day. Charlotte doubted she could survive a week of Carrie's life. But she would need to, if . . .

She reminded herself not to be a fool. Their kiss, all she had felt in it . . . so many people would brush that off, let it blow away with the fog. She had always been too susceptible to feelings, hers and everyone else's. She'd see something in a man's eyes and respond to it, only to have him deny it as loudly as if he'd been accused of a crime. Maybe she was prone to hallucination; maybe she recognized things before others were conscious of them. It hardly mattered—if Darryl didn't feel the way she did, then she'd rather never see him again. It wasn't hard to avoid someone in Wellfleet, and she had come to the SixMart now because she knew it was after his coffee break time.

Bud sighed. "I'll be in suspense till March," he said. "I don't get it. They were giving frost, not six inches of solid ice." He sounded comfortable, though, buckled in for his ride through life, ready for this next bump. He worked when the tide was low, slept when it was high, drank through the winter months, got by. Matty and Jake had oyster grants, and sterile rooms to wash and sort their harvest, and refrigerator trucks to take the oysters to market . . . modern, likely profitable operations. And of course Matty had Soule Propane and Jake his lobster operation, and Jake was a painter too—small, close views of the tide bottom that seemed to get every inch exact: the sparkle of the water among the brown and gray stones, the dull red seaweed, the vein of rust running through the wet sand. Standing in front of one of those paintings, you'd feel that every square foot of the world had a sacred beauty.

"How's Tim?" Bud asked Carrie.

"How d'ya think?" she said. "No one asks how I am, with three kids at home and two jobs and the claim and the truck a total loss and—"

"Bite my head off, why don't ya?"

"He'll be out in February; then you can ask him yourself."

"Hi, Carrie," Charlotte said, setting the milk on the counter. Carrie looked as if the quart of milk must have spoken.

"A dollar ninety-nine," she told it. She might have fallen on hard times, but she had not gotten so low she had to acknowledge a washashore like Charlotte Tradescome.

Ada came in, chipper in her red wool coat, smiling, her cheeks glowing from the cold, talking to herself in her bright, curious voice. ". . . but I suppose that's the way things always are. I was too young to know, then, and of course later I was too old to care. . . ."

"Hello, Ada," Charlotte and Carrie said at once.

"Hello, ladies." Ada sounded kind, concerned, as if she guessed both were suffering, because people generally were. "We're having a real winter, aren't we? Like we used to . . ."

"Is this unusual now?" Charlotte asked.

"I don't remember when the bay froze so hard so early."

"The year the *Mary Belle* went down," Carrie said to Ada, keeping her glance averted from Charlotte, as if to say it was none of her business. Did Carrie realize that Ada had joined the lawsuit, signed the petition to get the sea farmers out of Mackerel Bay? If so, she didn't care. Ada had been born here. Charlotte was the interloper and she had better keep that in mind.

"That's right," Ada said, nodding. "Doesn't seem long ago."

"Icing," Carrie said, nodding toward a yellowed clipping framed on the back wall.

"What's that?" Charlotte asked. Carrie frowned, as if this were an impertinent question.

"My father used to say the ocean was the real cemetery here," Ada said. "Only the women are buried in the churchyard; the men were all lost at sea . . . and the women lost on land . . ." she continued, to herself, counting out exact change from her coin purse. "Thank you, dear." With the *Boston Globe* and the *Wellfleet Oracle* folded under her arm, she set back off toward home, picking her way across the icy parking area, looking up and down Route 6, then crossing it with her firm, measured step as if it were still the lazy tourist trail it had been in the fifties, not a highway traveled by all manner of trucks and cranes and whatever heavy equipment was necessary to construct the dream houses (second . . . no, third houses) of the very rich. Charlotte took a deep breath and dashed after her, like a good reporter, getting across just before a cement truck barreled over the top of the hill.

"Miss Town?"

Ada looked surprised, and not particularly pleased, but she was, of course, polite. Charlotte looked into her eyes like a burglar at a jewelry store window—what was in there, how best to snatch it? What had gone wrong with Henry that he'd been left in such a bleak state? Wasn't there some way to save the oyster farms? Ada's posture warned her against direct questions—she was like the ladies on Marlboro Street who'd had them in for a glass of Dubonnet after Henry's father died. The first thing Charlotte did wrong that day was to mention his death; the ladies had ignored this as they would if she had belched. She tried compliments, saying what a lovely home they had, asking about the tapestries that covered the walls, but a stern look passed between them: Why was she prying? A mention of the weather elicited a quiet protest—damp was common in harbor towns. Giving up, she had said, "What crisp saltines," and saw them relax. They talked on for half an hour without saying a thing, and at the end of it they seemed to feel young Henry had married well.

"What is 'icing'?" she asked Ada.

"Oh, the spray off the waves freezes on the rigging in the winter. It happens on the windward side, so the boat lists—the *Mary Belle* rolled onto its side and sank. When I was young, it wasn't so bad; the boats would just come straight in on a bad day. With the new fishing rules, they only have so many days, and they can't afford to lose one. So they take more chances. . . ." She shook her head, walking along, disappearing into her own thoughts. "How long has it been since anyone had a new boat?" she asked herself. "These draggers, they're thirty or forty years old. . . ."

"So they're in mortal danger when they fish at sea, so they turn to farming, but the city people move in and try to pull the flats out from under them—because they don't like the way they look," Charlotte said.

"Change is the nature of a seagoing place." Ada sighed. "Everyone leaves their mark here."

"The Narvilles lived in their house for about two minutes before they dreamed up this lawsuit." Ada turned up her driveway, and Charlotte went with her—it was a sand path, hardened with oyster shell, that ran through a thicket of chokecherry and then turned to curve alongside the marsh. The tide was out; the winding channel was empty except for a trickle, coated with smooth ice at the sides.

"Someone else would have done this if Jeb Narville hadn't," Ada said. "It was bound to happen."

"So you don't mind that Carrie and the others are likely to lose their farms?"

Ada stopped walking. "How long have you lived here now?" she asked.

"We moved in last April, so, almost nine months," Charlotte said, with the pride she'd heard in other people's voices, people who could say "almost six years" or "almost a decade" or "almost a lifetime."

"Not much longer than Jeb Narville."

"No, but . . . I'm speaking for people who've lived here all their lives," Charlotte protested.

"My dear," Ada said, "they don't want you to speak for them. They don't want you here at all." They were standing on Ada's front step, and Charlotte shuddered, letting herself feel the cold now that the house stood between them and the wind. It was a half cape, covered in cedar shingles like everything out here—cedar was the only thing that would stand the salt. The wooden storm door was freshly painted dark red, the windows looked newly washed, the garden was covered with a thick layer of salt hay for the winter. Inside it would be low and dark— those old places always were—but if you'd begun life in a dory on a rough sea, a neat, small life in a house like this might be just the thing.

"Nice of you to walk me home, dear," Ada said.

"Not at all," Charlotte said, not budging. "What do you mean, they don't want me here?"

"Oh," Ada said, starting to open the door and then letting go of the latch, not wanting to invite Charlotte in. "It's a dead culture and it's left them all ashamed," she said in a distant voice.

"What?"

"Oh! Nothing, dear, I get lost in my thoughts."

Charlotte recalled a time when she had brightly asked an old man with a thick accent what it had been like to flee Berlin during the city's last free hours. She'd seen in his eyes, for a half second, what it had been like, and what it was like to have a silly, apparently pitiless girl ask him to recount it as a piece of cocktail conversation. "Miss

Town, I don't mean to be rude, I just . . . I feel bad. It seems like it's my fault that all this is happening."

Ada shook her head. "No, no . . . something will always be going wrong for Carrie; that's the way it is with the Steads . . . generation after generation—their lives move from one accident to the next. . . ." Her voice drifted; it seemed she was thinking aloud.

"What do you mean, a dead culture?" Charlotte asked very quietly, so as not to wake Ada out of her thoughts.

"Fishing, fishing . . . Zeke Stead, the grandfather, he was a good man. Rough—but you had to be rough. Out to Georges Bank every day, no matter what—pride was measured in pounds of cod back then—a full net. It still would be, still is . . . but the fish aren't there, and the men don't quite understand that. They come back with a quarter of what their fathers got; all they feel is small."

Charlotte thought of Henry, trying to live up to what he expected of himself, demanded of himself. His mind was supposed to become invincible, to make up for his body's fragility. An impossible goal, but he despised himself for failing to reach it.

"Amos Stead—Darryl's father—came by to see me," Ada said. "When he was shipping out for Vietnam . . . He was radiant; he was going to be a hero. When he got back, I don't know. He was drinking, he got into fights, he took chances. . . . I'll never forget those men's faces the day he fell into the net. Marlene just said, 'I knew he'd die some fool way.'"

This was pretty much what Henry had predicted in *Dread and the Common Man.*

"But Darryl . . . Ada, Darryl still has a whole spirit; he's working up from a pit, and he'll lose everything if Jeb Narville wins."

"None of those Steads was worth a cent, except Zeke," Ada said.

"My father was over there taking care of them, more than he was at the church. . . . She died of drink; she left them alone."

"Over where? Who died of drink?"

"Oh, Emmy . . ." Ada said, shaking her head, looking around as if she'd just woken from a trance. "Another Stead. Years and years ago now. She lived in this house, left it to my father—to repay him for his years of care. Now I must take leave of you, my dear."

Charlotte turned to go, turned back. "Darryl's worth a cent," she said.

Ada's glance was sharp. "He's a handsome man," she allowed.

"He's more than that, way more," Charlotte said. "Have you ever seen him work?" She wanted to make a speech to Ada, to say that Darryl had looked at his life of wrong and failure straight on, with a courage such as few people could muster. The light, understanding, thoughtfulness that shone from his face—these qualities were hard-earned. Ada didn't seem interested to hear.

"It's not just Steads and Cloutiers who'll lose their livelihood. . . . It's Buzz, and the Soules, and the Bethels. . . ."

"The Bethels are down at Indian Neck. No one's claiming that land," Ada said. "Tim Cloutier doesn't care about anyone but himself, believe me. He's a renegade. We'll be lucky to be rid of him."

"Someone will claim the Indian Neck flats. Some couple from New York will buy Westie Small's house for a million dollars, and . . ."

Ada smiled at this idea—it was impossible for her to imagine anyone wanting to buy Westie's cottage, which was no bigger than the stacks of lobster traps beside it. She was so used to seeing the bay gleaming around every turn that she couldn't imagine what that sight might be worth . . . and so used to the Wellfleet hardscrabble she didn't guess how little a million dollars meant to some people. Narville couldn't believe the bargain he'd gotten from Charlotte, and there were thousands of guys like Narville—guys "in asphalt," or copper, scions of supermarket chains and heavy-equipment companies, inventors of tiny devices to keep arteries clear, or computers cool. The man who figured out how to shrink-wrap things and the guy who thought up Velcro while combing the burrs out of his German shepherd's fur. Whales, spices, bananas from the islands, those had been the basis of Wellfleet's wealth. Then it was fish, and now it was tourism and real estate.

"... and tear it down and spend another million on some hideous palace with a 'destination hot tub' from which they will not want to look out and see people breaking their backs on the tide flats ..."

Ada was shaking her head, as if poor Charlotte were crazy.

"You know it's true," she said, with more heat than she meant to show. "And the precedent will be set; the flats will belong to ... Mr and Mrs. Abercrombie and Fitch! And that will be the end of it. They'll have fashion shows out there. The town will be quaint, nothing more."

"Darryl is a reliable worker," Ada said. "He'll find something else. The birds were here long before any of us, and someone needs to speak for them. Good-bye, dear, give my best regards to your husband."

She said this pointedly, as if Charlotte needed a reminder.

19

AT SEA

Fiona knelt in front of her dollhouse, explaining to the dolls in a very calm, motherly voice why she had to rearrange their lives. All the furniture was going, to make way for a pasture in the living room, where a goat, sheep, and cow who had been liberated from their positions as Christmas tree ornaments were going to graze. The dolls would sleep together in a makeshift manger. Charlotte had discovered the dollhouse in the attic—it must have belonged to Henry's mother. It was made of wooden liquor crates nailed together, so was taller than Fiona, and it had real wallpaper and braided rugs, handmade lace curtains on the windows. The furniture was from FAO Schwarz; the dolls were wire with molded heads, father in a felt sweater and suit pants, mother with an apron over her gingham dress. A baby swaddled in white lace was glued in the cradle, which Fiona lifted now to kiss the baby, setting it in the goat pasture and rocking it to sleep. Across the room, Henry was reading *The Well Wrought Urn*, drinking a glass of Jameson. He didn't seem to hear the phone when it rang, so Charlotte, who was stirring a pot of black beans with one hand, picked it up with the other.

"Charlotte?" It was Darryl. His voice was raw, as if her name tore his throat, and hearing this, a softness came over her; everything else fell away.

"Hi," she said, barely audibly, but Fiona looked up like she'd heard a shot.

"Where've you been?" he asked.

"I . . . let me go upstairs and check. . . ." This sounded ordinary enough, and Fiona returned to her menagerie. Charlotte turned the beans off and ran up the stairs with the phone, wedging herself in on the floor of the linen closet.

"I've been . . . hiding, I guess . . ." she admitted.

He laughed. "Me too."

This seemed to be all she needed. She would just stay here, with her knees pulled up and the phone to her ear in the dark, and they could tell each other how lost they were, how frightened, how grateful to have found another honest soul. So much of life—riding up in the elevator, eyes fixed on the others' ten pairs of competitively glamorous shoes, or listening to Henry on the phone as he decided whether this or that life merited inclusion in the Mirror's obituaries— "Prolific, yes, but hardly a first-rate mind"—was a false construction, fitted over the crooked, messy, half-assed truth. Darryl was real.

"Charlotte? Are you there?"

"Yes, yes . . . I just . . . didn't know what to say. . . ."

"I'm sorry," he said. "I know I shouldn't call."

"No, no, you should! I mean, I shouldn't want you to call, but . . ."

"I just want . . ." he said. "Can I tell you the truth?"

"Of course. Always." She said this bravely, because in her experience, a person who wanted to tell you the truth was about to hurt you.

"I just want to come over there and drag you up the stairs and . . .

make love to you. . . ." He spoke so roughly she likely should have been frightened, but naturally she was thrilled. Those sweet confidences, the shyness, the hope shining there between them had generated a want more violent than the dainty phrase *make love* could describe.

"Darryl . . ." she said hopelessly, so he started to apologize.

"No!" she said, too loudly, and closed her eyes, drew her knees up so she could pull the closet door shut. "I want you just as badly! I think about you all the time. I think, if we'd met each other when we were younger . . . but . . ." She heard herself whispering with the urgent intensity of a teenager—lost in the enchanted forest at the end of childhood, dreaming of a rescue by love. Crosby, Stills, and Nash echoed in her head: "Say, can I have some of your purple berries . . . prob'ly keep us both alive." Everything flooded back in on her, the music, the smell of the incense burning in her bedroom while she wrote poems about horses and swans and her mother drifted under morphine in the next room; the way the snow fell in New Hampshire, the lush cloak over every tree.

"Oh, if only you'd been there," she said.

"If you knew me back then you'd have spit in my face."

"I'd have made love to you like it was my religion." She could hear him breathe; she fitted her breaths to his. "If only we'd known each other before our misspent youths."

"You didn't misspend your youth."

This sounded like a rebuke: *He* was the prodigal. She was living in the lighted window while he worked and worked and worked, seven days a week though his back hurt, and now he never went on the flats without expecting trouble, someone who'd want to pick a fight. The guy he was building for on Try Point had signed the petition that went with the suit, asking the town to void the shellfish grants. Darryl heard him talking while he shingled the roof in a bitter wind, dark coming on. He had a painting job too, indoor work he could do in the evenings. He was calling from that phone, so his name wouldn't show on the caller ID, not that Henry knew what caller ID was. His voice echoed in the empty house as they talked.

"Not the same way you did, no," Charlotte said. "Maybe in a worse way—too dutiful, too anxious to please, too grateful for Henry's shelter." This was the best she could do to explain herself. "I married too young."

"Like Carrie and Tim . . ."

"Exactly. Too exactly." She was not going to expound on the class differences while she was hiding in a linen closet. Tim used his fists, Henry his tongue—the effects were the same. Darryl drew a ragged breath on the other end of the line. They were two miserable creatures, shivering together now that they were in from the cold.

"I'm so glad I kissed you," she said.

"I thought you'd forgotten."

"Forget the nicest day of my life?" But he meant forgotten on purpose, because forgetting was the right thing to do.

"What are we going to do?" she asked, picking at a thread on her knee, glad he couldn't see her.

"Nothing," he said, with absolute conviction. "I've done enough wrong for a lifetime already."

She heard emphatic little footsteps coming up the stairs and pushed the closet door open, but before she could stand up Fiona was there, hands over her mouth, laughing in surprise.

"Boo!" Charlotte said.

"You're funny, Mama!"

"I am a riot."

"Mama, his head came off." She held out the father doll, in two pieces. The wire neck had snapped and there was nothing to stitch or glue. It seemed nothing less than a death. Fiona had never yet brought her a problem she couldn't solve.

"Sweetheart . . ." she began, but Fiona, who had rarely seen Charlotte show consternation, brightened.

"Don't worry, Mama. I know what to do. I'll put ice on it," she said, and went off on her healing mission with precise, confident steps.

Charlotte leaned back against the wall. "Talk," she said to Darryl, sounding like a reasonable adult again. "That's what we need to do. Talk, get to know each other better."

"I guess," he said, doubtful, as if she'd said they ought to leap off a bridge together.

"Listen, I take Fiona to Mrs. Carroll's, down in Paine Hollow, every morning at nine. You still take your coffee break at nine thirty?"

"It depends. . . ."

"Tell me when, and I'll meet you . . . at the SixMart. . . ."

"Might as well broadcast it on the national news," he said.

"Oh . . . So, at Shadblow Pond."

"The gate's locked for the winter over there."

"Where, then?" she asked.

"Somewhere where no one will see us, but where we won't be, you know . . . alone."

"At the Blind Person Crossing sign over on the Sneed Cartway?"

"Okay," he said, laughing. "I see your point."

"I mean, I suppose we could write to each other. . . . That's it; I'll write you a letter." This mess, in which she barely knew herself and might start sobbing or praying or panting any minute . . . why not turn it into an English project? She was good at English projects.

It struck him differently. "Okay, Wednesday morning, nine

thirty. I'll meet you in the smallpox graveyard. Do you know where that is? Off the Old King's Highway, in the woods there. You turn onto the first fire road, and park right behind the embankment. . . . But I'll have to leave by nine forty-five. Right now I gotta go pick up my mom from a meeting; I'm late already."

And then the conversation was over and Charlotte blinked and saw she was crouched in her own linen closet and had nearly forgotten who she was. She took a deep breath, then another, going to stand at the dormer window to look toward Try Point and the empty house Darryl had called from. A fishing dragger was crossing the mouth of the bay. There was a lighted Christmas tree affixed to its mast—one defiant bright spot in fifty miles of darkness. Each of the Lemon Pie Cottages was edged with lights too, and back in Fox Hollow someone's boat, up on blocks in the driveway, had the whole hull and wheelhouse outlined in big bright bulbs. Jake had drawn a lobster in red lights on his shed. In town the captains' houses might have an electric candle in each window, but out here the gaiety was both a cry in the wilderness and a statement of solidarity: *We're here, way out here at sea, but we're not quite alone.*

"Who was that?" Henry asked when she came down. He had set the table, washed the lettuce, started the rice.

"Darryl." She couldn't think of another answer.

"What did he want?"

"He . . . he's afraid the pipes are going to freeze." Her cheeks were blazing, and Henry squinted at her, puzzled.

"That's why I went upstairs, to start the water running. He thinks we should leave the faucet on, just a trickle, you know, overnight, just to be sure."

Fiona was whispering to her doll on its bed in the dollhouse, its head beside it in a miniature bowl. Charlotte could see that this life of hers was very beautiful. Everywhere her eye lit—on Fiona's head bent to attend to her dolls, the bowl of oranges on the table, on her book, the life of Martha Gellhorn, open on the couch beside Fiona's, *Spot Goes to the Beach*, on the Indian carpet worn soft as old denim, the floorboards salvaged from the old salt mill that were so salty the paint wouldn't stick to them —there was something solid and good. Only one piece was missing, and it was something she had believed she should learn to do without.

"It *is* cold," Henry said cozily. "I think I'll build a fire after dinner, put my feet up, and read about the interrogation martyrdom of the Russian intelligentsia."

It was genius, the idea of meeting in the smallpox cemetery, which had been hidden in the woods more than a century ago out of fear of contagion. She found the fire road without trouble, and the parking spot, but from there, there was no clear pathway. A tough green vine with half-inch thorns looped through the trees like razor wire. The sun was so low the trees cast endless shadows, and she scanned between them until finally she picked out a headstone and made her way toward it. The stones were eroded into shapelessness, with long grass matted between them. Something—deer or coyotes, maybe—had slept here, without fear of men. Nine thirty-five—it wasn't just Darryl she was waiting for; it was that old hope, the thing that seized her once she realized her mother would die: She'd felt sure then that if she was good, if she bore up bravely, some cosmic gift would come to her to make up for it all. And it would be a huge gift; it would have to be, to balance such a loss. Something really wonderful was going to happen to Charlotte Pelletier. She'd had a radiance about her then, which came from this expectation, and the radiance itself took her a long way, through high school and college and all the way to her desk at the *East Village Mirror*.

The cemetery ground was wet, so she crouched to read the names on the stones. They'd been chiseled by hand, and if that hand had been weak, the record it made had worn away. JEB CROL, she could make out, and HANA STED. BABY TIBBO, with some kind of shape inscribed below, so faint now she had to trace it with her finger—a lamb. A long needle of fear went through Charlotte's heart and she fought the impulse to race over to Mrs. Carroll's and be sure Fiona was safely stringing the fat wooden beads she loved, her head bent in concentration.

She heard a car, not Darryl's truck with its coughing motor. It passed without slowing. Nine fifty-five—she'd been waiting half an hour. He was delayed. Henry had used to stand her up, and was always furious that this upset her. Things came up at the paper, important things, and yes, he could have called, but he hadn't thought of it; he was preoccupied with world affairs. Darryl wasn't like that; if he didn't come there was bound to be a reason.

She got home to an empty house, called down to Henry with no answer. The living room was flooded with light: The ice in the bay would melt a little every afternoon and freeze again every night, so a hard, smooth layer frosted the icebergs and doubled the sun's effect. "Henry?" she tried again. Silence.

Then she heard a splash from the bathroom. She went to the staircase, smelled a faint, old-fashioned fragrance wafting down, light and sweet. "Henry?" A big slosh—he was in the bathtub, in the middle of the day. "Henry?"

At the top of the stairs the fragrance was stronger, but not unpleasant—there was no musk in it, none of that essence-of-Venus-flytrap that made her avoid the atomizer ladies in the department stores. The bathroom door was open a crack, and she heard Henry scoop a pitcher of water and pour it over his head. A lighthearted sound. She knocked on the bathroom door, and pushed it open. There he was, wet and bright-eyed, like a fledgling.

"Hi!"

"Hi," he said.

"Everything okay?"

"Oh, fine . . . I was getting a washcloth from the linen closet and the phone rang. . . . I knocked a bottle of perfume off the shelf. . . . I suppose you can smell it."

"I can . . . it's nice."

"Good, because I think the smell is there for the rest of our lives. . . . I mopped it up but it soaked in between the floorboards."

"Was that your mother's scent?"

"Mother? A scent? I can't quite imagine it. Anyway, I had to take a bath; it was overpowering."

"Who called? I mean, that made you break the perfume?"

"Oh . . . Darryl Stead. He was checking on the pipes again. It's very moving, the concern he has for this place. The Steads had a great respect for Father. . . ."

The bathroom being on the east side of the house, she took the phone out the kitchen door, facing west, and scrolled back to find the number he'd called from.

"What happened?" she asked when he picked it up.

"Wait . . . just a minute . . . let me just . . ."

She waited.

"Listen, I can't talk now." He was whispering. "The guys are all here. I couldn't get away. It would have looked fishy."

"It would have looked fishy for you to get coffee at coffee break?"

"Kara came by with a thermos and muffins. . . . Westie's wife."

"But . . . when can we . . . ?"

"I gotta go, I gotta go . . . bye."

Henry came down, scrubbed and shining, redolent of lilacs.

"What a day!" he said.

"Bright," Charlotte said. "But cold."

"I don't know," Henry said, standing by the front window, a towel around his hips, both hands proudly on his belly as if all his worldly substance were contained therein. He took a deep breath, as if it were the first day of spring. "There's just something in the air."

"It's your mother's perfume," Charlotte said.

"Very funny," he said. "I really don't think that was Mother's."

"Are you telling me your father wore lilac perfume?"

He sighed. "When do you pick Fiona up?"

"Noon."

"I'll go."

"What?"

"I'll go get her. I'd like to see the place."

"And a partridge in a pear tree!" Charlotte said.

Henry laughed. "Exactly."

In other words, yes, this was an odd little gift, his showing this interest in Fiona—a gift prompted by what? A scent, a fog, a half-remembered dream wafting in the air, more powerful than anything you could touch or see. When Charlotte said, out of nowhere, A partridge in a pear tree, Henry didn't have to ask what she meant. They'd known each other that long.

When he arrived home with Fiona, she bounded in from the car talking so fast Charlotte could hardly understand her, about how she had shown him the hamster, the fish, and the snake.

"He had a pet snake when he was little," Fiona told Charlotte knowingly. "Daddy! Let's paint a picture!"

"Oh, no, no, I've got to finish Mailer's obituary. He's in the hospital. He could go any day," Henry said, disappearing down the stairs like the white rabbit, with Bunbury at his heels.

"I love him!" Fiona said, peering down into the basement, then back at her mother with her little hands sprung open in surprise.

20

LONG NIGHT MOON

Mailer recovered, allowing some further edits. Charlotte found a Mulligan to rig a shower in the bathtub. January was cold and clear; the fire department opened the gates and plowed the snow off Shadblow Pond and on Friday nights turned the fire truck's floodlights on the ice. The whole town came out to skate. Betsy Godwin floated and spun, way off in the middle of the pond, and Carrie, who had played on a girls' ice hockey team when she was young, skirted the edge in quick, powerful strokes. Fiona, Alexis, and Crystal stayed together close to shore, skating in little clicking steps, falling, laughing, falling again just for fun. Charlotte stood near the campfire, pouring cocoa and looking for Darryl. She hadn't heard from him; she should try to keep from thinking of him, but that didn't seem possible.

She worked on the house with a vengeance. Taking a corner of the bedroom wallpaper, she pulled as hard as if it were the only thing getting in the way of her happiness. The sheet came off whole, bringing down hunks of plaster so she coughed in the dust. It felt almost wrong, as if she were disturbing the souls who had lived here before her. Henry's grandmother, tired from a journey, so glad to be back in the salt air, would have pulled out her hatpin at the oval mirror of the dressing table. The cameo Charlotte had found in the safe-deposit box, of the brave woman with bare feet and a spear, must have belonged to her. Her gloves were still in the top drawer—kid leather with six buttons along the wrist, the same blushing gray as the wallpaper background. The paper on the inner walls was stained so lightly it was only romantic; Charlotte decided to leave it up and took the gloves to the hardware store, to find paint to match.

It had been snowing lightly all morning and now a squall blew up; no one was on the road and there was not a car in the hardware store parking lot. As she was opening the door, a snowball hit her, softly, just at her collar. She turned around but there was no one—it must have slipped from the overhang. Then came another, just grazing the top of her head.

"What the hell . . . ?" She looked up to see Darryl astride the roof of the house next door, packing a soft snowball. "What are you doing?"

"A leak," he said. "A rotten fascia board right under the peak here."

His sweatshirt hood was cinched tight around his face; the snow was blowing off the harbor directly at him.

"In this weather?"

"It came up kind of quick."

"Darryl Stead, I have *never*!" No, never ever, not once, felt such elation. She packed a big snowball and threw it up toward him but it fell apart midair.

"Has no one ever shown you how to make a snowball?" He pulled his leg back over the ridge and let himself down to the ladder, and there he was beside her, with the snow sifting down over them.

"No," she said, "I guess no one did."

He looked up and down the street—not a soul. "How are you?"

"I'm good . . . how are you?"

"I'm . . . Charlotte, did you . . ."

"Did I what?"

"Nothing. I just . . . thought you'd said you'd write to me. I checked my P.O. box like twice a day until Leslie Harding asked if I was already expecting my tax refund. . . . Then I thought, maybe, maybe you didn't want to send it in the mail. You might have slipped it in my glove compartment while I was away from the truck. Then I saw something under the windshield wiper and my heart leaped and . . . it was a parking ticket." He laughed. "Of course."

"You never came, and I called you and you said you couldn't talk, and . . ."

"The cemetery was a bad idea. It's a good place to hide—hardly anyone even knows it's out there. Rob and I used to meet our customers there when we were dealing. I don't want to go back there."

"Darryl, everyone has stuff they regret in their past. Selling pot in high school—it's like baseball, a national pastime."

His smile was pained, a recognition that she didn't understand

"My last day in the halfway house," he said, needing to shock her, glad to see her take it in, "I asked my counselor, 'How will I know if I'm going down the wrong path?' He said—'If you can't be open about something, don't do it.'"

"So why should I write to you, if it's so wrong?"

"Because . . ." His hands were inches from her two arms, and she could feel the circuit that would connect if he touched her. His eyes, his face showed everything, how much he felt, how little he dared.

Westie Small's van came around the corner into the parking lot and there was just a quarter second to glance a good-bye to each other as they turned back into their public selves.

"So what are you here for?" Darryl asked, in his hearty carpenter's voice.

"Paint," she said, holding out the gloves.

"Gloves need a new coat of paint?"

"No, but they match the wallpaper in the upstairs bedroom, you know, with the peonies?"

"Yeah," he said, "I've thought a lot about that room." He caught her eye one last time before Westie got out of the van. "Hey, Westie . . . a nice snow, eh?"

Westie grumbled that it might be snow but he didn't see anything nice about it.

"About those pipes," Darryl said to Charlotte, "call me if you have any more problems."

"Oh, thanks, I will." The snow glittered everywhere, over the roofs of the Lemon Pie Cottages, on the sides of the wavy locust trees, like physical proof that he loved her.

Driving home, she saw a truck stopped dead, half in, half out of the breakdown lane. Carrie's truck. Charlotte pulled over just in front of her.

"What happened?"

Carrie, who had just put the hood up, turned and looked at her without interest.

"Died," she said, turning back to the engine.

"Can I help?"

"No-o-o."

"Give you a ride?"

"Naw, I'll wait here. Someone will come along." Charlotte wasn't someone.

"Did you call for help?"

"No," Carrie said, as if this were just the kind of idea to be expected from a spoiled bitch like Charlotte, who probably had a cell phone in every pocket.

"Well, let me take you then. . . ."

It was about to become awkward when Westie drove up behind them.

"First one Stead, then the other," he said to Charlotte, and to Carrie: "Whadaya need here?"

Carrie laughed, a dry hoot. "A joint would have done me, in the old days," she said. "Rob's got a speed trap going back at the church, so there'd be no worries."

"How 'bout a jump?"

"We're way past that," she said. "The battery's about the only thing that does work."

"Well, let's get 'er outta the way here," he said, rubbing his beard. They went to work together, opening both doors and rolling the truck carefully forward, Westie, the gentleman, taking the roadward side. "Easy does it," he said, as if the truck were a balky horse. "That's a girl, here we go." Charlotte stood there with her arms hanging useless, like Henry.

"Okay, now back to the garage, we'll get a tow, we'll see what needs to happen," he said. To Charlotte, whose name he didn't know, he touched his forehead, like a cap. "Nice of you to stop."

"Of course," Charlotte said. Carrie glanced at her, wary. "Would you like me to bring Timmy home from Mrs. Carroll's later?" she asked.

"No, thanks," Carrie said. "Desiree'll be home from school by then." Desiree was her oldest, a bouncy blond thing, no relation of Tim Cloutier. Carrie had married him years later, when she was expecting the middle boy, Matt.

Carrie cast an acerbic smile toward Charlotte as they drove away.

How had that happened exactly—that she stopped to help and ended up standing here alone? But the snow, the snow! She started back toward the Volvo and saw Betsy coming along the other way, driving home from Orleans.

"Charlotte!" Betsy stopped cold in her lane and there was a terrible screech of brakes behind her—some young guy in an old sports car who had no doubt been following too closely.

Charlotte rushed into the road as if she thought she could shield the two cars from each other. Betsy screamed. The guy in the sports car, who had skidded to the side and stopped just before he hit her, rolled down the window and yelled, "Assholes, New York whores, fuck, fuck you!" Betsy looked as alarmed as if she'd just discovered a blatant run in her stocking, pulled off to the side, and the guy backed up and screeched away, his middle finger out the window.

"I'm sorry," Betsy said. "I was just wondering if you needed help and instead I almost got you killed."

"Danger is my business," Charlotte said. Her heart was beating as if it were trying to escape. "I'm fine. I've got to learn not to throw myself between colliding automobiles; no good can come. You okay?"

"I'm fine!" Betsy said. "I almost got to try out the air bags. New York whores, are we?"

"I guess so. . . ."

"Wanna get a cup of coffee?"

"I'd love to," Charlotte said. In the circumstances she liked Betsy better than just about anyone. "Let's try the new place . . . Della's." Della was Jamaican—she'd come to work one summer and stayed, heaven knew how. Her new place was right on the highway and had a sign advertising DELLA'S COUNTER SERVICE; FRESH BREAD AND MEAT. Charlotte had not seen trucks in the driveway there—the oystermen went to the Wicked Oyster. Darryl hadn't wanted to be seen with her; she didn't want to be seen with Betsy. She parked around the back, where a cat was sitting patiently by the kitchen door, hoping for a fish.

Inside, Della's was painted a brilliant yellow, with pineapples and watermelons dancing along the walls. The music was an infectious rap-reggae version of "A Hard Rain's A-gonna Fall," and the coffee was indeed strong—Charlotte remembered that she'd gotten high the first time she drank coffee, interviewing a dairy farmer for the local newspaper, an internship in high school. Sitting at that kind man's kitchen table, listening to his story in the morning sunlight, she'd thought how wonderful it would be to be a reporter and do this all the time.

Betsy had an unself-conscious ease about her. It didn't occur to her that one might feel uncertain or out of place—she was small and pretty and had been welcome as an ornament all her life. She was warm to Della, who had worked for her at the jewelry shop one summer, and settled in with Charlotte at the one little table as if they'd been girlfriends for years.

"We ought to get the girls together more often," she said, sipping her coffee. "They'll be growing up together—it won't be long before they're shopping for prom dresses together. Alexis's already sweet on Dylan Mulligan. You can practically see hearts bubbling up over her head when she's with him."

"I hope it won't all go quite that fast," Charlotte said.

"Oh, I know," Betsy said. "Back in Rochester—that's where my family is—you should see; they're wearing little white satin corsets to their first communion!" She shuddered. "Boy, am I glad I got out of there."

"How did you?" It was the first question on everyone's lips; no one ever moved to Wellfleet to study, or take a better job, or any of the usual things—you came because you lucked out, like Charlotte, or lost out, like Darryl, and couldn't get away.

"Oh, I came out for the summer, met Skip, and the rest is history. Sometimes I wonder whether I married him or the town. What about you?"

"Oh, it's all because of Henry. I grew up in New Hampshire . . . near Manchester. . . ." The name itself gave her claustrophobia—the old mills looming, graffitied over with the names of the kids who scuffled in their shadows, barely aware of the life in the larger world.

Betsy laughed. "You're kidding," she said. "I figured you for Scarsdale, like Skip. My father's a butcher," she confided suddenly. "His brother was a priest, so we didn't have to go to church to confess. We went into the meat locker! That's right, and my uncle would sit on a stool, with a side of beef hanging between us on a hook, and I'd confess all my sins to this hunk of meat."

Charlotte covered her mouth with both hands.

"Yes," Betsy said, delighting in her story.

"It's a wonder you're not insane!"

Betsy made a comic face and leaned back in her chair. "You can't get much farther from a butcher shop than a jewelry store. I used to dream about it—these sparkling glass cases, all the gold on blue velvet, the clean little tools."

"I dreamed of hanging laundry out to dry, looking out over the sea."

"We got our wishes," Betsy said. "Not like it was easy. That first year when I was pregnant and Skip was really just doing title searches, his parents weren't charging us rent, but the heating oil was more than we could afford. But now . . ." She leaned across the table to confide. "I'm redoing the kitchen. Wait till you see. Granite counters, a chef's stove, and a fireplace in the corner so there'll be a little sitting area there for the kids. It'll be crazy for a while, but by summer the dust will have settled, hopefully it'll be a good season, the coffers will fill, everyone will be in a better mood. We fall apart in the winter around here. In the summer everyone's so busy, but January comes, they've got time to think . . . they go a little crazy." She stretched her hand out in front of her—admiring it. It was a very small and delicate hand. "In the winter the slightest thing blows up into a scandal."

"Like the Narvilles' lawsuit . . ."

"Yeah, that seems to be what everybody's talking about. Skip's gotten some pretty upsetting phone calls. I mean, he's a lawyer; he's doing a job he was hired to do."

But her voice was tight; she had some qualm of her own. Charlotte would have liked to say: *And what Darryl and the others do: They raise oysters.* She was too timid, so she told herself she was just gathering information. It turned out that she didn't have to say anything. Betsy kept defending herself point by point.

"It's not like the outcome would be different. They'd have hired someone else if Skip had refused," Betsy went on. "I feel bad for Carrie; she's got way more than she can handle. Desiree's expecting, did you know?"

"I did not," Charlotte said, heart sinking, thinking of Ada's saying that birth by neglect led to death by neglect in the Stead family. "Desiree's still in high school, isn't she?"

"Yeah, she's not graduating till next year. But a new baby, a new life in the house, it'll be nice for them, exciting."

"Not if they can't afford it."

"Honey," Betsy said, "by the time those oysters are sold, for forty or forty-five cents apiece, so much effort has gone into them . . . bagging groceries at Stop and Shop pays better. No one's been allowed to raise shellfish in Truro for years, you know. And everything seems to work out fine. Yes, you can fish on private land, but aquaculture is farming. It's from *Pazolt versus the Division of Marine Fisheries,* 1994. Pa-

zolt v. the Town of Truro, 1993. Jeb Narville, and the rest of them, they paid a lot of money for their land. They deserve—"

"What about work?" Charlotte asked suddenly. "What about all the labor that . . . Carrie . . . and the others have put in? A guy like Narville—he paid a lot of money but he hasn't lived in that house a whole month yet. The Steads, and the others, they've been working that land for years and years."

"You do realize that if you were lying in the street, Tim Cloutier would drive right over you? I mean, you understand that?"

"Yes," Charlotte said. "I know he's trouble. I just wish . . . Why couldn't Skip have argued the oystermen's side?"

"It's not what he was paid to do," Betsy said simply. A question crossed her face. "People don't blame you, you know, honey," she said. "There's nobody here who wouldn't have sold that piece of land."

"It's just . . . I'm so glad to have a little part of this town. I don't want to have had a bad effect here."

"You didn't," Betsy said, her voice full of kindness, as if she were talking to a child. "You have nothing to do with it. Things change. Wellfleet has changed a million times; it's always changing. No one ever got rich oystering—you break your back year in and year out; then a red tide wipes you out and you start over. The Narvilles, the other new people coming into town, they'll change our fortunes. Boating people tie up at the marina and take their credit cards for a walk through town—a thousand dollars for a pair of earrings, it isn't a big deal for them. They're opening a Marc Jacobs on Commercial Street. And a new steak-and-seafood place down where the Dairy Queen used to be, by the wharf. There're going to be jobs, jobs that really pay. I hear," she said, leaning in for a delicious confidence, "that Blair Settenbee, the publisher, bought the site of the old Sea Witch Inn, out on Try Point. His architect is flying in from Easthampton."

"There goes the neighborhood," Charlotte said. Blair Settenbee was the publisher of *Celeb*, and *SportsNow*, and *Summit Design*, which was the thickest, glossiest magazine with the highest advertising rates in the business. Charlotte had ridden in an elevator with him once—he glowed as if he were made out of something harder and brighter than most people. If he did build a house on Try Point, he would occupy it only a few weeks a year. He had his place overlooking the Bosphorus and the flat beside Le Jardin du Luxembourg. And the villa on Mustique.

"A rising tide lifts all boats!" Betsy said. "There's going to be plenty for everyone."

"I used to work for Blair Settenbee," Charlotte said.

Betsy blinked and looked at her as if for the first time. "You did?" Charlotte could almost see her wondering if she'd been a governess.

"I wrote for *Celeb*."

"Get out!" Betsy said. "You did not! I love *Celeb*."

"I was on the style beat."

"Gee, I never miss that section," Betsy said, scrutinizing her again. What had she missed? What clue was there to show that Charlotte had once been chic? "I probably bought some of the things you recommended," she said, looking disillusioned.

"I'm so glad we got to know each other a little," Betsy said, pushing a ten-dollar bill into Della's tip jar and heading down the front steps. "It's lonely out here in the winter. People like us have to stick together. Sorry about the near-death experience, though . . ."

"All's well that ends well," Charlotte said, watching Betsy hop into the BMW and pull blithely back onto the road, causing a gravel truck to downshift loudly behind her. She was probably right: The oystermen were fighting a losing battle—it was a romantic notion that you could farm the edge of the sea, live by the tides, and really make a living at it. Farmers never made a decent living. . . . Certainly the dairy farmers she'd grown up among had suffered one hard time after another, and without government milk subsidies, she'd hate to think. But to be able to say, "I raise oysters," was a little like being able to say you were a mom, or that you wrote a column for the *East Village Mirror*—there was not much outward glory in it, but at the end of the day you could be proud of what you'd done.

And it was the same for the town as for a person—the Wellfleet where oysters grew just beneath the surface of the bay was an infinitely more vital place than the Wellfleet where grandiose houses muscled into one another's views on the hillsides. To live by the waters, according to the tides and the seasons and the phases of the moon, to see by the light of the long narrative of the town's history and the complicated story of these neighbors' interlocking lives, was to see more, feel more, be more alive. That was why she had torn her family up by the roots and set them down here. That was why Darryl could get well here—strong enough to look life in the eye.

Home, finally, she pushed the dresser and the washstand away from the walls and draped them with sheets, ran masking tape along the window frames and the molding, stirred the paint and poured it into the roller tray. It was one of those smells, like the first cut grass of the year, or the bay during a plankton bloom on a cold spring day— so fresh and hopeful that it changed everything the minute it was set loose in the room. Charlotte sat down on the bed: Darryl had been waiting for a letter she'd never thought of writing. Searching for it, disappointed again and again. She could see him standing there on the tide flats, one arm stretched out toward her. He had nothing, not even a halfway decent truck, and he knew he had no one but himself to blame. To be in such a humble position was to be in company with everyone on earth.

21

WISTERIA

Dear Darryl,

I can't stand thinking that you were waiting for a letter and I didn't send one. When I think of the chance anyone takes, falling in love—I hardly know how anyone manages. When you're twenty you've got hormones, and maybe bourbon . . . and that sense of immortality that causes so many motorcycle crashes and marriages. I suppose I ought to be tough as an old rhinoceros by now, but really I seem more fragile, since I know how much it can hurt. I took the upstairs wallpaper down without wrecking the walls; you'd be proud! You and I are so different that to find this green thing growing between us is a kind of miracle. I can't take my eyes off it; I want to see what kind of flowers it will have . . . and . . . I want it to become strong as a wisteria. Nothing kills a wisteria; you probably know that. Darryl, we have everything good between us—we have to find a way to let it grow.

Love,

Charlotte

This half page took two hours to write. In the first draft, the white horses and swans from her old poems came into it—steeds to carry a schoolgirl away. That girl had to be kept hidden from Henry, but she'd crept out to meet Darryl. Charlotte would have liked to write pages—volumes—to explain herself, to justify herself, saying that she, like Darryl, was past forty and still a raw newcomer to life, just hatched out of a protective madness, determined now to build something solid and real. But half a page was risk enough. She put the letter in an *East Village Mirror* envelope so it would look like business correspondence, and pushed it into the post office mail slot so it would go into his P.O. box without ever leaving the building.

It came out of the box along with a notice from the Department of Motor Vehicles saying that as six weeks had passed since Darryl's truck had failed to pass inspection, the registration had been revoked. And his health insurance bill—higher than his rent. And the March issue of *Playboy*—his mother, who had given him a subscription the year he turned thirteen (*It's perfectly normal, honey—Love, Mom*), had repeated the gesture this Christmas . . . to signify a fresh start? In hopes that he would never see a naked woman without thinking of her? He let it slip out of its wrapper into the garbage, and folded the brown paper into his pocket to burn at home. Then he saw the address on the envelope—the *East Village Mirror*—and a scalding sensation shriveled his guts. He tore it open right there, though it was indiscreet. *Keep your hands off my wife*, was what he expected to see.

By the time he realized it wasn't a threat, he felt too ill to read it. What had he gotten himself into? *The rich are different from you and me.* Where had he heard that, and why was it echoing in his mind now? It made him ache to watch her with Fiona, to see her blush at his flirtations. Thrilling to push a little farther, and farther, to see how far he could go with her. She laughed so easily; life was a sparkling fascination to her.

For most of the women he knew, life was a force they only just managed to bear. They laughed when they guessed he meant to be funny, because they needed help and he looked so strong. He needed a wife, and his time of illusions had passed—the choices were few: Dawn, with her twelve-year-old son who wouldn't be allowed to play sports again until he finished anger-management classes; Nikki, who could work harder than any woman he'd ever met, whose green eyes were as distant as if she were looking up at him from the bottom of the sea; Kim, the dental assistant; possibly Lisa Gonsalves from the bait shop. He had to pick one of them and settle down, make a life. And one of them had to pick him—to say, *Yes, he used to be a drug addict but he seems to have it beat, and he hasn't even got a decent truck, but he works so steadily I think he'll come out ahead, and I'd rather him than Bud Rivette.* Charlotte, by the luck of her marriage, had been lifted above such calculations. When he was working on the flats in the evening he'd see her at the kitchen window—it was a vision of happiness, goodness, hope. The house itself, the books on the shelves, the Persian rug passed down through the generations, Fiona's strewn toys—any man who lived there would be a whole man, unafraid of life, with no need of the supplemental courage and energy you could get through a needle.

It had been like being young again, telling her his secrets, taking these stealthy steps into her heart. With every glance he'd forced another door, and she was always there, laughing, glad to see him. He'd been bold as a lion. Why? Because she was married to Henry Tradescome and there was no earthly chance . . . though he'd dreamed there might be, had imagined . . . He laughed to himself. *Playboy* wouldn't touch what he'd imagined, couldn't, because there would be that look in her eyes. Yes, he'd looked for her letter . . . he'd pulled up the floor mats in the truck, hoping she might have hidden it there. What he'd found was that the floor was rusted through. And he'd felt relief as much as disappointment. She wasn't in love with him, she wouldn't pull him closer so she wouldn't hurt him, he wouldn't hurt her. How his heart had turned over, out on the tide flats when he saw it was true, that she was going to let him kiss her, going to let something wild loose.

He spread the letter across the steering wheel but he could hardly dare read it, for fear it would show something he didn't want to see— her sticky womanly need, an intelligence that could overwhelm his, something false that he'd find himself hating . . . or all three. Her handwriting was spiky, messy, difficult to decipher; not, thank God, Dawn's round, regular script. He read it through once, then again. She was, by some miracle or calamity, in love with him, and for a second he felt only contempt—could she be such a fool? Then he felt again how the ground had gone out from under him that day in the fog. She'd seen the best things in him and it made her the most seductive and dangerous woman on earth. That picture she carried around in her head was something he *had* to have.

A familiar feeling. He distrusted it absolutely. He folded the letter and stuck it inside the flap of his checkbook, which he kept in the breast pocket of his winter jacket. After this he would find himself reaching to touch it absently, when he was worried about the future or guilty about the past. But to unfold it, to read it again—that seemed a sin, for which he would be punished by finding that he had only imagined the letter, had kept a fold of blank paper next to his heart all that time.

22

AN UNEXPLODED BOMB

It seemed to Charlotte that she had been watching Henry through a telescope all the years in New York, focused so closely she could see him only piece by piece. Here in Wellfleet she looked through the other way and saw him distant but whole, set in his own landscape—cold, staunch New England—and, it seemed, his own time. His father had been born in 1910, his grandfather in 1885. Even his mother, born Priscilla Standish, the only child of a Presbyterian minister and his wife, had been raised with a steely ideal.

Cross-legged on the living room rug, drinking tea from a porcelain cup that Priscilla had tagged as *Seventeen hundreds, estate of Auntie Experience*, Charlotte was reading her mother-in-law's letters. Expecting a letter herself, and with it, the real beginning of love, she was blind and dizzy with hope. She could barely think; she lost track of conversations, laughed at the wrong moments, stood at the kitchen window for half an hour at a time until she shook herself back to reality and washed another dish. The rote work of going through the old trunks was a comfort; the stacks of little envelopes, each promising a glimpse into another life, another time. Bunbury stretched out, on his back, in the swath of sunlight that fell across the couch. Charlotte opened another letter.

> Dear Henry,
>   We are having the finest weather of the summer, I do believe. Young Henry has been up the marsh in the canoe all day. Viola and Ted Hawkins won the duplicate competition last night. Viola's cousin will be here for the first two weeks in August and would like to play. I thought Ada Town might make a fourth. It must be hot there. I hope you have some of the light shirts back from Mr. Chun.
>   Yours fondly,
>   Priscilla

There were hundreds of these monstrously appropriate little missives, dutiful and empty—*emptied*, it seemed—of hope or disappointment, judgment or observation, any human detail. Most were sent from Wellfleet to her husband, at work in the city, but there was a boxful addressed to Henry at college, and beneath those, letters to her parents in Maine. Then, at the bottom of the trunk, there was a letter addressed to Priscilla—a very young Priscilla, who needed to have a tooth pulled. Her father, whose handwriting, like Henry's, was full of slashing downward strokes, exhorted her to stoicism: *We must expect suffering in this world. We must face it down.*

The sunlight that Bunbury had been sleeping in had shifted and was reflecting off the gong now, so brightly Charlotte turned it sideways to avoid the glare. The gong disk swayed, the reflection veering crazily; Charlotte saw that Priscilla had taped one of her notes to the underside of the sandalwood frame: *Gong from Simeulue, Indonesia.* **Kingfisher** *held in quarantine there; plague. Also clove oil.* She could have made lists, an inventory of these things that would explain their provenance for posterity, or she could have typed up a little history of each object, as if this were a museum. But she hadn't valued the story she was trying to tell, not enough to really set it down and take care that it was passed along. Instead she'd scrawled it on torn scraps, hoping someone—Henry—would see and understand.

Henry didn't want to see. There was a photograph at the very bottom of the trunk, one Charlotte hadn't seen before, of Priscilla holding a young Henry on her lap. She looked fashionable and un-happy; he looked irritated but obedient. Maybe Henry had been one of those babies who didn't want to be soothed; Charlotte had read about them. Maybe his mother had been waiting for affection all her life, and when her own child didn't seem to warm naturally, it had broken her. Or worse: She'd been waiting to feel affection in her own heart, and had found that her child didn't move her as she'd expected he would. Whatever, it had ended with Priscilla taping her little mes-sages to the furniture.

Or maybe every guess Charlotte made was wrong. Henry had al-most never spoken of his mother, except to say something like, "Mother loved a good lamb chop," or "Mother was very partial to cats, in her own peculiar way." He did not recall seeing his parents kiss, nor had he ever heard them argue. Charlotte's interest in them made him queasy. When she said she was just trying to get to know him, he maintained that this was a bad idea. This was the great thing about the Mermaid, and McClellan's, his corner bar back in the city. Thanks to whiskey, he could skip the squeamish-making process of friendship and go straight to the meat of a conversation—politics, literature, the weather. He always left feeling the deepest bond with the man on the next stool, something that would hardly have been true if he'd "gotten to know" the fellow.

Still, Charlotte *had* gotten to know Henry, thus becoming dangerous to him. There she was reading his mother's letters, making her assumptions, thinking she understood something! Yesterday it was the bottle of lilac water, which she was determined must have meaning to him; but she was wrong, and worse than that, she was trespassing, prying in places he didn't even allow himself to go.

"Here, smell it again, Henry. . . . It must remind you of *something*." It had seemed to change him, that day he took the bath—at least for a minute. As if he'd awoken, looked around, noticed his daughter . . . It seemed there was some genie in that bottle that might change their lives.

He sighed. He knew what she wanted; it wasn't an unreasonable desire. It just happened to be something he didn't have. The perfume bottle was made of frosted glass, with lilacs hand-painted on the side and a green glass stopper in the shape of two leaves. He sniffed. "It reminds me of old ladies," he said.

"It has to have belonged to your mother . . . or your grand-mother?"

"I suppose," he said. He was trying to get downstairs to his desk, to safety, but she stood in the door.

"Did she like lilacs? Your mother?"

"Mother? Mother liked . . . What did Mother like?" He stepped back, leaning against the kitchen sink with a furrowed brow and a smile twitching at the corner of his mouth.

"Mother was a very reserved person," he said finally. "She took a great interest in antique furniture, but beyond that . . . I don't know, and I'm not sure I ever did." Bunbury rubbed up against his legs and he saw an easy escape. "Do you want to go out?" he asked, looking down at the cat as if he expected an answer. "Oh, yes, do you want to go out? It's cold out there, but you'd probably like to go out." He opened the door. "Here you go; is that what you want, to go out?"

Bunbury put his nose out and sniffed the air, turning to gaze mildly up at Henry. Bunbury was not given to hinting: When he wanted to go out he sat with his nose to the doorjamb; if he wanted to come in, he jumped onto the porch railing to tap the window with his paw. But Henry kept up the one-sided conversation, in hopes Charlotte would desist.

If he had asked her what her mother had liked—well, she knew every single thing: little bouquets of wildflowers, handmade quilts.... Her mother would always, always stop at a child's lemonade stand.... There was a sadness in her that was quieted by simple, homey things. When she died the worst part was that Charlotte couldn't protect her from that sadness anymore. Thinking of her made Charlotte feel as if she were standing at the edge of a dizzying precipice, so she tried not to. Maybe the same was true for Henry, who was entirely absorbed in the cat now, petting him, scratching behind his ears, while Bunbury purred and stretched his neck, angling his head to take fuller advantage of the attention.

"You said once that she liked cats . . ." Charlotte said.

"Yes, old mister," Henry continued, to Bunbury. "Yes, you like a nice scratch."

"Henry?"

"What?" He shook his head; he seemed surprised she was still there.

"I was saying that you'd told me your mother liked cats."

"I suppose I might have."

"Did you have a cat when you were little?"

"Oh, we had a number of cats. Mother liked a kitten. She got one every spring. Then in the fall she'd have it put away."

"You're not serious."

He had that look of suppressed delight he got when he'd been able to shock her. "Ye-es, he's such a good kitty," he said to Bunbury. "She liked what she liked, Mother did," he added.

"She killed your pet once a year?"

"She only liked kittens."

"She killed your pet kitten the minute it wasn't a cute baby anymore, year in and year out?"

"Don't make a federal case out of it," he said. "It was her pet kitten, not mine. It controlled the mice. We didn't have mice back in Boston, so she didn't need a cat there. People weren't so sentimental back then."

"Well, pardon my sentimentality." The things people can't bear to remember are supposed to be loud and dramatic—obvious, like incest, or beatings. They're not supposed to be sitting there neat and reasonable among the antique teacups a child is taught never to touch. To think of Henry, the lonely child in the picture, growing up in a cold, cold house, with a burning faith in God as his comfort and an obsession with baseball because the best thing about him seemed to be his pitching arm . . . how, if that child became ill, and the spirit went out of the arm, and a bleak clarity dawned as he heard the tired old pieties from the mouth of his minister . . . the bleakness itself might become the solid center, the thing that child could trust.

"I used to write their obituaries," Henry said, staring out toward the bay through the branches of the oak tree. "I suppose you could say that was my juvenilia." Then, turning the subject: "The cardinal's been right there on that branch for hours, calling for his mate. I haven't seen the female all day."

23

SEPTEMBER TWELFTH

"You know who lives in town?" Henry asked. "Selwyn Latrousse, from the *Nation*."

"Do we know him?"

"Well, we're part of his community." Henry spoke stiffly—the great community of arts and letters did not conform to conventional boundaries, as Charlotte ought to have known. "We're invited for dinner Friday night."

"When did he write for the *Nation*?" Charlotte asked, politely not inquiring whether dinosaurs had still roamed the earth at the time. She had heard in Henry's voice that ironclad reverence he held for the generation before him, or at least the part of that generation that had disagreed with his Republican father.

"He's emeritus, of course." Case closed. They had escaped New York, but they would never escape the damned intelligentsia, the very circle Charlotte had once dreamed of entering. On Friday she dressed as for a funeral—her own—but standing in front of the clouded mirror, over which she had folded the dove gray gloves, she felt a spring of rebellion start to bubble and went back to the closet, from which a

brown dress with big polka dots and a cinched waist was loudly calling. Wearing it she looked dangerous—as if she were on the lam
from another decade, making use of a very old-fashioned weapon
(red lipstick) to cause unmentionable trouble wherever she went.
Henry looked grim when he saw her come down the stairs. He had
on the one suit jacket he possessed, the one they had bought him
when he went to Andover. Charlotte was his only ornament and he'd
have preferred something more dignified. Well, he should have married Susan Sontag.

They picked Orson up on the way to the Latrousses'. His house,
like his person, was very small but very ornate—a Queen Anne fantasia complete with miniature turret and gothic windows that sat at
the crest of Pennyfarthing Hill. He came down the stairs with a
springy step, and settled himself in the backseat with a flourish, orga-
nizing his cape carefully, to prevent wrinkles.

"Orson, I haven't seen you all winter," Charlotte said. "Have you
been hibernating?"

"Something like it," he said, with grave wit. "I have been reha-
bilitated."

Unsure of the etiquette, Charlotte took her cue from his tone.
"Congratulations!"

"Or condolences," Orson said. "It's hard to know."

"Where did you go . . . Bridgewater, is it?"

Orson chuckled. "Heavens, no, my dear. Bridgewater is where
they put you. *I* was at McLean, where you check *yourself* in. *Very* interesting group this time . . . a painter, a couple of jazz musicians . . . the
weeks *flew*."

"Sounds lovely," Charlotte said. They were driving through town,
down the main street with its shuttered clothing shops and restaurants, past the church where Ada's father had been pastor. AA met

there on Friday evenings, and there was Darryl, holding the door for another man, clapping him on the back as he went in. It was a month since Charlotte had sent the letter, with no response, and seeing him, she felt a twinge like a probe gone deep into some festering abscess— a sick joy.

"I tried AA once," Orson said, as if he'd read her mind. "It was over a man, of course. . . ." He laughed to himself, with lascivious melancholy. "The shoulders of a stevedore and the mouth of a Michelangelo . . . I'd have paid to watch him sleep. Alas, I was not invited to partake of such bliss, but . . . he had given up drinking and saw AA as his salvation. Naturally, he wanted to help the fallen." Orson patted his bow tie happily, proud of his membership in this society.

"So I agreed to go to a few of their gatherings. It was simple enough—after all, they meet at the Masonic lodge three times a week. So I would take my customary constitutional, and instead of crossing Point Road to the Mermaid, I'd join the Friends of Bill across the way. The manly companionship so intoxicated me, I barely missed my gin. And this fellow, whose beauty was equaled only by his kindness, would pay me the most generous attention, bringing me coffee, listening to my abject stories. . . ." Orson smiled, speaking the word *abject* with sweet irony.

"But one night, as I gave the familiar introduction: 'I'm Orson, and I'm an alcoholic'—I experienced a revelation. I thought, By God, that's the truth. I'm an alcoholic! I don't belong here. I ought to be across the street at the Mermaid. So there I went, and there I drank. Happily ever after. With the occasional vacation at McLean."

The Volvo was chugging up the very steep Latrousse driveway, and they found themselves on a hilltop that looked down over the town center, the harbor, and across the bay to Provincetown, a narrow band of lights in a wide darkness, like a sheltering arm around the bay. To have been a sailor, weeks at sea, and finally see Cape Cod, literally beckoning—yes, it was easy to imagine a ship anchoring on a windless night, the men uncertain with their parcel, a wide-eyed baby. . . . How had they cared for her during the voyage? Was her mother on board? Some salty old cook heating milk in the galley? And where would such milk have been gotten? Where had the ship sailed from? Spain? Cape Verde? Jamaica? Ada looked entirely northern, born to wear her tartan. These questions fell aside, though, when you looked down to see the steps leading up from the harbor, straight to the church—the spire shining in the same moonlight that would have lit the path that night. Real life can never stand up against a story. Still, Ada must wonder about it every minute of her life, though she insisted that she did not, that her own life was no different from any life, a mystery from beginning to end.

Selwyn Latrousse, portly and bright-eyed, took Charlotte's hand with warmth. "I'm so glad you could come," he said, looking at her as if he were drinking up her youth like medicine. His wife, Natasha, took her and the polka-dot dress in, in one sardonic glance. "A bit much, *mais non?*" she said over her shoulder to a woman in an immense caftan, and to Charlotte, "You needn't have gone to such trouble. This is just a little dinner for friends." She meant that it was very rude of Charlotte to be young still, when the rest of them had lived their lives already.

"Oh, I was just feeling lighthearted," Charlotte said, not entirely without spite.

Natasha made a little face, but Selwyn said, "I'm glad to hear it. Lightheartedness is in short supply around here these days."

There were twelve for dinner, in a glass and concrete house that seemed conceived to thwart comfort—designed by Wuidenueven, (or that was what she thought she had heard Orson say in a reverent hush), one of his very few private homes. Charlotte supposed he had designed mostly airplane hangars. Henry's generation had embraced modernism in reaction against what went before. They'd all wanted to smash up their parents' teacups with baseball bats, to claw down the flocked wallpaper and chop up the Chippendale dressers for kindling. . . . *They* lived among ideas, not furniture. Their ideas, by now, seemed like their furniture—sad and spindly, attempts to strip life of its emotional welter, reduce it to something clean-lined and reasonable. Charlotte, who had never felt suffocated by a house full of colonial assumptions and tasseled draperies, felt lonely amid the spare, sleek tables and chairs. She looked around at Mrs. Latrousse's paintings—huge citrus-colored abstracts—while the others ate marinated fava beans and discussed architecture, naming men she thought she'd never heard of until she began to penetrate their language and realized they were having skirmishes of pronunciation, so *Weed-ah-noo-ven* became V*weed-ech-noo-ay-ven* and then V*wid-aa-noy-ven*, and Latrousse shook his head and said, "He himself preferred *Woy-dan'-ach-wen*."

Charlotte laughed out loud, certain this was a joke, but everyone looked at her as if she must be mentally defective, which, probably, she was.

A baked fish was set out, with a special white-corn polenta and broccolini. The conversation turned to politics, and the Republicans were eviscerated in a few quick phrases. All too easy, just another way of looking away from problems too frightening to approach. President Bush talked about *the enemy* without being able to say who the enemy was. People believed him because they didn't know enough to doubt him, and they needed something to believe in. The money that could have been spent on education was spent on war . . . in which the ignorant were dying. The Democrats weren't doing any more about it than the Republicans, and Charlotte wasn't doing any more about it than the Latrousses. Probably that was why they infuriated her. She missed Fiona sharply and glanced around, spotting things she'd like to bring home for her—a malachite frog crouched in a potted plant; a molted horseshoe crab shell, thin as parchment, that she could have slipped into her pocket unnoticed.

"My cleaning lady's brother comes home next week," Mrs. Latrousse was saying, in her deep, cultivated, savage voice. "*Not* in a box, though he'll wish he were. Head wound. Pass the broccolini, Selwyn. Twenty-three years old, enlisted September twelfth. His parents are gone; his sister will have to manage it, somehow. Selwyn, the broccolini . . . ?"

Across the table someone was speaking of Joan Didion with a tender disapprobation, as if she were a rebellious niece. Over the salad Latrousse got in that Salman Rushdie had blurbed his son's book. However, there was a professor of physics two seats down whose son had a blurb from Coetzee.

"What is it about?" Charlotte asked.

"Who can say what a book is about?" Henry said, irritated. She was constantly pulling a conversation down out of the theoretical stratosphere. He was always in danger of embarrassment. She blushed—it was true no one else had asked; maybe the man's son, and the book, were so famous it was wrong of her not to know.

"It's a history of man's relation to the animal kingdom," the physicist said, his eyes brighter for Charlotte's interest.

"*Disgrace*—what a book," Henry said. "Coetzee doesn't waste a word."

"And certainly he doesn't waste a feeling," Charlotte said. "In fact, there's no feeling in that book at all." Poor Coetzee was about to take the blows she meant for Henry. "Really, it was less a book than a dia-

gram." This might have crossed her mind once before, but she felt it
with a vengeance now, and saying it was nearly as effective a rebellion as putting two carrot sticks in her nostrils and intoning, "I am
the walrus," something she dearly wished to do. Henry looked as if
she had, but the physicist, having begun to tell his story, was ready to
continue, and she turned to him.

"Why did your son take up that subject?" she asked him, and
while the others discussed Coetzee he told her how as a very young
child his son would pull caterpillars apart as if they were toys; then
empathy came over him, and his curiosity, interwoven with guilt, became a larger fascination. The physicist had a large, bald head and
gray complexion, and he had made Charlotte think of a mushroom,
but as he talked about his son, his face came alive and it was only
natural to love him.

"I'll get a copy," Charlotte said. "Henry's writing about cruelty
too."

"Coffee?" Mrs. Latrousse was asking. The physicist asked for
cream, but the cream had turned.

"I'll run to SixMart," Charlotte said. "It will only take a minute."

"I think I have some Cremora," Mrs. Latrousse said, rooting in
the back of a cabinet.

"Really," Charlotte insisted, thinking greedily of all the air she
was about to breathe. "I'm happy to go."

She resisted the urge to run home and give Fiona a quick kiss. Or to run
home, grab Fiona, and head away, away, away. But you can't run away
from the place you've just run away to. And she wanted to bring the
physicist some little gift, in return for his being so human. The SixMart
smelled of gasoline and coffee; she loved it. And the rack of tabloid
newspapers, and the jar of bloated pickles in brine. Della was at the

cash register; her café was struggling, so she was doing some nights at SixMart to make ends meet. The bus from Boston had just pulled away, and the people who'd gotten off—a middle-aged couple who looked as if they must have been homeless for some time—made their way to the back of the store and began kissing each other against the dairy case. The man pushed the woman's gray, greasy hair back with both hands so he could look into her eyes. Neither of them noticed Charlotte, lingering beside the Doritos, not wanting to interrupt them.

The bell on the door jingled: Darryl.

"Della!" he said. "Any winners so far?" Everyone asked, on the guess that there must only be a few winning scratch tickets on each roll.

"No, darlin'," Della said. "We save all the winners for you."

"Hello," Charlotte said, from behind him.

He wheeled around. Her voice had an effect on him too. She had her parka on, but he took in the polka-dot dress, the high-heeled boots. He was wearing a green sweater with his name machine-stitched above the logo of a local electrician.

"We were at a dinner party. They needed some cream for the coffee, so I . . ." She explained and explained, as if she were very, very guilty—of course, she'd grabbed the chance to go to SixMart because she'd seen him going into AA, and known he would likely stop there after. His eyes darted around the room as if he were checking for spies. They'd both have been less jumpy if they were stealing plutonium to sell on the international black market.

Darryl glanced purposefully toward the door and Charlotte nodded, following him out to his truck.

She took a deep breath. "Did you get my letter?"

He nodded. "I didn't . . . I couldn't think how to respond," he said. "I can't stand to call; certainly I couldn't write . . . I . . ."

"Darryl, do you not want to see me?" An idiotic question. He'd kissed her. He'd stood her up. He'd breathed his hopes and fears into her ear over the phone. He'd avoided her as if she were a live wire carrying about a hundred thousand volts.

"Oh, my God—no, no, I don't. I don't. I mean—I do, but . . ." Whatever he said in words, his eyes were telling a larger truth. Or that was what it seemed like to a woman who had just gulped down a great deal of Gewürztraminer, umlaut and all. The heels made her tall enough to kiss his mouth without getting up on her toes. The Gas sign blurred overhead.

"It's all wrong, Charlotte."

"Darryl Stead, it is not wrong. It is a gorgeous, amazing, beautiful thing." She started laughing. "All through history," she said, shaking her head, "starting with Eve and Adam, up through every religion, every civilization, women have trusted their senses, and men have lived by, or against, the rules."

But Darryl tensed, as if she were laughing at him.

"It's not all nice," he said, angry, ready to blurt his worst thoughts, how he'd noticed her tits first—that reflexive little rush of lust while she was standing there imperious on this land he'd worked and known all his life; he'd thought of pulling her into that shuttered, creaking old house and fucking her until she was shaken free of all her New York assumptions, gasping and crying and wanting more, Then there was the question of how exactly a strange old man like Henry Tradescome could have come into possession of such a wife, the pleasure Darryl would have finally in saying, *Take the land, the house, the birthright; I've got her.* That was the beginning. It was only after this that he'd seen the way she talked to Fiona, and listened to Fiona, as if a four-year-old's prattle really meant something to her. And found her shaking after the run-in with Tim. The play of interest and concern over her face, the sense that she had seen the best in him, in one glance . . . the shock of love; they would feel it together. . . .

"I haven't got the courage," he said. "That's the truth."

"For you to admit that . . . takes more courage than I have," she said, so quietly she doubted he'd hear. But he was a man who had worked to re-create the sound of snow falling, and he listened to her so well he could barely hear anything else.

He was looking at the ground; he couldn't meet her eyes. She picked at the sleeve of his sweater, where the hem was unraveling.

"Oh . . . oh, I see . . ."

"We're lucky to get out of it now," he said, his arms coming around her waist, pulling her in, to console her. "The deeper we got, the worse it would be in the end. Or, maybe not for you . . ."

"I can't sleep; I can't think about anything else," she admitted, talking into his collarbone. "I think, if we got *married* . . ." This was the bitterest word she'd ever spoken. "I'm too old—you have to have children; I see that—you need someone younger, and how on earth would we make ends meet, and then I think, We'd manage, it would be worth it, because—"

"I've gotta go forward," he said, almost angry. "I've got to . . . find someone, first of all, never mind the rest." The harshness went out of his voice. "Every time I meet someone, I think . . . I feel like it's wrong, like I'm betraying you."

"Darryl, you don't owe me anything," she said.

"I know." He nodded. He dropped his arms and stepped away from her and this was intolerable, like being plunged into ice water, and they pulled each other back to safety. It was some minutes later that Charlotte heard loud, scratchy laughter and saw that the grimy old people who'd been necking in front of the refrigerator case were watching them from the market door. She and Darryl had been there under the Gas sign, kissing as if they had nothing to hide at all.

She arrived back at the Latrousse house with cheeks flushed, hair tangled, and an expression of stricken dazzlement, but no one seemed to notice.

"I'm sorry," she said, proffering the cream. "There were these people kissing against the refrigerator and I didn't want to bother them."

"We're not above a little Cremora," said the stoic Mrs. Latrousse. "Poached pear?"

"No, thank you." She sat sipping espresso on the Eames-era chair, listening to the Eames-era voices around her overlap, each more deeply certain than the last. They had spent their lives acquiring knowledge, the way other people acquired stock options or antiques, and now here they were, showing it off to one another. Henry admired them, and they were certainly admirable, but Charlotte could see only their pretenses, their lack of vital interest in one another, in life. But it didn't matter now her heart was beating with such joy and excitement she could barely hear what anyone else was saying. They might as well have been speaking Middle English. Then she realized they *were* speaking Middle English, quoting one of the lesser-known Canterbury Tales.

24

THE GHOST NET

Charlotte was unloading groceries in the sidelong sunlight of a March afternoon when she heard a sound she'd almost forgotten: the tide sloshing in the bay. She set the bags back in the car and walked down to the water. The ice had softened and begun to break, the pieces swaying together on the movement of the tide. Spring was beginning. She'd lived in Wellfleet for nearly a year. She had a sense of the people around her, even people she barely knew, just from seeing them go through their mail at the post office, or push their children on the swings. When Nikki Miles's brother came home from Iraq, Fiona heard it first.

"Guess what," she said, as soon as she got in the car after school, with big round eyes and the earnest excitement that was her most essential trait. "There's a hero! A war hero, here! His sister is Mrs. Carroll's friend Nikki, and she's going to help him learn to talk again . . . and then, when he can talk, he's coming to tell us about the war!" Of course, Darryl had said Nikki's brother was in Iraq, and it was entirely likely that Nikki was Mrs. Latrousse's cleaning lady, in addition to being the receptionist for the crane company. No one in Wellfleet had only one job.

Charlotte hadn't spoken to Darryl since the night of the Latrousse party. They found a kind of balance, like performers on a
high wire: As long as each kept utterly aware of the other, they lived
in a state of grace. Passing him on the highway, Charlotte would
guess from the tilt of his head that he was worried, or was having a
good day. He was doing his work, she hers. She had started tomato
seeds under grow lights in the extra bedroom; as they unfurled she
felt a little pride, the way she had when she and Darryl were working
together. She told herself that this was enough, but now a soft breeze
was blowing, and half her life was behind her, full of men who had
protested that they didn't really care, men with theories against mo-
nogamy, men who preferred their motorcycles, their newspapers,
who didn't seem to want a woman so much as a doll. Darryl had
kissed her as if his life depended on it. To refuse to take a man like
that straight to your heart . . . well, you'd have to be a fool!

"The cherry blossoms are out in Washington, D.C.," said Henry with
mortal dread, from behind the newspaper.

"Is that a bad thing?"

"It's *three weeks* early." Of course, global warming. No one would
feel this quite as deeply as Henry, who peeked out at life through his
wall of ice. If it melted, the world would end. Of course he was afraid.
Charlotte poured out the last of the cereal—half a bowl of crumbs.

"Would you like a poached egg, Henry?"

He put down the paper and looked at her as if she'd casually
shown him the back road into paradise.

"A poached egg on toast," he said. "When did I last have a poached
egg?"

"Sometime before the cholesterol hysteria. You used to love
them."

Henry pricked his egg and found the yolk just liquid at the center, cut it into halves, then quarters, then eighths, took a bite.

"My father loved a poached egg," he said, his voice thin suddenly. The lines in his face, already so deep they might have been marked with a knife, went deeper.

"My life," he said. "Where did it go?"

"Henry . . ." Charlotte reached across the table toward him with both hands, but the distance was too great, and she had been trying to cross it for too long. She picked up the salt and pepper and blew on them, as if that was what she had intended.

"I guess no one's immune," he said, with a surprised little laugh, shaking off the burst of feeling. "A poached egg is truly a marvelous thing."

"Some of the finest mediums in history have relied on the humble poached egg," Charlotte said. He allowed a smile. Charlotte pulled Fiona onto her lap, rocking her, holding her tight.

"Daddy's remembering your grandpa," she said.

"Crystal's grandpa lives right in the same house with her," Fiona said bitterly. "And they have a ferret too."

"What else did your father like, Henry?"

"Oh, the stock market. Propriety. A really good game of bridge. And . . . trees. I'd forgotten. He knew every tree in the forest. He'd show me how to identify them—the bark and such. The sassafras has mitten-shaped leaves. It bored me silly; I never paid attention. A lot of the trees on Point Road were salvaged from a shipwreck—all those apple and pear trees that bloom in the spring."

"I guess you paid some attention."

"You can't help it; your parents get into you." He cleared his plate and began to wash up. Bad enough that his parents had gotten into him; Charlotte wasn't to join them.

"He loved this house," he said suddenly, turning back to them. "He'd ... I don't know what he'd think if he saw I was living here now, after all I did to break away. And with my *family* . . . my daughter? I swore to him I would beget nothing but books."

A shadow passed over him, a cloud from another century. He turned to the sink again, leaning over it in a little spasm. Then he came back to the table suddenly and kissed Fiona on the top of her head, looking as startled as if he'd just done a cartwheel. And then, searching for something to absorb the excess tenderness, he scooped Bunbury up and kissed him between his pricked-up ears. "Yes, you like the warm weather, don't you, Mr. Puss ... you like to feel the wind in your fur. . . ."

The tide ebbed, taking the ice with it, icebergs the size of trucks that bobbed companionably in the water, like boats when the striped bass—stripers, everyone called them, but Charlotte didn't feel entitled to the word yet—were running. One by one the oystermen came to survey the scene: Bud in the old red pickup he used only for the flats; Jake, whose truck had a cap on the back so he could take his paintings around in it; Trent Mulligan in a huge, gleaming new Chevy 4 x 4. They stood conferring as the flats came into view, like continents on a map, for the first time that year. The familiar landscape had returned, and with it the familiar routine. Carrie drove in with Desiree, rolled down her window to talk to the men, then turned around and gunned the truck up the driveway. The oysters wouldn't go back in for a couple weeks. There wasn't much to do but check the clams, see what the winter had wrought. Someone found a broken lobster trap sticking out of the sand and threw it in his truck bed. Jake started driving all the way around the water's edge, looking for other flotsam.

As the rest were leaving, Darryl arrived. He'd put it off, having

begun to feel about Charlotte's house as he did about the Mermaid—
that it was a seductive place that must be avoided. He watched for
Charlotte always, and a glimpse of her counted as a good sign, like
finding a penny heads-up on the sidewalk. One morning he'd been
passing the preschool and seen her lift Fiona up for a good-bye kiss,
and it gave him a burst of confidence so that he dared call Matty Soule
and take up the matter of the money he was owed for putting the new
deck on Matty's house. Darryl had expected Matty to complain that
the bill was inflated or the workmanship poor, but in fact Matty was
sheepish, said he was sorry and would get it in the mail that day. The
most ordinary, daily magic, and it would work as long as he kept
Charlotte at the proper distance. Get too close and . . . well, look at
Dev, who'd made it through rehab by reciting his mother's recipe for
biryani. Dev went home to his wife clean and sober, and stayed that
way two years, until she left him. Six months later Dev was dead of
an OD. Love was a life-or-death matter; that Darryl had come to
understand.

He waved to Bud and Westie as he drove down to the flats: a com-
radely half salute. As he saw the water stretching away toward the
pinkened western sky, his heart moved with something more solid
than joy. He belonged here: He knew the place by its smell, by the
color of the water and angle of the sun. The seagulls were gliding
over, back to their nests on Try Point; you could set your watch by
them. He parked as far out as he dared—the tide was coming in. Another few months, just to fatten up after the winter, and his clams
would be ready for sale. That would be a big step toward a down payment. . . . The rest of the summer could fill it out so he'd own land by
winter, start to build next year.

As he walked out to the claim, he could see something was different. The sand had shifted over the winter, of course—but he scored

the rake along the top without finding the net. Deeper: Still no net, no clams. He knelt, and began to dig with both hands, at first gently, then like a dog, pulling up handfuls of muck. A foot deep, his hand closed on a shell—round and heavy. Yes. He pulled it up, let a little wave rinse over it—it flipped right open; it was full of mud. A few feet farther on, he dug two fingers in and found the piece of net he and Charlotte had left on the claim back in December. It had become a ghost net, moving with the water, icing over whenever it bobbed to the top until it rolled into a frigid tumbleweed and the withdrawing tide pulled it over his grant like a harrow, catching on the nets over the clam beds, tearing them up so the sand beneath them washed away. In summer the clams would have dug themselves farther down, but now, dormant, they floated up and were caught in the flux of the tide. What few were left had been drilled by moonsnails—every one had a neat hole, as if some ticket collector had come through with a paper punch.

He took one corner of the net and yanked, unearthing it bit by bit. The best he could do was to get it out before it did any more harm. Thinking back, he could see himself there with Charlotte, unable to pull away so those last minutes, as the tide closed over the claim, were lost. By the time he noticed the net, they were balancing the overloaded canoe between them. Charlotte didn't know the waters; if he'd let go of his end, the whole thing could have tipped and all of his oysters spilled into the bay. He knew her well enough to fall in love with her, to feel as if he were pulling bliss itself toward him when he kissed her; he just didn't know her well enough to trust her with the damned canoe. So he had left the net in the water. If the cold hadn't come so fast, it would likely have washed out with the tide, become another piece of flotsam in the vast continent of junk swirling in the sea. If . . . Oh, he could feel it now, how easy it would have been to take the few steps over to retrieve it. He'd been wrong to leave the net, wrong in the smallest way, and still it had come back to get him. Two years' crop, two years' labor, two years of reminding himself every day that if he worked patiently the results would confirm him as a solid, honest man. All of it was gone.

Charlotte had kept away from the window. The house was a fishbowl with its big old windows set across from one another; it seemed that if Darryl looked up from the beach, he would see right through to her heart. And the loneliness, the yearning there . . . no one would want to see that. So she kept busy in the kitchen, making brownies with Fiona, thinking of the biryani that had saved Darryl's friend's soul. Almonds, raisins, jasmine rice—she could see how a man could find his way out of a wilderness by repeating such a recipe over and over. The thought of Darryl planting his oysters had the same effect on her. That he was out there working meant there was an orderly goodness in life, just as the crocus tips proved that spring, and hope, would always come around again. She would not have believed that he could lose half of all he'd worked for without her sensing it. When she heard his truck come up the driveway she steeled herself, knowing he wouldn't stop—but she felt as if some thread of herself were caught on his button and she would unravel as he drove away.

The sunset cast a pink light over everything, with blue shadows behind it. Some of the icebergs had been left on the beach and caught the colors in every hollow, like Monet's haystacks. Once the men were gone, Charlotte took Fiona out to explore them.

"It's spring, it's spring!" Fiona cried, climbing to the top of the highest one, twirling, sliding down the side. "Oh, Mom, I forgot there was anything but winter!"

She ran along the beach, trying every iceberg, like Goldilocks—on a flat-topped one she made a snow angel; on another they drew a door and windows, then burrowed in until it collapsed around them. The tide was coming in; the first wave turned, then another, the sound of the world starting up again. Everything was possible. It was cowardly to let love lie around unused. She ought to find Darryl, insist on ... well, something. A heron coasted down, landing at the edge of the Narvilles' koi meditation pond, leaving with a long and undoubtedly very pricey goldfish wriggling in its bill.

When they got inside the phone was ringing.

"Andrea, hi!" Charlotte said. "How are you? How was the Georgia winter?"

"Oh, it's drab down here," Andrea said. "No snow, none of the atmosphere you get up there. Charlotte, I've got a favor to ask you."

"Of course." Favors were good—they implied trust, kindnesses given, bound to be returned. "What can I do?"

"Listen, honey, can you keep Fiona off our part of the beach? I mean, really we don't mind a child, and especially when we're not even there." She gave a dizzy, nervous little laugh. "But right now, with the decision just in, we've got to enforce it pretty strictly. You know what I mean—first it's a child playing, then a family walking by on the beach; then suddenly they're counting it as an easement and farming on *our land!*"

The floor dropped from beneath Charlotte's feet. "So, you won the case?"

"Well, it's pretty cut-and-dried," Andrea said. "Truro's just ten miles up the beach. It's not likely they'd have a different rule for Wellfleet."

"I suppose not."

"Those icebergs do look pretty tempting," Andrea said, changing the subject.

"What? How do you know?"

"My security cam," she said brightly.

"Your security cam?"

"Yeah, you know, the little cam that scans for burglars? We got one for the waterside too." Charlotte tried to think of a reply and failed.

"Don't you have a cam?" Andrea asked. "I don't know anyone who doesn't have one down here."

"I don't know anyone who does."

"Listen," Andrea said, her velvet glove slipping, her voice harsh. "No one benefits more from this ruling than you do. The size of your property just doubled. I'd think you'd be grateful."

"I don't want that land!" Charlotte said. "I have no use for a piece of tide bottom. I like seeing the oystermen out there."

"So I hear."

25

A TOURIST

The Driftwood Cabins were laid out along a grid of rutted dirt roads on the back side of Point Road, the side away from the water. It was better than the trailer park, or that's what people said. At least these were houses, or miniature replicas of houses, with peaked roofs and real front porches. The driveways held pickup trucks whose ladder rails, like antlers, communicated their owners' station in life. Charlotte could easily have walked there, but it felt so foreign, she was glad to be safe in the car. Some boys were kicking a soccer ball back and forth across the road and they stopped to let her through, their postures wary and menacing. The second she passed, one kicked the ball straight at the car, and a cheer went up as it bounced off the bumper.

The Very Honorable Truck, with its very modest ladder rails, sat beside the plainest of the cottages, and when Charlotte saw it, fear spilled through her. But then, fear was always spilling through her— if she allowed it to stop her she'd be living under the bed. She ought to tell Darryl about Andrea's call. And she had to see him, to look into his eyes and be sure his feelings hadn't changed. In the rearview mirror she saw the boys watching her, wondering—a strange car was news here. She pulled in behind the truck, got out, and, feeling almost too self-conscious to walk, went up the front steps. The storm door had no glass in it, so she reached through it to knock.

No answer, but the truck was here and Darryl must be with it. She tried again. The dog in the next yard barked cholerically, wagging its tail at the same time. The world was backward, upside down, she was wrong to be here; everything was wrong. She kept knocking, for lack of a better plan.

A woman popped her head out the next-door window. "Shut up, Digger," she said wearily to the dog, and to Charlotte: "You looking for Darryl? I think he's at Carrie's." She pointed across the road to one of the larger cabins, a buzzing hive with an old Chevy in the yard, oyster gear brimming out of the garage, a faded plastic playhouse lying on its side in the last little crust of snow. A diapered creature came flying out of the house toward Charlotte, followed by little Timmy, then Carrie.

"Mrs. Tradescome," Carrie said—sneered.

"I . . ." Charlotte said to Darryl, who was last out the door, his face unreadable . . . or no, unwelcoming. "I . . . I came about the oysters."

"What?"

"You were going to sell me some oysters?" she said, lying by impulse. Business between them wasn't as suspicious as friendship.

"At this time of year?" He squinted, scratching under his chin, trying to figure it out. He seemed nothing like the man who had whispered his secrets into her hair.

An old white van came jouncing up the road and the driver jumped out almost before it had stopped. Desiree, Carrie's daughter, ran past them carrying a fishbowl tight against her pregnant belly. "It spilled when I stopped at the light," she said, leaping up the front steps into the house. "How long can a fish live out of water?"

"You can't just run tap water over a fish, can you?" Charlotte asked, but no one answered.

"Let's go across the way to my place," Darryl said carefully. "I do have a barrel of oysters out back. I'd be happy to sell you some. How'd you find me?" This he said loudly, to show everyone he hadn't given her his address. She looked at him, questioning, and his face warned her of something, so she kept quiet, kept a distance behind him as they crossed back to his place.

"They know," he said, as soon as they were inside.

"What do you mean, they know? Know what?"

"About us," he said, pulling her into the living area to stand in the corner between the windows so no one would see her. The curtains were stapled to the window frames; the walls were one board thick. For one week in the summer, it would have been sweet. After that the ceilings would seem lower, the rooms darker every day, and when you swatted a fly and the whole place shook, or the shower pipe froze because it was right against the outer wall so the heat from the woodstove couldn't compete with the icy air outside . . . you'd be reminded every day that you lived here because you didn't have anyplace else to go.

"Well, could they tell me? I mean, is there an *us*?"

Darryl had backed against the far wall, to stay safe from physical magnetism.

"Carrie saw us the other night."

"What other night?"

"At the SixMart. *Outside* the SixMart? She drove by . . . and now they all know."

"But . . . we barely know it ourselves."

True, but they were living it; Carrie had only been driving by. In the pool of light under the Gas sign, she had seen something so ordinary as to be perfectly recognizable—an unreasoning kiss, the kind that happens in a gas station parking lot because it has nowhere else to go. It would have caught Carrie's eye in any case. Wellfleet was a small town; it worked like a novel—when Jake had tea instead of coffee at the SixMart one morning, word had gotten around pretty quickly that he was seeing the British woman who'd rented the house on the end of Try Point, hoping to recover from her broken marriage. How else would tea even cross his mind? The speculation had, as usual, been true.

"It makes good gossip," Darryl said.

Charlotte's heart sank to think how true this was. When Carrie was young, women from out of town were spoken of as "New York whores," as casually as they were called washashores now. Carrie had never been to New York. And Darryl—well, he'd gotten off-cape, all right. All the way to Hollywood, with the result that he had his detox at Betty Ford, while Tim got his in the Barnstable County jail.

"We're innocent?" she tried. Darryl shot her a fond, skeptical smile.

"We are!" she insisted. "We can't help what we feel, and we can hardly be accused of *doing* anything."

He pulled the curtain over the couch back and checked out the window to be sure no one was looking—not the gesture of an innocent man.

"We were both wearing down jackets!" Charlotte protested. "It was, like, us and twelve geese! *That* is innocence. Either innocence or, you know, bestiality." Talking steadied her; she wasn't sure she could stop.

He laughed. "You'd make a good lawyer," he said, shaking his head. "Everyone is talking about it. Rob Welch says, 'You've got something going with Charlotte Tradescome, eh?'"

"Rob Welch is the cop whose ear got bitten off?"

"Well, not all the way off."

"Oh, that's okay then . . ."

"Of course, I told him I had no idea what he was talking about," Darryl said, righteously. "I mean, I suppose he could have meant something else . . ." he said.

"Like what, that we've got a money-laundering business together?"

He smiled and shook his head.

"I don't care if they do know," she protested. "We like each other more than we're supposed to. I'm not going to feel guilty about it."

"Feelings aren't facts," Darryl said. He was wearing his canvas jacket, and as he spoke he reached into the pockets and turned them out in a gesture so eloquent it was hard to believe it was unconscious. He couldn't afford her. "I learned that in rehab. . . . I mean, it's not like we're . . . adulterers, or anything. It's just a feeling."

An AA platitude; it cut her heart. To reckon with feeling, awkward and foolish as such reckoning would always be . . . to work to be honest and good and aware of your own naked humanness . . . and not have a single shred of Yeats to cover yourself . . .

"You're an angel . . ." she said, reaching toward him.

He flinched back. "Everything's against us."

"What do you mean?" She spoke quietly; his frustration seemed at the point of exploding.

"I wiped out my clams," he said. "That I've been growing two years . . . the day we went out, in the fog, we . . . I . . . left the net out there and it froze and tore up the whole claim."

"Oh."

"A mistake I wouldn't have made if I'd been paying attention and not screwing around with you."

"I . . . I'm sorry."

"It's not your fault," he said, stoic. "But the clams are gone and they're half my crop. It's just . . . it's like the clearest sign."

"The Narvilles won the suit," she blurted. "Speaking of bad signs."

"Where'd you hear that?"

"Andrea called. She's got a little security camera focused on the beach. She wanted me to keep Fiona off her land."

"You're kidding."

"I couldn't think something like that up."

He smiled. They were on the same side again and both relaxed, so that all the natural affection came back into their hearts, and their faces. "Could you move your claim so it's in front of our place?" she asked.

"That's where Westie and Jake are. . . ." That's right, she was really the mistress of the big house now, in charge of their fates—they'd be coming to hate her, if they didn't already.

"There's some space on the south side of Try Point. Nobody's been using it, probably because it's a lousy spot . . . but I think some of us can get grants over there."

"Won't it be the same problem eventually?"

His shoulders dropped. "I can't worry about 'eventually,'" he said. "So, why'd you come over?"

"I . . . I had an epiphany. You know, where a truth just pops into your mind?"

"I did go to college."

"I'm sorry."

"Don't be. People assume I'm stupid all the time."

"God damn it," she said. "I thought I should tell you what Andrea said. And . . ." There was nothing to lose; she blurted the truth. "Actually, I came over to throw myself at you. Because I like stupid guys."

He squinted at her as if he thought she might mean it.

"Never mind," she said. Everything was off-key, out of sync, but she pushed on. She'd gone too far not to.

"I had a moment yesterday, while the sun was setting and Fiona was playing on the icebergs . . . or I guess I should say trespassing on private property . . . Oh, you know, the bay was that soft summer blue, and the air was full of hope, and I thought, We can't just let all this feeling go; we've got to get up our courage and take this chance with each other." She was telling it as a story because that was the only way she could keep a little distance. She didn't dare feel it; she was already dizzy and off balance and she wanted to go home. "Because we've been our real selves with each other, and that . . . it's kind of rare. So it seemed wrong to pass it by."

"I wouldn't know what's rare," he said bitterly. "I missed fifteen fucking years."

"I missed them too," she admitted. Safely married, as he'd been safely high. "Shouldn't we be brave enough to at least see where the road might take us?"

"Let me tell you about courage," he said, with an edge of fury that struck a spark in her.

"No, let me tell you. Do you think I've never done anything brave? Every damn step I took after my mother died . . . well, it was like a space walk, that's what. And grad school, New York, getting married, how's that for courage? Having Fiona? While you were sticking a needle in your arm?"

She heard herself fighting with him the way she used to fight with Henry, for some reason she barely understood. "I'm sorry," she said. "I know you've been brave, really brave. I just . . . I want us to talk all day and all night—get to know each other."

They stayed in their corners, looking across at each other.

"Actually," she admitted, "by *talk*, I guess I meant *kiss*."

There was a kind of fluttering, as when a bird is startled out of its nest, and they rushed together. His hand was so sharp in the small of her back that instinct swept over, and everything was as clear and natural as could be. They were lost in the kiss until finally they had to breathe. The air was full of reason and caution and doubt.

"Listen," he said. "We'll talk. Tomorrow or . . . whenever. But we can't talk here."

"Why? Why? Has no one in the Driftwood Cabins ever had a love affair? Are you, like . . . Shakers?"

"This is an adventure for you," he said, not unkindly. "You're like . . . a tourist here. In my life. Here, take some oysters." He made a motion for her to stay still and went out the kitchen door to the back stoop, where there was a rubber trash can filled with oysters, and began to fill a paper bag with them, working so fast you'd have thought there was a train bearing down on him. She stood at the sink, watching him out the window—there were years of grease absorbed in the ruffled kitchen curtains, a tide chart on the wall, and a copy of the *Big Book*, the AA bible, on the table. An old afghan covered the couch; the radio had a wire hanger for an antenna.

"Here," he said, thrusting the bag into her hands.

The cottage was at the back of the land, pushed up against the woods, where the late sunlight angled through the trees. Three glossy black crows dropped from a high branch, flapping to slow their descent.

"You've got a nice spot," she said. "It's pretty here."

"That's National Seashore back there. There's a blackberry patch must be half an acre. Good mushrooming in there too . . . boletus mushrooms and even chanterelles. And the asparagus just keeps coming up—in another month or so I'll be eating right out of the front yard."

He seemed proud, suddenly, of what he had to offer, and his face, which had been shuttered a minute ago, glowed. It felt certain, as natural as a leaf unfolding, that they would walk into each other's arms and make a true beginning together.

"I'm sorry," he said, barely audible. "I can't take the chance."

He peeked out through the curtain again, like a fugitive. A taboo had been broken, a loyalty betrayed . . . not hers, but his. If he could have answered with a nasty laugh, saying yeah, he had something going with Charlotte Tradescome—if he'd been a creep, that would have been fine. The real feeling . . . the man and woman each with half a life's mistakes behind them, who had found each other like two children, without knowing anything except what they could see in each other's eyes . . . that he was ashamed to admit to. If Tim and the others knew he was so fragile as that, they'd never let him live that down. The way Henry's schoolmates had laughed at his hopeless hand.

"Go," Darryl said, and she went, down his steps, feeling as if there were a spotlight on her.

"That's eight dollars," he called after her. For show, of course, but her cheeks burned.

"I'll send you a check," she called over her shoulder as if it were the worst insult she knew. And drove away, home to the house with the tall windows looking out on the bay.

26

A CRIME

He went straight out to the truck. He'd intended to use the last hour of light to build gear in preparation for setting the oysters out, and that was what he was determined to do. The work might be pointless but it was repetitive, anesthetic. He had a roll of the plastic-coated wire mesh—three hundred dollars' worth. He would cut it into three-foot lengths, fold each one, and crimp the edges tight together so it became a bag for the quarter-size, year-old animals. He'd made three when he saw the cop car coming down the road. Somehow he knew it was coming for him, though he hadn't, as far as he knew, done anything wrong. Not in the last three years, anyway. What went before, though . . . any of it could have come back to bite him, and his first instinct was to take off into the woods, but he steeled himself. He turned to face the cruiser as it pulled in behind the truck. It was driven by Rob Welch, of course—he was the only year-round cop the town had.

Rob got out of the car stiffly, slowly. He had a big, soft gut under his shiny-buttoned uniform; police work was about the most sedentary job a man in Wellfleet could do, driving up and down the same eight miles of Route 6 all day. It was a long time since he'd been Darryl's sidekick, growing dope in the National Seashore, way off the trails where no one would find it, selling it to . . . well, there was almost no one they hadn't sold to back then. Rob made most of the deliveries, sticking his neck out because he was too stupid to protect it. They used to call him Backward Bob, because his transmission had malfunctioned and he tried to drive home from school in reverse. No one would have imagined he'd be the one who made good.

"Hey, pal," he said, awkward. "Long time no see."

"Very long time," Darryl said, wiping his hands on his pants, though they weren't dirty, before shaking his hand. Rob's hair, which used to cause an arc of pimples where he habitually swept it off his forehead, was cut to bristles now, exposing the torn ear.

"Got something here for ya, buddy," he said, sheepishly proffering an envelope.

"What, I finally won an Oscar?"

"Yeah . . . that's what it is. Actually, it's a warning. For trespassing. First offense, no biggie."

Darryl laughed. "Trespassing?" He'd half expected the charge to be murder. Or the smash-and-grab on Charlotte Tradescome's heart. He and Rob had a girl they used to visit after school—she was fourteen. They'd smoke dope together and she let them do whatever they wanted. One day she'd tried to talk to him at school; he'd acted like he didn't know her. The look on her face . . . He shuddered. He wondered what Rob remembered. Maybe nothing; he had a wife and two kids, a home of his own on a dirt road off the highway. License to forget.

"Where've I been trespassing?"

"On property owned by Mr. and Mrs. Jebediah Narville, 9 Point Road, Wellfleet. I'm just the delivery guy here, Darryl. You know I don't like it. If you want to keep working that land, I think you've gotta find a lawyer."

"I can't afford a lawyer," Darryl said. He could see himself holding out that handful of half-grown oysters to Charlotte last summer, as if they were proof of the kingdom he had to offer her. Fool.

Rob hitched up his pants. "You've gotta sign that you've read it, while I'm here."

Darryl signed.

"What now?"

"Stay off the flats, that's all. Listen, I hear they're going to open up the flats south of Try Point."

"Thanks, Rob," Darryl said. Rob had a little motorboat; he liked to fish for stripers—he wouldn't have any idea that the bay south of Try Point was short and narrow, with no movement of salt and freshwater, nothing like Mackerel Bay. "I appreciate it."

"We gotta have a beer one of these days. For old times' sake."

Darryl nodded. It wasn't a real invitation and didn't need to be refused. He watched Rob back the cruiser around and bump out of the driveway; then he took the filthy curtains with their neat, once yellow rickrack trim in one hand and pulled them off the window, rod and all. He threw them out the back door, and while he was there he heaved the oyster barrel down the stairs, and was about to rip the door off its hinges when he realized that it was too damned easy. There was as much satisfaction in destroying this place as there would have been in tearing up a sheet of paper. If he was going to satisfy his fury, he needed to fight something live.

He wanted a drink more than anything. Just one. Right. He'd drink himself sick, he'd drink himself to death, he'd be done. And then what about his mother and Carrie? Carrie had Tim, and his mother had her new religion—the Cape Cod Church of the Risen

Christ; she'd been baptized in the Holiday Inn swimming pool with fifty other poor, sad souls looking for a reason to hope. He laughed out loud suddenly, mirthlessly. What good could he do for his mother? She had a one-room apartment in the "affordable housing" complex, supplemented her social security by working as a companion to an elderly painter who'd lost his eyesight and was willing to pay her under the table. She hadn't had a drink in eight years and was hoping her boyfriend, a scrap metal dealer up in Hyannis, would marry her. Every Sunday Darryl had dinner with her, though it made his heart race just to smell the old-lady sadness, the smallness of the place.

He sat down on the couch and opened the *Big Book,* but all its petty wisdoms looked foolish and prim. He decided to drive to Chatham, where he could probably buy a bottle of Jack Daniel's without seeing anyone he knew. When he opened the front door, though, Carrie was standing there.

"Look at this, brother," she said, waving an arm toward the driveway, where Tim stood, with a blank face and rigid bearing. "Look who's home."

"'Lo, Darryl," he said, and walked toward his house, toward little Timmy standing tough in the doorway, watching without a word.

27

TRY AGAIN

Charlotte went straight from Darryl's to pick Fiona up at the God-wins'. She was early, but Fiona was her center of gravity; she had to see her. Betsy's new kitchen was in progress, sealed off behind a tarp, but the appliances had already been delivered and stood magnificently in the center of the living room. The girls were playing hide-and-seek while Betsy considered tile samples she had spread out on plywood on top of the stove.

"Hi, everybody!" Charlotte said in a very cheerful voice, though her face was blotchy, her hair looked insane, and her eyes seemed to be focused in different directions—she could feel a migraine starting up in her temple. Betsy took one quick look, saw that the problem was beyond her, and got busy packing up Fiona's things. Alexis kept a cool eye on Charlotte, though—she was a quiet child, always watching. "What's wrong?" she asked finally, without sympathy.

"I think I'm coming down with something, Alexis," she said. "Or getting over something. A psychosis probably."

"Is that when worms get in your eyes?"

"No. No, it's not."

This apparently was satisfying, and Alexis returned to a favorite theme. "Fiona doesn't know how to play hide-and-seek."

This was true. Fiona's idea of hide-and-seek was that she stood in the middle of the room while Charlotte made a huge drama out of searching for her. She hated being stuffed into closets and under furniture by Alexis, who was brilliant at hide-and-seek and had nearly tricked them into calling the police the week before by burrowing into the laundry basket and refusing to come out when she was called.

"None of us is perfect," Charlotte said, wanting to add: *And you talk just like a spider.*

Henry had been having a good day. There was a new young writer at the *Mirror*—one Moishe Nakamura—"A Japanese Israeli!"—whose perspective was so fresh and his prose so muscular, he was going to draw a brand-new readership. "A paper like the *Mirror* is vitally important in times like these," Henry said, while Charlotte peered into the refrigerator so he wouldn't see her face, which must have looked like a Picasso.

"The *Times* called Moishe up, but he was having none of it," Henry said. "He feels the way I do."

He had not looked at her since he came in. He always averted his eyes from hers. She and Darryl could have been working through the Kama Sutra on the living room floor and Henry would have stepped over them to get his copy of *The Economist* off the coffee table.

"I brought oysters," she said. "Westie was selling them out of the back of his truck. Eliminating the middleman." How she lied! But then, she'd been lying to Henry every day for years, when she didn't tell him something for fear of his condescension, or when he was too busy to answer her and she pretended not to care. The day she stopped her mindless, and no doubt tuneless, singing around the house was the beginning of a long, long lie.

"We don't have an oyster knife," he said. "Not much we can do with 'em."

"Are you kidding? Did the seafaring Tradescomes do without an oyster knife? All their silverware is still in the drawers. We have monogrammed lobster picks, enameled crab crackers, and a sterling silver fish fork in the shape of a cod with gilded scales! Yes, we have an oyster knife!"

Oh, she needed to jam a knife into something. She scrubbed the oysters violently, cleaning them with a wire brush under water so cold her fingers went numb. "You say oyster, and I say erster . . ." she began, and she went on, very loudly. Fiona came running over and peered up at her, to see if Charlotte might have gone mad. By "tomato, tomahto" she was singing along.

Charlotte had seen Darryl open oysters—you held it down with one hand, pushed the point of the knife in hard beside the hinge, and twisted it to pop the shell apart. Like this.

Or . . . like *this* . . .

No . . . like *this* . . .

"Ow, ow, oh, my God, oh, God, *ow* . . ." She had borne down on the oyster with all her strength, and the knife had slipped and gouged her left hand, in the soft place above her thumb. She balled it up tight in her fist—really she'd rather cut off the whole hand now, so as not to have to look at the wound.

"Mama!" Fiona rushed to help, with Henry behind her.

"We'd better go to the emergency room," Henry said.

"Is it that bad?" Charlotte had kept her eyes squeezed shut. Now she opened them just enough for a quick peep. "It's all the way in Hyannis. I had a tetanus shot last summer."

"A tetanus shot," he said. "Do those even work anymore? The diseases are winning; antibiotics are losing their power...."

Eyes shut tight, Charlotte heard him better than usual—he sounded less like a punishing patriarch and more like a frightened child. The planet was too hot, the deficit too big, obesity ballooning, diseases winning out against cures.... You never knew when suddenly you'd be imprisoned in an iron lung ... by parents who didn't know what a child was ... who wouldn't think you might be lonely and terrified, who would tell you how lucky you were.

"Henry, was the iron lung here, in this room?"

"What? Yes, right in the middle. At night I'd hear the mice running over the rafters.... What does that have to do with this?"

"Oh, never mind." She sat up and opened her eyes. "Bleccch—it looks awful, but it doesn't look life-threatening. Fiona, can you get me a Band-Aid, and the ointment I use for your cuts?"

Fiona set off like Joan of Arc. Henry looked inconsolable. "Would you mind making dinner?" she asked him.

"Of course not," he said, happy as could be. She was going to live. She needed him. "Omelette?"

He settled her on the couch and poured her a glass of wine. Shock after shock ran through her: Darryl had acted as if he didn't know her, kissed her as if she were all he wanted, pushed her angrily away. She was back from throwing herself at him and Henry was making her an omelette. Fiona returned, brandishing her first-aid items.

"Here, I'll put on the Band-Aid," Henry said.

"I'll put on the Band-Aid," Fiona said.

"No, no, I'll put on the Band-Aid."

Fiona started to cry. "I got the Band-Aid; I get to put it on."

"Henry, I think Fiona's old enough to put on my Band-Aid, don't you?" She gave him a fond, laughing glance to say it would be good for Fiona to feel she could take an important part, but he had that stiff, hurt look he could get so easily. *He* wanted to take care of her. Charlotte's father had just said, "I can't cope," when her mother was ill. It was something he'd heard on a TV ad. Everyone had said how well Charlotte rose to the occasion, learning to change the IV bags, sitting with her mother hour on hour, and never late with a single homework assignment. She'd been frightened out of her wits, of course. Like Henry. Like everyone.

Henry brought the omelette. "Did I salt it enough?"

"Yes, it's good."

"Are you sure, because—"

"I'm sure, Henry. Thank you. You know, I keep trying to understand why, if the King's Law affects Truro *and* Wellfleet, they can move the grants south of Try Point. Shouldn't the laws be the same down there?"

"'The law is an ass,'" Henry quoted, glad for the opportunity.

"What if the court is wrong?"

He chuckled; she was so naive. "If the court is wrong, the law they make is still law. I mean, it can be appealed, I suppose, but it sounds pretty cut-and-dried to me. I'm sure a lawyer could explain it. I have no idea."

He said it as if it were inappropriate for her to have an idea. She wasn't a lawyer; she wasn't even much of a journalist. She was just a woman who used to be pretty, before he married her, and was in no position to have ideas.

"Of course *you* have no idea. All you ever do is touch up your obituary of Norman Mailer. I have an idea."

And he was just looking at her with that amusement he got when he gazed down, down from his great lofty perch to see her, wa-a-y below, shaking her little fist at him, when Fiona picked up the beater with both hands and struck the gong her great-great-grandfather had brought back from Indonesia, causing an earsplitting thunderclap that frightened her so badly she dove, shrieking, into Charlotte's lap, knocking the omelette off the plate onto the floor. Bunbury hissed and tore up the stairs, and Henry jumped, but in half a second he was composed and wry.

"Mother would be so pleased to see someone getting some use out of that gong," he said.

Love affairs, to judge by books, movies, operas, biographies, and gossip magazines, were so common you'd expect you could order one at a drive-through window. *One great suffering oysterman please, who's lived out his longings to the same music I have, who has the same secret dreams. Oh, thank you, I was just starving.* Russian nobility, French bourgeoisie, senators in high-end hotels, cowboys on the high sierra—how did they manage what Charlotte and Darryl could not? At two a.m., three a.m., while Henry slept with Bunbury curled in the crook at the back of his knees, Charlotte worried this question. Oh, to slip the skin of this marriage, its distance and disappointment! To escape Henry Tradescome, who despised her . . . and adored her, who had spent years now working around the stone of refusal in the center of his personality, to get just a little closer to his wife and child. Just one long night with Darryl, just one!

At four, she got up and went down to the kitchen, wrapped a dish towel around her right hand to protect it, and opened the oysters. It took half an hour to do all ten, but there they were, and she tipped her head back and gulped them one by one as if she were swallowing the sea. Thoughts that had been flitting at the edge of her mind for weeks found their way in finally. Tomorrow she would call Orson and try to figure out how the King's Law worked on Mackerel Bay, and whether there was anything she could do about it. And she was going to try to rent a refrigerated truck. If the restaurant that Rich, the financial manager, had taken them to had served Belon oysters for a price that made Charlotte dizzy, surely Wellfleet oysters would be welcome somewhere else. If Darryl could sell direct to the restaurants . . . then there was a chance to buy a house lot, have his own place, his own family.

The moonlight blazed a pale path across the water; the green light of the channel marker bobbed with the swells. She had spilled oyster juice down the front of her nightgown. She could still feel Darryl's hand at her back.

"I'm sorry, Orson, did I wake you?"

"You sound awfully chipper," he said. "What time is it?"

"Eleven thirty—a.m." And she had been waiting since dawn.

"I never rise before noon, darling," he said. "And may I know who's calling?"

"Orson, how can you call someone 'darling' before you know who they are?"

"Once you know a person, 'darling' never seems right," he lamented.

How had Orson ever been a lawyer? Charlotte tried to imagine him, armed with his squint and his fountain pen, dissecting dry and convoluted phrases, brandishing a telltale comma to prove his point.

"Can you talk, or do you want me to call back?"

"Let me just get my specs out. I find it difficult to hear without them."

"Do you remember the night we had dinner at the Wharf Grill, last fall?"

"Ahhh, calamari . . ."

"Does it come to mind . . . Didn't you say that night that you didn't think the Narvilles could win their case?"

"In matters of law, I am wrong only about half as often as in matters of love. A respectable record, when you consider it."

"So you were wrong?"

"Seems so . . ."

"But you said yourself that it was going to be about the judge's interpretation. . . ."

She could remember this as clearly as if it had just happened: hear Orson's fulsome voice enjoying his pronouncement; see Henry's face, glad as he always was for the company of men. Every moment surrounding that gift of calamari had been preserved exactly in her mind.

"It always is," he said. "But here, there's a clear precedent. . . ,"

"Orson, everyone talks about that precedent. But if it rules Mackerel Bay, what about the south shore of Try Point, where they're going to try to move the oysters? Why wouldn't the same law work there?"

"I . . ." He was going to tell her how wrong she was, how little she understood, how she ought to stay out of matters that were beyond her, and he was surely right. So she couldn't let him talk; she interrupted him and went on.

"Orson, the oystermen had no lawyer. The Narvilles had Skip Godwin, and judging by the new appliances in his new kitchen, he was working pretty hard. Surely a knowledgeable, accomplished attorney could have found something to tip the scales the right way."

"They can appeal that decision, of course."

"But they won't. Tim just got out of prison. Darryl's managing his rent, barely. Jake would stay home and paint all day if he could afford it, and Bud . . . They're all used to living on everyone else's left overs. They're not going to say, 'We have rights here and we're going to fight for them.' Jeb Narville is the kind of person who assumes he's entitled. He thinks, 'I want this,' and then he just figures out how to get it, whether it be a wife or a house or a hunk of money. If that means other people suffer, so what? People suffer everywhere, every day. Skip Godwin, he says to himself, 'I'm doing a job; I'm being paid for it; that's how the world works.' If no one stands up and tells them to look again, they'll all be right."

"I suppose." Orson sighed. "Now that you say it, that's why I retired when I did. I had expected that as I aged I would lose the idealism of youth, that I'd be able to say: 'Life is unfair, but I'm debonair,' or some such. I guess you could say I'm naïve. . . . I went to law school hoping to fight injustice, and then I seemed to find myself perpetuating it. . . ."

Orson had lost his haute-homosexual accent as he talked, and hearing himself sound so earnest, he laughed. "So, I decided to change the letters after my name from LLC to IFD . . . in flagrante delicto. Yes, there are many strange turns on the glorious path to the grave."

"Wanna take another one?"

"My dear, that sounds almost illicit. . . ."

There, she had him.

"Though I doubt there's much I can do."

"Oh, so it's 'not very much,' not 'nothing'!"

Henry had come up to get a cup of coffee and, hearing Charlotte on the phone, had lingered. *Who?* he mouthed.

Orson, she mouthed back, but he didn't take it in and asked aloud, "Who?"

"It's Orson," she said.

"Oh!" Henry reached for the phone.

"No, I called him." Henry's brows knit, and Charlotte motioned for him to go back downstairs, but when he was curious nothing could stop him. He'd gotten a big spurt of blood in the face the day Fiona was born.

"I do still have my license," Orson was saying. "I've never argued in land court, but naturally in my practice as a trust lawyer, the subject of real estate was not unknown to me. But what grounds are there for an appeal?"

"I only know one thing," Charlotte said. "There's land south of Try Point that Darryl said . . . It was mapped more recently, or zoned differently, or something, but somehow people say it's clear the upland owners don't own those flats. Maybe they're wrong, or maybe . . . I don't know, but it seems like, if the King's Law doesn't cover every piece of the waterfront, then . . . there's a chance it wouldn't work here."

Henry was goggling at her—what on earth did she imagine she was doing?

"It would require some serious research," Orson said.

"I'm good at research!"

The corner of Henry's mouth twitched. He had spent a night drinking with Bob Woodward once; Bob Woodward was good at research.

"Where do we begin?" she asked.

"Well, I've got a big book on littoral rights somewhere around here . . . and then I suppose we go down to the registry and undertake a title search."

"How about Friday?"

"*The Rose Tattoo* is playing at Cape Rep. I have two tickets for Friday night, and I don't, of course, drive. I had a different sort of date in mind, but . . ."

"It's a deal, Orson. Friday, the registry by day; then I'll take you out to dinner and we'll revel in Tennessee Williams."

"I shall wear my cloak."

28

THE SHORT HISTORY OF A WATERY PLACE

Charlotte wore the same dress she had when she went to the registry to meet Jeb Narville. She hadn't bought new clothes since they moved in, except the canvas jacket from the church thrift shop, and a serious pair of rubber knee boots from the marine supply store. Tying the dress at her waist, she felt pretty: lighthearted, openhanded, easily moved, likely to evoke tender feelings, to be loved. Why had she ever felt that dress was wrong? She found Orson standing on the tiny balcony of his tiny house, in white trousers, a navy jacket with brass buttons, and his fisherman's cap, and Charlotte couldn't help thinking of Stuart Little's yacht race.

"How natty!" she said.

Orson stood a little straighter. "Clothes make the man," he declared. "Come in for a minute; I'm still polishing my shoes."

The house had been a guest cottage, a tiny replica of a tycoon's Victorian folly, which had stood farther up the hill. The tycoon's son had inherited the big house and gone quietly insane there, driving to the dump every day to rescue broken chairs, lengths of rope, half-used cans of paint, and other perfectly useful but abandoned items, with which he stuffed every single room. When the sills rotted and the back part collapsed, he simply moved toward the front, and when he died, the place was condemned and razed. Orson bought the cottage, kept the exterior intact, tearing down the inner walls so the place felt like a studio apartment, all white and open with the bed in a loft space above the kitchen.

"Come up," Orson said. "From the balcony you can see whales frolicking." This seemed unlikely, as they were three blocks inland, but Charlotte went up the narrow staircase and found that by leaning out to the left she could see, over the rooftops, a wedge of sea. Suddenly a great cloud of mist puffed up in the middle of this view.

"Oh!"

"Did you see a spout? They've been having a marvelous time this morning. Here, what do you think?"

"Perfect," Charlotte said, as she could not say she thought he was a dead ringer for Stuart Little. The opera cloak was folded around a few sheets of tissue paper, its gold silk lining exposed.

"A bit dramatic for our purposes. I'll put it on later in the day."

Charlotte stopped to admire some black and white photographs that had looked botanical from a distance, mushrooms probably, but turned out to be penises of different sorts, in varying states of tumescence.

Orson made a ruminative sound, as if he'd had a second thought, an abashed moment. "My favorites," he said. "Though it's wrong to choose favorites, isn't it—when every variant has its allure. To the registry!"

If Orson looked like a white mouse, Charlotte felt like one. She stood trembling at the entrance to this great hall whose floor-to-ceiling shelves were filled with immense and nearly identical leather-bound volumes. Women ticked in and out on their heels, discovering facts, taking notes, calculating percentages. It seemed that in spite of the spiral notebook pressed to Charlotte's heart, they must see right through her and guess she was on a lover's errand, intent on peering into private matters out of motives most impure. Orson must have felt this way too, because his step was more than usually buoyant, and he looked around with bright, avid eyes.

"I . . . I need to look up a deed?" Charlotte asked of the pigeony-looking woman at the desk.

"Do you have the book and page number?" Her tone suggested that people who did not know their book and page number ranked with cockroaches and must be dutifully squished.

Charlotte blushed and shook her head. Henry's skepticism had been right; she was no more "good at research" than she was at flying. But no—she was timid, anxious to please, and having come from people who stayed carefully within the bounds of their postal route, she was easily convinced she'd done wrong. But it was that same distance from the world that made her so ravenous to know more. She'd been crazy to decipher the world, see how everything fit together. She'd wanted to lift up the roof of every one of those pretty places on Main Street, to see how their inhabitants lived, so she could do the same. And like everyone who was afraid to ask directions, she'd become exceedingly adept at reading maps.

"Then you'll have to look it up by address." The woman sighed.

"It doesn't have an address," Charlotte admitted. Her idea was about to be proven wrong; she would be revealed for the idiot that she was. . . . Henry had tried to save her but she had pushed ahead heedless. . . . "It . . . it's underwater most of the time."

The clerk gazed across at her, deadpan: "Do you know where it is, then?"

Charlotte nodded.

"Then you'll have to start with the maps. Over there."

She had so expected disappointment that she almost didn't know what to do with success. She went where the woman had pointed, knelt at the map drawers, and slid the book on Wellfleet out of its place. It was four feet wide and two feet high, like something in a dream, and opening it she felt small as a child. Here was Tradescome Point, seductive even in this dry portrait, its ragged southern edge torn by the glaciers, the soft northern sweep shaped by the sea. Here was the boat meadow— the grasslands that blazed green out of the creek in summer—and Point Road, with *Oyster Creek cartway* in parentheses, Fox Hollow, Mackerel Bay, Route 6 running just across one corner, and Try Point jutting at the bottom. The map was marked in a simple grid, each square having a number, which corresponded to one of the books on the shelves.

"In the eighteenth century," Orson explained, pulling down book number one ninety-four, going to page forty-three, "ownership was 'purely by use'—if you farmed it, it belonged to you. Ah, but here we are." He'd found a deed of sorts, dated 1824, covering Try Point, Mackerel Point, and Fox Hollow, *all land, islands, meadow ground, and sedge flats.*

"Sedge grows below the tide line," he told her, "so the tide flats, or a portion of the tide flats, were owned by . . . Nathaniel Bellwood, it says, at the time. So, did he sell the whole property to Luther Travis, or . . . ?"

They found nothing until the record of Luther Travis's sale to Isaiah Tradescome, in 1902. The registry had burned to the ground in 1900. "Their version of a computer crash," Orson said. "They had to reconstruct everything, bit by bit."

"So, what do we do?" Charlotte asked.

"Well, at the time, the probate court was in a different building. So the wills may tell the story."

He went up to the desk, threw his shoulders back, and became another man. "Can you direct me to the department of probate, my good woman? I need the records for Luther Travis, of Wellfleet, died ... 1930 or so." His voice was magisterial; it brooked no dissent—the woman who had sniffed at Charlotte became a marvel of helpful efficiency, leading them down the hall to the probate department herself.

"Naturally, given my interest in opera, I felt I should have some vocal training," Orson said sotto voce to Charlotte. "And you will imagine my pleasure at discovering a true baritone—nothing to fill a concert hall, of course, but a room such as this . . ." He smiled. The clerk returned with three thick volumes, for which he thanked her most eloquently.

"Here," he said, "Travis ... 1893 . . ."

Luther had inherited his father's "homestead" and his woodlots. Wood being the heating fuel of the time, these were his most valuable assets, though there was also a cranberry bog, a couple of useless lots on the desolate back-shore bluffs facing east over the Atlantic (ten dollars apiece; anyone who tried to live there would go mad with the isolation and incessant wind), two horses and a buggy, a skiff, and half interest in an oyster cellar. Also, he owned a spring, whose water he had bottled for sale.

That spring became Oyster Creek, a trickle that opened into the wide marsh full of serpentine channels, then onto the flats in the narrow bay. As the tide withdrew, it pulled the freshwater out with it through the oyster beds; as it rose, surging through the marsh, it bathed the oysters in minerals and salts. It was accidental, and perfect, and Luther had owned it all.

Charlotte looked back at Isaiah's deed—*by the waters of Mackerel Bay, extending eastward to a stake and stone marking the common beach, and westward to Sedgewick's Gutter.*

"Isn't it clear, then?" Charlotte asked. "By the waters, *beside* the waters. Not under them."

"That's not the way the courts interpreted the phrase in the Truro case."

"But . . ."

"Let's look a little further," Orson said.

"Why?"

"Because Luther *did* have title to that land. He owned Bushel Point, as it was called then, and Try Point, and the spring, and the marsh, and the bay. He owned it, and he could sell it. So, did he sell it to Isaiah Tradescome? Or someone else?"

"Wouldn't someone know that? Wouldn't it be part of the case?"

"Skip wouldn't want to know it, wouldn't want anyone to know it. And the oystermen, as you've said, don't have a lawyer. The judge saw whatever Skip showed him and that's all."

Charlotte was sitting at a Formica counter beside the window, the book open in front of her and her finger on the phrase *by the waters*. Orson stood behind her, looking over her shoulder. It had begun to snow, a quiet, delicate spring snow that seemed to cover the ground with lace. It was the height of satisfaction to be safe here in this big, sturdy building, beside the radiator, looking back into the world of Luther Travis, piecing together from these old documents how his actions a hundred years ago were dictating theirs now.

"So, we begin," Orson said. "Or should we lunch? The establishment across the street has an extraordinarily well-stocked bar."

They lunched. Orson had two Manhattans, because the restaurant was paneled with oak and had a brass bar rail, and he felt Manhattans fit best with such surroundings. Charlotte had a steak sandwich. Somehow a list of brandies and liqueurs materialized, but

Charlotte was able to slip her credit card to the waiter while Orson was still studying.

He looked up with a distant smile and said, "Courvoisier," as if from a dream.

"I'm sorry," she said. She was just finished signing. "But we don't want to peak too soon. We have an exciting afternoon ahead, and we have to be fresh for Tennessee Williams."

"Peak too soon?" he asked, woeful, but she doubted he was any match for a woman who could disengage a lollipop from Fiona's sticky little hands.

"I think I'll just visit the men's room for a moment," Orson said. "Why don't you go get started? I'll be over in just a bit."

So she returned alone to the probate court, to turn the pages and follow the fortunes of the Travis family of South Wellfleet, peeling up the layers of history one by one. Besides Tradescome Point, Luther had sold several pieces of land for resort hotels. The Sea Witch, the fantasia of turrets and gables set on the site of the old tryworks at the end of Try Point, had been the largest. Much of the Sea Witch had been built on piers and so was carried out to sea with the ice floes one year. Otherwise the only transactions recorded were sales of two cottages on the north side of Try Point to his sons, for one dollar apiece—wedding gifts, maybe—and the little wedge of land between the marsh and the King's Highway, which had become Route 6 later on. That must be Ada Town's house—it had been bought by someone named Carver. Luther died on V-E Day, leaving them the rest of the property, and as the war ended and prosperity returned, they became masters of subdivision. The back shore, with its wide, cold views, was not so frightening now—those ten-dollar scrub lots were split up and sold off, and Charlotte knew them as Sunrise Terrace and Beach Plum Lane, cul-de-sacs where knots of kids waited for the school bus in the mornings. Here was Fox Hollow, sold to the aspara-gus farmer; later, Patti Page would sing "Old Cape Cod" and the era of middle-class tourism began. Housewives who loved being house-wives would have hung their laundry on the pulley lines between the cottages; they'd have worn those dresses printed with morning glo-ries or fat cherries or lemon slices, dresses that just shouted the joy of being home with your family, growing your own little garden, stitch-ing up the rickrack curtains....

Charlotte had the most vivid picture, suddenly, of a little white cottage with blue shutters. There was a white kitten climbing one of the shutters, not a real one, but a porcelain sculpture, and her mother lifted her so she could touch it.... That's right, they had come to Cape Cod when she was very little . . . they had spent a week there in the summer. She might have been four? This one image was all that was left—and a sense of absolute happiness and the excitement of discov-ery, such as Fiona had now.

Henry would have just finished college that year.... They might even have crossed paths, the child and the young man. And Darryl . . . his father would have been just out of the army. Here was the deed to their little house on Shankpainter Road, and here the probate, when his wife inherited it. The mortgages, liens, discharges, as she tried to make her own way and failed, selling the house in 1985 for what did not look like very much. By then Darryl was a lost boy. As Charlotte had been a lost girl, rolling up joints at night and stashing them in the stone wall, to smoke while she waited for the school bus in the morn-ing. Those bleak, stony fields, the sense that she was growing into a world she didn't understand, with no one to guide her. If only there had been one other person, a hand to touch, someone to say, *Let's try it together, step by step; we'll keep each other brave.*

She looked up; the room was hot and stale; the snow melted

flake by flake as it touched the ground. She'd gotten off her subject, of course. She was searching for Darryl; she might look for him everywhere, every day, for the rest of her life. Orson returned, at something of an angle, and began to follow the story backward—to Luther's father, the ship's captain who had bought Try Point in the mid–eighteen hundreds, and further, to Nathaniel Bellwood, who seemed to have used it to pay off a debt. Orson's glasses lay beside his elbow on the counter and he looked up blearily, rubbing his eyes.

"Never study the history of a watery place," he said. "Men dig, they build, they engineer, but the sea overrules it all. Come here; let me show you. . . ."

The map on the wall was from 1884, and it showed, at the entry to Wellfleet Harbor, an island Charlotte had never seen.

"That's Billingsgate," Orson said. "You've heard of it? Billingsgate Light? It was due west of Tradescome Point; it acted as a wave break. Once it was gone, that water started to erode your beach. The landscape keeps changing; it always will."

"Is that why people are putting up seawalls?"

"Are people putting up seawalls?"

"That's what Darryl said. The Narvilles have a big one—Fiona used to catch crabs off it before they put up the camera."

Orson put on his glasses. "You say the Narvilles have a seawall?"

"Yes."

"A real seawall, with waves breaking?"

"At high tide."

"Good to know," Orson said, pressing his palm flat on the copy of Luther Travis's will. "Luther inherited it from his father. He sold the land to Isaiah Tradescome, the piece for the Sea Witch, then here. . . ."

He lifted the heavy book with Luther's will so it sat open between them, and Charlotte read aloud.

"'The eastern half of the Try Point property and one back-shore woodlot to Simon. The western part of Try Point and another woodlot to William.' And there's a rough sketch here that shows the piece he left to each one. It follows the outlines of the shore on both points. It doesn't show the tidal land at all."

"No," Orson said, with sudden understanding. "Because Luther forgot about the tidelands. The bay would have been much deeper when Luther inherited it. Deep and still, protected by Billingsgate Island. As Billingsgate broke down, Mackerel Bay silted up. It became too shallow for a proper mooring, and besides, by then boating was a hobby, not a necessity anymore. The bay was of no use to anyone, except as a view. So Luther forgot it, and when he drew the map, he left it out."

"He forgot it? How . . . ?"

"Look at this," Orson said. "Look at all he had—the stocks and bonds, the oyster cellar, the horses, a letter from Napoleon Bonaparte—I'd like to get a look at that!—paintings acquired in Shanghai and Brindisi. . . . What did he care about the mudflats of Mackerel Bay? And so . . . here it's explained: 'All that remains of my holdings, as may be fit for the use of man, I leave to Reverend Oliver Stewart of the First Congregational Church, in gratitude for his immense and selfless services rendered to the town of Wellfleet, and to my family in particular.'"

"So the tide flats belong to someone named Oliver Stewart?"

"They did forty years ago. Pastor Stewart was Ada Town's father . . . adoptive father, I mean."

Pastor Stewart's will was in another book, from a later time, and Charlotte was surprised to find that typescript looked just as old-fashioned by now as the scrolled handwriting of the earlier generations. More moving, in fact, because it reminded her of Henry.

Pastor Stewart had sold off most of his land before he died, and his will divided all of his considerable investments equally among his natural children.

Orson kept reading aloud: "'All that remains, including the parcel of land at the head of Mackerel Cove, known as the Red House and described in book six eleven, page three seventy-three of the Barnstable County registry of deeds, I leave to the foundling Ada Town.'"

"Mackerel Bay belongs to Ada Town?"

"He never sold it to anyone else, nor does he mention it in his bequests, and he left everything that was left over to Ada. He probably wasn't even aware he owned it."

"Orson! Then all we have to do is convince Ada to let them keep working the flats, and Darryl will be okay!"

Orson looked at her with great tenderness. "Is that what we've been doing?" he asked. "I wasn't sure."

Charlotte nodded involuntarily, looked quickly away.

"My dear," Orson said gently, formally touching her hand as he made his suggestion. "Would not one night of carnal ecstasy be a more appropriate remedy for this dilemma?"

"I'm not sure one would do...."

He nodded, in sympathy, and gave his own version of a prayer. "May we live forever to watch life unfold. And meanwhile, a drink."

"A drink!" Charlotte echoed. "To Darryl Stead, and all men and women who work daily for small gains!"

"And the beautiful shoulders they earn thereby!" Orson said, linking his arm in hers.

"You've got nice shoulders yourself, Orson," Charlotte said. "Especially after today."

29

ALL THAT REMAINS

"Oh, he didn't leave me anything but the house and the furniture, that sort of thing," Ada said. "I mean, he and his wife raised me along with their own children. I could hardly have asked for more." They were in her parlor, in the little red house looking out over the boat meadow. Ada sat in a straight-backed chair beside a secretary desk whose pigeonholes were crammed with old papers, Charlotte on the edge of a very hard velvet settee. This house, like Henry's, seemed arranged to thwart comfort, and Charlotte thought of the Narvilles' state-of-the-art hot tub—times had changed; they would change again.

"And I was a girl . . . he assumed I'd marry."

"But you never did."

Ada darted a quick look into Charlotte's face, but they were sitting up too straight for confidences. "No," she said quietly. "I never did."

"So you've always lived in this house."

"Yes," Ada said. "Or from the time I was about twelve, when we moved from the parsonage. Even when I was young I always preferred to be here, at home. I suppose my first few weeks had enough adventure for a lifetime."

So this door was open a little. "Is it true that someone brought you in from a ship?"

"That's what they say," Ada said. "Of course, I don't remember, but my father used to tell me it was a bright, moonlit night, and he thought he heard someone rowing in the harbor. Then he found me on the doorstep—all swaddled and nestled in a lifesaving ring."

"A lifesaving ring?"

"They were made of cork back then, you know. I don't suppose they had a basket on shipboard. They had to make do."

"Did it say the ship's name?"

"Not that I know of, but of course I never saw it."

"Your parents didn't save it?"

"They weren't sentimental," Ada said sharply, as if Charlotte had insulted them.

"Do you still wonder—about your real parents and everything?"

"Oh, no," Ada said quickly, her delicate hands folded in her lap. She was a lady, and if she wondered at all, she certainly would not be caught doing so in public. But her smile looked wistful. "It's so long in the past," she said. "There were lots of orphans back then. It was hardly worth remarking."

"That's funny," Charlotte said. "I grew up in the same house with my parents, and I still wonder about them all the time."

Ada's eyes sparkled. "I used to imagine they were from some exotic place, Japan or maybe India. . . ." She held out her translucent, thick-veined hand and smiled. "Not very likely. In fact, people who didn't know better were always telling me I resembled my father— Pastor Stewart, I mean. Most people don't look very closely at life . . . they only see what they expect to. After all, you're not supposed to stare." She spoke lightly, mischievously—then she blinked and her pale eyes focused out the window again.

"So you never found out . . ."

"I'm Ada Town," Ada said, almost by rote. "The town's daughter. The baker used to give me a slice of bread out of the oven whenever I went by—'I'm just one of your fathers, Ada,' he'd say. I suppose it made me think more about mothers and fathers and what they do, than most people. I always felt sad for my mother. I suppose she didn't believe she could care for me, so she sent me away."

"It changes you forever, having children," Charlotte said, with a moment's clear sense of this. "If I were young and alone, and it was the year nineteen . . ."

"Twelve," Ada finished. "I was born in 'twelve. Of course, we don't know when exactly, but I arrived on the church steps on Midsummer's Eve, so that was the day we celebrated."

"Why there?" Charlotte asked. "I mean, why do you suppose?"

"If the Congregational Church hadn't been built where it was, I might have been a Methodist. But you can see the Congregational steeple from all the way across the harbor, and if you moored east of the wharf in Duck Creek it would be the most natural thing in the world to go up the alley there. . . . It comes out right across from the church steps. Every kind of problem found its way to a church doorstep, back then. The pastor was doctor, lawyer, social worker, even a banker in hard times. The woman who owned this house left it to my father—he'd taken care of her during her illness."

"Who was that?"

"Emmy Carver. She was a Stead, somehow, I believe . . . but, oh, that was long ago, and she didn't have children, so I don't suppose anyone thinks of her anymore. It was a sad little house back then, and they built the highway right at the back of the yard, but what you see out the window . . . as my father used to say, God shows himself by the waters of Mackerel Bay."

It was high tide. The water had spilled from its winding channels and flooded to the tops of the spartina in the boat meadow. To see it was to feel what it would be to have all you wanted from life.

"It's true," Charlotte said, thinking of Darryl. "Did you know he was going to leave the house to you?"

"No, no. I admit I was surprised. He tried to divide his property fairly between the boys—they were men by the time he died, of course. I've wondered if he just forgot to put it down, when he was parceling everything out. He only left 'the rest' to me. He never mentioned any land."

"So, then, he didn't mention any water."

"What?" Ada looked up from her reverie.

"He . . . Ada, the land the Narvilles sued over—the tide flats at the mouth of Oyster Creek where the oyster grants are, I think they belong to you. Luther owned them, and it seems he left them to the church . . . without really thinking, because the land was underwater. So, when your father's will says 'all the rest' comes to you . . . well, that's a part of it."

"Oh, no," Ada said, with a quick glance toward the desk. "I don't think . . . I don't . . . at my age. I forget things, you know."

"You seem to remember a lot."

"Well, I miss appointments; I lose things. . . . It seems less that I've lost my memory and more that I'm lost *in* my memory. I remember much more vividly now—I can see my father's face as clearly as if he'd been here this morning, and it may be just that I heard the story so often, but I seem to remember the storm that took the lighthouse— that day after Christmas, it was. Deeds, wills, though . . . I'm helpless with these papers."

"I could help you," Charlotte said.

"I used to babysit for Henry, you know. He loved his little blue blanket. He couldn't bear to be parted from it."

"Really?" The image of Henry clinging to a soft little scrap, like Fiona with the lint from the dryer, struck Charlotte painfully. She had always understood that loving him was like nursing a wounded animal. You couldn't be surprised if he snapped at you; that was just the natural way.

"One didn't imagine he would marry," Ada mused. "Even before the illness, there was something . . . removed about him. Life was whirling around in front of him and he just stood there watching because he didn't know how to get on. I'd ask him to hand me the pins as I hung up the laundry, and he took it as an honor." She smiled at the little boy she remembered.

"Ada, let me help you now. I'd take it as an honor. Let's just start and see what we find. . . . We don't have to do anything. Wouldn't you like to know exactly what you own? I mean, we can begin right here. . . ."

Charlotte stood up, meaning to take some of the papers from the secretary, to show Ada how easy it could be. Had she learned nothing from the fox poised outside the window in the mornings? One must keep still, perfectly still. Ada jumped up and stepped firmly past her to show her the door. She wore a light perfume, and Charlotte asked her what it was to stall for time.

"Oh . . . it's very old-fashioned," she said. "Eau de Lilas . . . lilac water. My father bought me a little bottle when I was fifteen and I've always used it. When the company went out of business I bought a case, and I still have four bottles left. I suppose I'll die the day I use it up."

"Ada, did you sit for Henry often?"

"I kept watch over him when his parents were away."

"Where did they go?"

"They spent most of their weeks in Boston, came out for the weekends. But they liked Henry to be here, by the sea. He had a kitten he loved; I remember that."

"You must have been his second mother. Will you come and visit us? I expect he'd love to see you."

"Oh, I don't go out a lot, dear, but thank you." Her instinct was like Henry's: Keep your distance, even—no, especially—from those you love. "Preston Withers is coming to have a cup of tea with me this weekend, and I will speak to him about the land."

Preston Withers was the man who'd been with Ada at the Wharf Grill—director of the Wellfleet Ecological Life League, champion of sea turtles, piping plovers, and hognosed snakes. WELL was supported by donations, mostly from the wealthy owners of waterfront homes, whose interests seemed to coincide with those of the endangered species. Ada's tide flats would make a fine addition to the league's holdings. Charlotte remembered thinking that Preston Withers looked like a pastor—the kind of man Ada would trust. Why would she pay attention to Charlotte, who sat here with her jeans rolled up and her hair tied back in a shoelace, as if she were still sixteen? If she'd listen to Preston, though, she might listen to Henry too.

"It's been very nice to get to know you a little. I like to see you with your daughter—it's a lovely sight for an orphan and old maid."

Charlotte glanced away—the flash of Ada's loneliness was too painful, and the praise made her shy—but she felt the truth of it: She was uncertain partly because of her openness. Henry could press ahead and crush his opposition because he didn't stop to ask himself whether he might be wrong. Charlotte let life flow through and change her; and if this would have made her a very bad critic and a dreadful real estate developer, it had helped her become a good mother, the most ordinary, most important thing on earth.

She walked away down the driveway as the fog thickened into rain. The first green of spring seemed to bleed its tint into the air, and there was the fresh, fizzy smell of the plankton blooming. It filled her with hope, though she hardly knew what she was hoping for.

30

CLASS

She found Darryl in the house on Try Point, working down the punch list before the owners arrived. The smells of new wood and fresh paint, the whine of the saw, were more portents of spring— every shop downtown was getting reshingled or repainted, Sundae, Sundae had a new striped awning, and the Wharf Grill was adding a take-out window. With Speck dead and Godwin departed, Nittle had decided to retire, so Betsy had bought the storefront and moved the jewelry shop there. There was the feeling that a great curtain was about to go up and the town must be ready for its star turn.

Charlotte knocked on the door, though it was open. Darryl was planing a door set across two sawhorses, and he stood up and pulled his goggles off. He didn't seem glad to see her.

"Guess what? Guess what!"

"What?"

"I think everything's going to be fine!"

"Whadaya mean?"

"The lawsuit . . . the shellfish grants . . . you know."

"But how is it all going to be okay?" he asked, with a quiet con-

tempt toward anyone naive enough to make such a pronouncement.

"Orson and I went down to the registry and did a title search, and
that land doesn't belong to Jeb Narville, or to us, or anyone. Ada
owns it, Ada Town."

"How can that be?"

"It was willed to her by her father, by accident really. You can't
build on it, and back then oysters weren't farmed, so no one counted
it as being worth anything."

He smiled suddenly, as if he'd had the same thought she did. You
never knew what something, or someone, was worth.

"So," she went on, "there's more we have to do, but I think we
might be winning."

He was quiet, looking away out the window, and she felt she'd
presumed. "Or *you* might be winning."

"Charlotte, what is it?" he asked, careful not to meet her eyes.
"What's wrong between you and Henry?"

"Oh!" she said, surprised by the question, and surprised she had
an answer. "It's not Henry... It's... me and you, I feel..." Her throat
closed, and he reached across to touch her arm, to reassure her.
"There," she said, "just that, that's what it is."

He shook his head. "What?" He was naturally, mercurially responsive. He had no idea this was something to be proud of.

"It's just... life is so... frightening; there're so many mistakes you
can make, and to be able to be honest about it, so you're really together
in it... it feels like that would be the way with... with us. That's all."

His tension broke and all the sweetest things flooded in; the
room filled with hope and light and tenderness, a love untroubled by
reality. Darryl picked up the door he'd been planing and leaned it
against the wall, so he could walk through and hug her.

"I want to trust you," he admitted, bowing his head against hers. "I do. I . . . Charlotte, there's something . . . I . . . Do you know the letter you wrote me?"

"Um . . . by heart."

"Well, I had it in my checkbook, and I lost it."

"You saved it?"

He nodded. "So, I thought I'd lost the checkbook, but really my nephew took it—little Tim, Carrie's son."

"Why?"

"Who knows? He thought he could write a check on my account or something. You know how kids steal."

Charlotte tried to imagine Fiona stealing someone's checkbook, and failed.

"That's too bad. But you got it back and everything?"

"Yeah, yeah, I got it back. Carrie found it under the kid's mattress. But big Tim got the letter somehow, and . . ."

Charlotte laughed at the idea of Tim reading that letter—she saw a crocodile with a violet in its claw.

Darryl frowned as if she were very silly. "He's threatening to give it to Henry."

"Why?"

"Because he's trying to blackmail us," Darryl said.

"What? How would that work? I mean . . . it's just a little letter."

Darryl made a not very convincing laughing noise. "Do you know why Tim was on probation?" he asked.

"He bit off Rob Welch's ear."

"Yeah, because Rob was trying to keep him away from Carrie. She was bartending at the Mermaid back then and someone told Tim she was flirting with one of the guys over there. Tim hit her so hard he broke her cheekbone, Desiree called the cops, and when Rob got there Tim just went after him. It was when I was . . . away, so she didn't have anyone to look after her."

"She didn't leave Tim?"

He shook his head. "She says it's only that he's afraid of losing her, that he'll never do it again. But I feel a lot better knowing I'm right across the street. When I hear voices rising over there, I go over to borrow some rice or something. It kind of breaks the spell."

"Tim must be very fond of you."

Darryl laughed. "There's faces he'd rather see."

"So now he's turned the tables and you're the sinner."

"I guess."

Charlotte sat down on the front step. The marsh was greening up and the wind struck spray off the whitecaps in the bay. She could see her little world across it: the Narvilles' with the sun blazing off the copper roof on the tower; her house small and plain beside it, with the oak tree Henry had planted fifty years ago just beginning to leaf out.

"Blackmail!" she said. "It's so nineteenth century."

"You're not taking this the way I expected."

She laughed. "Does he suppose I'll pay him to keep Henry from hitting me?"

"Maybe."

"It might be worth a few thousand dollars to keep Henry from criticizing that letter," she said, thinking of the way he would slash his big editor's pen through anything he considered sentimental.

"You don't take this seriously."

"Well, my God . . . blackmail? I mean, we're not even lovers."

"It's the way we looked at each other," he said hopelessly. "Everybody knows."

This was true. Tim, Henry, Jeb Narville—their eyes were like two-way mirrors that allowed no glimpse into their hearts, while Charlotte and Darryl gave themselves away with every glance, and the more they kept apart, the more their feeling took on its own defiant life. If it was not to be acted upon, it demanded at least to be shown. Darryl might nod and say, "'Lo," to her, as he poured out his coffee at the SixMart, and she would answer softly, "Hi," and every single thing they felt would ring in the ears of whoever was standing in the lottery ticket line.

"This is about class," Charlotte said.

"Nah . . . don't be silly." But a contrary electricity had come over them; it made him restless and he went to the window. "What a view," he said. "What a job, looking out over this every day."

"What's it all costing?"

"Oh, God, you wouldn't believe it. Look at this—air-conditioning! Special ducts all through the walls for air-conditioning, in a seaside house. And then the Carrara marble for the shower; that was about thirty thousand dollars right there."

"Did you ever take a shower here?"

"No," he said. "Of course not."

"Right, you shower in a rusted tin box. And Tim wants to be sure you stay there. If he'd found us in a motel room together, he'd be glad you were getting a piece of ass. . . . It's not the sex; it's the love he minds. He thinks you've gotten above yourself. He wants to bring you down."

"All the time I was in L.A.," Darryl said, "Tim was here working, supporting my sister, raising those kids. . . . Now I'm back and you're here, and Tim and Carrie . . . well, maybe it is a class thing. Since before my father was born there've been the summer people and the locals, and we've done the work, and they've laid on the beach. They come and go while we act like the world over the bridge is a foreign . . .

planet... where we can't even breathe the air. And maybe we're right. After all, I left, and look what happened. Look around, Charlotte; do you see a lot of marriages between locals and washashores? No, they—your *class*"—bitter word this was, to him—"they use us for whatever they need us for. Sometimes they need us for love."

"I'm not... You don't know... My father was a mailman! I'm not using you!"

"You brought it up," he said, eyes flashing. Then he closed them, clenched his fists, and took a deep breath. "Ada's my great-aunt; did you know that?"

"Well, the *town's* great-aunt."

"No," he said. "Carrie's and mine. My grandmother's cousin. Her mother—Emmy Carver—fell in love with the Congregational minister; he knocked her up."

"But... the boat. They heard the oar...."

"Oh, Christ, that old story. Pastor Stewart was a very well-educated man. I mean, the guy was used to lying at quite some length every Sunday at eight and eleven. He was the most trusted man in town, and he knew how to make up a good story. He sent Emmy away to work for his brother in Virginia... then this baby arrived by ship. His wife must have guessed it—or maybe not. People don't guess very well about things they don't want to know. Anyway, she and the pastor raised Ada as their own, and the town saw a saint instead of a sinner. Emmy was broken, of course. She came back a drunk, and spent all those years under the minister's care."

"Ada doesn't know this?"

"I've seen things cross her face... but I'm not sure. Certainly no one's back is straighter than Ada's. She's her father's daughter—a Yankee all the way."

"A bibleface."

"What? I never heard that one." He smiled, and Charlotte remembered that he loved her. She had so much to give him, things he would love.

"I suppose it's just another word for a puritan," she said. "A person who's uncomfortable being happy, who believes it's a moral duty to suffer. Except Ada's very thoughtful, so I guess it doesn't fit."

"She's no friend to the Stead family. I suppose we embarrass her. She went to Mount Holyoke, you know. It was pretty unusual for a woman back then."

"So," Charlotte said, teasing, "another Stead who got over the bridge and came back with a college degree."

"She'd never admit to being a Stead," he said, laughing. "Not that I really blame her."

"Speaking of going over the bridge, what if we did?"

"Oh, no, no..." he said. "Oh, no."

"To sell oysters, I mean."

"I sell at the market in Chatham. Or the aquaculture consortium..."

"Wholesale."

"Yeah, wholesale."

"That's what I mean. I think we should take them to the restaurants. No middleman."

"Nah..."

"Why not try it? Why not just try?"

"Because..."

"Because the last time you took a step out beyond what was expected, you stumbled. But it won't happen this time; you've faced it down. It's the bravest thing a man can do, if you ask me."

A wondering tenderness lit his face. "I guess we could try," he said.

31

OVER THE BRIDGE

They set off for Boston on the morning of May's lowest tide. The oysters had been back in the water, south of Try Point now, for three weeks. They would grow slower and taste saltier because there was no spring to mix freshwater into the tide down there; but these had been nearly grown when Darryl set them back out, so they were fat and fresh and sweet. Henry had agreed to get Fiona dressed and off to school, and though he referred to the adventure as a wild-goose chase, he had an admiring gleam in his eye. His wife, who had so often stood still like a supplicant, hoping for his approval, his praise, his love—was becoming her own independent creature. She surprised him; she unnerved him. Even the way she moved had changed.

That morning, as soon as she heard the trees fill with the sharp whistles and cries, the *tick-ticks* and hoots and quibbles of the million morning birds, Charlotte pushed the covers back and left the bed in one swift motion, so as not to disturb her husband's sleep, and went silently down the dark hallway to wash, her feet loving the cool floor.

Darryl had the red canoe up on the rails of the truck and they drove up Point Road to the highway, crossing Oyster Creek and turning off through a grove of locust trees onto a grassy trail just wide enough for one car, then onto the beach. There was not the slightest breeze; the tide was receding without a ripple so it reflected exactly the pale rose and silver tints of the changing sky. A kingfisher was poised on a dead branch overhead, scanning. One plash: He dived, and came up with a fish clamped in his bill. The stillness felt sacred; Darryl and Charlotte kept silent. He poured coffee out of his thermos and she drank it down. They pulled the canoe behind them across the mud, then floated it out to the claim.

Charlotte went down the row, opening the pins, with Darryl behind her lifting bags of oysters into the canoe. By the time the sun was up it was nearly full. Darryl slid the closure off one bag, reached in, and took out a big oyster, holding it up to the eastern light. There was a frill of new shell, paper-thin, around the edge. "They're growing," he said. "They're off to a good start."

By eight they were out behind his place, not a bit shy as long as they kept working. The new leaves were just unfolding, pale green and deep red like flocks of butterflies all through the woods. Darryl put the power-wash nozzle on the hose and hit the oysters with it until most of the silt and muck was washed off, then began to chisel them apart, prying the small ones carefully off the shells of the larger ones and dropping them into bags to be returned to the water at the next tide. He sang as he worked:

> *Feet up on the dashboard,*
> *end of another long day.*
> *Drinking a beer in the church parking lot,*
> *Waitin' for Gramma to get out of AA.*

"Gracious, where does that come from?" Charlotte asked.

"Carrie," he said. "She was waiting to pick my mother up at the senior meeting; it gets out at six."

"I love it!"

"Yeah, there's only that one verse, but I do find myself singing it."

Charlotte sang too, scrubbing the oysters with a wire brush one by one.

"They're not goin' in a museum, you know," Darryl told her, but she liked to rub her thumb over each shell and feel how clean it was. In the end he took one bushel and scrubbed it himself in less time than she needed for a dozen. Charlotte hadn't been able to find a rental truck, so Darryl had lined his truck bed with a tarp and in Orleans they went around back of the rink and took pails full of ice shavings off the pile emptied from the Zamboni, packing it over the oysters, tying another tarp over the whole thing. Up-cape, cherry trees bloomed on the roadside, veiled by wisps of fog. At Charlotte's feet there were tools in case of car trouble—one of the truck's front springs was already broken, which magnified every bump they hit, adding to the general effervescence of the day. They were on an adventure together, the sun, by now, was blazing, and a tugboat was passing under the bridge as they crossed over.

"My heart's beating like we're running away," Charlotte said, laughing, but the minute it came out of her mouth she was sorry. "Not that we are running away, or anything like it," she said quickly.

"No." He watched the road. Everyone passed them; he didn't dare push the truck past fifty miles an hour. Charlotte had the feeling that if she said, "Turn off on 495 and go north," he would, and drive until nightfall, and they'd check in at whatever motel was nearest and have all they wanted of each other finally, and the next day wake up to a truck of oysters rotting in the sun.

"In fact," he said, "there's something I need to tell you. I . . . well, do you remember Nikki?"

"Nikki Miles? Whose brother got hurt in the war?"

"Yeah, that's her. You met her at the Wharf Grill with me last fall."

"I remember."

"Well, we're . . . you know . . . going out. He's younger, her brother; I knew him when he was little, so I've been going over to visit. I put in some handrails for him; he's not very steady on his feet right now. She's all alone with him; he has his veteran's benefits and nothing much else, and he has a grant out near Egg Island. She's been trying to manage it herself but it's pretty tough."

"That's nice," Charlotte said, frozen, stunned. This dream they'd created and kept aloft like a soap bubble between them—it was so fragile they'd barely dared touch it. And now he just popped it, without a thought? "That's very nice of you."

"Nice *for* me," he said.

"Yes, I'm sure."

"Charlotte . . ."

"Don't say anything. You don't need to, really. . . ."

"I know," he said quietly. "You've always understood."

She nodded. "I thought . . . I thought we'd get the oyster business thriving, and you'd get your general contractor's license, and I could write for the *Oracle*, and together we'd . . ."

"Wreck each other's lives," he finished.

"Or save them," she said.

"What about Fiona?" Darryl asked. "What would you have told her?" Past tense, aha. But past tense meant there was nothing to lose; they could talk.

"Honestly, Fiona started it! You watched her the way I did; when she did something funny or surprising, you noticed. You smiled over her little head at me. While Henry was reading the goddamned *Well Wrought Urn*."

"But he's her father."

"I'm not saying we ought to get married today," Charlotte said. "I'm not saying . . . anything . . . except, we like each other; I'd have liked it if we could have gotten to know each other." How reasonable this sounded, as if finally she had spoken a truth.

"Get to know each other!" he said. "I feel like I've swallowed a hook and every time you move it rips my guts."

They suffered one of those moments of knowing, and, turning to each other, nearly forgot everything else. The truck swerved; Darryl pulled it back too hard and it veered into the other lane, within inches of an Audi whose driver honked in outrage and made such a point of glaring that he nearly rear-ended the car in front of him.

"Do you know how many cars I wrecked, in the old days?" Darryl said, when the rush of fear had subsided and they could think again. "Six. Two of them were stolen. Once, I thought I saw some evil force coming at me, and I swerved off the road and went over an embankment onto a school playground. As it happened, it was a Sunday. Otherwise . . . you can imagine. Of the guys I was with in the halfway house, two died of AIDS, one OD'd, three are using again, and then there was Dev. His wife left; he couldn't bear it. One bad moment and you lose all you've gained, and more. I can't take another chance; I can't."

"Here, left lane, Route 93. So, what happened to Nikki's brother?" she asked. "What's his name? And how is he?"

"His name's Bart. His transport hit a land mine. . . . He was thrown from the vehicle, as they say. He's okay, he can walk, and sometimes he makes perfect sense. . . . His short-term memory is shot, though, and he has these hallucinations. . . . He can see light and dark; sometimes he can make out shapes. . . . They say physical therapy can help clear his vision somehow, but we'll see. It's hard on her. Her friends have been taking shifts with him, and there's the VNA nurse once a week, but it takes its toll. She's smoking too much and she's lost so much weight her wet suit's fallin' off her."

"Not good," Charlotte said. They were bumping along the Southeast Expressway while SUVs, eighteen-wheelers, even school buses zipped around them. Their first stops were in the South End—newly chic, with lots of little restaurants. Charlotte had been poring over menus all week, figuring out which places were pleased to be offering cheese from local farms and fish from the Gloucester pier. Full of excitement, imagining they were starting a business together, reminding herself it was no such thing.

"He's a big guy," Darryl said, "and when he loses his balance . . . it's tough."

"It's lucky you're there," Charlotte said blankly. "Here, Melnea Cass Boulevard, that's our turn."

The first place said they got all their oysters from Oregon. "Now, that's ridiculous," Charlotte said as they walked back to the truck, double-parked at a fire hydrant. It would have taken a speedy meter maid to catch them, though—their visit had been half a minute long. At the second place they had to park on the sidewalk, and the cook, who spoke no English, shooed them away on the assumption they were beggars. The third place felt just right: It was called the Sea Grill; there was a parking spot open right in front, and an awning over the sidewalk, as if it were Paris. Boston was farther into spring than Wellfleet; the maple leaves on the new little tree planted in front were fully open. Two young women sipped cappuccino at an outdoor table. In Wellfleet you could spend the morning watching a rabbit choose which blades of grass to nibble. Charlotte had forgotten the cheerful energy of cities: all the different people heading briskly toward their different aspirations. If you didn't keep your eye on your goal you'd be lost.

"Oysters, farm-fresh from Wellfleet," she said to the owner, who was lodged at a table in the dark back of the restaurant, poking at a calculator. "It's kind of the ultimate in local food." The man looked up; Charlotte discerned, amid the hair raging from his open shirt, the glint of a gold chain. She swallowed. "They take three years from seed to the final product, and every minute they're tended by hand."

"You sound like a telemarketer," the owner said.

"Well, it's something I'm proud of," she said, defensive. "Would you like to try one?"

"I'm getting a great deal on oysters," the owner said. "Up from Florida, they grow faster there; they're priced day-to-day."

"But . . ." She had exhausted the man's patience.

"I'm in business to make money," he said. "That's what we're all here for."

And they had a parking ticket. "What the hell?" Apparently there was no parking on alternate Thursdays, and this was an alternate Thursday . . . last Thursday would have been okay.

"It's been worth it," Darryl said, pulling back into the traffic. "We shouldn't see it as a failure. We've learned a lot—if nothing else, we're discovering that wholesale isn't such a bad deal."

"You mean you're going home, after three places?"

"Charlotte . . ."

"No. Darryl, you put in twelve-hour days, between the building and the oysters, all the time. You don't just try three times and give up."

"That's different. We're on a wild-goose chase here; he just explained it."

Charlotte remembered how Henry had called it a wild-goose chase, wry and tender, acknowledging that all life is a brave quest in a wrong direction. No one had chased his own personal wild goose more fiercely than Henry. Charlotte's throat tightened; she looked hard out the window.

"Yeah, he sure told us what big fools we are. I hate being told something I already know. We can't stop at three; we'll regret it forever. We've got something wonderful to sell here; we only have to find one person who recognizes that. I've got nine more places on the list. If none of them works out, we can give up and go home. Okay?"

North Wind wasn't on the list. It was halfway through its transformation from corner bar and sandwich joint to bistro, and Charlotte and Darryl were walking past, carrying the cooler of oysters between them, when Charlotte put her face to the window and saw the big wooden booths around the sides and the menu on a chalkboard—meaning it could change according to what was fresh that day. When they asked to speak to the manager, the waitress sent them around back and they found themselves in a tiny, dark kitchen where a man was sautéing mussels over a leaping flame.

"Mr. McConnell?"

"One second," he said, holding up a finger, sliding the mussels into a bowl. "Now, what's this? Wellfleet oysters?"

He was the first person to say he'd try one. Darryl opened one for him, then another.

"Not bad," he said. "Not bad at all."

"Fresh this morning," Darryl said, so simply, as a point of fact, with none of a salesman's bravado, that Charlotte saw trust begin to grow between the men.

"And how many . . . ?" McConnell asked.

"About a hundred in the cooler here. I've got eight bushels back in the truck."

"Let me talk to my partner." He looked over at an older man who was garnishing a tray of chocolate mousse on the other side of the room. "Why don't you wait in the barroom. Pretty quiet in there this time of day. Have whatever you like."

The bar was old Boston, old Irish, old, tenement South End. Henry would have loved it. Like all good bars it was a manly home, a place where men drank and talked together, feeling truly close to one another in some absolutely solitary way.

Darryl's hands shook; he looked as if he were whistling through a graveyard.

"Long time since I've been in a bar," he said.

"It's nice here," Charlotte said. "It's fine. Look at the jukebox. Look at all this old stuff. . . . God, was there really a time before Fiona?"

"A time before September eleventh. . . ."

"Where were you on 9/11?" she asked.

"Just moved back here. It was a good dry day; we were shingling. By the next day everyone else was flying an American flag on the back of his truck, and I was afraid they were going to lynch me when I said I didn't think we should go to war. What about you?"

"Nursing Fiona . . . at that exact moment. Then it was so loud . . . and then it was so quiet."

"Oh, that's right. You lived in New York."

"I kept thinking the Trade Center would fall like a tree, and the fire would spread like in an earthquake, so I wrapped Fiona up and I just started walking away. People were running, but I had this sense that I had to walk, because I had the baby. . . . I kept my head down,

like a horse in blinders. . . . I wasn't even thinking really, just following instinct—Guard the baby, guard the baby."

"Where'd you go?"

"Astor Place—Henry's office. I had the idea it would be safe
there . . . or we'd all be together. . . ."

He smiled sadly: She'd confirmed his suspicions.

"But . . ." she said, wanting to explain the other side, how by the
next day, caught in the apartment with the poison smell everywhere
and Henry out searching for an open bookstore so he could buy a
Koran, she had felt something bottomless open beneath her. She was
going to die one day, maybe tomorrow, and Henry's bleak love would
be the only one she'd known.

"We were working out by Mill Creek . . . you know it out there?
Big house, looks over the harbor, and it was that perfect day, and we
had the radio. . . . We just stopped still and listened, and after a while
I realized we were all right in the positions we'd been in half an hour
before. And I thought if I died right then, like all those people, my life
would have been worth nothing to anyone at all."

He had his restless look, his hands in front of him as if he needed
to use them as much as he needed to breathe. The bottles behind the
bar shone in rich colors like stained glass.

"Quarters," Charlotte said, motherhood having taught her the
value of distraction. "We need to play the jukebox."

"It takes dollars," the bartender said. He'd been so still there, she
hadn't noticed him—a pale young man with spiky hair and a long
nose, reading behind the bar—Kierkegaard probably, Charlotte
thought with a sinking heart.

"Could we get two ginger ales?" she asked. "Mr. McConnell said
he'd stand us a round."

"I don't think I've ever heard anyone actually say 'stand us a round before," the bartender said. She'd been wrong; he was reading Borges.

"Me neither," Darryl said. "She just blew in from the last century; she talks in iambic pentameter."

"Oh, I've had my shots for that," the barman said. "So, you guys have an oyster farm?"

"Yeah, yeah, we do," Darryl said, with a conspiratorial glance that made Charlotte feel as if the sun had just risen in the corner of the room. She was proud of herself, proud he loved her. "Not a huge operation, just, you know, a family farm."

She'd fed a five-dollar bill into the machine and started picking songs: "Refugee," "Runaway Train," "Crash into Me."

"About love they were never wrong, the old rockers," she said, as Tom Petty started wailing. "'How it arises in violence, out of despera- tion . . .'" This meant nothing to Darryl; he hadn't read Auden. She'd have to repeat it for Henry, who had never heard Tom Petty.

"You see what I told you," Darryl said to the bartender, but he'd gone back to his book. Charlotte found "Sugar Magnolia" and "Suite: Judy Blue Eyes."

"May I have this dance?" she asked him.

"What?"

"We can," she said. "I think we can. It's settled between us . . . we're not going to run off the rails with each other."

He stood there as if he were afraid to touch her, as he'd been afraid to walk into the bar, but she slipped an arm around his waist, took his other hand in hers.

"Lead," she said, and he smiled at her impertinence and did as she told him, his hand sharp at the small of her back, directing her in a waltz.

"Where did you learn to dance?" she asked.

"Oh, I've just seen a lot of movies." The truth was, he was a natural, instinctively responsive to the music, to life, to her. Box step by box step they held each other closer until they were like kids in a high school gymnasium, young again and so new to life they'd feel high on the spring air, and to be this close to each other was just sacred. Innocence—they'd lost it, both of them in different ways. Now here it was back again. And maybe the music would never stop. Darryl held her so tight, suddenly, it was like being clenched in his fist, and everything went raw and a prayer rose in the back of her throat. . . .

"Brian, maybe turn the jukebox down a little?" McConnell was standing in the doorway, and she and Darryl stepped apart, still holding hands for a second, like children. The music receded: Charlotte almost reached out as if she could catch the last notes in her hand. Then they remembered where they were and what they were doing.

"I'm George, by the way," McConnell said. "George McConnell. The oysters are amazing; that's the purest taste I've had in I don't know when. . . ."

"Darryl, Darryl Stead," Darryl said, shaking his hand. Charlotte stepped back; her job was done.

"I'll take them."

"The cooler full? Or a whole bushel?"

"Oh, no—all of them. How many did you say? Eight bushels? I'll make them the special this weekend. I'm not going to cook 'em—it would be a waste. It's just the thing—fresh, simple, memorable, right from the source. What's the name of your farm, by the way? I'll put it on the menu."

"Don't really have one. . . ."

"Red Canoe Sea Farm," Charlotte said. She hadn't worked on Madison Avenue for nothing. And she could still see the canoe full of oysters, floating behind them in the fog.

"Sounds great. Then, say, four bushels a week, until we figure out the demand?"

They walked back to the truck with a careful distance between them; good fortune was dangerous, and if they had brushed one hand against the other it might change everything so they'd drive away from home instead of toward it, into some future where they had each other and nothing else at all. Belted in, they breathed easier.

"Wild-goose chase, eh?" Charlotte said. "I *knew* it would work!"

"You were right," he said, too trusting.

"No," she admitted. "By the time we got the ticket I was sure it was hopeless. I just had to pray I might be wrong."

"A thousand dollars today . . . five hundred a week from now on . . . do you realize . . . ?"

"I see a solid truck in your future."

"I'm going to try to pay my mother back first," he said. Route 93 branched to the right, but they stayed on Route 3, heading south toward Cape Cod. "And maybe I can do something about Tim."

"Darryl, he doesn't really mean to blackmail me?"

"It's complicated," Darryl said. "He was holding the fort all that time I was away, and I'm supposed to have my tail between my legs now, and instead he went to prison and I got you, or that's the way it seems to him. So he likes seeing me squirm. I wish Carrie could get rid of him, find someone who showed her some love."

They drove for a long time, each in his own thoughts. Charlotte was singing the last song they'd danced to—"Runaway train, never going back, wrong way on a one-way track." But they were going back; here they were at the bridge. There was a new bouquet since the morning: crab-apple branches with a long blue ribbon fluttering.

Someone—some woman—honored a terrible grief here, week after week after week.

"It was the plainest little dream," Charlotte said after a long time, looking straight ahead down the highway. "Of just being two honest, searching people, doing the best we could together."

"And screwing up royally," Darryl said.

"Well, okay . . . so that could have been our motto. 'Red Canoe Sea Farm, raising oysters and living life together, one dumb mistake at a time.'" Laughing made it sadder, though.

"So," she said, "it was a dream of a working love."

"Yeah. It's just . . . it feels . . . it felt like a runaway train."

32

CHICKEN SOUP

"Henry? Fiona? I'm home!" Charlotte sank onto the couch. After the long day away her own living room looked like a perfect little chapel, the books stuffed into the dusty shelves, the painting of Billingsgate Light looking proudly over the sea, the vase of white daffodils on the table, from bulbs she'd planted last year. Henry had already set the table for dinner, and all the elephants were off the mantelpiece, grouped into families on the rug; he must have taken them down for Fiona. The clouds were low and ragged, but the sun was breaking through as it set—it was clearing from the west; it would be nice tomorrow. She loved this place, her family, her little spot on earth. She loved the damned *gong* from Indonesia, where the crew had been quarantined with plague, though she had put the beater out of Fiona's reach. A tear was stuck in her eyelashes; she blinked and it ran down her cheek.

Slowly she became aware of a rhythmic sound, a leisurely *thwack, thwack* coming from around the side of the house. It went on, absolutely regular, and Charlotte went to the kitchen window to see that Fiona was skipping rope—Henry had tied the rope to the banister and was turning it, evenly, with his good hand, while staring off across the bay.

"Ninety-eight, ninety-nine, one hundred!" Fiona said.

"That's very impressive," he said, gravely, and she said, "I can do more; just watch me. I bet I can do five hundred!"

"What's this? Do I have a star rope-jumper for a daughter?" Charlotte said.

They looked up and Fiona came running at her with such energy Charlotte was afraid she would bowl her over.

"Mama! I jumped a hundred times!"

"She did," Henry said. "You wouldn't have expected it, but being alone with a dry old soul all afternoon drove her to it."

He came up the steps and kissed her, quick, but urgent and tender, and he pushed her hair back from her forehead with his good hand as if she were an apparition he had to touch to believe.

"What? Is something wrong? Did . . . ?"

"Nothing. I missed you." He tossed this off with a certain defiance, as if to say: *Didn't think I could do it, did you?* The answer was no, she didn't think he could admit to missing her, or any such conventional fragility. He looked as if he'd seen a ghost—the ghost of his marriage, maybe.

"Did—did anyone call up?"

"Betsy, to say the Narvilles are arriving today."

"I guess that was unavoidable."

"So, how was Boston?" He sounded vague, and she realized he had very little idea what she had been doing—his book took up most of his mind and he hated to waste space on other things. All he knew was that some source of warmth had been missing, and now it was back.

"We did it," she said. "We sold 'em, every one." The tellable parts of the story began to perk in her mind—the dark kitchen with flames leaping, the barkeep and Borges, the way she'd guessed from the chalkboard menu that they'd found the right place. Henry always loved to hear her stories.

"Bad news here, I'm afraid."

So she'd been right. "What do you mean?"

"Did you see the *Times*?"

Charlotte shook her head, and Henry's shoulders dropped in disappointment. It was incomprehensible to him that a person could get through a day without reading the *Times*. He produced it, opened to page two, where the headline concerned Spain and socialism. The byline was Moishe Nakamura's.

"I don't suppose there could be two Moishe Nakamuras?" Charlotte asked, and burst into tears.

"Well, he's a man of the world," Henry said, to console her. "He speaks six languages, has a native understanding of two cultures—I suppose it was foolish to imagine we could keep him."

He thought she was crying over Moishe Nakamura. Of course he did. Charlotte gave a fresh sob.

"I'm afraid it's a bad move, though, for him. He's too young yet; he needs to develop a stronger spine. . . ."

They heard the flag whisk up the Narvilles' flagpole, then the whir and clank as the electric storm shutters were rolled back. Charlotte got her breath and went back to crying. "They think they own that land. We went down there to the registry and went through everything, and found out the truth and it didn't matter a bit. The oystermen are still in limbo and the Narvilles still don't even know anything has changed."

She had worked so hard; she had found the answer to every one of Darryl's problems—the lawsuit, the business. . . . Now he could get married—to Nikki. Charlotte sat down on the step. Fiona ran to get her teddy bear and thrust it into her hands for comfort.

"I poached some salmon," Henry said helplessly.

"How did you do that?"

"In a pan of water, like an egg. Isn't that what you do?"

"Yes," she sobbed. Great, her husband loved her. She cried harder, pulling Fiona into her lap with the bear. Henry patted the top of her head, with the hopeless look of a man bailing with a thimble.

"And toasted sesame seeds, on the salad?"

She nodded. The salmon was delicious, and by the time they finished she was calmer. For days, though, tears leaked down her face, welling and spilling, slipping silently down beside her nose. She wiped them away with the back of her hand, laughing, because they seemed to stream from such an abundant, inexhaustible source. She called Orson, who said they had done what they could. He had filed the results of the title search with the court, but for now Ada owned the tide flats and she would have to take the initiative to change things.

The Narvilles had to use Charlotte's driveway to put their boat in, for fear of scraping its bottom on the seawall. She watched from the kitchen yard, where she was digging in a gelatinous mix of watered peat and manure so as to transplant her lettuce seedlings. There was a long smear of dirt down her face where she wiped off the tears.

Henry stole quick, puzzled glances, but he'd have felt wrong bringing . . . anything . . . up. He himself had worked so carefully to keep sorrow at arm's length, he barely recognized it now. Whatever was wrong, it was, like most of life, a private matter. He offered to do the shopping, make the dinner, whatever would allow her a little peace. Tomorrow would bring a change. But tomorrow didn't, nor the day after, and on the third day, Charlotte was rinsing off a chicken to start a soup when she suddenly gave a sort of hissing sound, as if she might be deflating, and leaned against the sink in some kind of pain.

"Are you ill?" he asked.

"Oh, no," she said, grabbing a paper towel to blow her nose. "Allergies. The pollen. Look at Fiona." Fiona was on the beach, carrying armloads of seaweed and spreading them to dry on the lawn. She looked so earnestly absorbed, so purposeful and confident, as if she were quite sure that what she was doing was necessary and important . . . that Charlotte gave up and wept into her hands.

Henry stood behind her, his head bowed in a posture of apology. He didn't know what was wrong, but he was pretty sure it was all his fault.

"I know this . . . this whole land court problem is very upsetting for you," he said.

"That's kind of you, Henry. Don't worry; I'm fine."

"Should I peel the carrots?" She nodded and went out on the porch to sit in the wicker chair and cry. It was such a relief that for a minute it seemed she'd fallen in love solely for the purpose of weeping. Henry came out after a minute and patted her head, with a kind of modified dribbling motion.

"How many carrots?"

"Two is good."

"And celery?"

"Two stalks of celery, yes."

He kept standing there, looking uncertain.

"An onion?" he asked finally.

"Yes, an onion."

He took a step and then turned back.

"Do you want peppercorns?"

"I want love, Henry, and I have endeavored to get it in the most idiotic way, and now I'm apparently about to be blackmailed by a man who's been in jail for biting off a policeman's ear."

"Oh!" Henry sat down beside her, with a dry laugh. "I suppose the soup can wait, eh?"

She nodded.

"So, blackmail?"

"It's Tim Cloutier."

Henry looked absolutely appalled.

"Not that I was . . . involved, with . . . not that I've been really involved with anyone, or I have been, but not in such a way that . . . Oh, I wrote a letter, and Tim got hold of it, and he's said I have to buy it back at some awful cost or he's going to give it to you."

Henry nodded, stoic. Of course, she'd found a man with two arms. He pulled his bad one a little closer to his chest, to protect it.

"It's no surprise," he said, ". . . given the situation."

"What situation?"

"Me," he said, with disgust. He knew so much; it just didn't occur to him that things could change.

"It's not you," she said. "It's . . . oh, who ever knows."

He smiled, nodded. "Aphrodite is perverse," he said, apparently to comfort her. She waited for him to ask whom she had written to; how the letter had fallen into Tim's hands; anything at all. But he was a child of this house, these people. . . . Such questions didn't even form themselves in his mind.

"I will call Tim Cloutier," he said.

"Oh, no, don't. Wait. Maybe he'll back down, or . . . I don't know. Let's see what happens; maybe it will just blow over."

"He's been making threats against *my wife*," Henry said. His anger swung away from her, toward the easier target. A blow against Charlotte would damage his own life. "I'm not going to wait to see what he does next."

He was dialing. Charlotte worked mechanically, peeling the carrots, braced for a blow.

"I believe you've accidentally come into possession of something that belongs to my wife? A letter she wrote? Would you be so kind as to return it to her?"

He paused, listened. "The circumstances aren't of interest to me," he said. His voice was majestically cold; it allowed no argument.

Fiona came flying in the door just then, with her arms full of seaweed. "It's fish," she said. "I'm going to sell it at the market." She'd given up playing in the dollhouse—moving the dolls through life wasn't enough; she wanted to be the doll, to feel the experience, whatever it was. She was always wrapped in a shawl now, pretending to be an orphan scullery maid, or a Bengali spice merchant.

"Can the market be on the porch?" Charlotte asked.

Fiona considered, and deciding it could, hung the seaweed over the railings carefully and went upstairs to dress for her new job. Tim pulled into the driveway and came up the steps like a schoolboy on the principal's threshold, every muscle tense with defiance even as he did exactly what Henry had asked. Passing Fiona's market, he squinted for a second—did the Tradescomes know some way to get money out of seaweed? Henry opened the door before he could knock. Tim said nothing, just held the letter—folded in a tight triangle like a note passed in school—out to him.

"It belongs to my wife," Henry said. Charlotte took it, Tim glaring as if he'd like to spit on her. And on Henry—they were beneath his contempt, a pretty low spot to be in. Fiona came running down the stairs, wearing a makeshift burka, carrying a wicker basket over her arm. Tim looked as if he had never seen such depravity, and went away down the steps, shoulders straight and proud.

Charlotte put the chicken liver in Bunbury's bowl; then she pushed the letter in with the gizzard. It started to pinken with chicken seepage; she threw it away under the sink.

"I do love you, Henry," she said, just stating an old, obvious truth.

He nodded, and smiled at her . . . she'd have said he was shy.

"Either that," he said, "or you are the greatest actress the world has ever known."

33

DREAD AND THE COMMON MAN

On June 23, the second day in a row that Ada Town hadn't crossed the highway to buy her paper at the SixMart, Carrie called Rob Welch and asked him to check on her. He found Ada in bed, her book open on her chest, her reading glasses pushed up on her forehead; she seemed to have simply folded her hands and died. She was buried in the churchyard, beside Pastor Stewart, but she had not wanted a service, and only Alfred Nittle, her attorney, was there to see. She had called him just a week before to revise her will, leaving everything to the Wellfleet Ecological Life League, except for the house and the surrounding land. That was to pass to Carrie Cloutier.

"She's set for life. Ada saved her. She can get away from Tim; she can help Desiree with the baby when it comes. . . . But of all people, why Carrie? Did Ada even know Carrie, besides buying the paper from her every day?" Charlotte and Henry were sitting on the front porch steps with their coffee while Fiona gathered dandelions for the stew she was making. The air smelled of honey from the locust blossoms. Everything was shaggy with new foliage and flowers, and the early sunlight angled through the green shallows as the tide went out.

"Probably my suggestion," Henry said, as if he were admitting a fault. "I went to see her."

"What? When?"

"Oh, a few weeks ago. I took my walk early and stopped in there."

"You never told me."

"I don't suppose I did." Ada was part of a secret world, the world of his childhood. She was too close to his heart. He'd never let anyone see.

"I took her a copy of *Dread and the Common Man*. Obscene, really, that I hadn't done it before." He grimaced with a self-loathing he felt was entirely right and proper. Vestina would have approved. "We talked for half an hour, just the most conventional conversation. She's an admirable woman, you know, never marrying, making her own way. She agreed that Carrie's had a tough row. Ada was not about to sell any land to Tim, but she has something in common with Carrie. We talked about how the town takes care of its own, that kind of thing."

"You went over there and solved the whole problem and never said a word?"

"I'm a WASP!" he said, with mock horror. "Anyway, I didn't solve the problem; I just made a quiet suggestion. A suggestion you gave me. I didn't imagine it would have any effect."

"Was she glad to see you?"

"I suppose so."

"Were you glad to see her?"

"Would have been wrong not to go." That was what Henry had to say about his visit to the woman who had cared for him in place of his mother, whose lilac perfume could change his whole sense of life. Well, he was a WASP, skilled in the lost art of rectitude. He'd worked, after the polio, to become "hard as a ball bearing," so life couldn't take another bite out of him. And lost so much of himself in the process . . . Charlotte scooched over and put her arm around him.

"Was Ada around when you were sick?"

"She read to me," he said. "Hardy Boys. Book after book after book. Does it seem to you that the bay is much warmer this June than last?"

"It's warm when the high tide's in the afternoon, that's all. The sun heats the sand all morning and then the water comes in over it— it's heavenly."

"I don't remember it that way at all," he said, with some ghastly apprehension.

"Well, you never liked to swim. . . ."

"It's nothing like it used to be," Henry said, definitively, as if he'd just summed up someone's life in an obituary and there was nothing more to be said. "The hole in the ozone is much larger now even than they expected. . . ." Oh, he shook his head; he saw nothing but grief in the future. He'd been right all along.

"Was that what Ada was reading when she died?" Charlotte asked. "*Dread and the Common Man?*"

Henry gave a horrified giggle. "I hope not!" he said.

34

BY THE WATERS

"You have a tomato in your hair."

"What?"

"You've got a tomato tangled in your hair, right . . . back . . . here,"
Darryl said, reaching behind her. High summer, late July: Charlotte
had promised Fiona a Popsicle as soon as she was finished tying up
the tomato plants, but the box in the freezer was empty, so here they
were—where else?—at the SixMart. A minute later Darryl drove in,
in a new truck, a little refrigerator truck that still had the Bayside Ice
Company logo painted on the side.

"Gas," he explained. "It's on empty." It was important that she know
this, so she wouldn't think he'd stopped because he saw the Volvo. He
hadn't done that, or anything remotely like that, since the day they went
over the bridge. She'd seen him across the room at the VFW fund-raiser
for Nikki Miles's brother. He'd caught her eye during a speech about
courage and the price of freedom, shot her a quick fond glance that
seemed to encompass just about everything—regret, love, amazement
at the ineffable complications of life, and a certain peacefulness, as if he
knew he'd done the right thing. Then Nikki's brother had reached for

his beer bottle and missed, knocking it into his lap, so Darryl had to attend to him. And Charlotte had to attend to Henry, who, at the sight of a man wounded into clumsiness, had been seized by a fury and started muttering so loudly about impeaching George Bush that she'd been afraid he'd incite a riot.

The tomato was caught in the back, at the nape of her neck.

"Wow, it's really stuck."

"I was all tangled up in them," she said. "It's getting pretty jungly in there."

He worked carefully at the tangle, freeing one strand and then another until the tomato came loose in his hand. They looked down at the little unborn thing—milky green, veined like a gooseberry, tiny in his thick palm—and she almost bent to kiss it. Instead she smiled, feeling as always that he would understand the whole complicated story behind the smile, maybe better than if she'd tried to put it into words.

Fiona, absorbed in her Creamsicle, leaned back against her mother's legs and looked up at them, watching, taking it all in. There was the smell of fried fish in the air, and an unbroken procession of cars on the highway, with surfboards and bicycles and immense inflated beach toys bound on their roofs. Families sated with sun and salt water, returning to their rented cottages to grill hot dogs and watch the sunset—years later some of the children in those cars would remember this one day as an emblem of freedom and happiness.

Tim came out of the market, with sunglasses over his eye patch and a big shark's smile.

"Where's your truck?" Darryl asked.

Neither he nor Charlotte would have stopped at the SixMart if Tim's truck had been there.

"Carrie took it to the car wash," Tim said, wrinkling his nose.

"That's right; I heard you did pretty well," Darryl said.

"Four bluefin. They weren't biting at first; there was so much chum in the water they didn't care about the bait. But I waited 'em out. . . ." He lifted his sunglasses to shoot a glance at Charlotte, as if she would find his fisherman's prowess irresistible. "One was so fat, I got fifteen bucks a pound, for four hundred and seventy-three pounds."

"What a year you're having," Darryl said.

"Yeah, and I got somethin' to show ya."

An envelope, from the superior court. Everything else was forgotten; they gathered around to read it. Narville's claims had been summarily rejected.

"There is no issue as to material fact. This land is shown to be in possession of a third party, and cannot be claimed either by Mr. Narville or the town of Wellfleet," Tim read aloud.

"So, Ada was the owner; now it's Carrie, and the case is closed," Darryl said.

"Carrie and me; community property," Tim said. "I was out there at dawn; I've got half my oysters back in already. I can't wait to see the look on that bastard's face."

"Of course."

"So, you're my neighbor," Charlotte said, with a light irony that made Darryl smile and Tim bristle, a quick frown crossing his face. He'd heard the threat in it, and threat was his native language—but Charlotte's weapon—a hatpin—was unfamiliar.

"Damn right I am," he said. Charlotte could hear how he hated her.

None of them would speak of her letter to Darryl again. Tim would avoid even thinking of it, though he would suffer certain twinges, a vague shame gone to rage that left him contemptuous of

Henry, and New Yorkers, and newspaper people, and, of course, washashores. Charlotte would remember Henry's stoic face, the way he had borne her betrayal as he bore everything, in silence. Darryl thought of it every day: Charlotte had loved him, and he'd given her up, and with that sacrifice he hoped to have earned his way back into fate's good graces. If they'd been lovers, he'd have ended up ashamed. Now, every time he saw her, he felt proud.

"How's that Creamsicle?" he asked Fiona. He loved to see her— he had saved her from great harm.

"Good, Dar-r-ryl," she said, happy and shy, smiling at him while ice cream melted onto her shoes.

"Telegram!" Reggie the glass eater called, popping his head in through the door.

"Rhode Island Red," Fiona shot back, ready with the answer like the good schoolgirl she was.

"You're a regular 'fleetian!" Darryl told her, and she beamed.

"What does that mean?" Charlotte asked him. "Telegram, Rhode Island Red? Why does everyone say it? What's the joke?"

"Well, I have no idea," Darryl said. "All my life it's just been . . . he says telegram, you say Rhode Island Red. I have no idea what it means."

"You never asked?"

Darryl laughed. "It's just one of those things . . ." he said, looking quizzically at Tim. "Does anyone know?"

"I never paid any attention," Tim said. The three forty-five bus had pulled up outside and Orson appeared at the top of its steps, blinking in daylight, gathering his cape in as he came down the steps, with the aura of a dignitary descending from his private jet.

"A meeting of the St. Botolph Club," he said, holding his head. "Oh, Rémy Martin!"

"Do you have any idea about 'telegram . . . Rhode Island Red'?" Charlotte asked him. "What does everybody mean by that?"

Orson squinted at her. "Could you please direct me to the ibuprofen?" Then, with two fingers at his throat, "Good catch, I gather, Tim."

Tim gave a crisp nod.

"And congratulations on Carrie's inheritance."

"Thanks."

"Of course." Orson tried in vain to twist the childproof cap off the ibuprofen.

"I'll do it for you!" Fiona said, and quickly did.

Orson tossed four of them to the back of his throat and swallowed. "Of course, the really delicious thing is the seawall," he said.

"What do you mean?" Charlotte asked.

"The high tide hits the seawall, does it not?"

"It does," Charlotte answered.

"And the Narvilles' property line is 'by the waters,' in this case meaning to the mean high-tide line?"

"Yes . . ."

"So Carrie and Tim . . . own all the beach there, right up to the seawall. The Narvilles can stand on the seawall and look, but without your permission, sir, they can't swim there, nor moor their boat, nor take a little stroll. . . . Oh, my head. Skip was on his way over to explain that to them when I left yesterday. I didn't envy him."

Tim gave a low whistle. "Well, how d'ya like that?"

The silence that fell after this might have been unbreakable if Orson hadn't been there.

"What went around does seem to have come around," he said, and they all—Orson, Tim Cloutier, Darryl Stead, and Charlotte Tradescome—laughed together. They were not much alike, but they were alone with one another out here, and that bond was familial, unbreakable. As every drop that fell into the sea had its effect on the oysters, everything anyone did here affected the town. Ada's birth and the story that was made from it, Darryl's flight and his prodigal return, Charlotte's arrival, Tim's bite out of Rob Welch's ear . . . even such a pale, delicate thing as an embryonic love affair would change the climate here. They needed one another, knew one another; they would become closer to one another whether they wanted to or not.

"Jeb Narville's got his boat moored right in the middle of my property," Tim said. "I guess I'm going to have to take him to court."

They heard an ambulance wailing toward them.

"Car crash? Can't be too bad," Darryl said. "No one's going more than ten miles an hour."

They went to the doorway to watch it come, bumbling slow and clangorous between the two lanes of traffic, as cars grudgingly made way. Fiona clutched at Charlotte, burying her head in her mother's neck, and Charlotte felt the last of the Creamsicle spill down the front of her shirt.

"It's not going to hurt us, sweetie," she said. "Except maybe our eardrums."

It turned down Point Road.

"Shit," they all said, in perfect unison.

35

DEATH OF A VIKING

Jeb Narville's brick-red cheeks, which had made him look so greedy and angry to Charlotte, might have told a different story to a neurologist, but Jeb did not submit himself to doctors. He did not care to be regarded as a bundle of delicate interconnected membranes, each one vulnerable to its own sort of misery. He saw—had seen—himself as a solid entity, a steel-hulled ship slicing through the waves.

"The paramedic said his pupils had blown out," Andrea told Charlotte the next day. "Blown out, like a candle. It means they don't respond to light anymore. That even though he was breathing, he was pretty much gone. An aneurysm, it could have happened anytime."

She jumped up suddenly, as if she could escape this idea, sat instantly back down as if she'd hit her head on some other hard truth. Charlotte had wedged herself into a corner of the immense sofa, pressed as far back into the leather as she could get. She'd brought over a coffee cake, which she held on her lap as a kind of shield. Andrea's grief was so enormous and awful—compounded of shock and guilt and fury and fear—that it seemed almost physically dangerous, a giant, filthy wave that was about to crash down over them.

"He was here . . . right here," she kept saying angrily, as if demanding that Charlotte put him back. Her face was blotchy; there were dark circles under her eyes; she made a terrible sobbing sound but no tears came, and she clenched her fists. "Money was no object!" she said. "We could have appealed it right up to the Supreme Court!"

"Of course you could," Charlotte said, soothing, holding the coffee cake tight. "Of course."

"'No genuine issue as to material fact,' that's what they said in the judgment," Andrea said, twisting a Kleenex around her finger. "Because of . . . oh, some tiny little loophole. But Jeb says the court doesn't have jurisdiction; he would fight it on those grounds. Skip said he'd do it, but for now *they* . . . those men . . . have the rights to the land, and next morning there that guy was, putting all his *junk* out in front of our house."

Charlotte nodded, honestly sympathetic. She couldn't help it; it was virtually impossible for her to keep from sympathizing with any person who was in the same room with her.

"In the South, we have the welcome wagon," Andrea burst out. "When someone moves into town everyone goes over to meet them, brings them a little gift, just to make them feel at home. Here they seemed to hate us before we even moved in! They tricked us into thinking this was real waterfront. That woman at the SixMart, she acted like she couldn't see us! Over the winter they stole all the fish out of our koi pond! And Jeb had dreamed of this, he . . ."

Now the tears came, dammed up behind the mascara for a moment before they spilled down through Andrea's makeup so her whole face seemed to be coming apart, like the painting of Vestina when Charlotte dropped it. Andrea had made such a neat little package of herself—the frosted ponytail, the perfectly yoga-fied body—she had tried so hard, and still everything had come to ruin.

On the coffee table she had arranged a kind of shrine: a fat bronze Buddha and a group of votive candles around a photograph of a confident-looking young boy at the helm of a sailboat, facing into the wind.

"Is this Jeb?" Charlotte asked.

"His whole life he dreamed of having a summer place on Cape Cod," Andrea said, weeping. "He grew up in Eastlake Meadows—the projects, in Atlanta . . . you wouldn't guess, would you? He came up here for a week once, in the summer—it was a social services thing, a free camp program. He swore that once he made his fortune, he'd come back. So he did, and . . . ohhh."

Andrea bent over, her fists clenched, and Charlotte felt her own throat close on the same sorrow—if it had been Henry, cold, hard old Henry . . . her heart would have crumbled away just like this. She knew too well that a child was still alive in Henry, a child who needed so many things. She shuddered; she couldn't bear to think.

"The projects?" she echoed, stupidly. Of course, look around— that was why everything in the room screamed *money* the way it did, why even Andrea looked as if she might have been gotten for the highest bid. Money was freedom, safety, beauty, love, and if you'd begun in servitude, danger, ugliness, and need, you'd never be able to put enough layers of it between you and the past. It would just feel better to have another Hummer in the garage, for good measure, and you wouldn't want any mangy stand of lilacs marking the edge of your property, but a solid and preferably very expensive fence. You'd despise anyone who reminded you of those bad old days, and certainly you wouldn't want them desecrating your million-dollar view.

Henry wasn't so different, really, except that he had started with

enough money that he knew it wouldn't save him. He felt about ob-
scure poets the way Narville felt about high-end brand names.

"This house, it was supposed to be his dream come true," Andrea
said, weeping so openly and sadly now that Charlotte felt ready to
weep herself. "Every day he was going to sail in the bay the way he did
that week, forty years ago."

"Oh, oh, Andrea." Charlotte relinquished the coffee cake and
reached out to hug her. "I'm so sorry."

"Why did everybody *hate* us so?" Andrea asked. "Jeb, he does—
he did his best. Oh, he was the worst yoga student you ever saw!"
she said, laughing and crying at once. "He was stiff as a . . . well, he
reminded me of a gargoyle. He barely even tried to do the stretches.
Then it turned out he took the class because he'd seen *me*! That's the
way he is; he goes and gets what he wants. He wanted me so
much."

That made him indispensable. This, Charlotte could understand.

Jeb had been in a rage since Skip left. Everything had gone wrong,
all along the way. He watched Tim set out the racks that morning,
clipping the grow-out trays on them, and as soon as the truck was
gone, he'd set out to avenge himself, taking the oyster rack by its legs,
intending to wrench it out of the mud, pull it up and throw it over the
way you'd upend a table in a brawl. He had no way of knowing how
sharp a growing oyster could be, nor how the young ones clung to
the racks. The oyster shells sliced deep into both of his hands—
Andrea heard him cry out, looked out and saw him fall back into the
water. She ran to help him but the best she could do was to pull him
in toward the beach so he wouldn't drown as the tide came up. By
the time the rescue squad arrived, his pupils had blown out . . . he
was gone.

She grimaced with her whole body. "I guess it was there for years;

it was leaking blood into his brain. I guess I should be grateful it happened quick," she said.

"That's a blessing," Charlotte said, holding her tight. "At least he didn't suffer." She racked her mind for more of the phrases commonly used to put a patch on grief.

"He wanted a Viking funeral," Andrea said. "You know, in a burning boat?"

"No . . . I didn't know."

But Jeb had pillaged like a Viking, grown rich and fat like a Viking, and Charlotte supposed he ought to be borne into the next life in a flaming longship.

"They're pretty particular about what goes in the bay." She realized this wasn't the right thing only after she'd said it. "I mean, you'll need some kind of town approval. Maybe Skip could help?"

"Skip just put in a new kitchen with my inheritance," Andrea said sharply, and blew her nose.

"So you're not sorry the suit is over?"

Andrea looked at her wearily, then glanced around the room, the enormous furniture, the plasma TV screen covering the whole back wall, the bank of French doors, and the crystalline view. Finally she dropped her gaze—resigned, Charlotte thought at first, until she realized Andrea was stretching her leg out to contemplate a diamond ankle bracelet she was wearing.

"No," she said. "This just isn't the place for me."

36

A PERFECT BEACH DAY

A perfect beach day, a Saturday right in the middle of August, and inland the temperature was forecast to hit ninety-five. The tourists would be happy, and tonight they would arrive in the restaurants sleek from their showers, feeling smart and beautiful and a little richer than they did in the rain, ordering martinis and oysters, oysters, oysters, and after dinner they would stroll among the shops, buying linen ensembles and wide-brimmed hats for the lives they felt they were so very close to leading.

And jewelry.

"They don't need me until later. Tina will sit there all day alone," Betsy said, "but tonight they'll come in from the beach and they'll want to buy, buy, buy." She tilted the beach umbrella a little more toward the west and stretched deliciously, showing off the silver ring on her second toe.

"You can't ask for more than this," Charlotte said. "High tide at two p.m., not a cloud, barely a breeze . . ."

"Well, maybe one thing," Betsy said conspiratorially, pulling out a pink thermos. "Cosmopolitans!"

There were bright umbrellas tilted in the sand already, all around the bay. Everyone on earth would go to the beach today, and in the years and decades ahead, men and women would look back and stretch this and the few other days like it until they came to stand for whole summers of long, perfect days at the shore, days like the one Jeb Narville had hoped to replicate when he built his new house, like the one Charlotte remembered, when her parents had been happy and she'd been a little girl who didn't know the dangers of life. Someday Fiona might look back and remember this day, the light and freedom, Oreos and lemonade, the bright red beach pail with its yellow shovel.

"I'm going to feed one to the bordies!" she said, running toward a couple of seagulls that took flight in alarm. "Bordies, come back, bordies!" she cried.

"They don't like Oreos," Alexis said in her spider's voice, rolling her eyes. "They like clams, and dead meat, and things."

The little girls skittered along like sandpipers at the lacy edge of the water, and Betsy shaded her eyes with her hand, looking out to the mouth of the bay. Charlotte sipped. "God, what a day." There was a moment of blissful silence, marked only by terns crying.

"Is that a whale spout?"

"Where?"

"Over there, but it can't be; it would have blown away by now."

"It looks like smoke."

"Is it a boat on fire? Was it last summer, or . . . before you moved here, I guess, that the Muertaros' boat blew up in the harbor?" Betsy rummaged for her cell phone and dialed 911.

"It's what? What? Oh, no, come on . . ."

She covered her mouth with both hands and looked at Charlotte wide-eyed. "It's Jeb Narville! His Viking funeral!"

"Pass the potato chips," Charlotte said grimly.

Betsy shook her head. "That poor man."

"To Jeb," Charlotte said, lifting a Cosmo in a plastic glass.

"To Jeb!"

"I can't help but think it might all be the aneurysm; that if he were thinking clearly he never could have gotten so angry."

"You haven't been here long enough," Betsy said, shaking her head. "People get like this when they buy a place by the water. It's only natural, really: You invest a million dollars in a house, and it's supposed to be perfect, a dream house. They built those condos down by the wharf, advertised the view of the fishing boats, sold the places bing, bing, bing; then those people moved in, formed a condo association, and started trying to put the fishery out of business! They said it was ugly and it smelled bad and it was detrimental to their property values!"

"Life is hilarious."

"I'll drink to that," Betsy said. "I had a little fling with a guy who lived in those condos," she confided suddenly, much as she might have admitted to spending too much on a pair of shoes. "They've got amazing views, I'll say that."

Right. While Charlotte and Darryl suffered and yearned and steeled themselves against love, Betsy had been meeting some man for champagne and strawberries in his condo over the harbor. Of course.

"How did you manage it?"

"Oh, it was summer, and I'd just go over if the store was quiet, you know. It was . . . an interlude . . . that's all. I wasn't hung up on him or anything."

A sandpiper tiptoed nearly up to Charlotte's foot to take an Oreo crumb. They could see flames as well as smoke now, as the boat began to blaze.

"It's nice to smell woodsmoke," Charlotte said. "It makes me look forward to fall."

"Just think, you're breathing in a little of Jeb Narville."

"Betsy!"

"Well, it's true!"

"I don't know . . . now that Andrea told me all about him, I can't hate him anymore. It's discouraging."

"Have a sandwich," Betsy said kindly. "I've got cucumber and scallion cream cheese on whole wheat, or PB and J."

Fiona and Alexis were back, with seaweed. Alexis was modeling kelp around her shoulders like a brilliant green shawl, and Fiona had a bubbly, branched one arranged as a wig. Two little boys who'd run along the water's edge from the public beach stopped and pointed at the funeral boat. A flock of tiny sails flitted out from Try Point, turning abruptly with a shift in the wind.

Henry came up behind them, standing there on his stork legs, uncomfortable as always when he was away from his desk. He was taking a break from *The Torturer's Horse* to write a short biography of Ada Town, and this had lightened his mood.

"Is there something on fire out there?"

"It's Jeb," Charlotte said.

Suddenly the fire went out. The boat had broken and sunk out of sight.

"She's putting the house on the market," Betsy said.

"New neighbors," Charlotte said. "I hope they're nice."

Henry shook his head sadly. "It's not that kind of house," he said.

37

THE SOUND OF SNOW

"Now," the kindergarten teacher said kindly to Fiona, who was sitting at a tiny desk, alert and at the ready, as if she were about to pilot a space shuttle into the stratosphere. "Can you draw a picture of yourself for me?"

Fiona had passed the first test—piling four blocks on top of one another—and now she seized the crayon and with lips pursed in fierce concentration drew a face with hands and feet attached, then two larger faces hovering on either side.

"That's a very good picture," the teacher said, giving her a wide, lipsticky smile. "That's you?"

"Mama, Dad, me," Fiona said crisply. Then: "No, wait! I left out the water!" She grabbed the paper back and drew a long blue squiggle across the bottom of the page. "There: me." She folded her hands in her lap. She was a member of a family, a citizen of this place. That was her.

She couldn't wait another minute for school. All through Labor Day weekend she was tensed and ready to spring, and on Monday afternoon Charlotte took her on a last run into Hyannis for more school supplies, just to keep her from jumping out of her skin. They found themselves in something between a traffic jam and a parade—thousands leaving, hundreds standing on the bridges over Route 6, waving good-bye, holding signs that said, THANK YOU, and, COME BACK SOON! Red Cross tents were set up at the rest stops, offering coffee and doughnuts. The radio announced the length of the bridge backup: six miles, eight miles, then eleven. In Kmart they bought a Hello Kitty pencil box and erasers shaped like jungle animals, and headed home, nearly alone on the road.

As Charlotte tucked her into bed that night, Fiona grabbed her hand and refused to let it go.

"Mama, I want so much to be . . . what I'm supposed to be."

"Oh, my girl . . ." Charlotte sat down beside her. What was to become of a five-year-old who could know such a thing about herself, who already had the words to explain it? Her eyes sparkled so as she sat up against the pillow, clutching her bear tight, scarcely able to contain her excitement as she rushed off to meet life. To look at her was to believe the world must be entirely good, entirely.

"Fiona, you are so much more than what you're supposed to be." It was going to be a big part of Charlotte's job to make sure Fiona could go beyond what she was supposed to be; that, she knew.

In the morning they walked up Point Road, Fiona in her red plaid skirt, her hand so tight in her mother's, and here came the bus: Boat Meadow. In the afternoon Fiona would leap off, barely able to contain all her stories. The maple tree would turn red, the bay its deep fall blue, and later the oak leaves would get their Persian rug colors. By Thanksgiving, the marsh grasses would be as gold as Kansas wheat, and Charlotte would see Desiree pushing her new daughter in a carriage, walking the same route Ada used to take every day. One day there were three of them: the baby's father, who'd disappeared over the bridge when Desiree got pregnant, had come back and was walking along self-consciously beside her, beside his family. It was that or lose a piece of himself, Charlotte knew. At the new moon in December, she woke up to see headlights sweep over the ceiling as Tim and Bud and Westie headed out to the flats to take the oysters in. Darryl had been able to move his grant out next to Nikki's, near Egg Island.

The Narville house was sold to a barrel-chested guy from Quincy. "Great spot! Maximum potential!" he barked the day they met him. He intended to buy up a piece of the harbor for a marina, which pleased Betsy, because yacht people were also jewelry people. Of course he was having the house renovated, from stem to stern. Hot tub, koi pond . . . ridiculous. He was having a paddock put in—he liked the sound of hooves on stone. And he had a live-in cook, so the open-plan kitchen had to go.

The old town, the real town, was disappearing, little by little, day by day. The men gathered at the SixMart counter seemed to know they were becoming picturesque, like the last lions of Africa. One morning Charlotte went in for some coffee and found a photographer from the *National Geographic* setting up a time to go out on the flats with Bud and Jake. "You get some great light right *after* sunset," Jake was explaining. It was true—all the streams of the estuary would reflect the bright sky even after the sun was down.

The brilliant fall devolved into a warm, rainy winter. "Never should have taken the animals in," Bud kept saying. "All that work for nothing." In April the apple trees that had washed in from the wreck of the *Franklin* started to bloom, and the yellow shutters were off the windows at the Lemon Pie Cottages. Taking Fiona to her piano lesson, Charlotte passed Darryl on the highway—he was turning down Paine Hollow Road, talking on his cell phone, doing his job. As she was doing hers.

Then she came upon him in the hardware store, looking up the barrel of a socket wrench with a funny grin on his face. He blushed as if she'd caught him at something; then she blushed, and her knees started shaking so she had to press them tight together and talk very seriously about the tides.

"... and for the moment I can keep up with the orders," he said, looking away. "George always asks after you, by the way."

"George?"

"George McConnell? At the North Wind, in Boston? He had the idea we ..."

"Gee, where would he get that kind of idea?"

Darryl smiled. Everything was right there between them, just like always.

"Well, give him my regards when you see him," Charlotte said.

"I will. But I won't see him for a while. We're going away ... me and Nikki ... gettin' married and takin' her brother out west. There's a clinic out there, in Colorado—might be able to help him."

"That would be terrific," she said. The phrase *getting married* was folded so deep into the middle of the sentence, it was hard to get at it. "And congratulations on the wedding!" She surprised herself, chirping this out so brightly. She sounded like the kind of person who probably let days go by without thinking of Darryl Stead.

"It seems like the right thing," he said simply, as, when they'd been working together at the Narvilles', he'd run a board between two ladders for her to stand on while she painted, and had bounced on it lightly to test it. "Seems solid," he'd said then.

"I'm just—I'm so happy for you." The right words, but jealousy twisted them, made them syrupy, as if she were amazed someone would stoop to marry him. And then, trying to make up for that, she let her real feeling show on her face, and his face was crossed by a phantom suddenly, and he dropped the socket wrench back into the bin and said, "The bolt's in the truck," and was gone.

Standing there with her package of vacuum cleaner bags, a piece of screen to cut for patches, and a twenty-pound bag of potting soil, she felt she'd lost her life's best chance at love. But later, years later, it began to seem that she and Darryl had collaborated to make each other a gift—a memory preserved whole as in a snow globe, safe from the ordinary difficulties, the disappointments and uncertainties that corrode a love over time. They'd dreamed the same dream together; it helped them face their real lives.

There was the year of the red tide, a plume of toxic algae that streamed down from the Gulf of Maine on a spring nor'easter, hitting Wellfleet just before Memorial Day—the first day of the season, when coffers empty after the winter would have begun to fill. Every oyster and clam was tainted; it took most of the summer for the algae to clear. Then, just as things seemed to be getting back to normal, a crazy storm blew up with no warning and came in at just the right angle to drive a surge of water up the bay, carrying the oysters and their racks with it, smashing them against the seawall. Bud's whole crop was ruined. "I'm takin' the hint," he said, and put his house on the market and drove south to Pensacola to start a charter fishing business. The same storm unearthed the bones of a shipwreck at the back shore, stark as a skeleton in the desert. Skip and Betsy had bought the whole block Betsy's Fine Jewelry was on, renovated it with brilliant taste, and opened Alexis's Old Tyme Ice Cream Shoppe, a "country store" selling tin pails and cute aprons, and the Watermen's Grill, with a raw bar where you could taste oysters from every cove in Wellfleet.

EAT WHERE THE LOCALS DO! the sign proclaimed, though the locals couldn't really afford it, especially after it was hailed as "a taste of the authentic Wellfleet" in the New York Times.

Charlotte and Fiona frequented the clam shack at the Wharf Grill, because Desiree worked behind the counter. As she wrote up the orders and strung them on the line over the grill, she moved like Darryl, her face showing the same concentration. Tim and Carrie had sold Ada's house and were building their own on a lot beside the highway, while Desiree and her little family moved into Darryl's old place in Driftwood Cottages. One evening when Charlotte was waiting for a scallop roll and there was no one in line behind her, she asked what Desiree heard from her uncle.

"They like it out there—lotta construction work," Desiree said, looking down at her pad.

A job opened up at the *Oracle*, covering "land use and environmental issues." Charlotte wasn't sure how she would convince them that her study of celebrity style trends had prepared her for it, but no one even looked at her clippings. "Wow, *Celeb* magazine," the editor said when she went for the interview. "The salary for this position would be twenty-five thousand dollars." There was an awkward moment while he waited for Charlotte to pack up and go; then, realizing he had a living person who was willing to do the work, he added eagerly: "We do have a pair of chest waders for you; no need to spring for those."

"Oh, that's okay; I still have a pair from my last job."

He blinked.

"Joke."

"Right."

And she fastened her suspenders, pulling all ten pounds of this uniquely cumbersome garment up as high as she could. It felt like struggling into someone else's skin. Then it was out onto the tide flats to meet a team from the aquarium who'd come to do an autopsy on a beached whale. Her fingers froze as she noted down the findings, trying to angle upwind of the whale gut stench. She was developing bursitis, which the doctor said was exacerbated by the cold fog. But she loved the cold fog. She loved coming to know Wellfleet, down to who had bitten off whose earlobe, the salinity of the water in parts per million, and how to answer Reggie's cheerful, "Telegram." And Fiona would grow up knowing her mother was one thread in the weave of this town.

"That's the true work of journalism," Henry said, with honest pride. "The environment, climate change—most important issues out there right now. And you're right on the front line."

Henry. Her husband. A man so racked with grief, so steadfast in its face, that he seemed beyond reach of feeling, while his wife registered the emotional temperature as if there were mercury in her veins. Quite a couple, fast asleep with Bunbury tucked into the wide gap between them one night when Fiona ran in screaming as if her bed were on fire.

"What is it, what is it!" Charlotte said, and Henry jumped up, battle-ready, and hit his head on the lamp.

"They're going to steal me, take me away, the little lizard people!"

"It's okay, honey; it's just a dream," Charlotte said. "Here, come in with your mama and daddy."

Fiona got in between them, and Charlotte kissed her, seeing on Henry's face an unfamiliar expression—the look of a lonely child standing outside the circle, hoping for an invitation. "We're right here, sweetie, both of us," Charlotte said, not sure whether she was talking to her daughter or her husband. Henry kissed Fiona's forehead once, twice, three times—possessed by a tenderness that had to be gotten rid of, like an itch. Outside the coyote started howling and was joined by a whole yipping pack, but

Fiona, safe between her parents, Bunbury curled at her feet, was sound asleep.

Charlotte was shaking out the tablecloth one night after dinner, and having folded it over her arm, stood a minute looking over the bay in the last light, feeling the history and beauty of the place, undiminished by time (she was looking west, away from the Narville house), feeling as she would have in 1898, alone and strong here, facing into the wind. Though in 1898, Billingsgate Light would been flashing a slow, steady guiding signal over the water. As she turned back toward the house she saw Henry watching her from the top step.

"You look like you belong here," he said.

No one has ever received a better compliment than this. Under the layers of fury and sorrow and longing and distrust, her heart stirred, and she gave him a crooked little smile. What she dreamed of, yearned for, was so far outside the circle of Henry's understanding, it might have been the custom in some galaxy light-years away. She was here with him, warm and laughing; she made the spaghetti with clams, she came home with odd stories, she could alleviate some of his dread. Loneliness was natural, as familiar to him as the photograph of the *Kingfisher* among the towering waves. This . . . this wife, and the daughter no less . . . he could hardly believe it. His instinct was to stand back, keep a little distance, for fear they'd turn out to be a mirage.

Charlotte went up the steps and kissed him. Of all the kisses in her lifetime, she was least certain about this one, but she wasn't leaving, so she had to try to stay with her whole heart. When Fiona saw them hugging, she had to squeeze in between. "We're the best family ever," she said, causing a good laugh between her parents.

"Henry, if I get like your father when I'm old, so I'm living in a home and I don't really understand anything anymore—will you bring me things to smell? Basil and rosemary . . . and lemon oil. . . . and seaweed . . . and open an ear of corn right under my nose, okay? I think that would make me happy."

"Of course I will," he said, somber, touching his forehead to hers. After a long moment, he added, "And . . . you'd see the book gets printed? I mean, if anything happened to me. Just a hundred copies."

"Absolutely," Charlotte promised. "I'll make a thousand."

"I wonder what Joyce would have written next, if he'd lived?" she asked, to break the ceremonial mood.

"Well, I suppose . . ." Henry said, looking almost lighthearted, as if he knew his answer could go on for years.

Since the day her father admired her jump-rope skills, Fiona had started really working at them. A certain grace grew up alongside her clumsiness: She still fell off her chair at dinner, but she could do this while holding full a glass of milk, without spilling a single drop. Alexis, who could jump rope so easily, had lost interest, but Fiona needed to know she could master it and worked single-mindedly, always preparing a new trick to show Henry when he came up from his office. She'd convinced the school gym teacher to start a double-dutch team, and Charlotte was standing at the edge of the woods one winter evening, waiting for their practice to end, when she realized she was hearing the sound Darryl had once worked to re-create. Snow, the ocean-effect snow that the Boston weathermen never mentioned because they didn't believe there was really anyone out here, had been sifting over the town all day. Nothing was plowed, and from the hill beside the school she could see out over the harbor, the boats at anchor, the spires set among the hills around the bay. There was a thrill just to making a footprint—everything was so pure and smooth. A single car—Rob Welch's cruiser—was driving out onto the pier, but otherwise nothing moved. The storm was starting to pull away, leaving a sharp line where the clouds ended and the sky showed a deep evening blue. Charlotte felt a gentle blow at the back of her neck, as if someone had lobbed a soft snowball out of the woods. Not someone—Darryl. For the edge of a second she felt the old bliss rise in her chest, and she turned around, smiling, ready to reach out, as if she had known all along he'd be there.

Of course it was only a clump of snow that had slipped from a bough overhead. There was nothing but the forest behind her, stretching over the hill to the back shore: scrub oak with dry leaves still clinging; jack pine; a sassafras fallen crossways in one sharp, contrary stroke. Deeper in, she made out the silhouette of a hawk on a high branch, head tucked under and covered with snow like everything else around it. Otherwise, she was alone, without even a sound except the quiet patter as each flake touched down, and the wind sighing in the trees.

ACKNOWLEDGMENTS

Many, many thanks to my oyster advisers: William Walton of the Cape Cod Cooperative Extension Service; Andy Koch of the Wellfleet Shellfish Department; Provincetown Shellfish Constable Tony Jackett; and aquaculturists Laura Adams; Chip, Felicia, and Joel Benton; Richard Blakely; Nate Johnson; Meg Shields; and Pat and Barbara Woodbury. Attorney Marion Hobbs introduced me to the byzantine complexity of "littoral rights," and Tom Lindsay led me on a strangely exciting chase through the Barnstable County Registry of Deeds. I'm sure I've made mistakes in spite of all the good counsel; where I get it right, the thanks are due above.

No character or event here is intended to represent any actual person or story. Tradescome Point, Oyster Creek, all the surrounding area, and its citizens, its shops and organizations, and even some of its geology, are invented, an imaginary hamlet within the real town of Wellfleet, Massachusetts.

"Waiting on Gramma" is copyrighted by Jerry Beckham and used by permission.

Photo by Brad Fowler

HEIDI JON SCHMIDT is the author of *The Rose Thieves, Darling?,* and *The Bride of Catastrophe.* Her stories have been widely published, anthologized, and featured on National Public Radio. She has been a guest teacher of creative writing at many colleges and universities, and teaches in the summer program at the Fine Arts Work Center in Provincetown. She has lived on Cape Cod for twenty-five years. www. heidijonschmidt.com.

The House on Oyster Creek

HEIDI JON SCHMIDT

This Conversation Guide is intended to enrich the
individual reading experience, as well as encourage us
to explore these topics together—because books,
and life, are meant for sharing.

A CONVERSATION WITH HEIDI JON SCHMIDT

Q. *Why oysters?*

A. My sister is a shellfish farmer. I envy her life and admire it: She's out on the water all day and has the intimate knowledge of the natural world that can come only through hands-on, daily effort. It's backbreaking labor, and I feel sort of sheepish about having such a soft job myself. In one way, though, a day at the desk is like a day on the tide flats: You've felt a vital connection to life; you've worked at something worthwhile.

And Cape Cod is my home. I've been greatly affected by the struggles here between those who've been here for generations and those who've just moved in. So many people are barely scraping by, while others pop in, buy a house that costs a few million dollars, renovate it for a few million more, then decide they'd rather have a place in Provence. The estuaries, salt marshes, and the tide flats where oysters are farmed are the most fertile, beautiful places on earth, and it's painful to see them turned into a commodity, into "million-dollar views." I was excited to work on this book and think about it all in depth.

Q. *Is there really anything new to be said about love?*

A. My guess is that everyone alive has something new to say about love. Every love has so many layers—the hopes and dreams and fears of both lovers, their different experiences, the complications of class and culture and belief. *Oyster Creek* is centered on a marriage full of love *and* difficulty, like most marriages, and on a love affair that has great meaning even though it's unlikely to end well. And, of course, Fiona grows according to her parents' love, like a vine scrambling up a trellis.

Q. *Yes, maternal love is as important as romantic love here.*

A. The minute my daughter was alive in the world I became braver, more capable. Like Charlotte Tradescome, I wanted to "walk toward the light, keeping the little hand tight in mine." I saw that a huge part of motherhood was just being myself—the most honest self I could be—so my daughter could learn by osmosis. As I focused on that, I started taking more chances as a writer. I was truer to my own perceptions, less afraid to make mistakes. I want my daughter to feel comfortable being herself, and to dare to try things, even things that might not work out. In other words, I think a lot about motherhood, so I naturally end up writing about it.

Q. *Why do you call this an ecological novel?*

A. Every novel is its own ecosystem; it documents the immense effect each person has on others, and the ways these effects ripple out into the world. In Oyster Creek, one character's anger brings out the worst in the people around him, setting off a chain of troubling events. Another's generosity strengthens the community. "As every drop that fell into the sea had its effect on the oysters, everything anyone did here affected the town. Ada's birth and the story that was made from it, Darryl's flight and his prodigal return, Charlotte's arrival, Tim's bite out of Rob Welch's ear . . . even such a pale, delicate thing as an embryonic love affair would change the climate here. They needed each other, knew each other; they would become closer to each other whether they wanted to or not."

Q. *What kind of research did you have to do for* Oyster Creek?

A. I *loved* the research I had to do for *Oyster Creek*. I've always wanted to know how things work, and at first the idea that you could grow oysters in undersea gardens the way you might grow corn in a field was mind-boggling. I was so glad to have a good excuse to study it! I spent as much time on as many different oyster farms as I could, listening to what the farmers had to say, trying to get an intuitive sense of the work, the experience of it. We went out at sunset on an August evening, and before dawn on a November morning when the wind was as sharp as a knife and we had to work by the light of a miner's lamp. I've never felt so ridiculous, clomping around in a huge pair of waders, trying to maneuver a basket rake, or to pile bags of oysters into a canoe without tipping it. I wanted to really feel the work, in all its beauty and difficulty, and people were very, very kind in helping me do that.

Q. *What's it like to live on the Outer Cape in the winter?*

A. There's the strongest sense of community out here, because we're marooned together all winter when everything's boarded up. We rely on each other; we have to. Then we stick together to face the inundation of summer visitors. There's only one main road out here: Route 6. Everyone drives it: to work, to school, to the hospital. If you see someone turning off in an odd spot, you wonder why. Secrets don't keep very well, and when you can't keep secrets you're more aware of everyone's humanity, their fragility.

And human life is dwarfed by natural life. We're on a shifting sandbar, almost surrounded by water; the towns are fitted into the few spots best sheltered from the wind and waves. You learn to tell the temperature of the air by the color of the bay, and to understand what's going on in the water by the smell of the air. You develop a sixth sense for weather and tides.

Also, contemporary life is dwarfed by history. The Pilgrims landed here, did their laundry, and moved on. Half of our apple trees washed in from a shipwreck years ago. The towns look very much the same as they did during the Revolutionary War— the streets are so narrow, you can almost feel what it would have been like to live here in whaling times. And our shoreline is still controlled by the "King's Law." It makes a difference to be so close to nature, and so close to the past: You see how life is shaped by these immense forces, so much greater than yourself.

I love it here; I've wanted to bottle the experience so everyone could have some.

Q. *Any other experiences you've wanted to bottle?*

A. The real surprise of love—the absolute irrationality and deep meaning, and the way, when you look closer, it's all much more sensible than you'd ever think. The truth is, I want to bottle every experience. I wish I had an apothecary full of little bottles of different senses and feelings and adventures.

Q. *Can you tell us a little about how you came to be a writer, what you've written in the past and what you hope to write in the future?*

A. I grew up in a very isolated spot, down a dirt road, miles from anywhere. I was always inventing little societies: towns, families, schools, islands. I'd draw out the school bus routes and plan the menus. You could say it was a bad habit that got out of hand. I loved novels that had maps as endpapers—I'd pore over them to see how every piece of the imaginary world fit together. As I grew up I loved Faulkner and Jane Austen and the territories they invented based on the places they knew.

Oyster Creek is my fourth book (the others are: *The Rose Thieves, Darling?,* and *The Bride of Catastrophe*), and the first set on Cape Cod. The next will take place out here too. Painters talk about the inspiration they get from "cape light," the special quality of the light out here. Cape life is just as fertile for a writer. We have fishermen from the Azores and psychiatrists from Manhattan and everyone in between. We all see each other every day; our kids go to school together; we chafe against each other and learn from each other and fall in love with each other, and the stories just come bubbling up.

QUESTIONS FOR DISCUSSION

1. What experience would you bottle, and how would you do it? What are the particular details, the sights and sounds and smells that would really make that experience vivid for someone else?

2. As its title suggests, *Oyster Creek* is very much a novel of place. What place or places have strongly affected you, and why?

3. Charlotte's marriage to Henry evolves over the course of the book. At first Henry is almost a father figure, but after Fiona's birth Charlotte becomes the stronger partner, and husband and wife drift apart. Charlotte's love for Darryl has an intense, though unusual effect on her marriage. Do you think there are common stages of marriage, just like stages of life?

4. Henry Tradescome, glacial by nature, fears global warming above all things. Late in the book his wife finds out some things that change her understanding of his coolness. Have you known men, or women, like Henry, who keep themselves distant even from those they love most? Do you see this as a weakness or a strength?

5. Throughout *Oyster Creek*, the characters' lives are shaped by history, from the changes brought about by the sinking of Billingsgate Island to the effects of the King's Law to the ways the characters are influenced by their childhood experiences. Charlotte tries in many ways to have some good effect on the future, with only partial success. How has history affected your life? In what ways have your actions changed what may happen in the future?

6. The author suggests above that everyone has something new to say about love. What have you learned about love? How has love—romantic or familial—surprised you, changed you?

7. How do you imagine the lives in *Oyster Creek* will continue? What will become of the characters? What do you hope and fear for them? Are there things you wish you knew about the inhabitants of *Oyster Creek* and their lives?